ANDERSEN'S
FAIRY TALES

This Book Belongs To:

_____

_____

ANDERSEN'S FAIRY TALES

Illustrated by Troy Howell

LONGMEADOW PRESS

This book is printed on acid-free paper. It surpasses the standards set for Performance of Paper for Printed Library Materials.

Originally published under the title, *Faery Tales from Hans Andersen*, in a slightly different form.

Copyright © 1988 by dilithium Press, Children's Classics Division.
Color illustrations copyright © 1988 by Troy Howell.
All rights reserved.

This 1988 edition is published exclusively by Longmeadow Press, 201 High Ridge Road, P.O. Box 10218, Stamford, CT 06904, by arrangement with OBC, Inc., 225 Park Avenue South, New York, New York 10003.

Printed and bound in the United States of America

ISBN 0-681-40503-1

10 9 8 7 6 5 4 3 2 1

Cover design by Clair Moritz

CONTENTS

CONTENTS

LIST OF COLOR ILLUSTRATIONS

PREFACE

THIS edition of the fairy tales of Hans Christian Andersen is special in several ways. First, it includes the delightful, whimsical black-and-white drawings of Maxwell Armfield, originally published early in this century. Further, readers will find the classic translation to be distinctive, charming, and readable. Finally, the outstanding color illustrations by Troy Howell, specially commissioned for this Children's Classics edition, are the fruit of the artist's enduring passion for Andersen, nurtured over his many years as a distinguished illustrator of children's books.

Howell's strong feelings for Andersen are manifested in these meticulous, joyous paintings, expressing the gamut of emotion—from the stark beauty of a sleigh ride through the sky with the Snow Queen to the touching and warm humor of the Ugly Duckling shyly stumbling through the barnyard, while its denizens view him skeptically.

The publishers of Children's Classics celebrate this happy event together with the artist.

CLAIRE BOOSS
Series Editor

1988

viii

FOREWORD

Hans Christian Andersen's Fairy Tales are like exquisite jewels, drawing from us gasps of recognition and delight as we view their unexpected gleaming. Andersen created intriguing and unique characters—a tin soldier with only one leg but a big heart, a beetle nestled deep in a horse's mane but harboring high aspirations—whose struggles to come to terms with the world reflect our own dreams, hopes, and fears. Each one of us, at some time, has been touched by one of Andersen's fairy tales.

In these stories, we find everything—high comedy as well as gentle whimsy, romantic yearnings both satisfied and unrequited, moments of fear, and also revelations of poetry. We can almost hear Hans Christian Andersen speaking as naturally as if he were telling his tales to a beloved listener leaning forward eagerly at his knees. He spun stories of both the great and the lowly—from a Chinese emperor to an old bottle—that allow us to re-experience our own humanity. With startling humor, Andersen created the emperor tricked by his own comical insecurities into marching naked in an imperial procession in " The Emperor's New Clothes"—and with a rueful smile, we admit that we too have shared the emperor's weakness. In a more serious vein, we find ourselves drawn to " The Ugly Duckling" and its stirrings of hope. Banished from farmyard and hearth because of his gawky appearance, the duckling spies a flock of swans; and not realizing that he himself is a cygnet, there tears out of him " a shriek so piercing and so strange, that he was quite frightened by it himself." We stir to his call.

Andersen has the power to touch our hearts—a power he actually described in " The Nightingale." With gentle humor, he contrasted the artificiality of mere ingenuity to the unpredictability of the recognitions provided by the true artist. The Chinese emperor, on first hearing the tiny grey nightingale's song, has tears in his eyes, but is later seduced by the resplendent, jewel-encrusted mechanical nightingale sent to him by the Emperor of Japan. The music master prefers the manmade bird,

> " Because . . . . in the real nightingale you never know what you will hear, but in the artificial one everything is decided beforehand."

But the gears of the mechanical bird wear down. In one of Andersen's most haunting scenes, the dying emperor calls out,

> " Music, music! . . . . You precious little golden bird, sing, sing! I have loaded you with precious stones, and even hung my own golden slipper round your neck, sing, I tell you, sing!"
> But the bird stood silent, there was nobody to wind it up . . . . all was silent, so terribly silent.

But also, he used humor to draw us in. In " The Tinder Box," there is the delicious contrast between the mesmerizing presence of three dogs with huge eyes and the tongue-in-cheek humor of the soldier who finds them. The soldier's voice is a gentle, ironic one, which he does not lose, even in the most desperate situations. In a dungeon, waiting to be hanged, he says to a young boy rushing to the execution, " Don't be in such a hurry . . . Nothing will happen till I get there." Humphrey Carpenter and Mari Prichard in *The Oxford Companion to Children's Literature* (Oxford University Press, Oxford and New York, 1984), point out that " The Tinder Box" is based on a Scandinavian folk tale and bears similarities to " The Blue Light," a Grimm's fairy tale and to " Aladdin," from the *Arabian Nights*. But the voice we hear is Andersen's own—after the soldier loses his fortune and moves to a tiny, cold attic, and the friends he made when wealthy do not visit him, the author comments, " because there were far too many stairs."

Andersen also shows us the almost lyrical humor of the everyday. In " Olé Luköié, the Dustman," two dolls are to be married:

> The bridal pair sat upon the floor leaning against the leg of the table; they were very thoughtful, and they had reason to be.

The swallow tells them of the delights of the warm countries, urging them to travel, but the hen responds,

> " But they haven't got our green cabbage.... I was in
> the country all one summer with my chicks; there was a
> gravel pit that we scratched in all day, and then we got
> admission to a garden where the cabbage grew!.... I
> can't imagine anything more beautiful."

Andersen used humor to poke fun at the disparity between our
illusions of ourselves and our real worth. In "The Beetle," the
insect rests in the mane of the emperor's prized charger and
decides, "It was because of me that the horse was given gold
shoes." Within this straightforward adventure, Andersen
contrasts the beetle's self-involved universe, the cosmic world of
the Koran, and the often cruel world of humans. But here, as
elsewhere, Andersen shows us that it is our true natures that
determine the world we see.

This portrayal of different worlds and perspectives, universes
often included in, but ignorant of, each other, is a signature of
Andersen. In "The Pea Blossom," we are told:

> There were once five peas in one shell, they were green,
> the shell was green, and so they believed that the whole
> world must be green also.

In "The Goblin and the Huckster," the open book of a poor
student reveals to the imp a hitherto unguessed-at wealth of spirit:

> A mighty power surged around him, such as we feel
> when the Almighty moves over the face of the rolling
> waters in a storm, and he burst into tears.

The recognition of a new world is almost always a poignant
moment, the result of much yearning. In "The Mermaid," the
youngest of six mermaid princesses longs after the land above
the sea:

> Nothing gave her greater pleasure than to hear about
> the world of human beings above;.... above all it
> seemed strangely beautiful to her that up on the earth
> the flowers were scented,... also that the woods were
> green, and that the fish which were to be seen among the
> branches could sing so loudly and so sweetly that it was
> a delight to listen to them.

But she achieves a life on the earth only through great pain, and
her love is satisfied only with heartbreak.

Hans Christian Andersen himself had reason to know longing and the shadow-life of another world. Born in Odense, Denmark, in 1805, he was the son of a poor shoemaker who had convinced himself that he was of aristocratic origin. But if his father deluded himself, he was also a lover of literature, reading often to his son. He built toy theaters for Hans and took him to the playhouse. Carpenter and Prichard quote Andersen in his autobiography, *The Fairy Tale of My Life*, (Paddington Press Ltd, Two Continents Publishing Group, New York City), recalling that he made friends with the distributor of playbills of the many shows he could not afford to attend, was given a new playbill each day, and " with this I seated myself in a corner and imagined an entire play, according to the name of the piece and the characters in it. That was my first, unconscious poetizing."

Though his was a difficult personality, vain, and quick to take insult, Anderson also had the gift of being able to convince influential people to sponsor him. His life was replete with the sudden changes of fortune found in many of his stories. He first came to the notice of others through his lovely singing voice, but after it broke, received a royal grant to study at a state grammar school in Copenhagen. Much older than the other boys, he suffered abuse for both his age and his appearance—he had a long nose, and close-set eyes; his were the sufferings of " The Ugly Duckling." However, he passed his examinations at the age of twenty-three and chose to be a writer.

Among other things, Andersen wrote poetry and travel books. His first effort, " Tales Told for Children" was published as a small, cheap booklet in 1835, and further stories came out in small groups every Christmas. His tales were at first criticized for their colloquial style, by the end of ten years Andersen was recognized as a master of the fairy tale. His first stories were mostly retellings of stories told to him as a child; as he grew in confidence, he created more of his own.

Andersen never married, but suffered a series of unrequited loves. His heartache found expression in his stories—" The Steadfast Tin Soldier" and " The Mermaid," to name but two. His last unfulfilled love was the singer Jenny Lind, " The Swedish Nightingale," whose natural style he celebrated in his fairy tale, " The Nightingale." Andersen died in 1875.

Hans Christian Andersen often wrote of the truth of common things—the humble objects, ignored by us, that are the witnesses to our everyday life. In " The Bottle Neck," a glass bottle views both the tender, hopeful moment of a young girl's betrothal and her later, lonely spinster's existence. In his loving appreciation of even the most humble object, in the way he invested it with the dignity of story, Andersen sanctified the lives of common people. Hans Christian Andersen found a story in everything. Through his lens we see the world from the varied viewpoints of a beetle, a bottle, a mermaid, and an emperor—and perhaps we will never again turn our own doorknobs or wash our own cooking pots without pausing to ponder the tales they might tell.

ELLEN S. SHAPIRO

Brooklyn, New York
1988

Acknowledgment

The publishers gratefully acknowledge that this edition was prepared with the assistance and advice of Ellen S. Shapiro.

Editorial Note

The stories in this book were originally published in the first quarter of this century, and the modern reader may be surprised to discover old-fashioned styles of punctuation and spelling, but these have been retained in order to convey the flavor of the original work.

C.B.

ANDERSEN'S FAIRY TALES

The Mermaid

FAR out at sea the water is as blue as the bluest cornflower, and as clear as the clearest crystal; but it is very deep, too deep for any cable to fathom, and if many steeples were piled on the top of one another they would not reach from the bed of the sea to the surface of the water. It is down there that the Mermen live.

Now don't imagine that there are only bare white sands at the bottom; oh no! the most wonderful trees and plants grow there, with such flexible stalks and leaves, that at the slightest motion of the water they move just as if they were alive. All the fish, big and little, glide among the branches just as, up here, birds glide through the air. The palace of the Merman King lies in the very deepest part; its walls are of coral and the long pointed windows of the clearest amber, but the roof is made of mussel shells which open and shut with the lapping of the water. This has a lovely effect, for there are gleaming pearls in every shell, any one of which would be the pride of a queen's crown.

The Merman King had been for many years a widower, but his old mother kept house for him; she was a clever woman, but so proud of her noble birth that she wore twelve oysters on her tail, while the other grandees were only allowed six. Otherwise she was worthy of all praise, especially because she was so fond of the little mermaid princesses, her grandchildren. They were six beautiful children, but the youngest was the prettiest of all, her skin was as soft and delicate as a rose leaf, her eyes as blue as the deepest sea, but like all the others she had no feet, and instead of legs she had a fish's tail.

All the livelong day they used to play in the palace in the great halls, where living flowers grew out of the walls. When the great amber windows were thrown open the fish swam in, just as the swallows fly into our rooms when we open the windows, but the fish swam right up to the little princesses, ate out of their hands, and allowed themselves to be patted.

Outside the palace was a large garden, with fiery red and deep blue trees, the fruit of which shone like gold, while the flowers glowed like fire on their ceaselessly waving stalks. The ground was of the finest sand, but it was of a blue phosphorescent tint. Everything was bathed in a wondrous blue light down there; you might more readily have supposed yourself to be high up in the air, with only the sky above and below you, than that you were at the bottom of the ocean. In a dead calm you could just catch a glimpse of the sun like a purple flower with a stream of light radiating from its calyx.

Each little princess had her own little plot of garden, where she could dig and plant just as she liked. One made her flower-bed in the shape of a whale, another thought it nice to have hers like a little mermaid; but the youngest made hers quite round like the sun, and she would only have flowers of a rosy hue like its beams. She was a curious child, quiet and thoughtful, and while the other sisters decked out their gardens with all kinds of extraordinary objects which they got from wrecks, she would have nothing besides the rosy flowers like the sun up above, except a statue of a beautiful boy. It was hewn out of the purest white marble and had gone to the bottom from some wreck. By the statue she planted a rosy red weeping willow which grew splendidly, and the fresh delicate branches hung round and over it, till they almost touched the blue sand where the shadows showed violet, and were ever moving like the branches. It looked as if the leaves and the roots were playfully interchanging kisses.

Nothing gave her greater pleasure than to hear about the world of human beings up above; she made her old grand-mother tell her all that she knew about ships and towns, people and animals. But above all it seemed strangely beautiful to her that up on the earth the flowers were scented, for they were not so at the bottom of the sea; also that the woods were green, and that the fish which were to be seen among the branches could sing so loudly and sweetly that it was a delight to listen to them. You see the grandmother called little birds fish, or the mermaids would not have understood her, as they had never seen a bird.

"When you are fifteen," said the grandmother, "you will be allowed to rise up from the sea and sit on the rocks in the moonlight, and look at the big ships sailing by, and you will also see woods and towns."

One of the sisters would be fifteen in the following year, but the others—well, they were each one year younger than the other, so that the youngest had five whole years to wait before she would be allowed to come up from the bottom, to see what things were like on earth. But each one promised the others to give a full account of all that she had seen, and found most wonderful on the first day. Their grandmother could never tell them enough, for there were so many things about which they wanted information.

None of them was so full of longings as the youngest, the very one who had the longest time to wait, and who was so quiet and dreamy. Many a night she stood by the open windows and looked up through the dark blue water which the fish were lashing with their tails and fins. She could see the moon and the stars, it is true, their light was pale, but they looked much bigger through the water than they do to our eyes. When she saw a dark shadow glide between her and them, she knew that it was either a whale swimming above her, or else a ship laden with human beings. I am certain they never dreamt that a lovely little mermaid was standing down below, stretching up her white hands towards the keel.

The eldest princess had now reached her fifteenth birthday, and was to venture above the water. When she came back she had hundreds of things to tell them, but the most delightful of all, she said, was to lie in the moonlight, on a sandbank in a calm sea, and to gaze at the large town close to the shore, where the lights twinkled like hundreds of stars; to listen to music and the noise and bustle of carriages and people, to see the many church towers and spires, and to hear the bells ringing; and just because she could not go on shore she longed for that most of all.

Oh! how eagerly the youngest sister listened, and when, later in the evening she stood at the open window and looked up through the dark blue water, she thought of the big town with all its noise and bustle, and fancied that she could even hear the church bells ringing.

The year after, the second sister was allowed to mount up through the water and swim about wherever she liked. The sun was just going down when she reached the surface, the most beautiful sight, she thought, that she had ever seen. The whole sky had looked like gold, she said, and as for the clouds! well, their beauty was beyond description, they floated in red and violet splendour over her head, and, far faster than they went, a flock of wild swans flew like a long white veil over the water towards the setting sun; she swam towards it, but it sank and all the rosy light on clouds and water faded away.

The year after that the third sister went up, and being much the most venturesome of them all, swam up a broad river which ran into the sea. She saw beautiful green, vine-clad hills; palaces and country seats peeping through splendid woods. She heard the birds singing, and the sun was so hot that she was often obliged to dive, to cool her burning face. In a tiny bay she found a troop of little children running about naked and paddling in the water; she wanted to play with them, but they were frightened and ran away. Then a little black animal came up, it was a dog, but she had never seen one before; it barked so furiously at her that she was frightened and made for the open sea. She could never forget the beautiful woods, the green hills and the lovely children who could swim in the water although they had no fishes' tails.

The fourth sister was not so brave, she stayed in the remotest part of the ocean, and, according to her account, that was the most beautiful spot. You could see for miles and miles around you, and the sky above was like a great glass dome. She had seen ships, but only far away, so that they looked like sea-gulls. There were grotesque dolphins turning somersaults, and gigantic whales squirting water through their nostrils like hundreds of fountains on every side.

Now the fifth sister's turn came. Her birthday fell in the winter, so that she saw sights that the others had not seen on their first trips. The sea looked quite green, and large icebergs were floating about, each one of which looked like a pearl, she said, but was much bigger than the church towers built by men. They took the most wonderful shapes, and sparkled like diamonds. She had seated herself on one of the largest, and all the passing ships sheered off in alarm when they saw her sitting there with her long hair streaming loose in the wind.

In the evening the sky became overcast with dark clouds; it thundered and lightened, and the huge icebergs glittering in the bright lightning, were lifted high into the air by the black waves. All the ships shortened sail, and there was fear and trembling on every side, but she sat quietly on her floating iceberg watching the blue lightning flash in zigzags down on to the shining sea.

The first time any of the sisters rose above the water she was delighted by the novelties and beauties she saw; but once grown up, and at liberty to go where she liked, she became indifferent and longed for her home; in the course of a month or so they all said that after all their own home in the deep was best, it was so cosy there.

Many an evening the five sisters interlacing their arms would rise above the water together. They had lovely voices, much clearer than any mortal, and when a storm was rising, and they expected ships to be wrecked, they would sing in the most seductive strains of the wonders of the deep, bidding the seafarers have no fear of them. But the sailors could not understand the words, they thought it was the voice of the storm; nor could it be theirs to see this Elysium of the deep, for when the ship sank they were drowned, and only reached the Merman's palace in death. When the elder sisters rose up in this manner, arm-in-arm, in the evening, the youngest remained behind quite alone, looking after them as if she must weep, but mermaids have no tears and so they suffer all the more.

"Oh! if I were only fifteen!" she said, "I know how fond I shall be of the world above, and of the mortals who dwell there."

At last her fifteenth birthday came.

" Now we shall have you off our hands," said her grandmother, the old queen dowager. "Come now, let me adorn you like your other sisters!" and she put a wreath of white lilies round her hair, but every petal of the flowers was half a pearl; then the old queen had eight oysters fixed on to the princess's tail to show her high rank.

" But it hurts so! " said the little mermaid.

" You must endure the pain for the sake of the finery! " said her grandmother.

But oh! how gladly would she have shaken off all this splendour, and laid aside the heavy wreath. Her red flowers in her garden suited her much better, but she did not dare to make any alteration. " Good-bye," she said, and mounted as lightly and airily as a bubble through the water.

The sun had just set when her head rose above the water, but the clouds were still lighted up with a rosy and golden splendour, and the evening star sparkled in the soft pink sky, the air was mild and fresh, and the sea as calm as a millpond. A big three-masted ship lay close by with only a single sail set, for there was not a breath of wind, and the sailors were sitting about the rigging, on the cross-trees, and at the mast-heads. There was music and singing on board, and as the evening closed in, hundreds of gaily coloured lanterns were lighted —they looked like the flags of all nations waving in the air. The little mermaid swam right up to the cabin windows, and every time she was lifted by the swell she could see through the transparent panes crowds of gaily dressed people. The handsomest of them all was the young prince with large dark eyes; he could not be much more than sixteen, and all these festivities were in honour of his birthday. The sailors danced on deck, and when the prince appeared among them hundreds of rockets were let off making it as light as day, and frightening the little mermaid so much that she had to dive under the water. She soon ventured up again, and it was just as if all the stars of heaven were falling in showers round about her. She had never seen such magic fires. Great suns whirled round, gorgeous fire-fish hung in the blue air, and all was reflected in the calm and glassy sea. It was so light on board the ship that every little rope could be seen, and the people still better. Oh! how handsome the prince was, how he laughed and smiled as he greeted his guests, while the music rang out in the quiet night.

It got quite late, but the little mermaid could not take her eyes off the ship and the beautiful prince. The coloured lanterns were put out, no more rockets were sent up, and the cannon had ceased its thunder, but deep down in the sea there was a dull murmuring and moaning sound. Meanwhile she was rocked up and down on the waves, so that she could look into the cabin; but the ship got more and more way on, sail after sail was filled by the wind, the waves grew stronger, great clouds gathered, and it lightened in the distance. Oh, there was going to be a fearful storm! and soon the sailors had to shorten sail. The great ship rocked and rolled as she dashed over the angry sea, the black waves rose like mountains, high enough to overwhelm her, but she dived like a swan through them and rose again and again on their towering crests. The little mermaid thought it a most amusing race, but not so the sailors. The ship creaked and groaned, the mighty timbers bulged and bent under the heavy blows, the water broke over the decks, snapping the main mast like a reed, she heeled over on her side and the water rushed into the hold.

Now the little mermaid saw that they were in danger and she had for her own sake to beware of the floating beams and wreckage. One moment it was so pitch dark that she could not see at all, but when the lightning flashed it became so light that she could see all on board. Every man was looking out for his own safety as best he could, but she more particularly followed the young prince with her eyes, and when the ship went down she saw him sink in the deep sea. At first she was quite delighted, for now he was coming to be with her, but then she remembered that human beings could not live under water, and that only if he were dead could he go to her father's palace. No! he must not die; so she swam towards him all among the drifting beams and planks, quite forgetting that they might crush her. She dived deep down under the water, and came up again through the waves, and at last reached the young prince just as he was becoming unable to swim any further in the stormy sea. His limbs were numbed, his beautiful eyes were closing, and he must have died if the little mermaid had not come to the rescue. She held his head above the water and let the waves drive them whithersoever they would.

By daybreak all the storm was over, of the ship not a trace was to be seen; the sun rose from the water in radiant brilliance, and his rosy beams seemed to cast a glow of life into the prince's cheeks, but his eyes remained closed. The mermaid kissed his fair and lofty brow, and stroked back the dripping hair; it seemed to her that he was like the marble statue in her little garden, she kissed him again and longed that he might live.

At last she saw dry land before her, high blue mountains on whose summits the white snow glistened as if a flock of swans had settled there; down by the shore were beautiful green woods, and in the foreground a church or temple, she did not quite know which, but it was a building of some sort. Lemon and orange trees grew in the garden and lofty palms stood by the gate. At this point the sea formed a little bay where the water was quite calm, but very deep, right up to the cliffs; at their foot was a strip of fine white sand to which she swam with the beautiful prince, and laid him down on it, taking great care that his head should rest high up in the warm sunshine.

The bells now began to ring in the great white building and a number of young maidens came into the garden. Then the little mermaid swam further off behind some high rocks and covered her hair and breast with foam, so that no one should see her little face, and then she watched to see who would discover the poor prince.

It was not long before one of the maidens came up to him, at first she seemed quite frightened, but only for a moment, and then she fetched several others, and the mermaid saw that the prince was coming to life, and that he smiled at all those around him, but he never smiled at her, you see he did not know that she had saved him; she felt so sad that when he was led away into the great building she dived sorrowfully into the water and made her way home to her father's palace.

Always silent and thoughtful, she became more so now than ever. Her sisters often asked her what she had seen on her first visit to the surface, but she never would tell them anything.

Many an evening and many a morning she would rise to the place where she had left the prince. She saw the fruit in the garden ripen, and then gathered, she saw the snow melt on the mountain-tops, but she never saw the prince, so she always went home still sadder than before. At home her only consolation was to sit in her little garden with her arms twined round the handsome marble statue which reminded her of the prince. It was all in gloomy shade now, as she had ceased to tend her flowers and the garden had become a neglected wilderness of long stalks and leaves entangled with the branches of the tree.

At last she could not bear it any longer, so she told one of her sisters, and from her it soon spread to the others, but to no one else except to one or two other mermaids who only told their dearest friends. One of these knew all about the prince, she had also seen the festivities on the ship; she knew where he came from and where his kingdom was situated.

" Come, little sister! " said the other princesses, and, throwing their arms round each other's shoulders, they rose from the water in a long line, just in front of the prince's palace.

It was built of light yellow glistening stone, with great marble staircases, one of which led into the garden. Magnificent gilded cupolas rose above the roof, and the spaces between the columns which encircled the building were filled with life-like marble statues. Through the clear glass of the lofty windows you could see gorgeous halls adorned with costly silken hangings, and the pictures on the walls were a sight worth seeing. In the midst of the central hall a large fountain played, throwing its jets of spray upwards to a glass dome in the roof, through which the sunbeams lighted up the water and the beautiful plants which grew in the great basin.

She knew now where he lived and often used to go there in the evenings and by night over the water; she swam much nearer the land than any of the others dared, she even ventured right up the narrow channel under the splendid marble terrace which threw a long shadow over the water. She used to sit here looking at the young prince who thought he was quite alone in the clear moonlight.

She saw him many an evening sailing about in his beautiful boat, with flags waving and music playing, she used to peep through the green rushes, and if the wind happened to catch her long silvery veil and any one saw it, they only thought it was a swan flapping its wings.

Many a night she heard the fishermen, who were fishing by

torchlight, talking over the good deeds of the young prince; and she was happy to think that she had saved his life when he was drifting about on the waves, half dead, and she could not forget how closely his head had pressed her breast, and how passionately she had kissed him; but he knew nothing of all this, and never saw her even in his dreams.

She became fonder and fonder of mankind, and longed more and more to be able to live among them; their world seemed so infinitely bigger than hers; with their ships they could scour the ocean, they could ascend the mountains high above the clouds, and their wooded, grass-grown lands extended further than her eye could reach. There was so much that she wanted to know, but her sisters could not give an answer to all her questions, so she asked her old grandmother who knew the upper world well, and rightly called it the country above the sea.

"If men are not drowned," asked the little mermaid, "do they live for ever, do they not die as we do down here in the sea?"

"Yes," said the old lady, "they have to die too, and their life time is even shorter than ours. We may live here for three hundred years, but when we cease to exist, we become mere foam on the water and do not have so much as a grave among our dear ones. We have no immortal souls, we have no future life, we are just like the green sea-weed, which, once cut down, can never revive again! Men, on the other hand, have a soul which lives for ever, lives after the body has become dust; it rises through the clear air, up to the shining stars! Just as we rise from the water to see the land of mortals, so they rise up to unknown beautiful regions which we shall never see."

"Why have we no immortal souls?" asked the little mermaid sadly. "I would give all my three hundred years to be a human being for one day, and afterwards to have a share in the heavenly kingdom."

"You must not be thinking about that," said the grandmother, "we are much better off and happier than human beings."

"Then I shall have to die and to float as foam on the water, and never hear the music of the waves or see the beautiful flowers or the red sun! Is there nothing I can do to gain an immortal soul?"

"No," said the grandmother, "only if a human being so loved you, that you were more to him than father or mother, if all his thoughts and all his love were so centred in you that he would let the priest join your hands and would vow to be faithful to you here, and to all eternity; then your body would become infused with his soul. Thus and only thus, could you gain a share in the felicity of mankind. He would give you a soul while yet keeping his own. But that can never happen! That which is your greatest beauty in the sea, your fish's tail, is thought hideous up on earth, so little do they understand about it; to be pretty there you must have two clumsy supports which they call legs!"

Then the little mermaid sighed and looked sadly at her fish's tail.

"Let us be happy," said the grandmother, "we will hop and skip during our three hundred years of life, it is surely a long enough time, and after it is over, we shall rest all the better in our graves. There is to be a court ball to-night."

This was a much more splendid affair than we ever see on earth. The walls and the ceiling of the great ball room were of thick but transparent glass. Several hundreds of colossal mussel shells, rose-red and grass-green, were ranged in order round the sides holding blue lights, which illuminated the whole room and shone through the walls, so that the sea outside was quite lit up. You could see countless fish, great and small, swimming towards the glass walls, some with shining scales of crimson hue, while others were golden and silvery. In the middle of the room was a broad stream of running water, and on this the mermaids and mermen danced to their own beautiful singing. No earthly beings have such lovely voices. The little mermaid sang more sweetly than any of them and they all applauded her. For a moment she felt glad at heart, for she knew that she had the finest voice either in the sea or on land. But she soon began to think again about the upper world, she could not forget the handsome prince and her sorrow in not possessing, like him, an immortal soul. Therefore she stole out of her father's palace, and while all within was joy and merriment, she sat sadly in her little garden. Suddenly she heard the sound of a horn through the water, and she thought, "now he is out sailing up there; he whom I love more than father or mother, he to whom my thoughts cling and to whose hands I am ready to commit the happiness of my life. I will dare anything to win him and to gain an immortal soul! While my sisters are dancing in my father's palace, I will go to the sea witch of whom I have always been very much afraid, she will perhaps be able to advise and help me!"

Thereupon the little mermaid left the garden and went towards the roaring whirlpools at the back of which the witch lived. She had never been that way before; no flowers grew there, no seaweed, only the bare grey sands stretched towards the whirlpools, which like rushing mill-wheels swirled round, dragging everything that came within reach down to the depths. She had to pass between these boiling eddies to reach the witch's domain, and for a long way the only path led over warm bubbling mud, which the witch called her " peat bog." Her house stood behind this in the midst of a weird forest. All the trees and bushes were polyps, half animal and half plant; they looked like hundred-headed snakes growing out of the sand, the branches were long slimy arms, with tentacles like wriggling worms, every joint of which from the root to the outermost tip was in constant motion. They wound themselves tightly round whatever they could lay hold of and never let it escape. The little mermaid standing outside was quite frightened, her heart beat fast with terror and she nearly turned back, but then she remembered the prince and the immortal soul of mankind and took courage. She bound her long flowing hair tightly round her head, so that the polyps should not seize her by it, folded her hands over her breast, and darted like a fish through the water, in between the hideous polyps which stretched out their sensitive arms and tentacles towards her. She could see that every one of them had something or other, which they had grasped with their hundred arms, and which they held as if in iron bands. The bleached bones of men who had perished at sea and sunk below peeped forth from the arms of some, while others clutched rudders and sea chests, or the skeleton of some land animal; and most horrible of all, a little mermaid whom they had caught and suffocated. Then she came to a large opening in the wood where the ground was all slimy, and where some huge fat water snakes were gambolling about. In the middle of this opening was a house built of the bones of the wrecked; there sat the witch, letting a toad eat out of her mouth, just as mortals let a little canary eat sugar. She called the hideous water snakes her little chickens, and allowed them to crawl about on her unsightly bosom.

"I know very well what you have come here for," said the witch. "It is very foolish of you! all the same you shall have your way, because it will lead you into misfortune, my fine princess. You want to get rid of your fish's tail, and instead to have two stumps to walk about upon like human beings, so that the young prince may fall in love with you, and that you may win him and an immortal soul." Saying this, she gave such a loud hideous laugh that the toad and the snakes fell to the ground and wriggled about there.

"You are just in the nick of time," said the witch, "after sunrise to-morrow I should not be able to help you until another year had run its course. I will make you a potion, and before sunrise you must swim ashore with it, seat yourself on the beach and drink it; then your tail will divide and shrivel up to what men call beautiful legs, but it hurts, it is as if a sharp sword were running through you. All who see you will say that you are the most beautiful child of man they have ever seen. You will keep your gliding gait, no dancer will rival you, but every step you take will be as if you were treading upon sharp knives, so sharp as to draw blood. If you are willing to suffer all this I am ready to help you!"

"Yes!" said the little princess with a trembling voice, thinking of the prince and of winning an undying soul.

"But remember," said the witch, "when once you have received a human form, you can never be a mermaid again, you will never again be able to dive down through the water to your sisters and to your father's palace. And if you do not succeed in winning the prince's love, so that for your sake he will forget father and mother, cleave to you with his whole heart, let the priest join your hands and make you man and wife, you will gain no immortal soul! The first morning after his marriage with another your heart will break, and you will turn into foam of the sea."

" I will do it," said the little mermaid as pale as death.

" But you will have to pay me, too," said the witch, " and it is no trifle that I demand. You have the most beautiful voice of any at the bottom of the sea, and I daresay that you think you will fascinate him with it, but you must give me that voice, I will have the best you possess in return for my precious potion! I have to mingle my own blood with it so as to make it as sharp as a two-edged sword."

" But if you take my voice," said the little mermaid, " what have I left? "

" Your beautiful form," said the witch, " your gliding gait, and your speaking eyes, with these you ought surely to be able to bewitch a human heart. Well! have you lost courage? Put out your little tongue and I will cut it off in payment for the powerful draught."

" Let it be done," said the little mermaid, and the witch put on her cauldron to brew the magic potion. " There is nothing like cleanliness," said she, as she scoured the pot with a bundle of snakes; then she punctured her breast and let the black blood drop into the cauldron, and the steam took the most weird shapes, enough to frighten any one. Every moment the witch threw new ingredients into the pot, and when it boiled the bubbling was like the sound of crocodiles weeping. At last the potion was ready and it looked like the clearest water.

" There it is," said the witch, and thereupon she cut off the tongue of the little mermaid, who was dumb now and could neither sing nor speak.

" If the polyps should seize you, when you go back through my wood," said the witch, " just drop a single drop of this liquid on them, and their arms and fingers will burst into a thousand pieces." But the little mermaid had no need to do this, for at the mere sight of the bright liquid which sparkled in her hand like a shining star, they drew back in terror. So she soon got past the wood, the bog, and the eddying whirlpools.

She saw her father's palace, the lights were all out in the great ballroom, and no doubt all the household was asleep, but she did not dare to go in now that she was dumb and about to leave her home for ever. She felt as if her heart would break with grief. She stole into the garden and plucked a flower from each of her sister's plots, wafted with her hand countless kisses towards the palace, and then rose up through the dark blue water.

The sun had not risen when she came in sight of the prince's palace and landed at the beautiful marble steps. The moon was shining bright and clear. The little mermaid drank the burning, stinging draught, and it was like a sharp, two-edged sword running through her tender frame; she fainted away and lay as if she were dead. When the sun rose on the sea she woke up and became conscious of a sharp pang, but just in front of her stood the handsome young prince, fixing his coal black eyes on her; she cast hers down and saw that her fish's tail was gone, and that she had the prettiest little white legs any maiden could desire, but she was quite naked, so she wrapped her long thick hair around her. The prince asked who she was and how she came there, she looked at him tenderly and with a sad expression in her dark blue eyes, but could not speak. Then he took her by the hand and led her into the palace. Every step she took was, as the witch had warned her beforehand, as if she were treading on sharp knives and spikes but she bore it gladly; led by the prince she moved as lightly as a bubble, and he and every one else marvelled at her graceful gilding gait.

Clothed in the costliest silks and muslins she was the greatest beauty in the palace, but she was dumb and could neither sing nor speak. Beautiful slaves clad in silks and gold came forward and sang to the prince and his royal parents; one of them sang better than all the others, and the prince clapped his hands and smiled at her; that made the little mermaid very sad, for she knew that she used to sing far better herself. She thought, "Oh! if he only knew that for the sake of being with him I had given up my voice for ever!" Now the slaves began to dance, graceful undulating dances to enchanting music; thereupon the little mermaid lifting her beautiful white arms and raising herself on tiptoe glided on the floor with a grace which none of the other dancers had yet attained. With every motion her grace and beauty became more apparent, and her eyes appealed more deeply to the heart than the songs of the slaves. Everyone was delighted with it, especially the prince, who called her his little foundling, and she danced on and on, notwithstanding that every time her foot touched the ground it was like treading on sharp knives. The prince said that she should always be near him, and she was allowed to sleep outside his door on a velvet cushion.

He had a man's dress made for her, so that she could ride about with him. They used to ride through scented woods, where the green branches brushed her shoulders, and little birds sang among the fresh leaves. She climbed up the highest mountains with the prince, and although her delicate feet bled so that others saw it, she only laughed and followed him until they saw the clouds sailing below them like a flock of birds, taking flight to distant lands.

At home in the prince's palace, when at night the others were asleep, she used to go out on to the marble steps; it cooled her burning feet to stand in the cold sea water, and at such times she used to think of those she had left in the deep.

One night her sisters came arm in arm; they sang so sorrowfully as they swam on the water that she beckoned to them and they recognised her, and told her how she had grieved them all. After that they visited her every night, and one night she saw, a long way out, her old grandmother (who for many years had not been above the water), and the Merman King with his crown on his head; they stretched out their hands towards her, but did not venture so close to land as her sisters.

Day by day she became dearer to the prince, he loved her as one loves a good sweet child, but it never entered his head to make her his queen; yet unless she became his wife she would never win an everlasting soul, but on his wedding morning would turn to sea foam.

"Am I not dearer to you than any of them?" the little mermaid's eyes seemed to say when he took her in his arms and kissed her beautiful brow.

"Yes, you are the dearest one to me," said the prince, "for you have the best heart of them all, and you are fondest of me; you are also like a young girl I once saw, but whom I never expect to see again. I was on board a ship which was wrecked, I was driven on shore by the waves close to a holy Temple where several young girls were ministering at a service; the youngest of them found me on the beach and saved my life;

I saw her but twice. She was the only person I could love in this world, but you are like her, you almost drive her image out of my heart. She belongs to the holy Temple, and therefore by good fortune you have been sent to me, we will never part!"

"Alas! he does not know that it was I who saved his life," thought the little mermaid. "I bore him over the sea to the wood, where the Temple stands. I sat behind the foam and watched to see if any one would come. I saw the pretty girl he loves better than me." And the mermaid heaved a bitter sigh, for she could not weep.

"The girl belongs to the holy Temple, he has said, she will never return to the world, they will never meet again, I am here with him, I see him every day. Yes! I will tend him, love him, and give up my life to him."

But now the rumour ran that the prince was to be married to the beautiful daughter of a neighbouring king, and for that reason was fitting out a splendid ship. It was given out that the prince was going on a voyage to see the adjoining countries, but it was without doubt to see the king's daughter; he was to have a great suite with him, but the little mermaid shook her head and laughed; she knew the prince's intentions much better than any of the others. "I must take this voyage," he had said to her; "I must go and see the beautiful princess; my parents demand that, but they will never force me to bring her home as my bride; I can never love her! She will not be like the lovely girl in the Temple whom you resemble. If ever I had to choose a bride it would sooner be you with your speaking eyes, my sweet, dumb foundling!" And he kissed her rosy mouth, played with her long hair, and laid his head upon her heart, which already dreamt of human joys and an immortal soul.

"You are not frightened of the sea, I suppose, my dumb child?" he said, as they stood on the proud ship which was to carry them to the country of the neighbouring king; and he told her about storms and calms, about curious fish in the deep, and the marvels seen by divers; and she smiled at his tales, for she knew all about the bottom of the sea much better than any one else.

At night, in the moonlight, when all were asleep, except

the steersman who stood at the helm, she sat at the side of the
ship trying to pierce the clear water with her eyes, and fancied
she saw her father's palace, and above it her old grandmother
with her silver crown on her head, looking up through the cross
currents towards the keel of the ship. Then her sisters rose
above the water, they gazed sadly at her, wringing their white
hands; she beckoned to them, smiled, and was about to tell
them that all was going well and happily with her, when the cabin
boy approached, and the sisters dived down, but he supposed
that the white objects he had seen were nothing but flakes of
foam.

The next morning the ship entered the harbour of the neighbouring king's magnificent city. The church bells rang and
trumpets were sounded from every lofty tower, while the soldiers
paraded with flags flying and glittering bayonets. There was
a *fête* every day, there was a succession of balls, and receptions
followed one after the other, but the princess was not yet present,
she was being brought up a long way off, in a holy Temple they
said, and was learning all the royal virtues. At last she came.
The little mermaid stood eager to see her beauty, and she was
obliged to confess that a lovelier creature she had never beheld.
Her complexion was exquisitely pure and delicate, and her
trustful eyes of the deepest blue shone through their dark lashes.

" It is you," said the prince, " you who saved me when I
lay almost lifeless on the beach? " and he clasped his blushing
bride to his heart. " Oh! I am too happy! " he exclaimed
to the little mermaid.

" A greater joy than I had dared to hope for has come to
pass. You will rejoice at my joy, for you love me better than
any one." Then the little mermaid kissed his hand, and felt
as if her heart were broken already.

His wedding morn would bring death to her and change her
to foam.

All the church bells pealed and heralds rode through the
town proclaiming the nuptials. Upon every altar throughout
the land fragrant oil was burnt in costly silver lamps. Amidst
the swinging of censers by the priests, the bride and bridegroom
joined hands and received the bishop's blessing. The little
mermaid dressed in silk and gold stood holding the bride's

train, but her ears were deaf to the festal strains, her eyes saw nothing of the sacred ceremony, she was thinking of her coming death and of all that she had lost in this world.

That same evening the bride and bridegroom embarked, amidst the roar of cannon and the waving of banners. A royal tent of purple and gold softly cushioned was raised amidships where the bridal pair were to repose during the calm cool night.

The sails swelled in the wind and the ship skimmed lightly and almost without motion over the transparent sea.

At dusk lanterns of many colours were lighted and the sailors danced merrily on deck. The little mermaid could not help thinking of the first time she came up from the sea and saw the same splendour and gaiety; and she now threw herself among the dancers, whirling, as a swallow skims through the air when pursued. The onlookers cheered her in amazement, never had she danced so divinely; her delicate feet pained her as if they were cut with knives, but she did not feel it, for the pain at her heart was much sharper. She knew that it was the last night that she would breathe the same air as he, and would look upon the mighty deep, and the blue starry heavens; an endless night without thought and without dreams awaited her, who neither had a soul, nor could win one. The joy and revelry on board lasted till long past midnight, she went on laughing and dancing with the thought of death all the time in her heart. The prince caressed his lovely bride and she played with his raven locks, and with their arms entwined they retired to the gorgeous tent. All became hushed and still on board the ship, only the steersman stood at the helm, the little mermaid laid her white arms on the gunwale and looked eastwards for the pink tinted dawn; the first sunbeam she knew would be her death. Then she saw her sisters rise from the water, they were as pale as she was, their beautiful long hair no longer floated on the breeze, for it had been cut off.

" We have given it to the witch to obtain her help, so that you may not die to-night! she has given us a knife, here it is, look how sharp it is! Before the sun rises, you must plunge it into the prince's heart, and when his warm blood sprinkles your feet they will join together and grow into a tail, and you will once more be a mermaid; you will be able to come down into the water to us, and to live out your three hundred years before you are turned into dead, salt, sea-foam. Make haste! you or he must die before sunrise! Our old grandmother is so full of grief that her white hair has fallen off as ours fell under the witch's scissors. Slay the prince and come back to us! Quick! Quick! do you not see the rosy streak in the sky? In a few moments the sun will rise and then you must die!" saying this they heaved a wondrous deep sigh and sank among the waves.

The little mermaid drew aside the purple curtain from the tent and looked at the beautiful bride asleep with her head on the prince's breast; she bent over him and kissed his fair brow, looked at the sky where the dawn was spreading fast; looked at the sharp knife, and again fixed her eyes on the prince who, in his dream called his bride by name, yes! she alone was in his thoughts!—For a moment the knife quivered in her grasp, then she threw it far out among the waves now rosy in the morning light and where it fell the water bubbled up like drops of blood.

Once more she looked at the prince, with her eyes already dimmed by death, then dashed overboard and fell, her body dissolving into foam.

Now the sun rose from the sea and with its kindly beams warmed the deadly cold foam, so that the little mermaid did not feel the chill of death. She saw the bright sun and above her floated hundreds of beauteous ethereal beings through which she could see the white ship and the rosy heavens, their voices were melodious but so spirit-like that no human ear could hear them, any more than an earthly eye could see their forms. Light as bubbles they floated through the air without the aid of wings. The little mermaid perceived that she had a form like theirs, it gradually took shape out of the foam. "To whom am I coming?" said she, and her voice sounded like that of the other beings, so unearthly in its beauty that no music of ours could reproduce it.

"To the daughters of the air!" answered the others, "a mermaid has no undying soul, and can never gain one without winning the love of a human being. Her eternal life must depend upon an unknown power. Nor have the daughters of the air an everlasting soul, but by their own good deeds they may create one for themselves. We fly to the tropics where mankind is the victim of hot and pestilent winds, there we bring cooling breezes. We diffuse the scent of flowers all around, and bring refreshment and healing in our train. When, for three hundred years, we have laboured to do all the good in our power we gain an undying soul and take a part in the everlasting joys of mankind. You, poor little mermaid, have with your whole heart struggled for the same thing, as we have struggled for. You have suffered and endured, raised yourself to the spirit world of the air; and now, by your own good deeds you may, in the course of three hundred years, work out for yourself an undying soul."

Then the little mermaid lifted her transparent arms towards God's sun, and for the first time shed tears.

On board ship all was again life and bustle, she saw the prince with his lovely bride searching for her, they looked sadly at the bubbling foam, as if they knew that she had thrown herself into the waves. Unseen she kissed the bride on her brow, smiled at the prince and rose aloft with the other spirits of the air to the rosy clouds which sailed above.

" In three hundred years we shall thus float into Paradise."

" We might reach it sooner," whispered one. " Unseen we flit into those homes of men where there are children, and for every day that we find a good child who gives pleasure to its parents and deserves their love, God shortens our time of probation. The child does not know when we fly through the room, and when we smile with pleasure at it, one year of our three hundred is taken away. But if we see a naughty or badly disposed child, we cannot help shedding tears of sorrow, and every tear adds a day to the time of our probation."

HANS CLODHOPPER

THERE was once an old mansion in the country, in which an old squire lived with his two sons, and these two sons were too clever by half. They had made up their minds to propose to the king's daughter, and they ventured to do so, because she had made it known that she would take any man for a husband who had most to say for himself. These two took a week over their preparations; it was all the time they had for it, but it was quite enough with all their accomplishments, which were most useful. One of them knew the Latin Dictionary by heart, and the town newspapers for three years either forwards or backwards. The second one had made himself acquainted with all the statutes of the Corporations, and what every alderman had to know. So he thought he was competent to talk about affairs of state; and he also knew how to embroider harness, for he was clever with his fingers.

"I shall win the king's daughter," they both said, and their father gave each of them a beautiful horse. The one who could repeat the Dictionary and the newspapers had a coal-black one, while the one who was learned to Guilds and embroideries had a milk-white one. Then they smeared the corners of their mouths with oil to make them more flexible. All the servants were assembled in the court-yards to see them mount, but just then the third brother came up, for there were three, only nobody made any account of this one, Hans Clodhopper, as he had no accomplishments like his brothers.

" Where are you going with all your fine clothes on? " he asked.

" To court, to talk ourselves into favour with the princess. Haven't you heard the news which is being drummed all over the country? " And then they told him the news.

" Preserve us! then I must go too," said Hans Clodhopper. But his brothers laughed and rode away.

" Father, give me a horse. I want to get married too. If she takes me, she takes me, and if she doesn't take me, I shall take her all the same."

" Stuff and nonsense," said his father, " I will give no horse to you. Why you have got nothing to say for yourself, now your brothers are fine fellows."

" If I mayn't have a horse," said Hans Clodhopper, " I'll take the billy-goat, he is my own and he can carry me very well! " And he seated himself astride the billy-goat, dug his heels into its sides, and galloped off down the high road. Whew! what a pace they went at.

" Here I come," shouted Hans Clodhopper, and he sang till the air rang with it.

The brothers rode on in silence, they did not say a word to each other, for they had to store up every good idea which they wanted to produce later on, and their speeches had to be very carefully thought out.

" Halloo! " shouted Hans Clodhopper, " here I come; see what I've found on the road," and he showed them a dead crow.

" What on earth will you do with that, Clodhopper? " said they.

" I will give it to the king's daughter."

" Yes, I would do that," said they, and they rode on laughing.

" Halloo, here I come; see what I have found; one doesn't find such a thing as this every day on the road." The brothers turned round to see what it was.

" Clodhopper," said they, " it's nothing but an old wooden shoe with the upper part broken off. Is the princess to have that too? "

" Yes indeed she is," said Hans, and the brothers again rode on laughing.

" Halloo, halloo, here I am," shouted Hans Clodhopper. " Now this is famous."

" What have you found this time? " asked the brothers.

" Won't the princess be delighted! "

" Why," said the brothers, " it's only sand picked up out of the ditch! "

" Yes, that it is," said Hans Clodhopper, " and the finest kind of sand, too. You can hardly hold it." And he filled his pockets with it. The brothers rode on as fast as they could, and arrived at the town gates a whole hour before him. At the gate the suitors received tickets, in the order of their arrival, and they were arranged in rows, six in each file, and so close together that they could not move their arms which was a very good thing, or they would have torn each others garments off, merely because one stood in front of the other. All the other inhabitants of the town stood round the castle, peeping in at the windows to see the king's daughter receive the suitors, and as each one came into the room he lost the power of speech.

" No good," said the princess, " away with him! "

Now came the brother who could repeat the Lexicon, but he had entirely forgotten it while standing in the ranks. The floor creaked and the ceiling was made of looking-glass, so that he saw himself standing on his head; and at every window sat three clerks and an alderman, who wrote down all that was said, so that it might be sent to the papers at once, and sold for a halfpenny at the street corners. It was terrible, and the stoves had been heated to such a degree that they got red-hot at the top.

" It is terribly hot in here," said the suitor.

" That is because my father is roasting cockerels to-day," said the princess.

Bah! There he stood like a fool; he had not expected a conversation of this kind, and he could not think of a word to say, just when he wanted to be specially witty.

" No good," said the king's daughter, " away with him," and he had to go.

Then came the second brother. " There's a fearful heat here," said he.

" Yes, we are roasting cockerels to-day," said the king's daughter.

" What did—what? " said he, and all the reporters duly wrote " What did—what."

" No good," said the king's daughter, " away with him."

Then came Hans Clodhopper. He rode the billy-goat right into the room.

" What a burning heat you have here," said he.

" That is because I am roasting cockerels," said the king's daughter.

" That is very convenient," said Hans Clodhopper; " then I suppose I can get a crow roasted, too."

" Yes, very well," said the king's daughter: " but have you anything to roast it in? For I have neither pot nor pan."

" But I have," said Hans Clodhopper. " Here is a cooking pot." And he brought out the wooden shoe and put the crow into it.

" Why you have enough for a whole meal," said the king's daughter; " but where shall we get any dripping to baste it with? "

" Oh, I have some in my pocket," said Hans Clodhopper; " I have enough and to spare," and he poured a little of the sand out of his pocket.

" Now I like that," said the princess; " you have an answer for everything, and you have something to say for yourself. I will have you for a husband. But do you know that every word we have said will be in the paper to-morrow, for at every window sit three clerks and an alderman, and the alderman is the worst, for he doesn't understand." She said this to frighten him. All the clerks sniggered and made blots of ink on the floor.

" Oh, those are the gentry," said Hans Clodhopper; " then I must give the alderman the best thing I have," and he turned out his pockets and threw the sand in his face.

" That was cleverly done," said the princess, " I couldn't have done it, but I will try to learn."

So Hans Clodhopper became king, gained a wife and a crown and sat upon the throne. We have this straight out of the alderman's newspaper, but it is not to be depended upon.

THE FLYING TRUNK

THERE was once a merchant who was so rich that he might have paved the whole street, and a little alley besides, with silver money. But he didn't do it—he knew better how to use his money than that: if he laid out a penny, he got half a crown in return, such a clever man of business was he—and then he died.

His son got all the money, and he led a merry life; he used to go to masquerades every night, made kites of bank notes, and played ducks and drakes with gold coins instead of stones. In this way the money soon went. At last he had only a penny left, and no clothes except an old dressing-gown and a pair of slippers. His friends cared for him no longer, they couldn't walk about the streets with him; but one of them who was kind sent him an old trunk, and said, "Pack up." Now this was all very well, but he had nothing to pack, so he got into the trunk himself.

It was a most peculiar trunk. If you pressed the lock the trunk could fly; and this is what happened: with a whiz it flew up the chimney, high above the clouds, further and further away. The bottom of it cracked ominously, and he was dreadfully afraid it would go to pieces, and a nice fall he would have had! Heaven preserve us! At last he arrived in the country of the Turks. He hid the trunk in a wood under the dead leaves, and walked into the town; he could easily do that, as all the Turks wear dressing-gowns and slippers, you know, just like his. He met a nurse with a baby. " I say, you Turkish nurse," said he, " what is that big palace close to the town, where all the windows are so high up? "

" That's where the king's daughter lives," said she; " it has been prophesied that she will be made very unhappy by a lover, so no one is allowed to visit her except when the king and the queen go with them."

" Thank you," said the merchant's son, and then he went back to the wood and got into his trunk again, and flew on to the roof of the palace, from whence he crept in at the princess's window.

She was lying on a sofa, fast asleep. She was so very beautiful that the merchant's son was driven to kiss her. She woke up and was dreadfully frightened, but he said that he was the Prophet of the Turks and he had flown down through the air to see her, and this pleased her very much.

They sat side by side and he told her stories about her eyes; he said they were like the most beautiful deep, dark lakes, in which her thoughts floated like mermaids; and then he told her about her forehead, that it was like a snow mountain, adorned with a series of pictures. And he told her all about the storks, which bring beautiful little children up out of the rivers. No end of beautiful stories he told her, and then he asked her to marry him, and she at once said " Yes." " But you must come here on Saturday," she said, " when the king and the queen drink tea with me. They will be very proud when they hear I am to marry a prophet; but mind you have a splendid story to tell them, for my parents are very fond of stories: my mother likes them to be grand and very proper, but my father likes them to be merry, so that he can laugh at them."

" Well, a story will be my only wedding-gift! " he said, and then they separated: but the princess gave him a sword encrusted with gold. It was the kind of present he needed badly.

He flew away and bought himself a new dressing-gown, and sat down in the wood to make up a new story; it had to be ready by Saturday, and it is not always so easy to make up a story.

However he had it ready in time, and Saturday came.

The king, the queen and the whole court were waiting for him round the princess's tea-table. He had a charming reception.

" Now will you tell us a story," said the queen, " one which is both thoughtful and instructive."

" But one that we can laugh at too," said the king.

" All right! " said he, and then he began: we must listen to his story attentively.

" There was once a bundle of matches, and they were frightfully proud because of their high origin. Their family tree, that is to say the great pine tree of which they were each a little splinter, had been the giant of the forest. The matches now lay on a shelf between a tinder-box and an old iron pot, and they told the whole story of their youth to these two. ' Ah, when we were a living tree,' said they, ' we were indeed a green branch! Every morning and every evening we had diamond-tea, that was the dew-drops. In the day we had the sunshine, and all the little birds to tell us stories. We could see, too, that we were very rich, for most of the other trees were only clad in summer, but our family could afford to have green clothes both summer and winter. But then the wood-cutters came, and there was a great revolution, and our family was sundered. The head of the tribe got a place as mainmast on a splendid ship, which could sail round the world if it chose; the other branches were scattered in different directions, and it is now our task to give light to the common herd, that is how such aristocratic people as ourselves have got into this kitchen.'

" ' Now my lot has been different! ' said the iron pot, beside which the matches lay. ' Ever since I came into the world I have passed the time in being scoured and boiled, over and over again! Everything solid comes to me, and in fact I am the most important person in the house. My pleasure is when the dinner is over, to lie clean and bright on the shelf, and to have a sensible chat with my companions; but with the exception of the water-bucket, which sometimes goes down into the yard, we lead an indoor life. Our only newsmonger is the market-basket, and it talks very wildly about the Government and the People. Why the other day an old pot was so alarmed by the conversation, that it fell down and broke itself to pieces! It was a Liberal you see!'

" 'You are talking too much,' said the tinder-box, and the steel struck sparks on the flint. 'Let us have a merry evening.'

" 'Yes, pray let us settle which is the most aristocratic among us,' said the matches.

" 'No, I don't like talking about myself,' said the earthen pipkin; 'let us have an evening entertainment! I will begin. I will tell you the kind of things we have all experienced; they are quite easy to understand, and that is what we all like: By the eastern sea and Danish beeches—'

" 'That's a nice beginning to make!' said all the plates; 'I am sure that will be a story I shall like!'

" 'Well, I passed my youth there, in a very quiet family; the furniture was bees-waxed, the floors washed, and clean curtains were put up once a fortnight!'

" 'What a good story-teller you are,' said the broom; 'one can tell directly that it's a woman telling a story, a vein of cleanliness runs through it!'

" 'Yes, one feels that,' said the water-pail, and for very joy it gave a little hop which clashed on the floor.

" The pipkin went on with its story, and the end was much the same as the beginning.

" All the plates clattered with joy, and the broom crowned the pipkin with a wreath of parsley, because it knew it would annoy the others; and it thought, 'If I crown her to-day, she will crown me to-morrow.'

" 'Now I will dance,' said the tongs, and began to dance; heaven help us, what a way into the air she could get her leg. The old chair-cover in the corner burst when she saw it! 'Mayn't I be crowned too,' said the tongs, so they crowned her.

" 'They're only a rabble after all,' said the matches.

" The tea-urn was called upon to sing now, but it had a cold, it said; it couldn't sing except when it was boiling; but that was all because it was stuck-up; it *wouldn't* sing except when it was on the drawing-room table.

" There was an old quill pen, along on the window-sill, which the servant used to write with; there was nothing extraordinary about it, except that it had been dipped too far into the ink-pot, but it was rather proud of that. ' If the tea-urn won't sing, it can leave it alone,' it said. ' There is a nightingale hanging outside in a cage, it can sing; it certainly hasn't learnt anything special, but we needn't mind that to-night.'

" ' I think it is most unsuitable,' said the kettle, which was the kitchen songster, and half-sister of the urn, ' that a strange bird like that should be listened to! Is it patriotic? I will let the market-basket judge.'

" ' I am very much annoyed,' said the market-basket. ' I am more annoyed than any one can tell! Is this a suitable way to spend an evening? Wouldn't it be better to put the house to rights? Then everything would find its proper place, and I would manage the whole party. Then we should get on differently! '

" ' Yes, let us make a row! ' they all said together.

" At that moment the door opened, it was the servant, and they all stood still, nobody uttered a sound. But not a pot among them which didn't know its capabilities, or how distinguished it was, ' If *I* had chosen, we might have had a merry evening, and no mistake,' they all thought.

" The servant took the matches and struck a light; preserve us! how they spluttered and blazed up.

" ' Now everyone can see,' they thought, ' that we are the first. How brilliantly we shine! What a light we shed around! ' —And then they were burnt out."

" That was a splendid story," said the queen; " I quite felt that I was in the kitchen with the matches. Yes indeed you shall marry our daughter."

" Certainly! " said the king. " Thou shalt marry her on Monday! " They said " du " (thou) to him now, as they were to be related.

So the wedding was decided upon, and the evening before the town was illuminated. Buns and cakes were scattered broadcast; the street boys stood on tiptoe and shouted hurrah, and whistled through their fingers. Everything was most gorgeous.

" I suppose I shall have to do something too," said the merchant's son; so he bought a lot of rockets, squibs, and all sorts of fireworks, put them in his trunk, and flew up into the air with them.

All the Turks jumped at the sight, so that their slippers flew up into the air, they had never seen a flight of meteors like that before. They saw now without doubt that it was the prophet himself, who was about to marry the princess.

As soon as the merchant's son got down again into the wood with his trunk, he thought, "I will just go into the town to hear what was thought of the display," and it was quite reasonable that he should do so.

Oh, how every one talked, every single man he spoke to had his own opinion about it, but that it had been splendid was the universal opinion.

"I saw the prophet myself," said one; "his eyes were like shining stars, and his beard like foaming water."

"He was wrapped in a mantle of fire," said another. "The most beautiful angels' heads peeped out among the folds." He heard nothing but pleasant things and the next day was to be his wedding-day. He went back to the wood to get into his trunk—but where was it? The trunk was burnt up. A spark from the fireworks had set fire to it and the trunk was burnt to ashes. He could not fly any more, or reach his bride. She stood all day on the roof waiting for him; she is waiting for him still, but he wanders round the world telling stories, only they are no longer so merry as the one he told about the matches.

The rose elf

IN the middle of a garden grew a rose tree; it was full of roses, and in the loveliest of them all lived an elf. He was so tiny that no human eye could see him. He had a snug little room behind every petal of the rose. He was as well made and as perfect as any human child, and he had wings reaching from his shoulders to his feet. Oh, what a delicious scent there was in his room, and how lovely and transparent the walls were, for they were palest pink rose petals. All day he revelled in the sunshine, flew from flower to flower, and danced on the wings of fluttering butterflies. Then he would measure how many steps he would have to take to run along all the high roads and paths on a linden leaf. These paths were what we call veins, but they were endless roads to him. Before he came to the end of them the sun went down, for he had begun rather late.

It became very cold, the dew fell and the wind blew; it was high time for him to get home. He hurried as much as ever he could, but the rose had shut itself up, and he could not get in, —not a single rose was open. The poor little rose elf was dreadfully frightened, he had never been out in the night before; he had always slept so safely behind his cosy rose leaves. Oh, it would surely be his death!

At the other end of the garden he knew there was an arbour

32

covered with delicious honeysuckle, the flowers looked like beautiful painted horns. He would get into one of those and sleep till morning.

He flew along to it. Hush! There were already two people in the arbour, a young handsome man and a lovely maiden. They sat side by side and wished they might never more be parted, so tenderly did they love each other. They loved each other more dearly than the best child can even love its father and mother.

" Still, we must part," said the young man: " your brother is not friendly to us, therefore he sends me on such a distant errand, far away over mountains and oceans. Good-bye, my sweetest bride, for you are that to me, you know!"

Then they kissed each other, and the young girl wept, and gave him a rose, but before she gave it to him she pressed a kiss upon it, a kiss so tender and impassioned that the rose spread its petals. Then the little elf flew in and leant his head against the delicate fragrant walls, but he could hear them saying, " Farewell, farewell," and he felt that the rose was placed upon the young man's heart—ah, how it beat! The little elf could not go to sleep because of its beating.

The rose did not remain long undisturbed on that beating heart; the young man took it out, as he walked alone through the dark wood, and kissed it passionately many, many times; the little elf thought he would be crushed to death. He could feel the young man's burning lips through the leaves, and the rose opened as it might have done under the midday sun.

Then another man came up behind, dark and angry; he was the pretty girl's wicked brother. He took out a long sharp knife, and while the other was kissing the rose the bad man stabbed him. He cut off his head and buried it with the body in the soft earth under the linden tree.

" Now he is dead and done with," thought the wicked brother. " He will never come back any more. He had a long journey to take over mountains and oceans where one's life may easily be lost, and he has lost his. He will never come back, and my sister will never dare to ask me about him."

Then he raked up the dead leaves with his foot, over the earth where it had been disturbed, and went home again in the darkness of the night. But he was not alone, as he thought; the little elf went with him. He was hidden in a withered linden leaf which had fallen from the tree on to the bad man's head while he was digging the grave. It was covered by his hat now, and it was so dark inside, where the little elf sat trembling with fear and anger at the wicked deed. The bad man got home in the early morning; he took off his hat, and went into his sister's bedroom. There lay the pretty, blooming girl dreaming about her beloved, whom she thought was so far away, beyond mountains and woods. The wicked brother leant over her with an evil laugh, such as a fiend might laugh. The withered leaf fell out of his hair upon the counterpane; but he never noticed it, and went away to get a little sleep himself. But the elf crept out of the dead leaf, and into the ear of the sleeping girl, and told her, as in a dream, the tale of the terrible murder. He described the place where her brother had committed the murder, and where he had laid the body; he told her about the flowering linden tree, and said, " So that you may not think all I have told you is a mere dream, you will find a withered leaf upon your bed."

This she found, as he had said, when she woke. Oh! what bitter, bitter tears she shed. To no one did she dare betray her grief. Her window stood open all day, and the little elf could easily have got into the garden to the roses and all the other flowers, but he could not bear to leave the sorrowing girl. A monthly rose-bush stood in the window, and he took up his place in one of the flowers, whence he could watch the poor girl. Her brother often came into the room. He was merry with an evil mirth, but she dared not say a word about the grief at her heart.

When night came she stole out of the house, and into the wood, to the place where the linden tree stood. She tore away the leaves from the ground and dug down into the earth, and at once found him who had been murdered. Oh how she wept and prayed to God, that she too might soon die. Gladly would she have taken the body home with her could she have done so. But she took the pale head with the closed eyes, kissed the cold lips and shook the earth out of his beautiful hair.

" This shall be mine! " she said, when she had covered up

the body with earth and leaves. Then she took the head home
with her and a little spray of the jasmine tree which flowered
in the wood where he was killed.

As soon as she reached her room she fetched the biggest
flower pot she could find, and laid the head of the dead man in
it, covered it with earth, and planted the sprig of jasmine in
the pot.

" Farewell, farewell! " whispered the little elf. He could no
longer bear to look at such grief, so he flew away into the garden
to his rose, but it was withered, and only a few faded leaves
hung round the green calyx. " Alas! how quickly the good
and the beautiful pass away! " sighed the elf. At last he found
another rose, and made it his home. He could dwell in safety
behind its fragrant petals.

Every morning he flew to the poor girl's window, and she
was always there, weeping by the flower pot. Her salt tears
fell upon the jasmine, and for every day that she grew paler
and paler the sprig gained in strength and vigour. One shoot
appeared after another, and then little white flower buds showed
themselves, and she kissed them; but her wicked brother scolded
her, and asked if she was crazy. He did not like to see, and
could not imagine why, she was always hanging weeping over
the flower pot. He did not know what eyes lay hidden there,
closed for ever, nor what red lips had returned to dust within
its depths. She leant her head against the flower pot, and the
little elf found her there, fallen into a gentle slumber. He crept
into her ear, and whispered to her of that evening in the arbour,
about the scented roses, and the love of the elves. She dreamt
these sweet dreams, and while she dreamt her life passed away.
She was dead—she had died a peaceful death, and had passed
to heaven to her beloved! The jasmine opened its big white
blossoms, and they gave out their sweetest scent. They had
no other way of weeping over the dead.

The wicked brother saw the beautiful flowering plant, and
he took it for himself as an inheritance. He put it into his own
bedroom, close by his bedside, because it was so beautiful to
look at, and smelt so sweet and fresh. The little rose elf accompanied it and flew from blossom to blossom; in each lived a
little elf, and to each one he told the story of the murdered man

whose head now rested under the earth. He told them about the wicked brother and his poor sister.

"We know it," said each little creature. "We know it; did we not spring from those murdered eyes and lips? We know it, we know it!" and then they nodded their heads so oddly.

The rose elf could not understand how they could be so quiet about it, and he flew to the bees who were gathering honey. He told them the story about the wicked brother, and the bees told it to their queen, who commanded them all to kill the murderer next morning.

But in the night, the first night after his sister's death, when the brother was asleep in his bed, close to the fragrant jasmine tree, every blossom opened wide its petals, and out of every flower stepped invisibly, but armed each with a tiny poisoned spear, the little spirits from the flower. First they took their places by his ear, and told him evil dreams; then they flew over his mouth and pierced his tongue with their poisoned darts.

"Now we have revenged the dead!" said they, and crept back again into the white bells of the jasmine.

When morning came, the window all at once flew open, and in flew the rose elf and all the swarm of bees with their queen to kill him.

But he was already dead; people stood round the bed and said, "The scent of the jasmine has killed him!"

Then the rose elf understood the vengeance of the flowers, and told it to the queen bee, and she with all her swarm buzzed round the flower pot; the bees would not be driven away. Then a man took up the flower pot, and one of the bees stung his hand, and he let the flower pot fall, and it was broken to bits.

Then they saw the whitened skull, and they knew that the dead man lying on the bed was a murderer. The queen bee hummed in the air, and sang about the vengeance of the flowers to the rose elf, and that behind each smallest leaf lurks a being who can discover and revenge every evil deed.

THE WILD SWANS

FAR away, where the swallows take refuge in winter, lived a king who had eleven sons and one daughter, Elise. The eleven brothers—they were all princes—used to go to school with stars on their breasts and swords at their sides. They wrote upon golden slates with diamond pencils, and could read just as well without a book as with one, so there was no mistake about their being real princes. Their sister Elise sat upon a little footstool of looking-glass, and she had a picture-book which had cost the half of a kingdom. Oh, these children were very happy; but it was not to last thus for ever.

Their father, who was king over all the land, married a wicked queen who was not at all kind to the poor children; they found that out on the first day. All was festive at the castle, but when the children wanted to play at having company, instead of having as many cakes and baked apples as ever they wanted, she would only let them have some sand in a tea-cup, and said they must make-believe.

In the following week she sent little Elise into the country to board with some peasants, and it did not take her long to make the king believe so many bad things about the boys, that he cared no more about them.

"Fly out into the world and look after yourselves," said the wicked queen; "you shall fly about like birds without voices."

But she could not make things as bad for them as she would have liked; they turned into eleven beautiful wild swans. They flew out of the palace window with a weird scream, right across the park and the woods.

It was very early in the morning when they came to the place where their sister Elise was sleeping in the peasant's house. They hovered over the roof of the house, turning and twisting their long necks, and flapping their wings; but no one either heard or saw them. They had to fly away again, and they soared up towards the clouds, far out into the wide world, and they settled in a big, dark wood, which stretched down to the shore.

Poor little Elise stood in the peasant's room, playing with a green leaf, for she had no other toys. She made a little hole in it, which she looked through at the sun, and it seemed to her as if she saw her brothers' bright eyes. Every time the warm sunbeams shone upon her cheek, it reminded her of their kisses. One day passed just like another. When the wind whistled through the rose-hedges outside the house, it whispered to the roses, " Who can be prettier than you are? " But the roses shook their heads and answered, " Elise! " And when the old woman sat in the doorway reading her Psalms, the wind turned over the leaves and said to the book, " Who can be more pious than you? " " Elise! " answered the book. Both the roses and the book of Psalms only spoke the truth.

She was to go home when she was fifteen, but when the queen saw how pretty she was, she got very angry, and her heart was filled with hatred. She would willingly have turned her into a wild swan too, like her brothers, but she did not dare to do it at once, for the king wanted to see his daughter. The queen always went to the bath in the early morning. It was built of marble and adorned with soft cushions and beautiful carpets.

She took three toads, kissed them, and said to the first, " Sit upon Elise's head when she comes to the bath, so that she may become sluggish like yourself. Sit upon her forehead," she said to the second, " that she may become ugly like you, and then her father won't know her! Rest upon her heart," she whispered to the third. " Let an evil spirit come over her, which may be a burden to her." Then she put the toads into the clean water, and a green tinge immediately came over it.

She called Elise, undressed her, and made her go into the bath; when she ducked under the water, one of the toads got among her hair, the other got on to her forehead, and the third on to her bosom. But when she stood up three scarlet poppies floated on the water; had not the creatures been poisonous, and kissed by the sorceress, they would have been changed into crimson roses, but yet they became flowers from merely having rested a moment on her head and her heart. She was far too good and innocent for the sorcery to have any power over her. When the wicked queen saw this, she rubbed her over with walnut juice, and smeared her face with some evil-smelling salve. She also matted up her beautiful hair; it would have been impossible to recognise pretty Elise. When her father saw her, he was quite horrified and said that she could not be his daughter. Nobody would have anything to say to her, except the yard dog, and the swallows, and they were only poor dumb animals whose opinion went for nothing.

Poor Elise wept, and thought of her eleven brothers who were all lost. She crept sadly out of the palace and wandered about all day, over meadows and marshes, and into a big forest. She did not know in the least where she wanted to go, but she felt very sad, and longed for her brothers, who, no doubt, like herself had been driven out of the palace. She made up her mind to go and look for them, but she had only been in the wood for a short time when night fell. She had quite lost her way, so she lay down upon the soft moss, said her evening prayer, and rested her head on a little hillock. It was very still and the air was mild, hundreds of glow-worms shone around her on the grass and in the marsh like green fire. When she gently moved one of the branches over her head, the little shining insects fell over her like a shower of stars. She dreamt about her brothers all night long. Again they were children playing together: they wrote upon the golden slates with their diamond pencils, and she looked at the picture-book which had cost half a kingdom. But they no longer wrote strokes and noughts upon their slates as they used to do; no, they wrote down all their boldest exploits, and everything that they had seen and experienced. Everything in the picture book was alive, the birds sang, and the people walked out of the book, and spoke to Elise and her brothers. When she turned over a page, they skipped back into their places again, so that there should be no confusion among the pictures.

When she woke the sun was already high; it is true she could not see it very well through the thick branches of the lofty forest trees, but the sunbeams cast a golden shimmer around beyond the forest. There was a fresh delicious scent of grass and herbs in the air, and the birds were almost ready to perch upon her shoulders. She could hear the splashing of water, for there were many springs around, which all flowed into a pond with a lovely sandy bottom. It was surrounded with thick bushes, but there was one place which the stags had trampled down and Elise passed through the opening to the water side. It was so transparent, that had not the branches been moved by the breeze, she must have thought that they were painted on the bottom, so plainly was every leaf reflected, both those on which the sun played and those which were in shade.

When she saw her own face she was quite frightened, it was so brown and ugly, but when she wet her little hand and rubbed her eyes and forehead, her white skin shone through again. Then she took off all her clothes and went into the fresh water. A more beautiful royal child than she could not be found in all the world.

When she had put on her clothes again, and plaited her long hair, she went to a sparkling spring and drank some of the water out of the hollow of her hand. Then she wandered further into the wood, though where she was going she had not the least idea. She thought of her brothers, and she thought of a merciful God who would not forsake her. He let the wild crab-apples grow to feed the hungry. He showed her a tree, the branches of which were bending beneath their weight of fruit. Here she made her midday meal, and, having put props under the branches, she walked on into the thickest part of the forest. It was so quiet that she heard her own footsteps, she heard every little withered leaf which bent under her feet. Not a bird was to be seen, not a ray of sunlight pierced the leafy branches, and the tall trunks were so close together that when she looked before her it seemed as if a thick fence of heavy beams hemmed her in on every side. The solitude was such as she had never known before.

It was a very dark night, not a single glow-worm sparkled in the marsh; sadly she lay down to sleep, and it seemed to her as if the branches above her parted asunder, and the Saviour looked down upon her with His loving eyes, and little angels' heads peeped out above His head and under His arms.

When she woke in the morning she was not sure if she had dreamt this, or whether it was really true.

She walked a little further, when she met an old woman with a basket full of berries, of which she gave her some. Elise asked if she had seen eleven princes ride through the wood. " No," said the old woman, " but yesterday I saw eleven swans, with golden crowns upon their heads, swimming in the stream close by there."

She led Elise a little further to a slope, at the foot of which the stream meandered. The trees on either bank stretched out their rich leafy branches towards each other, and where, from their natural growth, they could not reach each other, they had torn their roots out of the ground, and leant over the water so as to interlace their branches.

Elise said good-bye to the old woman, and walked along by the river till it flowed out into the great open sea.

The beautiful open sea lay before the maiden, but not a sail was to be seen on it, not a single boat. How was she ever to get any further? She looked at the numberless little pebbles on the beach; they were all worn quite round by the water. Glass, iron, stone, whatever was washed up, had taken their shapes from the water, which yet was much softer than her little hand. " With all its rolling, it is untiring, and everything hard is smoothed down. I will be just as untiring! Thank you for your lesson, you clear rolling waves! Some time, so my heart tells me, you will bear me to my beloved brothers! "

Eleven white swans' feathers were lying on the sea-weed; she picked them up and made a bunch of them. There were still drops of water on them. Whether these were dew or tears no one could tell. It was very lonely there by the shore, but she did not feel it, for the sea was ever-changing. There were more changes on it in the course of a few hours than could be seen on an inland fresh-water lake in a year. If a big black cloud arose, it was just as if the sea wanted to say, " I can look black too," and then the wind blew up and the waves showed their white crests. But if the clouds were red and the wind dropped, the sea looked like a rose-leaf, now white, now green. But, however still it was, there was always a little gentle motion just by the shore, the water rose and fell softly like the bosom of a sleeping child.

When the sun was just about to go down, Elise saw eleven wild swans with golden crowns upon their heads flying towards the shore. They flew in a swaying line, one behind the other, like a white ribbon streamer. Elise climbed up on to the bank and hid behind a bush; the swans settled close by her and flapped their great white wings.

As soon as the sun had sunk beneath the water the swans shed their feathers and became eleven handsome princes; they were Elise's brothers. Although they had altered a good deal, she knew them at once; she felt that they must be her brothers and she sprang into their arms, calling them by name. They were delighted when they recognised their little sister who had grown so big and beautiful. They laughed and cried, and told each other how wickedly their step-mother had treated them all.

" We brothers," said the eldest, " have to fly about in the guise of swans, as long as the sun is above the horizon. When it goes down we regain our human shapes. So we always have to look out for a resting place near sunset, for should we happen to be flying up among the clouds when the sun goes down, we should be hurled to the depths below. We do not live here; there is another land, just as beautiful as this, beyond the sea; but the way to it is very long and we have to cross the mighty ocean to get to it. There is not a single island on the way where we can spend the night, only one solitary little rock juts up above the water midway. It is only just big enough for us to stand upon close together, and if there is a heavy sea the water splashes over us, yet we thank our God for it. We stay there over night in our human forms, and without it we could never revisit our beloved Fatherland, for our flight takes two of the longest days in the year. We are only permitted to visit the home of our fathers once a year, and we dare only stay for eleven days. We hover over this big forest from whence we catch a glimpse of the palace where we were born, and where our father lives; beyond it we can see the high church towers where our mother is buried. We fancy that the trees and bushes here are related to us; and the wild horses gallop over the moors, as we used to see them in our childhood. The charcoal burners still sing the old songs we used to dance to when we were children. This is our Fatherland, we are drawn towards it, and here we have found you again, dear little sister! We may stay here two days longer, and then we must fly away again across the ocean, to a lovely country indeed, but it is not our own dear Fatherland! How shall we ever take you with us, we have neither ship nor boat!"

"How can I deliver you!" said their sister, and they went on talking to each other, nearly all night, they only dozed for a few hours.

Elise was awakened in the morning by the rustling of the swans' wings above her; her brothers were again transformed and were wheeling round in great circles, till she lost sight of them in the distance. One of them, the youngest, stayed behind. He laid his head against her bosom, and she caressed it with her fingers. They remained together all day; towards evening the others came back, and as soon as the sun went down they took their natural forms.

"To-morrow we must fly away, and we dare not come back for a whole year, but we can't leave you like this! Have you courage to go with us? My arm is strong enough to carry you over the forest, so surely our united strength ought to be sufficient to bear you across the ocean."

"Oh yes! take me with you," said Elise.

They spent the whole night in weaving a kind of net of the elastic bark of the willow bound together with tough rushes; they made it both large and strong. Elise lay down upon it, and when the sun rose and the brothers became swans again, they took up the net in their bills and flew high up among the clouds with their precious sister, who was fast asleep. The sunbeams fell straight on to her face, so one of the swans flew over her head so that its broad wings should shade her.

They were far from land when Elise woke; she thought she

must still be dreaming, it seemed so strange to be carried through the air so high up above the sea. By her side lay a branch of beautiful ripe berries, and a bundle of savoury roots, which her youngest brother had collected for her, and for which she gave him a grateful smile. She knew it was he who flew above her head shading her from the sun. They were so high up that the first ship they saw looked like a gull floating on the water. A great cloud came up behind them like a mountain, and Elise saw the shadow of herself on it, and those of the eleven swans looking like giants. It was a more beautiful picture than any she had ever seen before, but as the sun rose higher, the cloud fell behind, and the shadow picture disappeared.

They flew on and on all day like an arrow whizzing through the air, but they went slower than usual, for now they had their sister to carry. A storm came up, and night was drawing on; Elise saw the sun sinking with terror in her heart, for the solitary rock was nowhere to be seen. The swans seemed to be taking stronger strokes than ever; alas! she was the cause of their not being able to get on faster; as soon as the sun went down they would become men, and they would all be hurled into the sea and drowned. She prayed to God from the bottom of her heart, but still no rock was to be seen! Black clouds gathered, and strong gusts of wind announced a storm; the clouds looked like a great threatening leaden wave, and the flashes of lightning followed each other rapidly.

The sun was now at the edge of the sea. Elise's heart quaked, when suddenly the swans shot downwards so suddenly, that she thought they were falling, then they hovered again. Half of the sun was below the horizon, and there for the first time she saw the little rock below, which did not look bigger than the head of a seal above the water. The sun sank very quickly, it was no bigger than a star, but her foot touched solid earth. The sun went out like the last sparks of a bit of burning paper; she saw her brothers stand arm in arm around her, but there was only just room enough for them. The waves beat upon the rock, and washed over them like drenching rain. The heaven shone with continuous fire, and the thunder rolled, peal upon peal. But the sister and brothers held each other's hands and sang a psalm which gave them comfort and courage.

The air was pure and still at dawn. As soon as the sun rose the swans flew off with Elise, away from the islet. The sea still ran high, it looked from where they were as if the white foam on the dark green water were millions of swans floating on the waves.

When the sun rose higher, Elise saw before her half floating in the air great masses of ice, with shining glaciers on the heights. A palace was perched midway a mile in length, with one bold colonnade built above another. Beneath them swayed palm trees and gorgeous blossoms as big as mill wheels. She asked if this was the land to which she was going, but the swans shook their heads, because what she saw was a mirage; the beautiful and ever changing palace of Fata Morgana. No mortal dared enter it. Elise gazed at it, but as she gazed the palace, gardens and mountains melted away, and in their place stood twenty proud churches with their high towers and pointed windows. She seemed to hear the notes of the organ, but it was the sea she heard. When she got close to the seeming churches, they changed to a great navy sailing beneath her; but it was only a sea mist floating over the waters. Yes, she saw constant changes passing before her eyes, and now she saw the real land she was bound to. Beautiful blue mountains rose before her with their cedar woods and palaces. Long before the sun went down, she sat among the hills in front of a big cave covered with delicate green creepers. It looked like a piece of embroidery.

" Now we shall see what you will dream here to-night," said the youngest brother, as he showed her where she was to sleep.

" If only I might dream how I could deliver you," she said, and this thought filled her mind entirely. She prayed earnestly to God for His help, and even in her sleep she continued her prayer. It seemed to her that she was flying up to Fata Morgana in her castle in the air. The fairy came towards her, she was charming and brilliant, and yet she was very like the old woman who gave her the berries in the wood, and told her about the swans with the golden crowns.

" Your brothers can be delivered," she said, " but have you courage and endurance enough for it? The sea is indeed softer than your hands, and it moulds the hardest stones, but it does not feel the pain your fingers will feel. It has no heart, and does not suffer the pain and anguish you must feel. Do you see this stinging nettle I hold in my hand? Many of this kind grow round the cave where you sleep; only these and the ones which grow in the churchyards may be used. Mark that! Those you may pluck although they will burn and blister your hands. Crush the nettles with your feet and you will have flax, and of this you must weave eleven coats of mail with long sleeves. Throw these over the eleven wild swans and the charm is broken! But remember that from the moment you begin this work, till it is finished, even if it takes years, you must not utter a word! The first word you say will fall like a murderer's dagger into the hearts of your brothers. Their lives hang on your tongue. Mark this well!"

She touched her hand at the same moment, it was like burning fire, and woke Elise. It was bright day-light, and close to where she slept lay a nettle like those in her dream. She fell upon her knees with thanks to God and left the cave to begin her work.

She seized the horrid nettles with her delicate hands, and they burnt like fire; great blisters rose on her hands and arms, but she suffered it willingly if only it would deliver her beloved brothers. She crushed every nettle with her bare feet, and twisted it into green flax.

When the sun went down and the brothers came back, they were alarmed at finding her mute; they thought it was some new witchcraft exercised by their wicked step-mother. But when they saw her hands, they understood that it was for their sakes; the youngest brother wept, and wherever his tears fell, she felt no more pain, and the blisters disappeared.

She spent the whole night at her work, for she could not rest till she had delivered her dear brothers. All the following day while her brothers were away she sat solitary, but never had the time flown so fast. One coat of mail was finished and she began the next. Then a hunting-horn sounded among the mountains; she was much frightened, the sound came nearer, and she heard dogs barking. In terror she rushed into the cave and tied the nettles she had collected and woven, into a bundle upon which she sat.

At this moment a big dog bounded forward from the thicket,

and another and another, they barked loudly and ran backwards and forwards. In a few minutes all the huntsmen were standing outside the cave, and the handsomest of them was the king of the country. He stepped up to Elise: never had he seen so lovely a girl.

"How came you here, beautiful child?" he said.

Elise shook her head; she dared not speak; the salvation and the lives of her brothers depended upon her silence. She hid her hands under her apron, so that the king should not see what she suffered.

"Come with me!" he said; "you cannot stay here. If you are as good as you are beautiful, I will dress you in silks and velvets, put a golden crown upon your head, and you shall live with me and have your home in my richest palace!" Then he lifted her upon his horse, she wept and wrung her hands, but the king said, "I only think of your happiness; you will thank me one day for what I am doing!" Then he darted off across the mountains, holding her before him on his horse, and the huntsmen followed.

When the sun went down, the royal city with churches and cupolas lay before them, and the king led her into the palace, where great fountains played in the marble halls, and where walls and ceilings were adorned with paintings, but she had no eyes for them, she only wept and sorrowed; passively she allowed the women to dress her in royal robes, to twist pearls into her hair, and to draw gloves on to her blistered hands.

She was dazzlingly lovely as she stood there in all her magnificence; the courtiers bent low before her, and the king wooed her as his bride, although the archbishop shook his head, and whispered that he feared the beautiful wood maiden was a witch, who had dazzled their eyes and infatuated the king.

The king refused to listen to him, he ordered the music to play, the richest food to be brought, and the loveliest girls to dance before her. She was led through scented gardens into gorgeous apartments, but nothing brought a smile to her lips, or into her eyes, sorrow sat there like a heritage and a possession for all time. Last of all, the king opened the door of a little chamber close by the room where she was to sleep. It was adorned with costly green carpets, and made to exactly resemble the cave where he found her. On the floor lay the bundle of flax she had spun from the nettles, and from the ceiling hung the shirt of mail which was already finished. One of the huntsmen had brought all these things away as curiosities.

"Here you may dream that you are back in your former home!" said the king. "Here is the work upon which you were engaged; in the midst of your splendour, it may amuse you to think of those times."

When Elise saw all these things so dear to her heart, a smile for the first time played upon her lips, and the blood rushed back to her cheeks. She thought of the deliverance of her brothers, and she kissed the king's hand; he pressed her to his heart, and ordered all the church bells to ring marriage peals. The lovely dumb girl from the woods was to be queen of the country.

The archbishop whispered evil words into the ear of the king, but they did not reach his heart. The wedding was to take place, and the archbishop himself had to put the crown upon her head. In his anger he pressed the golden circlet so tightly upon her head as to give her pain. But a heavier circlet pressed upon her heart, her grief for her brothers, so she thought nothing of the bodily pain. Her lips were sealed, a single word from her mouth would cost her brothers their lives, but her eyes were full of love for the good and handsome king, who did everything he could to please her. Every day she grew more and more attached to him, and longed to confide in him, tell him her sufferings; but dumb she must remain, and in silence must bring her labour to completion. Therefore at night she stole away from his side into her secret chamber, which was decorated like a cave, and here she knitted one shirt after another. When she came to the seventh, all her flax was worked up; she knew that these nettles which she was to use grew in the churchyard, but she had to pluck them herself. How was she to get there? "Oh, what is the pain of my fingers compared with the anguish of my heart," she thought. "I must venture out, the good God will not desert me!" With as much terror in her heart, as if she were doing some evil deed, she stole down one night into the moonlit garden, and through the long alleys out into the silent streets to the churchyard. There she saw, sitting on a gravestone, a group of hideous ghouls, who took off their tattered garments, as if they were about to bathe, and then they dug down into the freshly-made graves with their skinny fingers, and tore the flesh from the bodies and devoured it. Elise had to pass close by them, and they fixed their evil eyes upon her, but she said a prayer as she passed, picked the stinging nettles and hurried back to the palace with them.

Only one person saw her, but that was the archbishop, who watched while others slept. Surely now all his bad opinions of the queen were justified; all was not as it should be with her, she must be a witch, and therefore she had bewitched the king and all the people.

He told the king in the confessional what he had seen and what he feared. When those bad words passed his lips, the pictures of the saints shook their heads as if to say: it is not so, Elise is innocent. The archbishop however took it differently, and thought that they were bearing witness against her, and shaking their heads at her sin. Two big tears rolled down the king's cheeks, and he went home with doubt in his heart. He pretended to sleep at night, but no quiet sleep came to his eyes. He perceived how Elise got up and went to her private closet. Day by day his face grew darker, Elise saw it but could not imagine what was the cause of it. It alarmed her, and what was she not already suffering in her heart because of her brothers? Her salt tears ran down upon the royal purple velvet, they lay upon it like sparkling diamonds, and all who saw their splendour wished to be queen.

She had, however, almost reached the end of her labours, only one shirt of mail was wanting, but again she had no more flax and not a single nettle was left. Once more, for the last time, she must go to the churchyard to pluck a few handfuls. She thought with dread of the solitary walk and the horrible ghouls; but her will was as strong as her trust in God.

Elise went, but the king and the archbishop followed her, they saw her disappear within the grated gateway of the churchyard. When they followed they saw the ghouls sitting on the gravestone as Elise had seen them before; and the king turned away his head, because he thought she was among them, she, whose head this very evening had rested on his breast.

" The people must judge her," he groaned, and the people judged. " Let her be consumed in the glowing flames! "

She was led away from her beautiful royal apartments to a dark damp dungeon, where the wind whistled through the grated window. Instead of velvet and silk they gave her the bundle of nettles she had gathered to lay her head upon. The hard burning shirts of mail were to be her covering, but they could have given her nothing more precious.

She set to work again with many prayers to God. Outside her prison the street boys sang derisive songs about her, and not a soul comforted her with a kind word.

Towards evening she heard the rustle of swans' wings close to her window; it was her youngest brother, at last he had found her. He sobbed aloud with joy although he knew that the coming night might be her last, but then her work was almost done and her brothers were there.

The archbishop came to spend her last hours with her as he had promised the king. She shook her head at him, and by looks and gestures begged him to leave her. She had only this night in which to finish her work, or else all would be wasted, all —her pain, tears and sleepless nights. The archbishop went away with bitter words against her, but poor Elise knew that she was innocent, and she went on with her work.

The little mice ran about the floor bringing nettles to her feet, so as to give what help they could, and a thrush sat on the grating of the window where he sang all night, as merrily as he could to keep up her courage.

It was still only dawn, and the sun would not rise for an hour when the eleven brothers stood at the gate of the palace, begging to be taken to the king. This could not be done, was the answer, for it was still night; the king was asleep and no one dared wake him. All their entreaties and threats were useless, the watch turned out and even the king himself came to see what was the matter; but just then the sun rose, and no more brothers were to be seen, only eleven wild swans hovering over the palace.

The whole populace streamed out of the town gates, they were all anxious to see the witch burnt. A miserable horse drew the cart in which Elise was seated. They had put upon her a smock of green sacking, and all her beautiful long hair hung loose from the lovely head. Her cheeks were deathly pale, and her lips moved softly, while her fingers unceasingly twisted the green yarn. Even on the way to her death she could not abandon her unfinished work. Ten shirts lay completed at her feet—she laboured away at the eleventh, amid the scoffing insults of the populace.

" Look at the witch how she mutters. She has never a book of psalms in her hands, no, there she sits with her loathsome sorcery. Tear it away from her, into a thousand bits! "

The crowd pressed around her to destroy her work, but just then eleven white swans flew down and perched upon the cart flapping their wings. The crowd gave way before them in terror.

" It is a sign from Heaven! She is innocent! " they whispered, but they dared not say it aloud.

The executioner seized her by the hand, but she hastily threw the eleven shirts over the swans, who were immediately transformed to eleven handsome princes; but the youngest had a swan's wing in place of an arm, for one sleeve was wanting to his shirt of mail, she had not been able to finish it.

" Now I may speak! I am innocent."

The populace who saw what had happened bowed down before her as if she had been a saint, but she sank lifeless in her brother's arms; so great had been the strain, the terror and the suffering she had endured.

" Yes, innocent she is indeed," said the eldest brother, and he told them all that had happened.

Whilst he spoke a wonderful fragrance spread around, as of millions of roses. Every faggot in the pile had taken root and shot out branches, and a great high hedge of red roses had arisen. At the very top was one pure white blossom, it shone like a star, and the king broke it off and laid it on Elise's bosom, and she woke with joy and peace in her heart.

All the church bells began to ring of their own accord, and the singing birds flocked around them. Surely such a bridal procession went back to the palace as no king had ever seen before!

The Elf Hill

SOME lizards were nimbly running in and out of the clefts in an old tree. They understood each other very well, for they all spoke lizard language.

"What a rumbling and grumbling is going on inside the old Elf-hill," said one of the lizards. "I have not closed my eyes for the last two nights for the noise. I might just as well be having toothache, for all the sleep I get!"

"There is something up inside," said the other lizard. "They propped up the top of the hill on four red posts till cockcrow this morning, to air it out thoroughly; and the elf maidens had been learning some new dancing steps, which they are always practising. There certainly must be something going on."

"Yes, I was talking to an earthworm of my acquaintance about it," said the third lizard. "He came straight up out of the hill, where he had been boring into the earth for days and nights. He had heard a good deal, for the miserable creature can't see, but it can feel its way, and plays the part of eaves-dropper to perfection. They are expecting visitors in the Elf-hill, grand visitors; but who they are the earthworm refused to say, or perhaps he did not know. All the will-o'-the-wisps are ordered for a procession of torches, as it is called; and the silver and gold plate, of which there is any amount in the hill, is all being polished up and put out in the moonlight."

" Whoever can the strangers be? " said all the lizards together.

" What on earth is happening? Hark! what a humming and buzzing? "

At this moment the Elf-hill opened, and an elderly elf-maiden tripped out. She was hollow behind,[1] but otherwise quite attractively dressed. She was the old elf-king's house-keeper, and a distant relative. She wore an amber heart upon her forehead. She moved her legs at a great pace, " trip, trip." Good heavens! how fast she tripped over the ground; she went right down to the night-jar in the swamp.

" You are invited to the Elf-hill for to-night," said she to him. " But will you be so kind as to charge yourself with the other invitations. You must make yourself useful in other ways, as you don't keep house yourself. We are going to have some very distinguished visitors, goblins, who always have something to say, and so the old elf-king means to show what he can do."

" Who is to be invited? " asked the night-jar.

" Well, everybody may come to the big ball, even human beings, if they can only talk in their sleep, or do something else after our fashion. But the choice is to be strictly limited for the grand feast. We will only have the most distinguished people. I have had a battle with the elf-king about it; because I hold that we musn't even include ghosts. The merman and his daughters must be invited first. I don't suppose they care much about coming on dry land, but I shall see that they each have a wet stone to sit on, or something better; so I expect they won't decline this time. All the old demons of the first-class, with tails, the river-god, and the wood-sprites. And then I don't think we can pass over the grave-pig,[2] the hell-horse, and the church-grim, although they belong to the clergy, who are not of our people; but that is merely on account of their office, and they are closely connected with us, and visit us very frequently."

" Croak," said the night-jar, and he flew off to issue the invitations.

[1] According to a superstition these elf-maidens are hollow, like the inside of a mask.
[2] According to Danish superstition, a living horse or pig has been buried under every church; their ghosts are said to walk at night.

The elf-maidens had already begun to dance, and they danced a scarf dance, with scarves woven of mist and moonshine; these have a lovely effect to those who care for that kind of thing. The great hall in the middle of the Elf-hill had been thoroughly polished up for the occasion. The floor was washed with moonshine, and the walls were rubbed over with witches' fat, and this made them shine with many colours, like a tulip petal. The kitchen was full of frogs on spits, stuffed snake skins, and salads of toadstool spawn, mouse snouts and hemlock. Then there was beer brewed by the marsh witch, and sparkling saltpetre wine from the vaults. Everything of the best, and rusty nails and church window panes among the kickshaws.

The old elf-king had his golden crown polished with pounded slate-pencil, ay, and it was a head-boy's slate-pencil too, and they are not so easy to get. They hung up fresh curtains in the bedroom, and fixed them with the slime of snails. Yes, indeed, there was a humming and a buzzing.

"Now we will fumigate with horse-hair and pig's bristles, and then I can do no more!" said the old elf-servant.

"Dear father!" said the youngest of the daughters, "are you not going to tell me who these grand strangers are?"

"Well, well," he said, "I suppose I must tell you now. Two of my daughters must prepare themselves to be married—two will certainly make marriages. The old Trold chieftain from Norway, that lives on the Dovrefield, among his many rock castles and fastnesses and gold works, which are better than you would expect, is coming down here with his two sons. They are coming to look for wives. The old Trold is a regular honest Norwegian veteran, straightforward and merry. I used to know him in the olden days, when we drank to our good fellowship. He came here to fetch a wife, but she is dead now. She was a daughter of the king of the chalk cliffs at Möen. As the saying is, 'he took his wife on the chalk,' viz., bought her on tick. I am quite anxious to see the old fellow. The sons, they say, are a pair of overgrown, ill-mannered cubs; but perhaps they are not so bad; I daresay they will improve as they grow older. See if you can't lick them into shape a bit."

"And when do they come?" asked one of the daughters.

"That depends upon wind and weather," said the elf-king. "They travel economically, and they will take their chance of a ship. I wanted them to come round by Sweden, but the old fellow can't bring himself to that yet. He doesn't march with the times, but I don't hold with that!"

At this moment two will-o'-the-wisps came hopping along, one faster than the other, so of course one arrived before the other.

"They are coming, they are coming!" they cried.

"Give me my crown, and let me stand in the moonlight," said the elf-king.

The daughters raised their scarves and curtseyed to the ground.

There stood the Trold chieftain from the Dovrefield; he wore a crown of hardened icicles and polished fir cones, and besides this, he had on a bearskin coat and snow-shoes. His sons, on the other hand, had bare necks and wore no braces, because they were strong men.

"Is that a hill?" asked the youngest of the brothers, pointing to the Elf-hill. "We should call it a hole in Norway."

"Lads!" cried the old man, "holes go inwards, hills go upwards! Haven't you got eyes in your heads?"

The only thing that astonished them, they said, was that they understood the language without any trouble.

"Don't make fools of yourselves," said the old man; "one might think you were only half-baked."

Then they went into the Elf-hill, where the company was of the grandest, although they had been got together in such a hurry; you might almost say they had been blown together. It was all charming, and arranged to suit everyone's taste. The merman and his daughters sat at table in great tubs of water, and said it was just like being at home. Everybody had excellent table manners, except the two young Norwegian Trolds; they put their feet up on the table, but then they thought anything they did was right.

"Take your feet out of the way of the dishes," said the old Trold, and they obeyed him, but not at once. They tickled the ladies they took into dinner with fir cones out of their pockets; then they pulled off their boots, so as to be quite comfortable, and handed the boots to the ladies to hold. Their father, the old Trold chieftain, was very different; he told no end of splendid stories about the proud Norwegian mountains, and the waterfalls dashing down in white foam with a roar like thunder. He told them about the salmon leaping up against the rushing water, when the nixies played their golden harps. Then he went on to tell them about the sparkling winter nights when the sledge bells rang and the lads flew over the ice with blazing lights, the ice which was so transparent that you could see the startled fish darting away under your feet. Yes, indeed, he could tell stories, you could see and hear the things he described; the sawmills going, the men and maids singing their songs and dancing the merry Halling dance. Huzza! All at once the old Trold gave the elf housekeeper a smacking kiss, such a kiss it was, and yet they were not a bit related. Then the elf-maidens had to dance, first plain dancing, and then step dancing, and it was most becoming to them. Then came a fancy dance.

Preserve us, how nimble they were on their legs, you couldn't tell where they began, or where they ended, you couldn't tell which were arms and which were legs, they were all mixed up together like shavings in a saw-pit. They twirled round and round so often that it made the hell-horse feel quite giddy and unwell and he had to leave the table.

" Prrrrr! " said the old Trold. " There is some life in those legs, but what else can they do besides dancing and pointing their toes and all those whirligigs? "

" We will soon show you! " said the elf-king, and he called out his youngest daughter; she was thin and transparent as moonshine, and was the most ethereal of all the daughters. She put a little white stick in her mouth and vanished instantly; this was her accomplishment.

But the Trold said he did not like that accomplishment in a wife, nor did he think his boys would appreciate it. The second one could walk by her own side as if she had a shadow, and no elves have shadows.

The third was quite different; she had studied in the marsh witches' brewery, and understood larding alder stumps with glow-worms.

" She will be a good housewife, " said the Trold, and then

he saluted her with his eyes instead of drinking her health, for he did not want to drink too much.

Now came the turn of the fourth; she had a big golden harp to play, and when she touched the first string everybody lifted up their left legs (for all the elfin folk are left legged). But when she touched the second string everybody had to do what she wished.

"She is a dangerous woman!" said the Trold, but both his sons left the hill, for they were tired of it all.

"And what can the next daughter do?" asked the old Trold.

"I have learnt to like the Norwegians," she said, "and I shall never marry unless I can go to Norway!"

But the smallest of the sisters whispered to the Trold, "that is only because she once heard a song which said that when the world came to an end, the rocks of Norway would still stand, and that is why she wants to go there, she is so afraid of being exterminated."

"Ho, ho!" said the Trold, "so that slipped out. But what can the seventh do?"

"The sixth comes before the seventh," said the elf-king, for he could reckon, but she would not come forward.

"I can only tell people the truth," she said. "Nobody cares for me, and I have enough to do in making my winding-sheet."

Now came the seventh and last, what could she do? Well she could tell stories as many as ever she liked.

"Here are my five fingers," said the old Trold, "tell me a story for each one."

The elf-maiden took hold of his wrist, and he chuckled and laughed, till he nearly choked. When she came to the fourth finger, which had a gold ring on it, as if it knew there was to be a betrothal, the Trold said, "Hold fast what you have got, the hand is yours, I will have you for a wife myself!" The elf-maiden said that the stories about Guldbrand, the fourth finger, and little Peter Playman, the fifth, had not yet been told.

"Never mind, keep those till winter. Then you shall tell us about the fir, and the birch, and the fairy gifts, and the tingling frost. You shall have every opportunity of telling us stories; nobody up there does it yet. We will sit in the Stone Hall, where the pine logs blaze, and drink mead out of the golden horns of the old Norwegian kings. The river god gave me a couple. When we sit there the mountain sprite comes to pay us a visit, and he will sing you the songs of the Sæter girls. The salmon will leap in the waterfalls, and beat against the stone wall, but it won't get in. Ah, you may believe me when I say that we lead a merry life there in good old Norway. But where are the lads? "

Yes, where were the lads? They were running about the fields, blowing out the will-o'-the-wisps, who came so willingly for the torchlight procession.

" Why do you gad about out there? " said the Trold. " I have taken a mother for you, now you can come and take one of the aunts."

But the lads said they would rather make a speech, and drink toasts; they had no wish to marry. Then they made their speeches, and drank toasts and tipped their glasses up to show that they had emptied them. After that they pulled off their coats and went to sleep on the table, to show that they were quite at home. But the old Trold danced round and round the room with his young bride, and exchanged boots with her, which was grander than exchanging rings.

" There is the cock crowing! " said the old housekeeper. " Now we must shut the shutters, so that the sun may not burn us up."

Then the hill closed up. But the lizards went on running up and down the clefts of the tree; and they said to each other, " Ah, how much I liked the old Trold."

" I liked the boys better," said the earthworm, but then it couldn't see, poor, miserable creature that it was.

the real princess

THERE was once a prince, and he wanted a princess, but then she must be a *real* princess. He travelled right round the world to find one, but there was always something wrong. There were plenty of princesses, but whether they were real princesses he had great difficulty in discovering; there was always something which was not quite right about them. So at last he had to come home again, and he was very sad because he wanted a real princess so badly.

One evening there was a terrible storm; it thundered and lightened and the rain poured down in torrents; indeed it was a fearful night.

In the middle of the storm somebody knocked at the town gate, and the old king himself went to open it.

It was a princess who stood outside, but she was in a terrible state from the rain and the storm. The water streamed out of her hair and her clothes, it ran in at the top of her shoes and out at the heel, but she said that she was a real princess.

"Well we shall soon see if that is true," thought the old queen, but she said nothing. She went into the bedroom, took all the bedclothes off and laid a pea on the bedstead: then she took twenty mattresses and piled them on the top of the pea, and then twenty feather beds on the top of the mattresses. This was where the princess was to sleep that night. In the morning they asked her how she had slept.

59

"Oh terribly badly!" said the Princess. "I have hardly closed my eyes the whole night! Heaven knows what was in the bed. I seemed to be lying upon some hard thing, and my whole body is black and blue this morning. It is terrible!"

They saw at once that she must be a real princess when she had felt the pea through twenty mattresses and twenty feather beds. Nobody but a real princess could have such a delicate skin.

So the prince took her to be his wife, for now he was sure that he had found a real princess, and the pea was put into the Museum, where it may still be seen if no one has stolen it.

Now this is a true story.

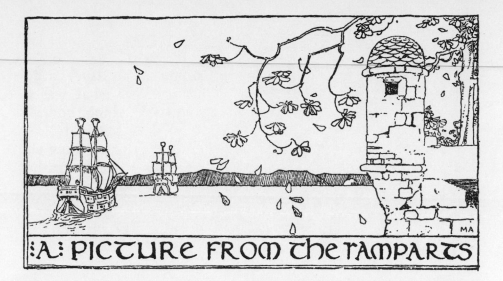

:A: PICTURE FROM The RAMPARTS

IT is autumn, and we are standing on the ramparts round the citadel, looking at the ships sailing on the Sound, and at the opposite coast of Sweden which stands out clearly in the evening sun-light. Behind us the ramparts fall away steeply; around are stately trees from which the golden leaves are falling fast. Down below us we see some dark and gloomy buildings, surrounded with wooden palisades, and inside these, where the sentries are walking up and down, it is darker still, yet not so gloomy as it is behind yon iron grating; that is where the worst convicts are confined. A ray from the setting sun falls into the bare room. The sun shines upon good and bad alike! The gloomy, savage prisoner looks bitterly at the chilly sunbeam. A little bird flutters against the grating. The bird sings to good and bad alike! It twitters softly for a little while, and remains perched, flutters its wings, picks a feather from its breast, and puffs its plumage up. The bad man in chains looks at it, a milder expression steals over his hideous face. A thought which is not quite clear to himself steals into his heart; it is related to the sunshine coming through the grating, related to the scent of violets, which in spring grow so thickly outside the window. Now is heard the music of a huntsman's horn clear and lively, the bird flies away from the grating, the sunbeam disappears and all is dark again in the narrow cell, dark in the heart of the bad man. Yet the sun has shone into it, and the bird has sung its song.

Continue ye merry notes! The evening is mild, the sea is calm and bright as any mirror.

61

THE RED SHOES

THERE was once a little girl; she was a tiny, delicate little thing, but she always had to go about barefoot in summer, because she was very poor. In winter she only had a pair of heavy wooden shoes, and her ankles were terribly chafed.

An old mother shoemaker lived in the middle of the village, and she made a pair of little shoes out of some strips of red cloth. They were very clumsy, but they were made with the best intention, for the little girl was to have them. Her name Karen.

These shoes were given to her, and she wore them for the first time on the day her mother was buried; they were certainly not mourning, but she had no others, and so she walked bare-legged in them behind the poor deal coffin.

Just then a big old carriage drove by, and a big old lady was seated in it; she looked at the little girl, and felt very very sorry for her, and said to the Parson, " Give the little girl to me and I will look after her and be kind to her." Karen thought it was all because of the red shoes, but the old lady said they were hideous, and they were burnt. Karen was well and neatly dressed, and had to learn reading and sewing. People said she was pretty, but her mirror said, " you are more than pretty, you are lovely."

At this time the queen was taking a journey through the country, and she had her little daughter the princess with her. The people, and among them Karen, crowded round the palace where they were staying, to see them. The little princess stood at a window to show herself. She wore neither a train nor a golden crown, but she was dressed all in white with a beautiful pair of red morocco shoes. They were indeed a contrast to those the poor old mother shoemaker had made for Karen. Nothing in the world could be compared to these red shoes.

The time came when Karen was old enough to be confirmed; she had new clothes, and she was also to have a pair of new shoes. The rich shoemaker in the town was to take the measure of her little foot; his shop was full of glass cases of the most charming shoes and shiny leather boots. They looked beautiful, but the old lady could not see very well, so it gave her no pleasure to look at them. Among all the other shoes there was one pair of red shoes like those worn by the princess; oh, how pretty they were. The shoemaker told them that they had been made for an earl's daughter, but they had not fitted. " I suppose they are patent leather," said the old lady, " they are so shiny."

" Yes, they do shine," said Karen, who tried them on. They fitted and were bought; but the old lady had not the least idea that they were red, or she would never have allowed Karen to wear them for her Confirmation. This she did however.

Everybody looked at her feet, and when she walked up the church to the chancel, she thought that even the old pictures, those portraits of dead and gone priests and their wives, with stiff collars and long black clothes, fixed their eyes upon her shoes. She thought of nothing else when the priest laid his hand upon her head and spoke to her of holy baptism, the covenant of God, and that from henceforth she was to be a responsible Christian person. The solemn notes of the organ resounded, the children sang with their sweet voices, the old precentor sang, but Karen only thought about her red shoes.

By the afternoon the old lady had been told on all sides that the shoes were red, and she said it was very naughty and most improper. For the future, whenever Karen went to the church, she was to wear black shoes, even if they were old. Next Sunday there was Holy Communion, and Karen was to receive it for the first time. She looked at the black shoes and then at the red ones—then she looked again at the red, and at last put them on.

It was beautiful, sunny weather; Karen and the old lady went by the path through the cornfield, and it was rather dusty.

By the church door stood an old soldier, with a crutch; he had a curious long beard, it was more red than white, in fact it was almost quite red. He bent down to the ground and asked the old lady if he might dust her shoes. Karen put out her little foot too. " See, what beautiful dancing shoes! " said the soldier. " Mind you stick fast when you dance," and as he spoke he struck the soles with his hand. The old lady gave the soldier a copper and went into the church with Karen. All the people in the church looked at Karen's red shoes, and all the portraits looked too. When Karen knelt at the altar-rails and the chalice was put to her lips, she only thought of the red shoes; she seemed to see them floating before her eyes. She forgot to join in the hymn of praise, and she forgot to say the Lord's Prayer.

Now everybody left the church, and the old lady got into her carriage. Karen lifted her foot to get in after her, but just then the old soldier, who was still standing there, said, " See what pretty dancing shoes! " Karen couldn't help it; she took a few dancing steps, and when she began her feet continued to dance; it was just as if the shoes had a power over them. She danced right round the church; she couldn't stop; the coachman had to run after her and take hold of her, and lift her into the carriage; but her feet continued to dance, so that she kicked the poor lady horribly. At last they got the shoes off, and her feet had a little rest.

When they got home the shoes were put away in a cupboard, but Karen could not help going to look at them.

The old lady became very ill; they said she could not live; she had to be carefully nursed and tended, and no one was nearer than Karen to do this. But there was to be a grand ball in the town, and Karen was invited. She looked at the old lady, who after all could not live; she looked at the red shoes; she thought there was no harm in doing so. She put on the red shoes, even that she might do; but then she went to the ball and began to dance! The shoes would not let her do what she liked: when she wanted to go to the right, they danced to the left: when she wanted to dance up the room, the shoes danced down the room, then down the stairs, through the streets and out of the town gate. Away she danced, and away she had to dance, right away into the dark forest. Something shone up above the trees, and she thought it was the moon, for it was a face, but it was the old soldier with the red beard, and he nodded and said, " See what pretty dancing shoes! "

This frightened her terribly and she wanted to throw off the red shoes, but they stuck fast. She tore off her stockings, but the shoes had grown fast to her feet, and off she danced, and off she had to dance over fields and meadows, in rain and sunshine, by day and by night, but at night it was fearful.

She danced into the open churchyard, but the dead did not join her dance, they had something much better to do. She wanted to sit down on a pauper's grave where the bitter wormwood grew, but there was no rest nor repose for her. When she danced towards the open church door, she saw an angel standing there in long white robes and wings which reached from his shoulders to the ground, his face was grave and stern, and in his hand he held a broad and shining sword.

" Dance you shall! " said he, " you shall dance in your red shoes till you are pale and cold. Till your skin shrivels up and you are a skeleton! You shall dance from door to door, and wherever you find proud vain children, you must knock at the door so that they may see you and fear you. Yea, you shall dance——"

" Mercy! " shrieked Karen, but she did not hear the angel's answer, for the shoes bore her through the gate into the fields over roadways and paths, ever and ever she was forced to dance.

One morning she danced past a door she knew well; she heard the sound of a hymn from within, and a coffin covered with flowers was being carried out. Then she knew that the old lady was dead, and it seemed to her that she was forsaken by all the world, and cursed by the holy angels of God.

On and ever on she danced; dance she must even through the dark nights. The shoes bore her away over briars and stubble till her feet were torn and bleeding; she danced away over the heath till she came to a little lonely house. She knew the executioner lived here, and she tapped with her fingers on the window pane and said,—

" Come out! come out! I can't come in for I am dancing! "

The executioner said, " You can't know who I am? I chop the bad people's heads off, and I see that my axe is quivering."

" Don't chop my head off," said Karen, " for then I can never repent of my sins, but pray, pray chop my feet off with the red shoes! "

Then she confessed all her sins, and the executioner chopped off her feet with the red shoes, but the shoes danced right away with the little feet into the depths of the forest.

Then he made her a pair of wooden legs and crutches, and he taught her a psalm, the one penitents always sing; and she kissed the hand which had wielded the axe, and went away over the heath.

" I have suffered enough for those red shoes! " said she. " I will go to church now, so that they may see me! " and she went as fast as she could to the church door. When she got there, the red shoes danced up in front of her, and she was frightened and went home again.

She was very sad all the week, and shed many bitter tears, but when Sunday came, she said, " Now then, I have suffered and struggled long enough; I should think I am quite as good as many who sit holding their heads so high in church! " She went along quite boldly, but she did not get further than the gate before she saw the red shoes dancing in front of her; she was more frightened than ever, and turned back, this time with real repentance in her heart. Then she went to the parson's house, and begged to be taken into service, she would be very industrious and work as hard as she could, she didn't care what wages they gave her, if only she might have a roof over her head and live among kind people. The parson's wife was sorry for her, and took her into her service; she proved to be very industrious and thoughtful. She sat very still, and listened most attentively in the evening when the parson read the Bible. All the little ones were very fond of her, but when they chattered about finery and dress, and about being as beautiful as a queen, she would shake her head.

Next Sunday they all went to church, and they asked her if she would go with them; but she looked sadly, with tears in her eyes, at her crutches, and they went without her to hear the word of God, and she sat in her little room alone. It was only big enough for a bed and a chair; she sat there with her prayer-book in her hand, and as she read it with a humble mind, she heard the notes of the organ, borne from the church by the wind; she raised her tear-stained face and said, "Oh, God help me!"

Then the sun shone brightly round her, and the angel in the white robes whom she had seen on yonder night, at the church door, stood before her. He no longer held the sharp sword in his hand, but a beautiful green branch, covered with roses. He touched the ceiling with it and it rose to a great height, and wherever he touched it a golden star appeared. Then he touched the walls and they spread themselves out, and she saw and heard the organ. She saw the pictures of the old parsons and their wives; the congregation were all sitting in their seats singing aloud—for the church itself had come home to the poor girl, in her narrow little chamber, or else she had been taken to it. She found herself on the bench with the other people from the Parsonage. And when the hymn had come to an end they looked up and nodded to her and said, "it was a good thing you came after all, little Karen!"

"It was through God's mercy!" she said. The organ sounded, and the children's voices echoed so sweetly through the choir. The warm sunshine streamed brightly in through the window, right up to the bench where Karen sat; her heart was so over-filled with the sunshine, with peace, and with joy, that it broke. Her soul flew with the sunshine to heaven, and no one there asked about the red shoes.

Thumbelina

THERE was once a woman who had the greatest longing for a little tiny child, but she had no idea where to get one; so she went to an old witch and said to her, "I do so long to have a little child, will you tell me where I can get one?"

"Oh, we shall be able to manage that," said the witch. "Here is a barley-corn for you; it is not at all the same kind as that which grows in the peasant's field, or with which chickens are fed; plant it in a flower-pot and you will see what will appear."

"Thank you, oh, thank you!" said the woman, and she gave the witch twelve pennies, then went home and planted the barleycorn, and a large, handsome flower sprang up at once; it looked exactly like a tulip, but the petals were tightly shut up, just as if they were still in bud. "That is a lovely flower," said the woman, and she kissed the pretty red and yellow petals; as she kissed it the flower burst open with a loud snap. It was a real tulip, you could see that; but right in the middle of the flower on the green stool sat a little tiny girl, most lovely and delicate; she was not more than an inch in height, so she was called Thumbelina.

Her cradle was a smartly varnished walnut shell, with the blue petals of violets for a mattress and a rose-leaf to cover her; she slept in it at night, but during the day she played about on the table where the woman had placed a plate, surrounded by a wreath of flowers on the outer edge with their stalks in water. A large tulip petal floated on the water, and on this little Thumbelina sat and sailed about from one side of the plate to the other; she had two white horsehairs for oars. It was a pretty sight. She could sing, too, with such delicacy and charm as was never heard before.

One night as she lay in her pretty bed, a great ugly toad hopped in at the window, for there was a broken pane. Ugh! how hideous that great wet toad was; it hopped right down on to the table where Thumbelina lay fast asleep, under the red rose-leaf.

"Here is a lovely wife for my son," said the toad, and then she took up the walnut shell where Thumbelina slept and hopped away with it through the window, down into the garden. A great broad stream ran through it, but just at the edge it was swampy and muddy, and it was here that the toad lived with her son. Ugh! how ugly and hideous he was too, exactly like his mother. "Koax, koax, brekke-ke-kex, that was all he had to say when he saw the lovely little girl in the walnut shell.

"Do not talk so loud or you will wake her," said the old toad; "she might escape us yet, for she is as light as thistle-down! We will put her on one of the broad water-lily leaves out in the stream; it will be just like an island to her, she is so small and light. She won't be able to run away from there while we get the state-room ready down under the mud, which you are to inhabit."

A great many water lilies grew in the stream, their broad green leaves looked as if they were floating on the surface of the water. The leaf which was furthest from the shore was also the biggest, and to this one the old toad swam out with the walnut shell in which little Thumbelina lay.

The poor, tiny little creature woke up quite early in the morning, and when she saw where she was she began to cry most bitterly, for there was water on every side of the big green leaf, and she could not reach the land at any point.

The old toad sat in the mud decking out her abode with grasses and the buds of the yellow water lilies, so as to have it very nice for the new daughter-in-law, and then she swam

out with her ugly son to the leaf where Thumbelina stood; they
wanted to fetch her pretty bed to place it in the bridal chamber
before they took her there. The old toad made a deep curtsey
in the water before her, and said, "Here is my son, who is to be
your husband, and you are to live together most comfortably
down in the mud."

"Koax, koax, brekke-ke-kex," that was all the son could say.

Then they took the pretty little bed and swam away with
it, but Thumbelina sat quite alone on the green leaf and cried
because she did not want to live with the ugly toad, or have
her horrid son for a husband. The little fish which swam about
in the water, had no doubt seen the toad and heard what she
said, so they stuck their heads up, wishing, I suppose, to see
the little girl. As soon as they saw her, they were delighted
with her, and were quite grieved to think that she was to go
down to live with the ugly toad. No, that should never happen.
They flocked together down in the water round about the green
stem which held the leaf she stood upon, and gnawed at it
with their teeth till it floated away down the stream carrying
Thumbelina away where the toad could not follow her.

Thumbelina sailed past place after place, and the little birds
in the bushes saw her and sang, "what a lovely little maid."
The leaf with her on it floated further and further away and
in this manner reached foreign lands.

A pretty little white butterfly fluttered round and round her
for some time and at last settled on the leaf, for it had taken
quite a fancy to Thumbelina: she was so happy now, because
the toad could not reach her and she was sailing through such
lovely scenes; the sun shone on the water and it looked like
liquid gold. Then she took her sash and tied one end round the
butterfly, and the other she made fast to the leaf which went
gliding on quicker and quicker, and she with it for she was
standing on the leaf.

At this moment a big cockchafer came flying along, he caught
sight of her and in an instant he fixed his claw round her slender
waist and flew off with her, up into a tree, but the green leaf
floated down the stream and the butterfly with it, for he was
tied to it and could not get loose.

Heavens! how frightened poor little Thumbelina was when

the cockchafer carried her up into the tree, but she was most of all grieved about the pretty white butterfly which she had fastened to the leaf; if he could not succeed in getting loose he would be starved to death.

But the cockchafer cared nothing for that. He settled with her on the largest leaf on the tree, and fed her with honey from the flowers, and he said that she was lovely although she was not a bit like a chafer. Presently all the other chafers which lived in the tree came to visit them; they looked at Thumbelina and the young lady chafers twitched their feelers and said, " she has also got two legs, what a good effect it has." " She has no feelers," said another. " She is so slender in the waist, fie, she looks like a human being." " How ugly she is," said all the mother chafers, and yet little Thumbelina was so pretty. That was certainly also the opinion of the cockchafer who had captured her, but when all the others said she was ugly, he at last began to believe it too, and would not have anything more to do with her, she might go wherever she liked! They flew down from the tree with her and placed her on a daisy, where she cried because she was so ugly that the chafers would have nothing to do with her; and after all, she was more beautiful than anything you could imagine, as delicate and transparent as the finest rose-leaf.

Poor little Thumbelina lived all the summer quite alone in the wood. She plaited a bed of grass for herself and hung it up under a big dock-leaf which sheltered her from the rain; she sucked the honey from the flowers for her food, and her drink was the dew which lay on the leaves in the morning. In this way the summer and autumn passed, but then came the winter. All the birds which used to sing so sweetly to her flew away, the great dock-leaf under which she had lived shrivelled up, leaving nothing but a dead yellow stalk, and she shivered with the cold, for her clothes were worn out; she was such a tiny creature, poor little Thumbelina, she certainly must be frozen to death. It began to snow and every snow-flake which fell upon her was like a whole shovelful upon one of us, for we are big and she was only one inch in height. Then she wrapped herself up in a withered leaf, but that did not warm her much, she trembled with the cold.

Close to the wood in which she had been living lay a large cornfield, but the corn had long ago been carried away and nothing remained but the bare, dry, stubble which stood up out of the frozen ground. The stubble was quite a forest for her to walk about in: oh, how she shook with the cold. Then she came to the door of a field-mouse's home. It was a little hole down under the stubble. The field-mouse lived so cosily and warm there, her whole room was full of corn, and she had a beautiful kitchen and larder besides. Poor Thumbelina stood just inside the door like any other poor beggar child and begged for a little piece of barley corn, for she had had nothing to eat for two whole days.

"You poor little thing," said the field-mouse, for she was at bottom a good old field-mouse. "Come into my warm room and dine with me." Then, as she took a fancy to Thumbelina, she said, "you may with pleasure stay with me for the winter, but you must keep my room clean and tidy and tell me stories, for I am very fond of them," and Thumbelina did what the good old field-mouse desired and was on the whole very comfortable.

"Now we shall soon have a visitor," said the field-mouse; "my neighbour generally comes to see me every week-day. He is even better housed than I am; his rooms are very large and he wears a most beautiful black velvet coat; if only you could get him for a husband you would indeed be well settled, but he can't see. You must tell him all the most beautiful stories you know."

But Thumbelina did not like this, and she would have nothing to say to the neighbour, for he was a mole. He came and paid a visit in his black velvet coat. He was very rich and wise, said the field-mouse, and his home was twenty times as large as hers; and he had much learning, but he did not like the sun or the beautiful flowers, in fact he spoke slightingly of them, for he had never seen them. Thumbelina had to sing to him and she sang both " Fly away cockchafer " and " A monk, he wandered through the meadow," then the mole fell in love with her because of her sweet voice, but he did not say anything, for he was of a discreet turn of mind.

He had just made a long tunnel through the ground from

his house to theirs, and he gave the field-mouse and Thumbelina leave to walk in it whenever they liked. He told them not to be afraid of the dead bird which was lying in the passage. It was a whole bird with feathers and beak which had probably died quite recently at the beginning of the winter, and was now entombed just where he had made his tunnel.

The mole took a piece of tinder-wood in his mouth, for that shines like fire in the dark, and walked in front of them to light them in the long dark passage; when they came to the place where the dead bird lay, the mole thrust his broad nose up to the roof and pushed the earth up so as to make a big hole through which the daylight shone. In the middle of the floor lay a dead swallow, with its pretty wings closely pressed to its sides, and the legs and head drawn in under the feathers; no doubt the poor bird had died of cold. Thumbelina was so sorry for it; she loved all the little birds, for they had twittered and sung so sweetly to her during the whole summer; but the mole kicked it with his short legs and said, " Now it will pipe no more! it must be a miserable fate to be born a little bird! Thank heaven! no child of mine can be a bird; a bird like that has nothing but its twitter and dies of hunger in the winter."

" Yes, as a sensible man, you may well say that," said the field-mouse. " What *has* a bird for all its twittering when the cold weather comes? it has to hunger and freeze, but then it must cut a dash."

Thumbelina did not say anything, but when the others turned their backs to the bird, she stooped down and stroked aside the feathers which lay over its head, and kissed its closed eyes. "Perhaps it was this very bird which sang so sweetly to me in the summer," she thought; "what pleasure it gave me, the dear pretty bird."

The mole now closed up the hole which let in the daylight and conducted the ladies to their home. Thumbelina could not sleep at all in the night, so she got up out of her bed and plaited a large handsome mat of hay and then she carried it down and spread it all over the dead bird, and laid some soft cotton wool which she had found in the field-mouse's room close round its sides, so that it might have a warm bed on the cold ground.

" Good-bye, you sweet little bird," said she, " good-bye, and thank you for your sweet song through the summer, when all the trees were green and the sun shone warmly upon us." Then she laid her head close up to the bird's breast, but was quite startled at a sound, as if something was thumping inside it. It was the bird's heart. It was not dead but lay in a swoon, and now that it had been warmed it began to revive.

In the autumn all the swallows fly away to warm countries, but if one happens to be belated, feels the cold so much that it falls down like a dead thing, and remains lying where it falls till the snow covers it up. Thumbelina quite shook with fright, for the bird was very, very big beside her who was only one inch high, but she gathered up her courage, packed the wool closer round the poor bird, and fetched a leaf of mint which she had herself for a coverlet and laid it over the bird's head. The next night she stole down again to it and found it alive, but so feeble that it could only just open its eyes for a moment to look at Thumbelina who stood with a bit of tinder-wood in her hand, for she had no other lantern.

"Many, many thanks, you sweet child," said the sick swallow to her; "you have warmed me beautifully. I shall soon have strength to fly out into the warm sun again."

"Oh!" said she, "it is so cold outside, it snows and freezes, stay in your warm bed, I will tend you." Then she brought water to the swallow in a leaf, and when it had drunk some, it told her how it had torn its wing on a blackthorn bush, and therefore could not fly as fast as the other swallows which were taking flight then for the distant warm lands. At last it fell down on the ground, but after that it remembered nothing, and did not in the least know how it had got into the tunnel.

It stayed there all the winter, and Thumbelina was good to it and grew very fond of it. She did not tell either the mole or the field-mouse anything about it, for they did not like the poor unfortunate swallow.

As soon as the spring came and the warmth of the sun penetrated the ground, the swallow said good-bye to Thumbelina, who opened the hole which the mole had made above. The sun streamed in deliciously upon them, and the swallow asked if she would not go with him, she could sit upon his back and they would fly far away into the green wood. But Thumbelina knew that it would grieve the old field-mouse if she left her like that.

"No, I can't," said Thumbelina.

"Good-bye, good-bye, then, you kind pretty girl," said the swallow, and flew out into the sunshine. Thumbelina looked after him and her eyes filled with tears, for she was very fond of the poor swallow.

"Tweet, tweet," sang the bird, and flew into the green wood.

Thumbelina was very sad. She was not allowed to go out into the warm sunshine at all; the corn which was sown in the field near the field-mouse's house grew quite long, it was a thick forest for the poor little girl who was only an inch high.

"You must work at your trousseau this summer," said the mouse to her, for their neighbour the tiresome mole in his black velvet coat had asked her to marry him. "You shall have both woollen and linen, you shall have wherewith to clothe and cover yourself when you become the mole's wife." Thumbelina had to turn the distaff and the field-mouse hired four spiders to spin and weave day and night. The mole paid a visit every evening, and he was always saying that when the summer came to an end, the sun would not shine nearly so warmly, now it burnt the ground as hard as a stone. Yes, when the summer was over he would celebrate his marriage; but Thumbelina was not at all pleased, for she did not care a bit for the tiresome mole. Every morning at sunrise and every evening at sunset she used to steal out to the door, and when the wind blew aside the tops of the corn-stalks so that she could see the blue sky, she thought how bright and lovely it was out there, and wished so much to see the dear swallow again; but it never came back; no doubt it was a long way off, flying about in the beautiful green woods.

When the autumn came all Thumbelina's outfit was ready.

"In four weeks you must be married," said the field-mouse to her. But Thumbelina cried and said that she would not have the tiresome mole for a husband.

"Fiddle-dee-dee," said the field-mouse; "don't be obstinate or I shall bite you with my white tooth. You are going to have a splendid husband; the queen herself hasn't the equal of his black velvet coat; both his kitchen and his cellar are full. You should thank heaven for such a husband!"

So they were to be married; the mole had come to fetch Thumbelina; she was to live deep down under the ground with him, and never to go out into the warm sunshine, for he could not bear it. The poor child was very sad at the thought of bidding good-bye to the beautiful sun; while she had been with the field-mouse she had at least been allowed to look at it from the door.

"Good-bye, you bright sun," she said as she stretched out her arms towards it and went a little way outside the field-mouse's house, for now the harvest was over and only the stubble remained. "Good-bye, good-bye!" she said, and threw her tiny arms round a little red flower growing there. "Give my love to the dear swallow if you happen to see him."

"Tweet, tweet," she heard at this moment above her head. She looked up; it was the swallow just passing. As soon as it saw Thumbelina it was delighted; she told it how unwilling she was to have the ugly mole for a husband, and that she was to live deep down underground where the sun never shone. She could not help crying about it.

"The cold winter is coming," said the swallow, "and I am going to fly away to warm countries. Will you go with me? You can sit upon my back! Tie yourself on with your sash, then we will fly away from the ugly mole and his dark cavern, far away over the mountains to those warm countries where the sun shines with greater splendour than here, where it is always summer and there are heaps of flowers. Do fly with me, you sweet little Thumbelina, who saved my life when I lay frozen in the dark earthy passage."

"Yes, I will go with you," said Thumbelina, seating herself on the bird's back with her feet on its out-spread wing. She tied her band tightly to one of the strongest feathers, and then the swallow flew away, high up in the air above forests and lakes, high up above the biggest mountains where the snow never melts; and Thumbelisa shivered in the cold air, but then she crept under the bird's warm feathers, and only stuck out her little head to look at the beautiful sights beneath her.

Then at last they reached the warm countries. The sun shone with a warmer glow than here; the sky was twice as high, and the most beautiful green and blue grapes grew in

clusters on the banks and hedgerows.   Oranges and lemons hung
in the woods which were fragrant with myrtles and sweet herbs,
and beautiful children ran about the roads playing with the
large gorgeously-coloured butterflies.   But the swallow flew on
and on, and the country grew more and more beautiful.   Under
magnificent green trees on the shores of the blue sea stood a
dazzling white marble palace of ancient date;   vines wreathed
themselves round the stately pillars.   At the head of these there
were countless nests, and the swallow who carried Thumbelina
lived in one of them.

"Here is my house," said the swallow; "but if you will
choose one of the gorgeous flowers growing down there, I will
place you in it, and you will live as happily as you can wish."

"That would be delightful," she said, and clapped her little
hands.

A great white marble column had fallen to the ground and
lay there broken in three pieces, but between these the most
lovely white flowers grew.   The swallow flew down with
Thumbelina and put her upon one of the broad leaves; what
was her astonishment to find a little man in the middle of the
flower, as bright and transparent as if he had been made of
glass.   He had a lovely golden crown upon his head and the
most beautiful bright wings upon his shoulders; he was no
bigger than Thumbelina.   He was the angel of the flowers.
There was a similar little man or woman in every flower, but
he was the king of them all.

"Heavens, how beautiful he is," whispered Thumbelina to
the swallow.   The little prince was quite frightened by the
swallow, for it was a perfect giant of a bird to him, he who
was so small and delicate, but when he saw Thumbelina he was
delighted; she was the very prettiest girl he had ever seen.
He therefore took the golden crown off his own head and placed
it on hers, and asked her name, and if she would be his wife, and
then she would be queen of the flowers!   Yes, he was certainly
a very different kind of husband from the toad's son, or the mole
with his black velvet coat.   So she accepted the beautiful prince,
and out of every flower stepped a little lady or a gentleman so
lovely that it was a pleasure to look at them. Each one brought
a gift to Thumbelina, but the best of all was a pair of pretty

wings from a large white fly; they were fastened on to her back, and then she too could fly from flower to flower. All was then delight and happiness, but the swallow sat alone in his nest and sang to them as well as he could, for his heart was heavy, he was so fond of Thumbelina himself, and would have wished never to part from her.

"You shall not be called Thumbelina," said the angel of the flower to her; " that is such an ugly name, and you are so pretty. We will call you May."

" Good-bye, good-bye," said the swallow, and flew away again from the warm countries, far away back to Denmark; there he had a little nest above the window where the man lived who wrote this story, and he sang his " tweet, tweet " to the man, and so we have the whole story.

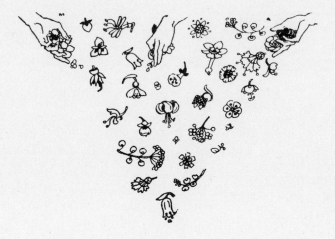

The GOBLIN & the huckster

THERE was once a real student who lived in an attic and possessed nothing at all. There was also a real huckster* who lived on the ground floor and owned the whole house. The goblin made friends with him, for every Christmas he was given a plateful of porridge with a lump of butter in it. The huckster could very well afford this, so the goblin stayed in the shop, which was a very instructive place.

One evening the student came in by the back door to buy himself some candles and cheese; he had no one to send, so he went himself. He got what he asked for and paid for it, and the huckster nodded to him and said "good evening" to him, and his wife did the same. She was a woman who could do more than nod, she had "the gift of the gab!" The student returned the nod, and then remained standing buried in something he found printed on the paper in which the cheese was wrapped. It was a page torn out of an old book, which ought never to have been torn up at all; it was an old book of poetry.

"There is more of it lying there," said the huckster. "I gave a few coffee beans to an old woman for it; if you will give me two pence you may have the rest of it."

"Thank you," said the student; "let me have it instead of the cheese! I can eat plain bread and butter just as well; it would be a sin if the whole of that book were to be torn to bits. You are a capital fellow and a practical man, but you know no more about poetry than that tub!"

Now this was a very rude speech, especially to the tub, but the huckster laughed; of course it was said as a kind of joke. But the goblin was much annoyed that anyone dared to say

*Old-fashioned word for grocer.

such a thing to a huckster who was a landlord and who sold the best butter.

At night when the shop was shut and everybody in bed except the student, the goblin went in and stole the goodwife's long tongue which she had no use for when she was asleep. On whatever object in the room he laid this article, it conferred the power of speech, and whatever the object, it became able to express its thoughts and feelings as glibly as the goodwife herself. But only one could have it at a time, and this was a very good thing or they would all have been talking at once.

The goblin laid the tongue down upon the tub which contained the old newspapers.

"Is it really true," asked he, "that you do not know what poetry is?"

"Of course I know," said the tub; "it is the kind of stuff which is printed at the foot of the newspaper columns, and is sometimes cut out. I imagine that I have more of it within me than the student has, and after all I am only a poor tub compared to the huckster."

Then the goblin put the tongue upon the coffee-mill, and what a pace it went at! He also put it on the butter cask and the cash-box. They were all of the same opinion as the tub; and what the majority agree upon must be respected.

"Now the student shall have it," said the goblin, and he stole silently up the back stairs to the attic where the student lived. There was a light burning, and the goblin peeped through the key-hole, and saw that the student was reading the tattered book from downstairs. But how bright the room was! A clear ray of light shot forth from the book, which widened out to a stem, and then to a mighty tree, which rose and spread its branches right over the student. The leaves were delightfully fresh, and every flower was like a lovely girl's face, some with dark and sparkling eyes, while others were wonderfully blue and clear. Every fruit was a shining star and the air was filled with music. No, the little goblin had never imagined, much less seen or taken part in such splendours. So then he stood on tip-toe peeping and peeping till the light was put out. The student blew out his lamp and went to bed, but the little goblin remained by the door, for the sweet songs still echoed through

Then the swallow flew away, high up in the air.

THUMBELINA

Page 76

"You shall dance in your red shoes till you are pale
and cold."

THE RED SHOES

the air, making a charming lullaby for the student who was taking his rest.

" This is splendid," said the goblin; " I hadn't expected anything of the kind!—I think I will stay with the student—! " and he thought—and thought again—and then he sighed, " but the student has no porridge! "—Then he went away—yes, he went back to the huckster, and it was a good thing he went, for the tub had almost used up the goodwife's volubility. He had given a description of all he contained from one side, and now he was just about to turn himself over to repeat the same from the other side, when the goblin came and took away the lady's tongue to return it to her. But the whole shop, from the cash drawer to the firewood, took their opinions from the tub from that time; and they respected it so highly and confided in it to such a degree, that when the huckster afterwards read the Art and Theatrical announcements in his *Times*, the evening one, they all thought that they came from the tub.

But the little goblin no longer sat quietly listening to all the wisdom and learning downstairs; no, as soon as a light appeared in the attic, it had the same effect upon him as if the rays of light had been stout anchor hawsers, for they drew him upwards and forced him to go and peep through the key-hole. A mighty power surged around him, such as we feel when the Almighty moves over the face of the rolling waters in a storm, and he burst into tears; he did not himself know wherefore, but there was some soothing in these tears. How splendid it must be to sit with the student under that tree, the tree of knowledge, but that might not be—he was glad even to stand at the key-hole.

He still came to peep through the key-hole when the autumn winds blew down upon it from the trap-door; it was cold, very cold, but the little creature did not feel it till the light went out in the attic and the sounds died away on the wind. Then how he shivered! he crept down again to his cosy corner, it was warm and comfortable there! And when the Christmas porridge appeared with a lump of butter in it—why then the huckster was master.

But in the middle of the night the goblin was roused up by a frightful uproar and banging on the window shutters; the people outside were thundering on them. The watchman was blowing his whistle; there was a great fire, the whole street was lighted up. Was it in this house, or the next? Where? It was terrible. The huckster's wife was so upset that she took the gold earrings out of her ears and put them into her pocket, so as at least to save something. The huckster ran to look for his bonds, and the maid-servant for the silk mantle she had just managed to afford herself. Everybody wanted to save the most precious thing he had, and the goblin wanted to do the same, so with a hop and a skip he was up the stairs and into the student's room. The student stood calmly at the window looking at the fire which was in the opposite house. The little goblin seized the marvellous book which was lying on the table, stuffed it into his red cap, and held it with both his hands; the greatest treasure in the house was saved! Then he rushed away, right out on to the roof to the very top of the chimney, and there he sat lighted up by the blaze opposite. He still held his red cap tightly grasped with both hands, in which the treasure was hidden.

Now he knew the leaning of his heart, and to whom he really belonged; but when the fire was out and he thought the matter over—why then—" I will divide myself between them," he said. " I can't give up the huckster, because of the porridge." In this he was quite human! We others go to the huckster too— for the porridge.

THE BOTTLE ‑ NECK

DOWN in a narrow crooked street among other poverty-stricken houses, stood a very high and narrow one, built of lath and plaster; it was in a very bad state and bulged out in every direction. It was entirely inhabited by poor people, but the attic looked the poorest of all. Outside the window in the sunshine hung a battered bird cage, which had not even got a proper drinking glass, but only the neck of a bottle turned upside down, with a cork at the bottom to serve this purpose. An old maid stood at the window, she had just been hanging chickweed all over the cage in which a little linnet hopped about from perch to perch, singing as gaily as possible.

"Ah, you may well sing!" said the bottle neck; but of course it did not say it as we should say it, for a bottle neck cannot talk, but it thought it within itself, much as when we inwardly talk to ourselves. "Yes, you may well sing, you who have all your limbs whole. You should try what it is like to have lost the lower part of your body like me, and only to have a neck and a mouth, and that with a cork in it, such as I have, and you wouldn't sing much. I have nothing to make me sing, nor could I if I would. But it is a good thing that somebody is pleased. I could have sung when I was a whole bottle and anyone rubbed me with a cork. I used to be called the real lark then, the big lark; and then I went to the picnic in the wood, with the furrier and his family, and his daughter was engaged—yes, I remember it as well as if it had been yesterday.

83

I have had no end of experiences when I begin to look back upon them. I have been through fire and water, and down into the black earth, and higher up than most people, and now I hang in the sunshine outside a bird cage. It might be worth while to listen to my story, but I don't speak very loud about it, for I can't."

Then it related within itself, or thought out its story inwardly. It was a curious enough story; the little bird twittered away happily enough, and down in the street people walked and drove as usual, all bent upon their own concerns, thinking about them, or about nothing at all; but not so the bottle neck. It recalled the glowing smelting furnace in the factory, where it had been blown into life. It still remembered feeling quite warm, and gazing longingly into the roaring furnace, its birthplace; and its great desire to leap back again into it. But little by little as it cooled, it began to feel quite comfortable where it was. It was standing in a row with a whole regiment of brothers and sisters, all from the same furnace, but some were blown into champagne bottles, and others into beer bottles, which makes all the difference in their after life! Later, when out in the world, a beer bottle may certainly contain the costliest Lacrimæ Christe, and a champagne bottle may be filled with blacking; but what one is born to may be seen in the structure. Nobility is nobility even if it has black blood in its veins!

All the bottles were soon packed up and our bottle with them. It never dreamt then of ending its days as a bottle neck serving as a drinking glass for a bird; but after all, that is an honourable position, so one is something after all. It first saw the light again, when with its other companions it was unpacked in the wine merchant's cellar. Its first rinsing was a peculiar experience. Then it lay empty and corkless, and felt curiously flat, it missed something, but did not know exactly what it was. Next it was filled with some good strong wine, was corked and sealed, and last of all it was labelled outside "first quality." This was just as if it had passed first class in an examination, but of course the wine was really good and so was the bottle. While one is young one is a poet! Something within it sang and rejoiced, something which it really knew nothing at all about; green sunlit slopes where the vine grew, merry girls and jovial youths singing and kissing each other. Ah, life is a heavenly thing! All this stirred and worked within the bottle just as it does in young poets, who very often know no more about it than the bottle.

At last one morning the bottle was bought by the furrier's apprentice; he was sent for a bottle of the best wine. It was packed up in the luncheon basket together with the ham, the cheese and the sausage; the basket also contained butter of the best, and various fancy breads. The furrier's daughter packed it herself, she was quite young and very pretty. She had laughing brown eyes, and a smile on her lips; her hands were soft and delicate and very white, yet not so white as her neck and bosom. It was easy to see that she was one of the town beauties, and yet she was not engaged. She held the provision basket on her lap during the drive to the wood. The neck of the bottle peeped out beyond the folds of the table-cloth. There was red sealing wax on the cork, and it looked straight up into the maiden's face; and it also looked at the young sailor who sat beside her, he was a friend of her childhood, the son of a portrait painter. He had just passed his examination for promotion with honour, and was to sail next day as mate on a long trip to foreign parts. There had been a good deal of talk about this journey during the packing, and while it was going on the expression in the eyes and on the mouth of the pretty girl had been anything but cheerful. The two young people walked together in the wood, and talked to each other. What did they talk about? Well, the bottle did not hear their conversation, for it was in the luncheon basket. It was a very long time before it was taken out, but when this did occur, it was evident that something pleasant had taken place. Everybody's eyes were beaming, and the furrier's daughter was laughing, but she talked less than the others, and her cheeks glowed like two red roses.

Father took up the bottle and the cork-screw—it was a curious sensation for the cork to be drawn from the bottle for the first time. The bottle neck never afterwards forgot the solemn moment when the cork flew out with a " kloop," and it gurgled when the wine flowed out of it into the glasses.

" The health of the betrothed," said father, and every glass was drained, while the young sailor kissed his lovely bride.

" Health and happiness! " said both the old people. The young man filled the glasses again and drank to the " home-coming and the wedding this day year." When the glasses were emptied, he took the bottle and held it up above his head. " You have shared my happiness to-day, and you shall serve nobody else," saying which he threw it up into the air. The furrier's daughter little thought she was ever to see it again; however this was to come to pass. It fell among the rushes by a little woodland lake. The bottle neck remembered distinctly how it lay there thinking over these events. " I gave them wine, and they gave me swamp water in return, but they meant it well." It could no longer see the betrothed pair or the joyous old people, but it could hear them for a long time gaily talking and singing. After a time two little peasant boys came along peering among the reeds where they saw the bottle and took it away with them, so it was provided for. At home in the forester's cottage where they lived, their eldest brother who was a sailor had been yesterday to take leave of them, as he was starting on a long voyage. Mother was now packing up a bundle of his things which father was to take to the town in the evening, when he went to see his son once more, and to take his mother's last greeting. A little bottle had already been filled with spiced brandy, and was just being put into the bundle when the two boys came in with the other larger bottle they had found. This one would hold so much more than the little one, and this was all the better, for it was such a splendid cure for a chill. It was no longer red wine like the last which was put into the bottle but bitter drops; however, these were good too—for the stomach. The large new bottle was to go and not the little one; so once more the bottle started on a new journey. It was taken on board the ship to Peter Jensen, and it was the very same ship in which the young mate was to sail. But the mate did not see the bottle, and even if he had he would not have known it, nor would he ever have thought that it was the one out of which they had drunk to his home-coming.

Certainly it no longer contained wine, but there was some-thing just as good in it. Whenever Peter Jensen brought it out, his shipmates dubbed it, " the apothecary." It contained good physic, and cured all their complaints as long as there was a drop left in it. It was a very pleasant time, and the bottle used to sing whenever it was stroked with a cork, so they christened it " Peter Jensen's lark."

A long time passed and it stood in a corner empty, when something happened—whether it was on the outward or the homeward journey, the bottle did not know, for it had not been ashore.

A storm rose, great waves dark and heavy poured over the vessel and tossed it up and down. The masts were broken and one heavy sea sprang a leak; the pumps refused to work; and it was a pitch dark night. The ship sank, but at the last moment the young mate wrote upon a scrap of paper, " In the name of Jesus, we are going down! " He wrote the name of his bride, his own, and that of the ship, put the paper into an empty bottle he saw, hammered in the cork, and threw it out into the boiling, seething waters. He did not know that it was the very bottle from which he had poured the draught of joy and hope for her and for himself. Now it swayed up and down upon the waves with farewells and a message of death.

The ship sank, and the crew with it, but the bottle floated like a bird, for it had a heart in it you know—a lover's letter. The sun rose and the sun set and looked to the bottle just like the glowing furnace in its earliest days, when it had a longing to leap back again. It went through calms and storms: it never struck against any rock, nor was it ever followed by sharks; it drifted about for more than a year and a day, first towards north and then towards south, just as the current drove it. It was otherwise entirely its own master, but one may get tired even of that.

The written paper, the last farewell from the bridegroom to the bride, could only bring grief, if it ever came into the right hands; but where were those hands, the ones which had shone so white when they spread the cloth upon the fresh grass in the green woods on the day of the betrothal? Where was the furrier's daughter? Nay, where was the land, and which land lay nearest? All this the bottle knew not; it drifted and drifted, till at last it was sick of drifting about; it had never been its own intention, but all the same it had to drift till at last it reached land—a strange land. It did not understand a word that was said; it was not the language it was accustomed to hear, and one loses much if one does not understand the language.

The bottle was picked up and looked at, the bit of paper inside was inspected, turned and twisted, but they did not understand what was written on it. They saw that the bottle had been thrown overboard, and that something about it was written on the paper, but what it was, this was the remarkable part. So it was put into the bottle again, and this was put into a large cupboard in a large room in a large house.

Every time a stranger came the slip of paper was taken out, turned and twisted, so that the writing which was only in pencil became more and more illegible. At last it was impossible even to make out the letters. The bottle stood in the cupboard for another year, then it was put into the lumber-room, where it was soon hidden with dust and spider's webs; then it used to think of the better days when it poured forth red wine in the wood, and when it danced on the waves and carried a secret, a letter, a farewell sigh within it.

Now it stood in the attic for twenty years, and it might have stood there longer, if the house had not been rebuilt. The roof was torn off, the bottle was seen and remarked upon, but it did not understand the language; one does not learn that by standing in a lumber-room, even for twenty years. "Had I remained downstairs," it thought indeed, "I should have learnt it fast enough!"

Now it was washed and thoroughly rinsed out, a process which it sorely needed; it became quite clear and transparent, and felt youthful again in its old age. The slip of paper it had contained within it so long had vanished in the rinsing.

The bottle was filled with seed corn, a sort of thing it knew nothing at all about. Then it was well corked and wrapped up tightly, so that it could neither see the light of lantern or candle, far less the sun or the moon—and one really ought to see something when one goes on a journey, thought the bottle. However, it saw nothing, but it did the most important thing required of it; that was to arrive at its destination, and there it was unpacked.

"What trouble these foreigners have taken with it!" was said, "but I daresay it is cracked all the same." However, it was not cracked. The bottle understood every single word that was said, it was all spoken in the language it had heard at the smelting furnace, at the wine merchant's, in the wood, and on board ship—the one and only good old language which it thoroughly understood. It had come home again to its own country, where it had a hearty welcome in the language. It nearly sprang out of the people's hands from very joy; it hardly noticed the cork being drawn. Then it was well shaken to empty it, and put away in the cellar to be kept and also forgotten. There is no place like home, even if it be a cellar. It never occurred to the bottle to think how long it lay there, but it lay there comfortably for many years; then one day some people came down and took away all the bottles and it among them.

In the garden outside everything was very festive. There were festoons of lamps and transparent paper lanterns like tulips. It was a clear and lovely evening; the stars shone brightly, and the slim crescent of the new moon was just up; in fact, the whole moon, like a pale grey globe, was visible with a golden rim to the half of it. It was a beautiful sight for good eyes.

There were also some illuminations in the side-paths, enough, at any rate, to see one's way about. Bottles were placed at intervals in the hedges, each with a lighted candle in it, and among them stood our bottle too, the one we know, which was to end its days as a bottle neck for a bird's drinking fountain. Everything here appeared lovely to the bottle, for it was once again in the green wood and taking part once more in merrymaking and gaiety. It heard music and singing once again, and the hum and buzz of many people, especially from that corner of the garden where the lanterns shone and the paper lamps gave their coloured light. The bottle was only placed in one of the side walks, but even there it had food for reflection. There it stood bearing its light aloft; it was being of some use as well as giving pleasure, and that was the right thing—in such an hour one forgets all about the twenty years passed in an attic—and it is good sometimes to forget.

A couple of persons passed close by it, arm in arm, like the betrothed pair in the woods, the sailor and the furrier's daughter. The bottle felt as if it were living its life over again. The guests walked about in the garden, and other people too, who had come to look at them and at the illuminations. Among them there was an old maid who was without kith or kin, but not friendless. She was thinking of the very same thing as the bottle; of the green wood and of a young pair very dear to her, as she herself was one of them. It had been her happiest hour, and that one never forgets, however old a spinster one may be. But she did not know the bottle, and it did not know her again; thus people pass one another in the world—till one meets again like these two who were now in the same town.

The bottle was taken from the garden to the wine merchant's, where it was again filled with wine and sold to an aeronaut who next Sunday was to make an ascent in a balloon. A crowd of people came to look on; there was a regimental band and many preparations. The bottle saw everything from a basket, where it lay in company with a living rabbit, which was much depressed, for it knew it was being taken up to be sent down in a parachute. The bottle knew nothing at all about it; it only saw that the balloon was being distended to a great size, and when it could not get any bigger it began to rise higher and higher, and to become very restive. The ropes which held it were then cut, and it ascended with the aeronaut, basket, bottle and rabbit. There was a grand clashing of music, and the people shouted "Hurrah!"

"It is a curious sensation to go up into the air like this!" thought the bottle. "It's a new kind of sailing, and there can't be any danger of a collision up here!"

Several thousands of persons watched the balloon, and among them the old maid. She stood by her open window, where the cage hung with the little linnet, which at that time had no drinking fountain, but had to content itself with a cup. A myrtle stood in a pot in the window, and it was moved a little to one side so as not to be knocked over when the old maid leant out to look at the balloon. She could see the aeronaut quite plainly when he let the rabbit down in the parachute; then he drank the health of the people, after which he threw the bottle high up into the air. Little did she think that she had seen the same bottle fly into the air above her and her lover on that happy day in the woods in her youth. The bottle had no time to think, it was so taken by surprise at finding itself suddenly thus at the zenith of its career. The church steeples and housetops lay far, far below, and the people looked quite tiny. The bottle sank with far greater rapidity than the rabbit, and on the way it turned several somersaults in the air; it felt so youthful, so exhilarated—it was half-drunk with the wine—but not for long did it feel so. What a journey it had! The sun shone upon the bottle, and all the people watched its flight; the balloon was already far away, and the bottle was soon lost to sight too. It fell upon a roof, where it was smashed to pieces, but there was such an impetus on the bits that they could not lie where they fell; they jumped and rolled till they reached the yard, where they lay in still smaller bits; only the neck was whole, and that might have been cut off with a diamond.

"That would do very well for a bird's drinking fountain!" said the man who lived in the basement; but he had neither bird nor cage, and it would have been too much to procure these merely because he had found a bottle neck which would do for a drinking fountain. The old maid in the attic might find a use for it, so the bottle neck found its way up there. It had a cork put into it, and what had been the top became the bottom, in the way changes often take place; fresh water was put into it, and it was hung outside the cage of the little bird which sang so merrily.

"Yes, you may well sing!" was what the bottle neck said; and it was looked upon as a very remarkable one, for it had been up in a balloon. Nothing more was known of its history. There it hung now as a drinking fountain, where it could hear the roll and the rumble in the streets below, and it could also hear the old maid talking in the room. She had an old friend with her, and they were talking, not about the bottle neck, but about the myrtle in the window.

"You must certainly not spend five shillings on a bridal

bouquet for your daughter," said the old maid. " I will give you a beauty covered with blossom. Do you see how beautifully my myrtle is blooming. Why it is a cutting from the plant you gave me on the day after my betrothal; the one I was to have had for my bouquet when the year was out—the day which never came! Before then the eyes which would have gladdened and cherished me in this life were closed. He sleeps sweetly in the depths of the ocean—my beloved! The tree grew old, but I grew older, and when it drooped I took the last fresh branch and planted it in the earth where it has grown to such a big plant. So it will take part in a wedding after all and furnish a bouquet for your daughter!" There were tears in the old maid's eyes as she spoke of her betrothal in the wood, and of the beloved of her youth. She thought about the toasts which had been drunk, and about the first kiss—but of these she did not speak, was she not an old maid! Of all the thoughts that came into her mind, this one never came, that just outside her window was a relic of those days, the neck of the bottle out of which the cork came with a pop when it was drawn on the betrothal day. The bottle neck did not recognise her either, in fact it was not listening to her conversation, partly, if not entirely, because it was only thinking about itself.

THE·STEADFAST·TIN·SOLDIER

THERE were once five and twenty tin soldiers, all brothers, for they were the offspring of the same old tin spoon. Each man shouldered his gun, kept his eyes well to the front, and wore the smartest red and blue uniform imaginable. The first thing they heard in their new world, when the lid was taken off the box, was a little boy clapping his hands and crying, "Soldiers, soldiers!" It was his birthday and they had just been given to him; so he lost no time in setting them up on the table. All the soldiers were exactly alike with one exception, and he differed from the rest in having only one leg. For he was made last, and there was not quite enough tin left to finish him. However, he stood just as well on his one leg as the others on two, in fact he is the very one who is to become famous. On the table where they were being set up, were many other toys; but the chief thing which caught the eye was a delightful paper castle. You could see through the tiny windows, right into the rooms. Outside there were some little trees surrounding a small mirror, representing a lake, whose surface reflected the waxen swans which were swimming about on it. It was altogether charming, but the prettiest thing of all was a little maiden standing at the open door of the castle. She, too, was cut out of paper, but she wore a dress of the lightest gauze, with a dainty little blue ribbon over her shoulders, by way of a scarf, set off by a brilliant spangle as big as her whole face. The little maid

93

was stretching out both arms, for she was a dancer, and in the dance one of her legs was raised so high into the air that the tin soldier could see absolutely nothing of it, and supposed that she, like himself, had but one leg.

" That would be the very wife for me! " he thought; " but she is much too grand; she lives in a palace, while I only have a box, and then there are five and twenty of us to share it.   No, that would be no place for her! but I must try to make her acquaintance! "   Then he lay down full length behind a snuff box, which stood on the table.   From that point he could have a good look at the little lady, who continued to stand on one leg without losing her balance.

Late in the evening the other soldiers were put into their box, and the people of the house went to bed.   Now was the time for the toys to play; they amused themselves with paying visits, fighting battles, and giving balls.   The tin soldiers rustled about in their box, for they wanted to join the games, but they could not get the lid off.   The nut-crackers turned somer-saults, and the pencil scribbled nonsense on the slate.   There was such a noise that the canary woke up and joined in, but his remarks were in verse.   The only two who did not move were the tin soldier and the little dancer.   She stood as stiff as ever on tip-toe, with her arms spread out: he was equally firm on his one leg, and he did not take his eyes off her for a moment.

Then the clock struck twelve, when pop! up flew the lid of the snuff box, but there was no snuff in it, no!   There was a little black goblin, a sort of Jack-in-the-box.

" Tin soldier! " said the goblin, " have the goodness to keep your eyes to yourself."

But the tin soldier feigned not to hear.

" Ah! you just wait till to-morrow," said the goblin.

In the morning when the children got up they put the tin soldier on the window frame, and, whether it was caused by the goblin or by a puff of wind, I do not know, but all at once the window burst open, and the soldier fell head foremost from the third storey.

It was a terrific descent, and he landed at last, with his leg in the air, and rested on his cap, with his bayonet fixed between two paving stones.   The maid-servant and the little boy ran down at once to look for him; but although they almost trod on him, they could not see him. Had the soldier only called out, "here I am," they would easily have found him, but he did not think it proper to shout when he was in uniform.

Presently it began to rain, and the drops fell faster and faster, till there was a regular torrent. When it was over two street boys came along.

"Look out!" said one; "there is a tin soldier! He shall go for a sail."

So they made a boat out of a newspaper and put the soldier into the middle of it, and he sailed away down the gutter; both boys ran alongside clapping their hands. Good heavens! what waves there were in the gutter, and what a current, but then it certainly had rained cats and dogs. The paper boat danced up and down, and now and then whirled round and round. A shudder ran through the tin soldier, but he remained undaunted, and did not move a muscle, only looked straight before him with his gun shouldered. All at once the boat drifted under a long wooden tunnel, and it became as dark as it was in his box.

"Where on earth am I going to now!" thought he. "Well, well, it is all the fault of that goblin! Oh, if only the little maiden were with me in the boat it might be twice as dark for all I should care!"

At this moment a big water rat, who lived in the tunnel, came up.

"Have you a pass?" asked the rat. "Hand up your pass!"

The tin soldier did not speak, but clung still tighter to his gun. The boat rushed on, the rat close behind. Phew, how he gnashed his teeth and shouted to the bits of stick and straw,—

"Stop him, stop him, he hasn't paid his toll; he hasn't shown his pass!"

But the current grew stronger and stronger, the tin soldier could already see daylight before him at the end of the tunnel; but he also heard a roaring sound, fit to strike terror to the bravest heart. Just imagine! Where the tunnel ended the stream rushed straight into the big canal. That would be just as dangerous for him as it would be for us to shoot a great rapid.

He was so near the end now that it was impossible to stop.

The boat dashed out; the poor tin soldier held himself as stiff as he could; no one should say of him that he even winced.

The boat swirled round three or four times, and filled with water to the edge; it must sink. The tin soldier stood up to his neck in water, and the boat sank deeper and deeper. The paper became limper and limper, and at last the water went over his head—then he thought of the pretty little dancer, whom he was never to see again, and this refrain rang in his ears,—

"Onward! Onward! Soldier!
For death thou canst not shun."

At last the paper gave way entirely and the soldier fell through—but at the same moment he was swallowed by a big fish.

Oh! how dark it was inside the fish, it was worse than being in the tunnel even; and then it was so narrow! But the tin soldier was as dauntless as ever, and lay full length, shouldering his gun.

The fish rushed about and made the most frantic movements. At last it became quite quiet, and after a time, a flash like lightning pierced it. The solider was once more in the broad daylight, and some one called out loudly, "a tin soldier!" The fish had been caught, taken to market, sold, and brought into the kitchen, where the cook cut it open with a large knife. She took the soldier up by the waist, with two fingers, and carried him into the parlour, where everyone wanted to see the wonderful man, who had travelled about in the stomach of a fish; but the tin soldier was not at all proud. They set him up on the table, and, wonder of wonders! he found himself in the very same room that he had been in before. He saw the very same children, and the toys were still standing on the table, as well as the beautiful castle with the pretty little dancer.

She still stood on one leg, and held the other up in the air. You see she also was unbending. The soldier was so much moved that he was ready to shed tears of tin, but that would not have been fitting. He looked at her, and she looked at him, but they said never a word. At this moment one of the little boys took up the tin soldier, and without rhyme or reason, threw him into the fire. No doubt the little goblin in the snuff box was to blame for that. The tin soldier stood there, lighted up by the flame, and in the most horrible heat; but whether it was the heat of the real fire, or the warmth of his feelings, he did not know. He had lost all his gay colour; it might have been from his perilous journey, or it might have been from grief, who can tell?

He looked at the little maiden, and she looked at him; and he felt that he was melting away, but he still managed to keep himself erect, shouldering his gun bravely.

A door was suddenly opened, the draught caught the little dancer and she fluttered like a sylph, straight into the fire, to the soldier, blazed up and was gone!

By this time the soldier was reduced to a mere lump, and when the maid took away the ashes next morning she found him, in the shape of a small tin heart. All that was left of the dancer was her spangle, and that was burnt as black as a coal.

THE PEA BLOSSOM
(FIVE PEAS IN A POD)

THERE were once five peas in one shell, they were green, the shell was green, and so they believed that the whole world must be green also, which was a very natural conclusion. The shell grew, and the peas grew, they accommodated themselves to their position, and sat all in a row. The sun shone without and warmed the shell, and the rain made it clear and transparent; it was mild and agreeable in the broad daylight, and dark at night as it generally is; and the peas as they sat there grew bigger and bigger, and more thoughtful as they mused, for they felt there must be something else for them to do.

" Are we to sit here forever? " asked one; " shall we not become hard by sitting so long? It seems to me there must be something outside, and I feel sure of it."

And as weeks passed by, the peas became yellow, and the shell became yellow.

" All the world is turning yellow, I suppose," said they,—and perhaps they were right.

Suddenly they felt a pull at the shell; it was torn off, and held in human hands, then slipped into the pocket of a jacket in company with other full pods.

" Now we shall soon be opened," said one,—just what they all wanted.

" I should like to know which of us will travel furthest," said the smallest of the five; " we shall soon see now."

" What is to happen will happen," said the largest pea.

" Crack" went the shell as it burst, and the five peas rolled out into the bright sunshine. There they lay in a child's hand. A little boy was holding them tightly, and said they were fine peas for his pea-shooter. And immediately he put one in and shot it out.

" Now I am flying out into the wide world," said he; " catch me if you can; " and he was gone in a moment.

" I," said the second, " intend to fly straight to the sun, that is a shell that lets itself be seen, and it will suit me exactly; " and away he went.

" We will go to sleep wherever we find ourselves," said the two next, " we shall still be rolling onwards; " and they did certainly fall on the floor, and roll about before they got into the pea-shooter; but they were put in for all that. "We shall go farther than the others," said they.

"What is to happen will happen," exclaimed the last, as he was shot out of the pea-shooter; and as he spoke he flew up against an old board under a garret-window, and fell into a little crevice, which was almost filled up with moss and soft earth. The moss closed itself round him, and there he lay, a captive indeed, but not unnoticed by God.

"What is to happen will happen," said he to himself.

Within the little garret lived a poor woman, who went out to clean stoves, chop wood into small pieces and perform such-like hard work, for she was strong and industrious. Yet she remained always poor, and at home in the garret lay her only daughter, not quite grown up, and very delicate and weak. For a whole year she had kept her bed, and it seemed as if she could neither live nor die.

"She is going to her little sister," said the woman; "I had but the two children, and it was not an easy thing to support both of them; but the good God helped me in my work, and took one of them to Himself and provided for her. Now I would gladly keep the other that was left to me, but I suppose they are not to be separated, and my sick girl will very soon go to her sister above." But the sick girl still remained where she was, quietly and patiently she lay all the day long, while her mother was away from home at her work.

Spring came, and one morning early the sun shone brightly through the little window, and threw its rays over the floor of the room. Just as the mother was going to her work, the sick girl fixed her gaze on the lowest pane of the window—"Mother," she exclaimed, "what can that little green thing be that peeps in at the window? It is moving in the wind."

The mother stepped to the window and half opened it. "Oh!" she said, "there is actually a little pea which has taken root and is putting out its green leaves. How could it have got into this crack? Well now, here is a little garden for you to amuse yourself with." So the bed of the sick girl was drawn nearer to the window, that she might see the budding plant; and the mother went out to her work.

"Mother, I believe I shall get well," said the sick child in the evening, "the sun has shone in here so brightly and warmly to-day, and the little pea is thriving so well: I shall get on better, too, and go out into the warm sunshine again."

" God grant it!" said the mother, but she did not believe it would be so. But she propped up with the little stick the green plant which had given her child such pleasant hopes of life, so that it might not be broken by the winds; she tied the piece of string to the window-sill and to the upper part of the frame, so that the pea-tendrils might twine round it when it shot up. And it did shoot up, indeed it might almost be seen to grow from day to day.

" Now really here is a flower coming," said the old woman one morning, and now at last she began to encourage the hope that her sick daughter might really recover.   She remembered that for some time the child had spoken more cheerfully, and during the last few days had raised herself in bed in the morning to look with sparkling eyes at her little garden which contained only a single pea-plant. A week after, the invalid sat up for the first time a whole hour, feeling quite happy by the open window in the warm sunshine, while outside grew the little plant, and on it a pink pea-blossom in full bloom. The little maiden bent down and gently kissed the delicate leaves. This day was to her like a festival.

" Our heavenly Father Himself has planted that pea, and made it grow and flourish, to bring joy to you and hope to me, my blessed child," said the happy mother, and she smiled at the flower, as if it had been an angel from God.

But what became of the other peas? Why the one who flew out into the wide world, and said, "Catch me if you can," fell into a gutter on the roof of a house, and ended his travels in the crop of a pigeon. The two lazy ones were carried quite as far, for they also were eaten by pigeons, so they were at least of some use; but the fourth, who wanted to reach the sun, fell into a sink and lay there in the dirty water for days and weeks, till he had swelled to a great size.

" I am getting beautifully fat," said the pea, "I expect I shall burst at last; no pea could do more than that, I think; I am the most remarkable of all the five which were in the shell." And the sink confirmed the opinion.

But the young maiden stood at the open garret window, with sparkling eyes and the rosy hue of health on her cheeks, she folded her thin hands over the pea-blossom and thanked God for what He had done.

" I," said the sink, "shall stand up for *my* pea."

THE BUTTERFLY

THE butterfly was looking out for a bride, and naturally he wished to select a nice one among the flowers. He looked at them, sitting so quietly and discreetly upon their stems, as a damsel generally sits when she is not engaged; but there were so many to choose among, that it became quite a difficult matter. The butterfly did not relish encountering difficulties, so in his perplexity he flew to the Daisy. She is called in France *Marguerite*. He knew that she could "spae," and that she did so often; for lovers plucked leaf after leaf from her, and with each a question was asked respecting the beloved:—"Is it true love?" "From the heart?" "Love that pines?" "Cold love?" "None at all"—or some such questions. Everyone asks in his own language. The butterfly came too to put his questions; he did not, however, pluck off the leaves but kissed them all one by one, with the hope of getting a good answer.

"Sweet Marguerite Daisy," said he, "you are the wisest wife among all the flowers; you know how to predict events. Tell me, shall I get this one or that? or whom shall I get? When I know, I can fly straight to the fair one, and commence wooing her."

But Marguerite would scarcely answer him; she was vexed at his calling her "wife." He asked a second time, and he asked a third time, but he could not get a word out of her; so he would not take the trouble to ask any more, but flew away without further ado on his matrimonial errand.

It was in the early spring, and there were plenty of Snowdrops and Crocuses. "They are very nice-looking," said the Butterfly, "charming little things, but somewhat too juvenile." He, like most very young men, preferred elder girls. Thereupon he flew to the Anemones, but they were rather too bashful for him; the Violets were too enthusiastic; the Tulips were too fond of show; the Jonquils were too plebeian; the Linden-tree blossoms were too small, and they had too large a family connection; the Apple blossoms were certainly as lovely as Roses to look at, but they stood to-day and fell off to-morrow, as the wind blew. It would not be worth while to enter into wedlock for so short a time, he thought. The sweet-pea was the one that pleased him most; she was pink and white, she was pure and delicate, and belonged to that class of notable girls who always look well, yet can make themselves useful in the kitchen. He was on the point of making an offer to her when at that moment he observed a pea-pod hanging close by, with a withered flower at the end of it. "Who is that?" he asked. "My sister," replied the Sweet - pea. "Indeed! then you will probably come to look like her, by-and-by," screamed the Butterfly as he flew on.

The Honeysuckles hung over the hedge; they were extremely ladylike, but they had long faces and yellow complexions. They were not to his taste. But who was to his taste? Ay! ask him that.

The spring had passed, the summer had passed, and autumn was passing too. The flowers were still clad in brilliant robes, but, alas! the fresh fragrance of youth was gone. Fragrance was a great attraction to him, though no longer young himself, and there was none to be found among the Dahlias and Hollyhocks.

So the Butterfly stooped down to the Wild Thyme.

"She has scarcely any blossom, but she is altogether a flower herself, and all fragrance—every leaflet is full of it. I will take her."

So he began to woo forthwith.

But the Wild Thyme stood stiff and still, and at length she said, "Friendship, but nothing more! I am old, and you are old. We may very well live for each other, but marry—no! Let us not make fools of ourselves in our old age!"

So the Butterfly got no one. He had been too long on the look-out, and that one should not be. The Butterfly became an old bachelor, as it is called.

It was late in the autumn, and there was nothing but drizzling rain and pouring rain; the wind blew coldly on the old willow trees till the leaves shivered and the branches cracked.

It was not pleasant to fly about in summer clothing; this is the time, it is said, when domestic love is most needed. But the Butterfly flew about no more. He had accidentally gone within doors, where there was fire in the stove—yes, real summer heat. He could live, but "to live is not enough," said he; "sunshine, freedom, and a little flower, one must have."

And he flew against the window pane, was observed, admired, and stuck upon a needle in a case of curiosities. There they could not do for him.

"Now I am sitting on a stem, like the flowers," said the Butterfly; "very pleasant it is not, however. It is almost like being married, one is tied so fast. And he tried to comfort himself with this reflection.

"That is poor comfort!" exclaimed the plants in the flower-pots in the room.

"But one can hardly believe a plant in a flower-pot," thought the Butterfly; "they are too much among human beings."

THE SNAIL AND THE ROSE-BUSH

AROUND a garden was a fence of hazel-bushes, and beyond that were fields and meadows, with cows and sheep; but in the centre of the garden stood a Rose-bush in full bloom. Under it lay a Snail, who had a great deal in him, according to himself. " Wait till my time comes," said he; " I shall do a great deal more than to yield roses, or to bear nuts, or to give milk as cows do."

" I expect an immense deal from you," said the Rose-bush. " May I ask when it is to come forth? "

" I shall take my time," replied the Snail. " You are always in such a hurry with your work, that curiosity about it is never excited."

The following year the Snail lay, almost in the same spot as formerly, in the sunshine under the Rose-bush; it was already in bud, and the buds had begun to expand into full-blown flowers, always fresh, always new. And the Snail crept half out, stretched forth its feelers, and then drew them in again.

" Everything looks just the same as last year; there is no progress to be seen anywhere. The Rose-bush is covered with roses—it will never get beyond that."

The summer passed, the autumn passed; the Rose-bush had yielded roses and buds up to the time that the snow fell. The weather became wet and tempestuous, the Rose-bush bowed down towards the ground, the Snail crept into the earth.

A new year commenced, the Rose-bush revived, and the Snail came forth again.

" You are now only an old stick of a Rose-bush," said he; " you must expect to wither away soon. You have given the world all that was in you. Whether that were worth much or not, is a question I have not time to take into consideration; but this is certain, that you have not done the least for your own improvement, else something very different might have been produced by you. Can you deny this? You will soon become only a bare stick. Do you understand what I say? "

104

"You alarm me," cried the Rose-bush. "I never thought of this."

"No, you have never troubled yourself with thinking much. But have you not occasionally reflected why you blossomed, and in what way you blossomed—how in one way and not in another?"

"No," answered the Rose-bush; "I blossomed in gladness, for I could not do otherwise. The sun was so warm, the air so refreshing; I drank of the clear dew and the heavy rain; I breathed—I lived! There came up from the ground a strength to me, there came a strength from above. I experienced a degree of pleasure, always new, always great, and I was obliged to blossom. It was my life; I could not do otherwise."

"You have had a very easy life," remarked the Snail.

"To be sure, much has been granted to me," said the Rose-bush, "but no more will be bestowed on me now. *You* have one of those meditative, deeply thinking minds, one so endowed that you will astonish the world."

"I have by no means any such design," said the Snail. "The world is nothing to me. What have I to do with the world? I have enough to do with myself, and enough in myself."

"But should we not in this earth all give our best assistance to others—contribute what we can? Yes! I have only been able to give roses; but you—you who have got so much—what have you given to the world? What will you give it?"

"What have I given? What will I give? I spit upon it! It is good for nothing! I have no interest in it. Produce your roses—you cannot do more than that—let the hazel bushes bear nuts, let the cows give milk! You have each of you your public; I have mine within myself. I am going into myself, and shall remain there. The world is nothing to me."

And so the Snail withdrew into his house, and closed it up.

"What a sad pity it is!" exclaimed the Rose-bush. "I cannot creep into shelter, however much I might wish it. I must always spring out, spring out into roses. The leaves fall off, and they fly away on the wind. But I saw one of the roses laid in a psalm-book belonging to the mistress of the house; another of my roses was placed on the breast of a young and beautiful girl, and another was kissed by a child's soft lips in an ecstasy of joy. I was so charmed at all this: it was a real happiness to me—one of the pleasant remembrances of my life.''

And the Rose-bush bloomed on in innocence, while the Snail retired into his slimy house—the world was nothing to him!

Years flew on.

The Snail had returned to earth, the Rose-bush had returned to earth; also the dried rose-leaf in the psalm-book had disappeared, but new rose-bushes bloomed in the garden, and new snails were there; they crept into their houses, spitting—the world was nothing to them!

Shall we read their history too? It would not be different.

THE NIGHTINGALE

IN China, as you know, the Emperor is a Chinaman, and all the people around him are Chinamen too. It is many years since the story I am going to tell you happened, but that is all the more reason for telling it, lest it should be forgotten. The emperor's palace was the most beautiful thing in the world; it was made entirely of the finest porcelain, very costly, but at the same time so fragile that it could only be touched with the very greatest care. There were the most extraordinary flowers to be seen in the garden; the most beautiful ones had little silver bells tied to them, which tinkled perpetually, so that one should not pass the flowers without looking at them. Every little detail in the garden had been most carefully thought out, and it was so big, that even the gardener himself did not know where it ended. If one went on walking, one came to beautiful woods with lofty trees and deep lakes. The wood extended to the sea, which was deep and blue, deep enough for large ships to sail up right under the branches of the trees. Among these trees lived a nightingale, which sang so deliciously, that even the poor fisherman who had plenty of other things to do, lay still to listen to it, when he was out at night drawing in his nets. "Heavens, how beautiful it is!" he said, but then he had to attend to his business and forgot it. The next night when he heard it again he would again exclaim, "Heavens, how beautiful it is!"

Travellers came to the emperor's capital, from every country in the world; they admired everything very much, especially the palace and the gardens, but when they heard the nightingale they all said, "This is better than anything!"

When they got home they described it, and the learned ones wrote many books about the town, the palace, and the garden, but nobody forgot the nightingale, it was always put above everything else. Those among them who were poets wrote the most beautiful poems, all about the nightingale in the woods by the deep blue sea. These books went all over the world, and in course of time some of them reached the emperor. He sat in his golden chair reading and reading, and nodding his head, well pleased to hear such beautiful descriptions of the town, the palace, and the garden. "But the nightingale is the best of all," he read.

"What is this?" said the emperor. "The nightingale? Why I know nothing about it. Is there such a bird in my kingdom, and in my own garden into the bargain, and I have never heard of it? Imagine my having to discover this from a book?"

Then he called his gentleman-in-waiting, who was so grand that when anyone of a lower rank dared to speak to him, or to ask him a question, he only would answer "P," which means nothing at all.

"There is said to be a very wonderful bird called a nightingale here," said the emperor. "They say that it is better than anything else in all my great kingdom! Why have I never been told anything about it?"

"I have never heard it mentioned," said the gentleman-in-waiting. "It has never been presented at court."

"I wish it to appear here this evening to sing to me," said the emperor. "The whole world knows what I am possessed of, and I know nothing about it!"

"I have never heard it mentioned before," said the gentleman-in-waiting. "I will seek it, and I will find it!" But where was it to be found? The gentleman-in-waiting ran upstairs and downstairs and in and out of all the rooms and corridors.

No one of all those he met had ever heard anything about the nightingale; so the gentleman-in-waiting ran back to the emperor, and said that it must be a myth, invented by the writers of the books. " Your imperial majesty must not believe everything that is written; books are often mere inventions, even if they do not belong to what we call the black art! "

" But the book in which I read it is sent to me by the powerful Emperor of Japan, so it can't be untrue, I will hear this nightingale, I insist upon its being here to-night. I extend my most gracious protection to it, and if it is not forthcoming, I will have the whole court trampled upon after supper! "

" Tsing-pe! " said the gentleman-in-waiting, and away he ran again, up and down all the stairs, in and out of all the rooms and corridors; half the court ran with him, for they none of them wished to be trampled on. There was much questioning about this nightingale, which was known to all the outside world, but to no one at court. At last they found a poor little maid in the kitchen. She said, " Oh heavens, the nightingale? I know it very well. Yes, indeed it can sing. Every evening I am allowed to take broken meat to my poor sick mother: she lives down by the shore. On my way back when I am tired, I rest awhile in the wood, and then I hear the nightingale. Its song brings the tears into my eyes, I feel as if my mother were kissing me! "

" Little kitchen-maid," said the gentleman-in-waiting, " I will procure you a permanent position in the kitchen and permission to see the emperor dining, if you will take us to the nightingale. It is commanded to appear at court to-night."

Then they all went out into the wood where the nightingale usually sang. Half the court was there. As they were going along at their best pace a cow began to bellow.

" O! " said a young courtier, " there we have it. What wonderful power for such a little creature; I have certainly heard it before."

" No, those are the cows bellowing, we are a long way yet from the place." Then the frogs began to croak in the marsh.

" Beautiful? " said the Chinese chaplain, " it is just like the tinkling of church bells."

"No, those are the frogs!" said the little kitchen-maid. "But I think we shall soon hear it now!"

Then the nightingale began to sing.

"There it is!" said the little girl. "Listen, listen, there it sits!" and she pointed to a little grey bird up among the branches.

"Is it possible?" said the gentleman-in-waiting. "I should never have thought it was like that. How common it looks. Seeing so many grand people must have frightened all its colours away."

"Little nightingale!" called the kitchen-maid quite loud, "our gracious emperor wishes you to sing to him!"

"With the greatest pleasure!" said the nightingale, warbling away in the most delightful fashion.

"It is just like crystal bells," said the gentleman-in-waiting. "Look at its little throat, how active it is. It is extraordinary that we have never heard it before! I am sure it will be a great success at court!"

"Shall I sing again to the emperor?" said the nightingale, who thought he was present.

"My precious little nightingale," said the gentleman-in-waiting, "I have the honour to command your attendance at a court festival to-night, where you will charm his gracious majesty the emperor with your fascinating singing."

"It sounds best among the trees," said the nightingale, but it went with them willingly when it heard that the emperor wished it.

The palace had been brightened up for the occasion. The walls and the floors which were all of china shone by the light of many thousand golden lamps. The most beautiful flowers, all of the tinkling kind, were arranged in the corridors; there was hurrying to and fro, and a great draught, but this was just what made the bells ring, one's ears were full of the tinkling. In the middle of the large reception-room where the emperor sat, a golden rod had been fixed, on which the nightingale was to perch. The whole court was assembled, and the little kitchen-maid had been permitted to stand behind the door, as she now had the actual title of .cook. They were all dressed in their best; everybody's eyes were turned towards the little grey bird at which the emperor was nodding. The nightingale sang delightfully, and the tears came into the emperor's eyes, nay, they rolled down his cheeks, and then the nightingale sang more beautifully than ever, its notes touched all hearts. The emperor was charmed, and said the nightingale should have his gold slipper to wear round its neck. But the nightingale declined with thanks, it had already been sufficiently rewarded.

" I have seen tears in the eyes of the emperor, that is my richest reward. The tears of an emperor have a wonderful power! God knows I am sufficiently recompensed! " and then it again burst into its sweet heavenly song.

" That is the most delightful coquetting I have ever seen! " said the ladies, and they took some water into their mouths to try and make the same gurgling, when anyone spoke to them, thinking so to equal the nightingale. Even the lackeys and the chambermaids announced that they were satisfied, and that is saying a great deal, they are always the most difficult people to please. Yes, indeed, the nightingale had made a sensation. It was to stay at court now, and to have its own cage, as well as liberty to walk out twice a day, and once in the night. It always had twelve footmen with each one holding a ribbon which was tied round its leg. There was not much pleasure in an outing of that sort.

The whole town talked about the marvellous bird, and if two people met, one said to the other " Night," and the other answered " Gale," and then they sighed, perfectly understanding each other. Eleven cheesemongers' children were called after it, but they had not got a voice among them.

One day a large parcel came for the emperor, outside was written the word " Nightingale."

" Here we have another new book about this celebrated bird," said the emperor. But it was no book, it was a little work of art in a box, an artificial nightingale, exactly like the living one, but it was studded all over with diamonds, rubies, and sapphires.

When the bird was wound up, it could sing one of the songs the real one sang, and it wagged its tail which glittered with silver and gold. A ribbon was tied round its neck on which was written, " The Emperor of Japan's nightingale is very poor compared to the Emperor of China's."

Everybody said, " Oh, how beautiful! "   And the person who brought the artificial bird immediately received the title of Imperial Nightingale-Carrier-in-Chief.

" Now, they must sing together; what a duet that will be."

Then they had to sing together, but they did not get on very well, for the real nightingale sang in its own way, and the artificial one could only sing waltzes.

" There is no fault in that," said the music master; " it is perfectly in time and correct in every way! "

Then the artificial bird had to sing alone. It was just as great a success as the real one, and then it was so much prettier to look at, it glittered like bracelets and breast-pins.

It sang the same tune three and thirty times over, and yet it was not tired; people would willingly have heard it from the beginning again, but the Emperor said that the real one must have a turn now—but where was it? No one had noticed that it had flown out of the open window, back its to own green woods.

" But what is the meaning of this? " said the emperor.

All the courtiers railed at it, and said it was a most ungrateful bird.

" We have got the best bird though," said they, and then the artificial bird had to sing again, and this was the thirty-fourth time that they heard the same tune, but they did not know it thoroughly even yet, because it was so difficult.

The music master praised the bird tremendously, and insisted that it was much better than the real nightingale, not only as regarded the outside with all the diamonds, but the inside too.

" Because you see, my ladies and gentlemen, and the emperor before all, in the real nightingale you never know what you will hear, but in the artificial one everything is decided beforehand! So it is, and so it must remain, it can't be otherwise. You can account for things, you can open it and show the human ingenuity in arranging the waltzes, how they go, and how one note follows upon another! "

They set him up on the table.

THE STEADFAST TIN SOLDIER

Page 96

The invalid sat up, feeling quite happy by the open window.

THE PEA BLOSSOM

Page 100

" Those are exactly my opinions," they all said, and the music master got leave to show the bird to the public next Sunday. They were also to hear it sing, said the emperor. So they heard it, and all became as enthusiastic over it as if they had drunk themselves merry on tea, because that is a thoroughly Chinese habit.

Then they all said " Oh," and stuck their forefingers in the air and nodded their heads; but the poor fishermen who had heard the real nightingale said, " It sounds very nice, and it is very like the real one, but there is something wanting, we don't know what." The real nightingale was banished from the kingdom.

The artificial bird had its place on a silken cushion, close to the emperor's bed: all the presents it had received of gold and precious jewels were scattered round it. Its title had risen to be " Chief Imperial Singer of the Bed-Chamber," in rank number one, on the left side; for the emperor reckoned that side the important one, where the heart was seated. And even an emperor's heart is on the left side. The music master wrote five and twenty volumes about the artificial bird; the treatise was very long, and written in all the most difficult Chinese characters. Everybody said they had read and understood it, for otherwise they would have been reckoned stupid, and then their bodies would have been trampled upon.

Things went on in this way for a whole year. The emperor, the court, and all the other Chinamen knew every little gurgle in the song of the artificial bird by heart; but they liked it all the better for this, and they could all join in the song themselves. Even the street boys sang " zizizi " and " cluck, cluck, cluck," and the emperor sang it too.

But one evening when the bird was singing its best, and the emperor was lying in bed listening to it, something gave way inside the bird with a " whizz." Then a spring burst, " whirr " went all the wheels and the music stopped. The emperor jumped out of bed and sent for his private physicians, but what good could they do? Then they sent for the watchmaker, and after a good deal of talk and examination, he got the works to go again somehow; but he said it would have to be saved as much as possible, because it was so worn out, and he could not renew the works so as to be sure of the tune. This was a great blow! They only dared to let the artificial bird sing once a year, and hardly that; but then the music master made a little speech using all the most difficult words. He said it was just as good as ever, and his saying it made it so.

Five years now passed, and then a great grief came upon the nation, for they were all very fond of their emperor, and he was ill and could not live, it was said. A new emperor was already chosen, and people stood about in the street, and asked the gentleman-in-waiting how their emperor was going on.

"P," answered he, shaking his head.

The emperor lay pale and cold in his gorgeous bed, the courtiers thought he was dead, and they all went off to pay their respects to their new emperor. The lackeys ran off to talk matters over, and the chambermaids gave a great coffee party. Cloth had been laid down in all the rooms and corridors so as to deaden the sound of footsteps, so it was very, very quiet. But the emperor was not dead yet. He lay stiff and pale in the gorgeous bed with its velvet hangings and heavy golden tassels. There was an open window high above him, and the moon streamed in upon the emperor, and the artificial bird beside him.

The poor emperor could hardly breathe, he seemed to have a weight on his chest, he opened his eyes and then he saw that it was Death sitting upon his chest, wearing his golden crown. In one hand he held the emperor's golden sword, and in the other his imperial banner. Round about, from among the folds of the velvet hangings peered many curious faces, some were hideous, others gentle and pleasant. They were all the emperor's good and bad deeds, which now looked him in the face when Death was weighing him down.

"Do you remember that?" whispered one after the other, "Do you remember this?" and they told him so many things that the perspiration poured down his face.

"I never knew that," said the emperor. "Music, music, sound the great Chinese drums!" he cried, "that I may not hear what they are saying." But they went on and on, and Death sat nodding his head, just like a Chinaman, at everything that was said.

" Music, music! " shrieked the emperor. " You precious little golden bird, sing, sing! I have loaded you with precious stones, and even hung my own golden slipper round your neck, sing, I tell you, sing! "

But the bird stood silent, there was nobody to wind it up, so of course it could not go. Death continued to fix the great empty sockets of its eyes upon him, and all was silent, so terribly silent.

Suddenly, close to the window, there was a burst of lovely song; it was the living nightingale, perched on a branch outside. It had heard of the emperor's need, and had come to bring comfort and hope to him. As it sang the faces round became fainter and fainter, and the blood coursed with fresh vigour in the emperor's veins and through his feeble limbs. Even Death himself listened to the song and said, " Go on little nightingale, go on! "

" Yes, if you give me the gorgeous golden sword; yes, if you give me the imperial banner; yes, if you give me the emperor's crown."

And Death gave back each of these treasures for a song, and the nightingale went on singing. It sang about the quiet churchyard, where the roses bloom, where the elder flowers scents the air, and where the fresh grass is ever moistened anew by the tears of the mourner. This song brought to Death a longing for his own garden, and like a cold grey mist, he passed out of the window.

" Thanks, thanks! " said the emperor; " you heavenly little bird, I know you! I banished you from my kingdom, and yet you have charmed the evil visions away from my bed by your song, and even Death away from my heart! How can I ever repay you? "

" You have rewarded me," said the nightingale. " I brought the tears to your eyes the very first time I ever sang to you, and I shall never forget it! Those are the jewels which gladden the heart of a singer; but sleep now, and wake up fresh and strong; I will sing to you! "

Then it sang again, and the emperor fell into a sweet refreshing sleep. The sun shone in at his window, when he woke refreshed and well; none of his attendants had yet come back to him, for they thought he was dead, but the nightingale still sat there singing.

"You must always stay with me!" said the emperor. "You shall only sing when you like, and I will break the artificial bird into a thousand pieces!"

"Don't do that!" said the nightingale, "it did all the good it could! keep it as you have always done! I can't build my nest and live in this palace, but let me come whenever I like, then I will sit on the branch in the evening, and sing to you. I will sing to cheer you and to make you thoughtful too; I will sing to you of the happy ones, and of those that suffer too. I will sing about the good and the evil, which are kept hidden from you. The little singing bird flies far and wide, to the poor fisherman, and the peasant's home, to numbers who are far from you and your court. I love your heart more than your crown, and yet there is an odour of sanctity round the crown too!— I will come, and I will sing to you!—But you must promise me one thing!"—

"Everything!" said the emperor, who stood there in his imperial robes which he had just put on, and he held the sword heavy with gold upon his heart.

"One thing I ask you! Tell no one that you have a little bird who tells you everything, it will be better so!"

Then the nightingale flew away. The attendants came in to see after their dead emperor, and there he stood, bidding them " good-morning! "

THE UGLY DUCKLING

THE country was lovely just then; it was summer. The wheat was golden and the oats still green; the hay was stacked in the rich low-lying meadows, where the stork was marching about on his long red legs, chattering Egyptian, the language his mother had taught him.

Round about field and meadow lay great woods, in the midst of which were deep lakes. Yes, the country certainly was delicious. In the sunniest spot stood an old mansion surrounded by a deep moat, and great dock leaves grew from the walls of the house right down to the water's edge; some of them were so tall that a small child could stand upright under them. In amongst the leaves it was as secluded as in the depths of a forest; and there a duck was sitting on her nest. Her little ducklings were just about to be hatched, but she was nearly tired of sitting, for it had lasted such a long time. Moreover, she had very few visitors, as the other ducks liked swimming about in the moat better than waddling up to sit under the dock leaves and gossip with her.

At last one egg after another began to crack. "Cheep, cheep!" they said. All the chicks had come to life, and were poking their heads out.

"Quack! quack!" said the duck; and then they all quacked their hardest, and looked about them on all sides among the green leaves; their mother allowed them to look as much as they liked, for green is good for the eyes.

"How big the world is, to be sure!" said all the young ones;

for they certainly had ever so much more room to move about than when they were inside in the egg shell.

"Do you imagine this is the whole world?" said the mother. "It stretches a long way on the other side of the garden, right into the parson's field; but I have never been as far as that! I suppose you are all here now?" and she got up. "No! I declare I have not got you all yet! The biggest egg is still there; how long is it going to last?" and then she settled herself on the nest again.

"Well, how are you getting on?" said an old duck who had come to pay her a visit.

"This one egg is taking such a long time," answered the sitting duck, "the shell will not crack; but now you must look at the others; they are the finest ducklings I have ever seen! they are all exactly like their father, the rascal! he never comes to see me."

"Let me look at the egg which won't crack," said the old duck. "You may be sure that it is a turkey's egg! I have been cheated like that once, and I had no end of trouble and worry with the creatures, for I may tell you that they are afraid of the water. I could not get them into it, I quacked and snapped at them, but it was no good. Let me see the egg! Yes, it is a turkey's egg! You just leave it alone and teach the other children to swim."

"I will sit on it a little longer, I have sat so long already, that I may as well go on till the Midsummer Fair comes round."

"Please yourself," said the old duck, and she went away.

At last the big egg cracked. "Cheep, cheep!" said the young one and tumbled out; how big and ugly he was! The duck looked at him.

"That is a monstrous big duckling," she said; "none of the others looked like that; can he be a turkey chick? well we shall soon find that out; into the water he shall go, if I have to kick him in myself."

Next day was gloriously fine, and the sun shone on all the green dock leaves. The mother duck with her whole family went down to the moat.

Splash, into the water she sprang. "Quack, quack!" she said, and one duckling plumped in after the other. The water dashed over their heads, but they came up again and floated beautifully; their legs went of themselves, and they were all there, even the big ugly grey one swam about with them.

" No, that is no turkey," she said; " see how beautifully he uses his legs and how erect he holds himself: he is my own chick! after all, he is not so bad when you come to look at him properly.   Quack, quack! Now come with me and I will take you into the world, and introduce you to the duckyard; but keep close to me all the time, so that no one may tread upon you, and beware of the cat! "

Then they went into the duckyard. There was a fearful uproar going on, for two broods were fighting for the head of an eel, and in the end the cat captured it.

" That's how things go in this world," said the mother duck, and she licked her bill, for she wanted the eel's head herself.

" Use your legs," said she; " mind you quack properly, and bend your necks to the old duck over there! She is the grandest of them all; she has Spanish blood in her veins and that accounts for her size, and, do you see? she has a red rag round her leg; that is a wonderfully fine thing, and the most extraordinary mark of distinction any duck can have. It shows clearly that she is not to be parted with, and that she is worthy of recognition both by beasts and men! Quack now! don't turn your toes in, a well brought up duckling keeps his legs wide apart just like father and mother; that's it, now bend your necks, and say quack! "

They did as they were bid, but the other ducks round about looked at them and said, quite loud; " Just look there! now we are to have that tribe! just as if there were not enough of us already, and, oh dear! how ugly that duckling is, we won't stand him! " and a duck flew at him at once and bit him in the neck.

" Let him be," said the mother; " he is doing no harm."

" Very likely not, but he is so ungainly and queer," said the biter; " he must be whacked."

" They are handsome children mother has," said the old duck with the rag round her leg; " all good looking except this one, and he is not a good specimen; it's a pity you can't make him over again."

"That can't be done, your grace," said the mother duck; "he is not handsome, but he is a thorough good creature, and he swims as beautifully as any of the others; nay, I think I might venture even to add that I think he will improve as he goes on, or perhaps in time he may grow smaller! He was too long in the egg, and so he has not come out with a very good figure." And then she patted his neck and stroked him down. "Besides he is a drake," said she; "so it does not matter so much. I believe he will be very strong, and I don't doubt but he will make his way in the world."

"The other ducklings are very pretty," said the old duck. "Now make yourselves quite at home, and if you find the head of an eel you may bring it to me!"

After that they felt quite at home. But the poor duckling which had been the last to come out of the shell, and who was so ugly, was bitten, pushed about, and made fun of both by the ducks and the hens. "He is too big," they all said; and the turkey-cock, who was born with his spurs on, and therefore thought himself quite an emperor, puffed himself up like a vessel in full sail, made for him, and gobbled and gobbled till he became quite red in the face. The poor duckling was at his wit's end, and did not know which way to turn; he was in despair because he was so ugly, and the butt of the whole duckyard.

So the first day passed, and afterwards matters grew worse and worse. The poor duckling was chased and hustled by all of them, even his brothers and sisters ill-used him; and they were always saying, "If only the cat would get hold of you, you hideous object!" Even his mother said, "I wish to goodness you were miles away." The ducks bit him, the hens pecked him, and the girl who fed them kicked him aside.

Then he ran off and flew right over the hedge, where the little birds flew up into the air in a fright.

"That is because I am so ugly," thought the poor duckling, shutting his eyes, but he ran on all the same. Then he came to a great marsh where the wild ducks lived; he was so tired and miserable that he stayed there the whole night.

In the morning the wild ducks flew up to inspect their new comrade.

"What sort of a creature are you?" they inquired, as the duckling turned from side to side and greeted them as well as he could. "You are frightfully ugly," said the wild ducks, "but that does not matter to us, so long as you do not marry into our family!" Poor fellow! he had no thought of marriage, all he wanted was permission to lie among the rushes, and to drink a little of the marsh water.

He stayed there two whole days, then two wild geese came, or rather two wild ganders, they were not long out of the shell, and therefore rather pert.

"I say, comrade," they said, "you are so ugly that we have taken quite a fancy to you; will you join us and be a bird of passage? There is another marsh close by, and there are some charming wild geese there; all sweet young ladies, who can say quack! You are ugly enough to make your fortune among them." Just at that moment, bang! bang! was heard up above, and both the wild geese fell dead among the reeds, and the water turned blood red. Bang! bang! went the guns, and whole flocks of wild geese flew up from the rushes and the shot peppered among them again.

There was a grand shooting party, and the sportsmen lay hidden round the marsh, some even sat on the branches of the trees which overhung the water; the blue smoke rose like clouds among the dark trees and swept over the pool.

The water-dogs wandered about in the swamp, splash! splash! The rushes and reeds bent beneath their tread on all sides. It was terribly alarming to the poor duckling. He twisted his head round to get it under his wing, and just at that moment a frightful, big dog appeared close beside him; his tongue hung right out of his mouth and his eyes glared wickedly. He opened his great chasm of a mouth close to the duckling, showed his sharp teeth—and—splash—went on without touching him.

"Oh, thank Heaven!" sighed the duckling, "I am so ugly that even the dog won't bite me!"

Then he lay quite still while the shot whistled among the bushes, and bang after bang rent the air. It only became quiet late in the day, but even then the poor duckling did not dare to get up; he waited several hours more before he looked about, and then he hurried away from the marsh as fast as he could. He ran across fields and meadows, and there was such a wind that he had hard work to make his way.

Towards night he reached a poor little cottage; it was such a miserable hovel that it could not make up its mind which way to fall even, and so it remained standing. The wind whistled so fiercely round the duckling that he had to sit on his tail to resist it, and it blew harder and harder; then he saw that the door had fallen off one hinge and hung so crookedly that he could creep into the house through the crack, and by this means he made his way into the room. An old woman lived there with her cat and her hen. The cat, which she called "Sonnie," could arch his back, purr, and give off electric sparks, that is to say if you stroked his fur the wrong way. The hen had quite tiny short legs, and so she was called "Chuckie-low-legs." She laid good eggs, and the old woman was as fond of her as if she had been her own child.

In the morning the strange duckling was discovered immediately, and the cat began to purr, and the hen to cluck.

"What on earth is that!" said the old woman looking round, but her sight was not good, and she thought the duckling was a fat duck which had escaped. "This is a capital find," said she; "now I shall have duck's eggs if only it is not a drake! we must find out about that!"

So she took the duckling on trial for three weeks, but no eggs made their appearance. The cat was the master of the house and the hen the mistress, and they always spoke of "we and the world," for they thought that they represented the half of the world, and that quite the better half.

The duckling thought there might be two opinions on the subject, but the cat would not hear of it.

"Can you lay eggs?" she asked.

"No!"

"Will you have the goodness to hold your tongue then!"

And the cat said, "Can you arch your back, purr, or give off sparks?"

"No."

"Then you had better keep your opinions to yourself when people of sense are speaking!"

The duckling sat in the corner nursing his ill-humour; then he began to think of the fresh air and the sunshine, an uncontrollable longing seized him to float on the water, and at last he could not help telling the hen about it.

"What on earth possesses you?" she asked; "you have nothing to do, that is why you get these freaks into your head. Lay some eggs or take to purring, and you will get over it."

"But it is so delicious to float on the water," said the duckling; "so delicious to feel it rushing over your head when you dive to the bottom."

"That would be a fine amusement," said the hen. "I think you have gone mad. Ask the cat about it, he is the wisest creature I know; ask him if he is fond of floating on the water or diving under it. I say nothing about myself. Ask our mistress yourself, the old woman, there is no one in the world cleverer than she is. Do you suppose she has any desire to float on the water, or to duck underneath it?"

"You do not understand me," said the duckling.

"Well, if we don't understand you, who should? I suppose you don't consider yourself cleverer than the cat or the old woman, not to mention me. Don't make a fool of yourself, child, and thank your stars for all the good we have done you! Have you not lived in this warm room, and in such society that you might have learnt something? But you are an idiot, and there is no pleasure in associating with you. You may believe me I mean you well, I tell you home truths, and there is no surer way than that of knowing who are one's friends. You just see about laying some eggs, or learn to purr, or to emit sparks."

"I think I will go out into the wide world," said the duckling.

"Oh, do so by all means," said the hen.

So away went the duckling, he floated on the water and ducked underneath it, but he was looked askance at by every living creature for his ugliness. Now the autumn came on, the leaves in the woods turned yellow and brown; the wind took hold of them, and they danced about. The sky looked very cold, and the clouds hung heavy with snow and hail. A raven stood on the fence and croaked Caw! caw! from sheer cold; it made one shiver only to think of it, the poor duckling certainly was in a bad case.

One evening, the sun was just setting in wintry splendour, when a flock of beautiful large birds appeared out of the bushes; the duckling had never seen anything so beautiful. They were dazzlingly white with long waving necks; they were swans, and uttering a peculiar cry they spread out their magnificent broad wings and flew away from the cold regions to warmer lands and open seas. They mounted so high, so very high, and the ugly little duckling became strangely uneasy, he circled round and round in the water like a wheel, craning his neck up into the air after them. Then he uttered a shriek so piercing and so strange, that he was quite frightened by it himself. Oh, he could not forget those beautiful birds, those happy birds, and as soon as they were out of sight he ducked right down to the bottom, and when he came up again he was quite beside himself. He did not know what the birds were, or whither they flew, but all the same he was more drawn towards them than he had ever been by any creatures before. He did not envy them in the least, how could it occur to him even to wish to be such a marvel of beauty; he would have been thankful if only the ducks would have tolerated him among them—the poor ugly creature!

The winter was so bitterly cold that the duckling was obliged to swim about in the water to keep it from freezing, but every night the hole in which he swam got smaller and smaller. Then it froze so hard that the surface ice cracked, and the duckling had to use his legs all the time, so that the ice should not close in round him; at last he was so weary that he could move no more, and he was frozen fast into the ice.

Early in the morning a peasant came along and saw him; he went out on to the ice and hammered a hole in it with his heavy wooden shoe, and carried the duckling home to his wife. There it soon revived. The children wanted to play with it, but the duckling thought they were going to ill-use him, and rushed in his fright into the milk pan, and the milk spurted out all over the room. The woman shrieked and threw up her hands, then it flew into the butter cask, and down into the meal tub and out again. Just imagine what it looked like by this time! The woman screamed and tried to hit it with the tongs, and the children tumbled over one another in trying to catch it, and they screamed with laughter—by good luck the door stood open, and the duckling flew out among the bushes and the new fallen snow—and it lay there thoroughly exhausted.

But it would be too sad to mention all the privation and misery it had to go through during that hard winter. When the sun began to shine warmly again, the duckling was in the marsh, lying among the rushes; the larks were singing and the beautiful spring had come.

Then all at once it raised its wings and they flapped with much greater strength than before, and bore him off vigorously. Before he knew where he was, he found himself in a large garden where the apple trees were in full blossom, and the air was scented with lilacs, the long branches of which overhung the indented shores of the lake! Oh! the spring freshness was so delicious!

Just in front of him he saw three beautiful white swans advancing towards him from a thicket; with rustling feathers they swam lightly over the water. The duckling recognised the majestic birds, and he was overcome by a strange melancholy.

" I will fly to them, the royal birds, and they will hack me to pieces, because I, who am so ugly, venture to approach them! But it won't matter; better be killed by them than be snapped at by the ducks, pecked by the hens, or spurned by the henwife, or suffer so much misery in the winter."

So he flew into the water and swam towards the stately swans; they saw him and darted towards him with ruffled feathers.

" Kill me, oh, kill me! " said the poor creature, and bowing his head towards the water he awaited his death. But what did he see reflected in the transparent water?

He saw below him his own image, but he was no longer a clumsy dark grey bird, ugly and ungainly, he was himself a swan! It does not matter in the least having been born in a duckyard, if only you come out of a swan's egg!

He felt quite glad of all the misery and tribulation he had gone through; he was the better able to appreciate his good fortune now, and all the beauty which greeted him. The big swans swam round and round him, and stroked him with their bills.

Some little children came into the garden with corn and pieces of bread, which they threw into the water; and the smallest one cried out: " There is a new one! " The other children shouted with joy, " Yes, a new one has come! " And they clapped their hands and danced about, running after their father and mother. They threw the bread into the water, and one and all said that " the new one was the prettiest; he was so young and handsome." And the old swans bent their heads and did homage before him.

He felt quite shy, and hid his head under his wing; he did not know what to think; he was so very happy, but not at all proud; a good heart never becomes proud. He thought of how he had been pursued and scorned, and now he heard them all say that he was the most beautiful of all beautiful birds. The lilacs bent their boughs right down into the water before him, and the bright sun was warm and cheering, and he rustled his feathers and raised his slender neck aloft, saying with exultation in his heart: " I never dreamt of so much happiness when I was the Ugly Duckling! "

GREAT CLAUS AND LITTLE CLAUS

IN a village there once lived two men of the self-same name. They were both called Claus, but one of them had four horses, and the other had only one; so to distinguish them people called the owner of the four horses " Great Claus," and he who had only one " Little Claus." Now I shall tell you what happened to them, for this is a true story.

Throughout the week Little Claus was obliged to plough for Great Claus, and to lend him his one horse; but once a week, on Sunday, Great Claus lent him all his four horses.

" Hurrah! " How Little Claus would smack his whip over all five, for they were as good as his own on that one day.

The sun shone brightly and the church bells rang merrily as the people passed by, dressed in their best, with their prayer-books under their arms. They were going to hear the parson preach. They looked at Little Claus ploughing with his five horses, and he was so proud that he smacked his whip and said, " Gee-up, my five horses."

" You mustn't say that," said Great Claus, " for only one of them is yours."

But Little Claus soon forgot what he ought not to say, and when anyone passed, he would call out, " Gee-up, my five horses."

" I must really beg you not to say that again," said Great Claus, " for if you do, I shall hit your horse on the head, so that he will drop down dead on the spot, and there will be an end of him."

127

"I promise you I will not say it again," said the other; but as soon as anybody came by nodding to him, and wishing him "Good-day," he was so pleased, and thought how grand it was to have five horses ploughing in his field, that he cried out again, "Gee-up, all my horses!"

"I'll gee-up your horses for you," said Great Claus, and seizing the tethering mallet he struck Little Claus' one horse on the head, and it fell down dead.

"Oh, now I have no horse at all," said Little Claus, weeping. But after a while he flayed the dead horse, and hung up the skin in the wind to dry.

Then he put the dried skin into a bag, and hanging it over his shoulder went off to the next town to sell it. But he had a long way to go, and had to pass through a dark and gloomy forest.

Presently a storm arose, and he lost his way; and before he discovered the right path evening was drawing on, and it was still a long way to the town, and too far to return home before nightfall.

Near the road stood a large farmhouse. The shutters outside the windows were closed, but lights shone through the crevices and at the top. "They might let me stay here for the night," thought Little Claus, so he went up to the door and knocked. The farmer's wife opened the door, but when she heard what he wanted, she told him to go away; her husband was not at home, and she could not let any strangers in.

"Then I shall have to lie out here," said Little Claus to himself as the farmer's wife shut the door in his face.

Close to the farmhouse stood a large haystack, and between it and the house there was a small shed with a thatched roof. "I can lie up there," said little Claus, as he saw the roof; "it will make a famous bed, but I hope the stork won't fly down and bite my legs." A live stork was standing up there who had his nest on the roof.

So Little Claus climbed on to the roof of the shed, and as he turned about to make himself comfortable he discovered that the wooden shutters did not reach to the top of the windows, so that he could see into the room, in which a large table was laid out, with wine, roast meat, and a splendid fish.

The farmer's wife and the sexton were sitting at table together, nobody else was there. She was filling his glass and helping him plentifully to fish, which appeared to be his favourite dish.

"If only I could have some too," thought Little Claus, and then as he stretched out his neck towards the window he spied a beautiful, large cake—indeed, they had a glorious feast before them.

At that moment he heard someone riding down the road towards the farm. It was the farmer coming home.

He was a good man, but he had one very strange prejudice —he could not bear the sight of a sexton. If he happened to see one he would get into a terrible rage. In consequence of this dislike, the sexton had gone to visit the farmer's wife during her husband's absence from home, and the good woman had put before him the best of everything she had in the house to eat.

When they heard the farmer they were dreadfully frightened, and the woman made the sexton creep into a large chest which stood in a corner. He went at once, for he was well aware of the poor man's aversion to the sight of a sexton. The woman then quickly hid all the nice things and the wine in the oven, because if her husband had seen it he would have asked why it was provided.

"Oh, dear!" sighed Little Claus, on the roof, when he saw the food disappearing.

"Is there anyone up there?" asked the farmer, peering up at Little Claus. "What are you doing up there? You had better come into the house."

Then Little Claus told him how he had lost his way, and asked if he might have shelter for the night.

"Certainly," said the farmer; "but the first thing is to have something to eat."

The woman received them both very kindly, laid the table, and gave them a large bowl of porridge. The farmer was hungry and ate it with a good appetite; but Little Claus could not help thinking of the good roast meat, the fish, and the cake, which he knew were hidden in the oven.

He had put his sack with the hide in it under the table by

his feet, for, as we remember, he was on his way to the town to sell it. He did not fancy the porridge, so he trod on the sack and made the dried hide squeak quite loudly.

"Hush!" said Little Claus to his sack, at the same time treading on it again, so that it squeaked louder than ever.

"What on earth have you go in your sack?" asked the farmer again.

"Oh, it's a Goblin," said Little Claus; "he says we needn't eat the porridge, for he has charmed the oven full of roast meat and fish and cake."

"What do you say!" said the farmer, opening the oven door with all speed, and seeing the nice things the woman had hidden, but which her husband thought the Goblin had produced for their special benefit.

The woman dared not say anything, but put the food before them, and then they both made a hearty meal of the fish, the meat, and the cake.

Then Little Claus trod on the skin and made it squeak again.

"What does he say now?" asked the farmer.

"He says," answered Little Claus, "that he has also charmed three bottles of wine into the oven for us."

So the woman had to bring out the wine too, and the farmer drank it and became very merry. Wouldn't he like to have a Goblin, like the one in Little Claus' sack, for himself?

"Can he charm out the Devil?" asked the farmer. "I shouldn't mind seeing him, now that I am in such a merry mood."

"Oh, yes!" said Little Claus; "my Goblin can do everything that we ask him. Can't you?" he asked, trampling up the sack till it squeaked louder than ever. "Do you hear what I say? But the Devil is so ugly, you'd better not see him."

"Oh! I'm not a bit frightened. Whatever does he look like?"

"Well, he will show himself in the image of a sexton."

"Oh, dear!" said the farmer; "that's bad! I must tell you that I can't bear to see a sexton! However, it doesn't matter; I shall know it's only the Devil, and then I shan't mind so much! Now, my courage is up! But he mustn't come too close."

" I'll ask my Goblin about it," said Little Claus, treading on the bag and putting his ear close to it.

" What does he say? "

" He says you can go along and open the chest in the corner, and there you'll see the Devil moping in the dark; but hold the lid tight so that he doesn't get out."

" Will you help me to hold it! " asked the farmer, going along to the chest where the woman had hidden the real sexton, who was shivering with fright.

The farmer lifted up the lid a wee little bit and peeped in. " Ha! " he shrieked, and sprang back. " Yes, I saw him, and he looked just exactly like our sexton! It was a horrible sight."

They had to have a drink after this, and there they sat drinking till far into the night.

" You must sell me that Goblin," said the farmer. " You may ask what you like for him! I'll give you a bushel of money for him."

" No, I can't do that," said Little Claus; " you must remember how useful my Goblin is to me."

" Oh, but I should so like to have him," said the farmer, and he went on begging for him.

" Well," said Little Claus at last, " as you have been so kind to me I shall have to give him up. " You shall have my Goblin for a bushel of money, but I must have it full to the brim! "

" You shall have it," said the farmer; " but you must take that chest away with you; I won't have it in the house for another hour; you never know whether he's there or not."

So Little Claus gave his sack with the dried hide in it to the farmer, and received in return a bushel of money for it and the measure was full to the brim. The farmer also gave him a large wheelbarrow to take the money and the chest away in.

" Good-bye! " said Little Claus, and off he went with his money and the big chest with the sexton in it.

There was a wide and deep river on the other side of the wood, the stream was so strong that it was almost impossible to swim against it. A large new bridge had been built across it, and when they got into the very middle of it, Little Claus said quite loud, so that the sexton could hear him—

" What am I to do with this stupid old chest? it might be

full of paving stones, it's so heavy! I am quite tired of wheeling it along; I'll just throw it into the river; if it floats down the river to my house, well and good, and if it doesn't, I shan't care."

Then he took hold of the chest and raised it up a bit, as if he was about to throw it into the river.

"No, no! let it be!" shouted the sexton; "let me get out!"

"Hullo!" said Little Claus, pretending to be frightened. "Why, he's still inside it, then I must have it into the river to drown him."

"Oh no, oh no!" shouted the sexton. "I'll give you a bushel full of money if you'll let me out!"

"Oh, that's another matter," said Little Claus, opening the chest. The sexton crept out at once and pushed the empty chest into the water, and then went home and gave Little Claus a whole bushel full of money: he had already had one from the farmer, you know, so now his wheelbarrow was quite full of money.

"I got a pretty fair price for that horse I must admit!" said he to himself when he got home to his own room and turned the money out of the wheelbarrow into a heap on the floor. "What a rage Great Claus will be in when he discovers how rich I am become through my one horse, but I won't tell him straight out about it." So he sent a boy to Great Claus to borrow a bushel measure.

"What does he want that for!" thought Great Claus, and he rubbed some tallow on the bottom, so that a little of whatever was to be measured might stick to it. So it did, for when the measure came back three new silver threepenny bits were sticking to it.

"What's this?" said Great Claus, and he ran straight along to Little Claus. "Where on earth did you get all that money?"

"Oh, that was for my horse's hide which I sold last night."

"That was well paid indeed," said Great Claus, and he ran home, took an axe and hit all his four horses on the head. He then flayed them and went off to the town with the hides.

"Skins, skins, who will buy skins?" he shouted up and down the streets.

All the shoemakers and tanners in the town came running up and asked him how much he wanted for them.

" A bushel of money for each," said Great Claus.

" Are you mad? " they all said; " do you imagine we have money by the bushel? "

" Skins, skins, who will buy skins? " he shouted again, and the shoemakers took up their measures and the tanners their leather aprons, and beat Great Claus through the town.

" Skins, skins! " they mocked him. " Yes, we'll give you a raw hide. Out of the town with him! " they shouted, and Great Claus had to hurry off as fast as ever he could go. He had never had such a beating in his life.

" Little Claus shall pay for this! " he said when he got home. " I'll kill him for it."

Little Claus' old grandmother had just died in his house; she certainly had been very cross and unkind to him, but now that she was dead he felt quite sorry about it. He took the dead woman and put her into his warm bed, to see if he could bring her to life again. He meant her to stay there all night, and he would sit on a chair in the corner; he had slept like that before.

As he sat there in the night, the door opened, and in came Great Claus with his axe; he knew where Little Claus' bed stood, and he went straight up to it and hit the dead grandmother a blow on the forehead, thinking that it was Little Claus.

" Just see if you'll cheat me again after that! " he said, and then he went home again.

" What a bad, wicked man he is," said Little Claus; " he was going to kill me there. What a good thing that poor old granny was dead already, or else he would have killed her."

He now dressed his old grandmother in her best Sunday clothes, borrowed a horse of his neighbour, harnessed it to a cart, and set his grandmother on the back seat, so that she could not fall out when the cart moved. Then he started off through the wood. When the sun rose he was just outside a big inn, and Little Claus drew up his horse and went in to get something to eat.

The landlord was a very, very rich man, and a very good

man, but he was fiery-tempered, as if he were made of pepper and tobacco.

"Good morning!" said he to Little Claus; "you've got your best clothes on very early this morning!"

"Yes," said Little Claus; "I'm going to town with my old grandmother, she's sitting out there in the cart, I can't get her to come in. Won't you take her out a glass of mead? You'll have to shout at her, she's very hard of hearing."

"Yes, she shall have it!" said the innkeeper, and he poured out a large glass of mead which he took out to the dead grandmother in the cart.

"Here is a glass of mead your son has sent!" said the innkeeper, but the dead woman sat quite still and never said a word.

"Don't you hear?" shouted the innkeeper as loud as ever he could; "here is a glass of mead from your son!"

Again he shouted, and then again as loud as ever, but as she did not stir, he got angry and threw the glass of mead in her face, so that the mead ran all over her, and she fell backwards out of the cart, for she was only stuck up and not tied in.

"Now!" shouted Little Claus, as he rushed out of the inn and seized the landlord by the neck, "you have killed my grandmother! Just look, there's a great hole in her forehead!"

"Oh, what a misfortune!" exclaimed the innkeeper, clasping his hands; "that's the consequence of my fiery temper! Good Little Claus, I will give you a bushel of money, and bury your grandmother as if she had been my own, if you will only say nothing about it, or else they will chop my head off, and that is so nasty."

So Little Claus had a whole bushel of money, and the inn-keeper buried the old grandmother just as if she had been his own.

When Little Claus got home again with all his money, he immediately sent over his boy to Great Claus to borrow his measure.

"What!" said Great Claus, "is he not dead? I shall have to go and see about it myself!" So he took the measure over to Little Claus himself.

"I say, wherever did you get all that money?" asked he, his eyes, round with amazement at what he saw.

"It was my grandmother you killed instead of me!" said Little Claus. "I have sold her and got a bushel of money for her!"

"That was good pay indeed!" said Great Claus, and he hurried home, took an axe and killed his old grandmother.

He then put her in a cart and drove off to the town with her where the apothecary lived, and asked if he would buy a dead body.

"Who is it, and where did the body come from?" asked the apothecary.

"It is my grandmother, and I have killed her for a bushel of money!" said Great Claus.

"Heaven preserve us!" said the apothecary. "You are talking like a madman; pray don't say such things, you might lose your head!"

And he pointed out to him what a horribly wicked thing he had done, and what a bad man he was who deserved punishment. Great Claus was so frightened that he rushed straight out of the shop, jumped into the cart, whipped up his horse and galloped home. The apothecary and everyone else thought he was mad, and so they let him drive off.

"You shall be paid for this!" said Great Claus, when he got out on the high road. "You shall pay for this, Little Claus!"

As soon as he got home, he took the biggest sack he could find, went over to Little Claus and said,—

"You have deceived me again! First I killed my horses, and then my old grandmother! It's all your fault, but you shan't have the chance of cheating me again!"

Then he took Little Claus by the waist and put him into the sack, put it on his back, and shouted to him—"I'm going to drown you now!"

It was a long way to go before he came to the river, and Little Claus was not so light to carry. The road passed close by the church in which the organ was playing, and the people were singing beautifully. Great Claus put down the sack with Little Claus in it close by the church door, and thought he would like to go and hear a psalm before he went any further. Little

Claus could not get out of the bag, and all the people were in church, so he went in too.

"Oh dear, oh dear!" sighed Little Claus in the sack. He turned and twisted, but it was impossible to undo the cord. Just then an old cattle drover with white hair and a tall stick in his hand came along. He had a whole drove of cows and bulls before him; they ran against the sack Little Claus was in, and upset it.

"Oh dear!" sighed Little Claus; "I am so young to be going to the Kingdom of Heaven!"

"And I," said the cattle drover, "am so old and cannot get there yet!"

"Open the sack!" shouted Little Claus. "Get in in place of me, and you will get to heaven directly!"

"That will just suit me," said the cattle drover, undoing the sack for Little Claus, who immediately sprang out. "You must look after the cattle now," said the old man as he crept into the sack. Little Claus tied it up and walked off driving the cattle before him.

A little while after Great Claus came out of the church, he took up the sack again on his back, and certainly thought it had grown lighter, for the old cattle drover was not more than half the weight of Little Claus. "How light he seems to have got; that must be because I have been to church and said my prayers!" Then he went on to the river, which was both wide and deep, and threw the sack with the old cattle drover in it into the water, shouting as he did so (for he thought it was Little Claus), "Now, you won't cheat me again!" Then he went homewards, but when he reached the crossroads he met Little Claus with his herd of cattle

"What's the meaning of this!" exclaimed Great Claus; "didn't I drown you?"

"Yes," said little Claus, "it's just about half an hour since you threw me into the river!"

"But where did you get all those splendid beasts?" asked Great Claus.

"They are sea-cattle," said Little Claus. "I will tell you the whole story, and indeed I thank you heartily for drowning me, I'm at the top of the tree now and a very rich man, I can

tell you.   I was so frightened when I was in the sack, the wind
whistled in my ears when you threw me over the bridge into the
cold water.   I immediately sank to the bottom, but I was not
hurt, for the grass is beautifully soft down there.   The sack
was opened at once by a beautiful maiden in snow-white clothes
with a green wreath on her wet hair;   she took my hand and said,
' Are you there, Little Claus?   Here are some cattle for you, and
a mile further up the road you will come upon another herd,
which I will give you too!"   Then I saw that the river was
a great highway for the sea-folk.   Down at the bottom of it they
walked and drove about, from the sea right up to the end of the
river.   The flowers were lovely and the grass was so fresh;   the
fishes which swam about glided close to me just like birds in the
air.   How nice the people were, and what a lot of cattle strolling
about in the ditches."

"But why did you come straight up here again then?"
asked Great Claus.   "I shouldn't have done that, if it was so
fine down there."

"Oh," said Little Claus, "that's just my cunning;   you
remember I told you that the mermaid said that a mile further
up the road—and by the road she means the river, for she can't
go anywhere else—I should find another herd of cattle waiting
for me.   Well, I know how many bends there are in the river
and what a roundabout way it would be.   It's ever so much
shorter if you can come up on dry land and take the short cuts,
you save a couple of miles by it, and get the cattle much sooner."

"Oh, you *are* a fortunate man!" said Great Claus;   "do
you think I should get some sea-cattle if I were to go down to
the bottom of the river?"

"I'm sure you would," said Little Claus;   "but I can't carry
you in the sack to the river, you're too heavy for me.   If you
like to walk there and then get into the sack, I'll throw you into
the river with the greatest pleasure in the world."

"Thank you," said Great Claus;   "but if I don't get any
sea-cattle when I get down there, see if I don't give you a sound
thrashing."

"Oh! don't be so hard on me."   They then walked off to
the river.   As soon as the cattle saw the water they rushed
down to drink, for they were very thirsty.   "See what a hurry

they're in," said Little Claus; "they want to get down to the bottom again."

"Now, help me first," said Great Claus, "or else I'll thrash you." He then crept into a big sack which had been lying across the back of one of the cows. "Put a big stone in, or I'm afraid I shan't sink," said Great Claus.

"Oh, that'll be all right," said Little Claus, but he put a big stone into the sack and gave it a push. Plump went the sack and Great Claus was in the river where he sank to the bottom at once.

"I'm afraid he won't find any cattle," said Little Claus, as he drove his herd home.

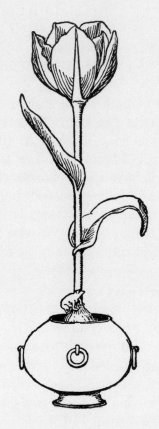

THE GARDEN OF PARADISE

THERE was once a king's son; nobody had so many or such beautiful books as he had. He could read about everything which had ever happened in this world, and see it all represented in the most beautiful pictures. He could get information about every nation and every country; but as to where the Garden of Paradise was to be found, not a word could he discover, and this was the very thing he thought most about. His grandmother had told him when he was quite a little fellow and was about to begin his school life, that every flower in the Garden of Paradise was a delicious cake, and that the pistils were full of wine. In one flower history was written, in another geography or tables, you had only to eat the cake and you knew the lesson. The more you ate, the more history, geography, and tables you knew. All this he believed then; but as he grew older and wiser and learnt more, he easily perceived that the delights of the Garden of Paradise must be far beyond all this.

"Oh, why did Eve take of the Tree of Knowledge! Why did Adam eat the forbidden fruit! If it had only been I it would not have happened! never would sin have entered the world!"

This is what he said then, and he still said it when he was seventeen; his thoughts were full of the Garden of Paradise.

He walked into the wood one day; he was alone, for that was his greatest pleasure. Evening came on, the clouds drew up, and it rained as if the whole heaven had become a sluice from which the water poured in sheets; it was as dark as it is otherwise in the deepest well. Now he slipped on the wet grass, and then he fell on the bare stones which jutted out of the rocky ground. Everything was dripping, and at last the poor Prince hadn't got a dry thread on him. He had to climb over huge rocks where the water oozed out of the thick moss. He was almost fainting; just then he heard a curious murmuring and saw in front of him a big lighted cave. A fire was burning in the middle, big enough to roast a stag, which was in fact being done; a splendid stag with its huge antlers was stuck on a spit, being slowly turned round between the hewn trunks of two fir trees. An oldish woman, tall and strong enough to be a man dressed up, sat by the fire throwing on logs from time to time.

"Come in by all means!" she said; "sit down by the fire so that your clothes may dry!"

"There is a shocking draught here," said the Prince, as he sat down on the ground.

"It will be worse than this when my sons come home!" said the woman. "You are in the cavern of the winds; my sons are the four winds of the world! Do you understand?"

"Who are your sons?" asked the Prince.

"Well that's not so easy to answer when the question is stupidly put," said the woman. "My sons do as they like, they are playing rounders now with the clouds up there in the great hall," and she pointed up into the sky.

"Oh indeed!" said the prince. "You seem to speak very harshly, and you are not so gentle as the women I generally see about me!"

"Oh I daresay, they have nothing else to do! I have to be harsh if I am to keep my boys under control! But I can do it, although they are a stiff-necked lot! Do you see those four sacks hanging on the wall? They are just as frightened of them as you used to be of the cane behind the looking-glass. I can double the boys up, I can tell you, and then they have to go into the bag; we don't stand upon ceremony, and there they have to stay; they can't get out to play their tricks till it suits me to let them. But here we have one of them." It was the Northwind who came in with an icy blast, great hailstones peppered about the floor and snowflakes drifted in. He was dressed in bearskin trousers and jacket, and he had a sealskin cap drawn over his ears. Long icicles were hanging from his beard, and one hailstone after another dropped down from the collar of his jacket.

" Don't go straight to the fire," said the Prince. " You might easily get chilblains! "

" Chilblains! " said the Northwind with a loud laugh. " Chilblains! they are my greatest delight! What sort of a feeble creature are you? How did you get into the cave of the winds? "

" He is my guest," said the old woman, " and if you are not pleased with that explanation you may go into the bag! Now you know my opinion! "

This had its effect, and the Northwind told them where he came from, and where he had been for the last month.

" I come from the Arctic seas," he said. " I have been on Behring Island with the Russian walrus-hunters. I sat at the helm and slept when they sailed from the north cape, and when I woke now and then the stormy petrels were flying about my legs; they are queer birds; they give a brisk flap with their wings and then keep them stretched out and motionless, and even then they have speed enough."

" Pray don't be too long-winded," said the mother of the winds. " So at last you got to Behring Island! "

" It's perfectly splendid! there you have a floor to dance upon, as flat as a pancake, half-thawed snow, with moss; there were bones of whales and Polar bears lying about, they looked like the legs and arms of giants covered with green mould. One would think that the sun had never shone on them. I gave a little puff to the fog so that one could see the shed. It was a house built of wreckage and covered with the skins of whales; the flesh side was turned outwards; it was all red and green; a living polar bear sat on the roof growling. I went to the shore and looked at the birds' nests, looked at the unfledged young ones screaming and gaping; then I blew down thousands of their throats and they learnt to shut their mouths. Lower down the walruses were rolling about like monster maggots with pig's heads and teeth a yard long! "

" You're a good story teller, my boy!" said his mother. " It makes my mouth water to hear you!"

" Then there was a hunt! The harpoons were plunged into the walruses' breasts, and the steaming blood spurted out of them, like fountains over the ice. Then I remembered my part of the game! I blew up and made my ships, the mountain-high icebergs, nip the boats; whew! how they whistled and how they screamed, but I whistled louder. They were obliged to throw the dead wulruses, chests and ropes out upon the ice! I shook the snowflakes over them and let them drift southwards to taste the salt water. They will never come back to Behring Island!"

" Then you've been doing evil!" said the mother of the winds.

" What good I did, the others may tell you," said he. " But here we have my brother from the west; I like him best of all, he smells of the sea and brings a splendid cool breeze with him!"

" Is that the little Zephyr?" asked the Prince.

" Yes, certainly it is Zephyr, but he is not so little as all that. He used to be a pretty boy once, but that's gone by!"

He looked like a wild man of the woods, but he had a padded hat on so as not to come to any harm. He carried a mahogany club cut in the American mahogany forests. It could not be anything less than that.

" Where do you come from?" asked his mother.

" From the forest wildernesses!" he said, " where the thorny creepers make a fence between every tree, where the water-snake lies in the wet grass, and where human beings seem to be superfluous!"

" What did you do there?"

" I looked at the mighty river, saw where it dashed over the rocks in dust and flew with the clouds to carry the rainbow. I saw the wild buffalo swimming in the river, but the stream carried him away, he floated with the wild duck, which soared into the sky at the rapids; but the buffalo was carried over with the water. I liked that and blew a storm, so that the primeval trees had to sail too, and they were whirled about like shavings."

" And you have done nothing else?" asked the old woman.

" I have been turning somersaults in the Savannahs, patting

the wild horse, and shaking down cocoa-nuts! Oh, yes, I have plenty of stories to tell! But one need not tell everything. You know that very well, old woman!" and then he kissed his mother so heartily that she nearly fell backwards; he was indeed a wild boy.

The Southwind appeared now in a turban and a flowing bedouin's cloak.

"It is fearfully cold in here," he said, throwing wood on the fire; "it is easy to see that the Northwind got here first!"

"It is hot enough to roast a polar bear," said the Northwind.

"You are a polar bear yourself!" said the Southwind.

"Do you want to go into the bag?" asked the old woman. "Sit down on that stone and tell us where you have been."

"In Africa, mother!" he answered. "I have been chasing the lion with the Hottentots in Kaffirland! What grass there is on those plains! as green as an olive. The gnu was dancing about, and the ostriches ran races with me, but I am still the fastest. I went to the desert with its yellow sand. It looks like the bottom of the sea. I met a caravan! They were killing their last camel to get water to drink, but it wasn't much they got. The sun was blazing above, and the sand burning below. There were no limits to the outstretched desert. Then I burrowed into the fine loose sand and whirled it up in great columns—that was a dance! You should have seen how despondently the dromedaries stood, and the merchant drew his caftan over his head. He threw himself down before me as if I had been Allah, his god. Now they are buried, and there is a pyramid of sand over them all; when I blow it away, sometime the sun will bleach their bones, and then travellers will see that people have been there before, otherwise you would hardly believe it in the desert!"

"Then you have only been doing harm!" said the mother. "Into the bag you go!" And before he knew where he was she had the Southwind by the waist and in the bag; it rolled about on the ground, but she sat upon it and then it had to be quiet.

"Your sons are lively fellows!" said the Prince.

"Yes, indeed," she said; "but I can master them! Here comes the fourth."

It was the Eastwind, and he was dressed like a Chinaman.

" Oh, have you come from that quarter? " said the mother. " I thought you had been in the Garden of Paradise."

" I am only going there to-morrow! " said the Eastwind. " It will be a hundred years to-morrow since I have been there. I have just come from China, where I danced round the porcelain tower till all the bells jingled. The officials were flogged in the streets, the bamboo canes were broken over their shoulders, and they were all people ranging from the first to the ninth rank. They shrieked ' Many thanks, Father and benefactor,' but they didn't mean what they said, and I went on ringing the bells and singing ' Tsing, tsang, tsu! ' "

" You're quite uproarious about it! " said the old woman. " It's a good thing you are going to the Garden of Paradise to-morrow; it always has a good effect on your behaviour. Mind you drink deep of the Well of Wisdom, and bring a little bottleful home for me."

" That I will," said the Eastwind. " But why have you put my brother from the south into the bag? Out with him! He must tell me about the phœnix; the Princess always wants to hear about that bird when I call every hundred years. Open the bag! then you'll be my sweetest mother, and I'll give you two pockets full of tea as green and fresh as when I picked it! "

" Well, for the sake of the tea, and because you are my darling, I will open my bag! "

She did open it and the Southwind crept out, but he was quite crestfallen because the strange Prince had seen his disgrace.

" Here is a palm leaf for the Princess! " said the Southwind. " The old phœnix, the only one in the world, gave it to me. He has scratched his whole history on it with his bill, for the hundred years of his life, and she can read it for herself. I saw how the phœnix set fire to his nest himself and sat on it while it burnt, like the widow of a Hindoo. Oh how the dry branches crackled, how it smoked, and what a smell there was. At last it all burst into flame, the old bird was burnt to ashes, but his egg lay glowing in the fire, it broke with a loud bang and the young one flew out. Now it rules over all the birds, and it is the only phœnix in the world. He bit a hole in the leaf I gave you, that is his greeting to the Princess."

" Let us have something to eat now! " said the mother of

the winds; and they all sat down to eat the roast stag, and the Prince sat by the side of the Eastwind, so they soon became good friends.

" I say," said the Prince, " just tell me who is this Princess, and where is the Garden of Paradise? "

" Oh ho! " said the Eastwind, " if that is where you want to go you must fly with me to-morrow. But I may as well tell you that no human being has been there since Adam and Eve's time. You know all about them, I suppose, from your Bible stories? "

" Of course," said the Prince.

" When they were driven away the Garden of Eden sank into the ground, but it kept its warm sunshine, its mild air, and all its charms. The queen of the fairies lives there. The Island of Bliss, where death never enters, and where living is a delight, is there. Get on my back to-morrow and I will take you with me; I think I can manage it! But you mustn't talk now, I want to go to sleep."

When the Prince woke up in the early morning, he was not a little surprised to find that he was already high above the clouds. He was sitting on the back of the Eastwind, who was holding him carefully! they were so high up that woods and fields, rivers and lakes, looked like a large coloured map.

" Good-morning," said the Eastwind. " You may as well sleep a little longer, for there is not much to be seen in this flat country below us, unless you want to count the churches. They look like chalk dots on the green board."

He called the fields and meadows " the green board."

" It was very rude of me to leave without saying good-bye to your mother and brothers," said the Prince.

" One is excused when one is asleep! " said the Eastwind, and they flew on faster than ever. You could mark their flight by the rustling of the trees as they passed over the woods; and whenever they crossed a lake, or the sea, the waves rose and the great ships dipped low down in the water, like floating swans. Towards evening the large towns were amusing as it grew dark, with all their lights twinkling now here, now there, just as when one burns a piece of paper and sees all the little sparks like children coming home from school. The Prince clapped his hands, but the Eastwind told him he had better leave off and hold tight, or he might fall and find himself hanging on to a church steeple.

The eagle in the great forest flew swiftly, but the Eastwind flew more swiftly still. The Kossack on his little horse sped fast over the plains, but the Prince sped faster still.

"Now you can see the Himalayas!" said the Eastwind. "They are the highest mountains in Asia; we shall soon reach the Garden of Paradise."

They took a more southerly direction, and the air became scented with spices and flowers. Figs and pomegranates grew wild, and the wild vines were covered with blue and green grapes. They both descended here and stretched themselves on the soft grass, where the flowers nodded to the wind, as much as to say, "Welcome back."

"Are we in the Garden of Paradise now?" asked the Prince.

"No, certainly not!" answered the Eastwind. "But we shall soon be there. Do you see that wall of rock and the great cavern where the wild vine hangs like a big curtain? We have to go through there! Wrap yourself up in your cloak, the sun is burning here, but a step further on it is icy cold. The bird which flies past the cavern has one wing out here in the heat of summer, and the other is there in the cold of winter."

"So that is the way to the Garden of Paradise!" said the Prince.

Now they entered the cavern. Oh, how icily cold it was, but it did not last long. The Eastwind spread his wings, and they shone like the brightest flame; but what a cave it was! Large blocks of stone, from which the water dripped, hung over them in the most extraordinary shapes; at one moment it was so low and narrow that they had to crawl on hands and knees, the next it was as wide and lofty as if they were in the open air. It looked like a chapel of the dead, with mute organ pipes and petrified banners.

"We seem to be journeying along Death's road to the Garden of Paradise!" said the Prince, but the Eastwind never answered a word, he only pointed before them where a beautiful blue light was shining. The blocks of stone above them grew dimmer and dimmer, and at last they became as transparent as a white cloud in the moonshine. The air was also deliciously soft, as fresh as on the mountain tops and as scented as down among the roses in the valley.

A river ran there as clear as the air itself, and the fish in it were like gold and silver. Purple eels, which gave out blue sparks with every curve, gambolled about in the water; and the broad leaves of the water-lillies were tinged with the hues of the rainbow, while the flower itself was like a fiery orange flame, nourished by the water, just as oil keeps a lamp constantly burning. A firm bridge of marble as delicately and skilfully carved as if it were lace and glass beads led over the water to the Island of Bliss, where the Garden of Paradise bloomed.

The Eastwind took the Prince in his arms and bore him over. The flowers and leaves there sang all the beautiful old songs of his childhood, but sang them more wonderfully than any human voice could sing them.

Were these palm trees or giant water plants growing here? The Prince had never seen such rich and mighty trees. The most wonderful climbing plants hung in wreaths, such as are only to be found in gold and colours on the margins of old books of the Saints or entwined among their initial letters. It was the most extraordinary combination of birds, flowers, and scrolls.

Close by on the grass stood a flock of peacocks with their brilliant tails outspread. Yes, indeed, it seemed so, but when the Prince touched them he saw that they were not birds but plants. They were big dock leaves, which shone like peacock's tails. Lions and tigers sprang like agile cats among the green hedges, which were scented with the blossom of the olive, and the lion and the tiger were tame. The wild dove, glistening like a pearl, beat the lion's mane with his wings; and the antelope, otherwise so shy, stood by nodding, just as if he wanted to join the game.

The Fairy of the Garden now advanced to meet them; her garments shone like the sun, and her face beamed like that of a happy mother rejoicing over her child. She was young and very beautiful, and was surrounded by a band of lovely girls, each with a gleaming star in her hair.

When the Eastwind gave her the inscribed leaf from the Phœnix her eyes sparkled with delight. She took the Prince's hand and led him into her palace, where the walls were the colour of the brightest tulips in the sunlight. The ceiling was one great shining flower, and the longer one gazed into it the deeper the calyx seemed to be. The Prince went to the window, and looking through one of the panes saw the Tree of Knowledge, with the serpent, and Adam and Eve standing by.

" Are they not driven out? " he asked, and the Fairy smiled and explained that Time had burned a picture into each pane, but not of the kind one usually sees; they were alive, the leaves moved, and people came and went like the reflections in a mirror.

Then he looked through another pane, and he saw Jacob's dream, with the ladder going straight up into heaven, and angels with great wings were fluttering up and down. All that had ever happened in this world lived and moved on these window panes; only Time could imprint such wonderful pictures.

The Fairy smiled and led him into a large, lofty room, the walls of which were like transparent paintings of faces, one more beautiful than the other. These were millions of the Blessed who smiled and sang, and all their songs melted into one perfect melody. The highest ones were so tiny that they seemed smaller than the very smallest rosebud, no bigger than a pinpoint in a drawing. In the middle of the room stood a large tree, with handsome drooping branches; golden apples, hung like oranges among its green leaves. It was the Tree of Knowledge, of whose fruit Adam and Eve had eaten. From every leaf hung a shining red drop of dew, it was as if the tree wept tears of blood.

" Now let us get into the boat," said the Fairy. " We shall find refreshment on the swelling waters. The boat rocks, but it does not move from the spot, all the countries of the world will pass before our eyes."

It was a curious sight to see the whole coast move. Here came lofty snow-clad Alps, with their clouds and dark fir trees. The horn echoed sadly among them, and the shepherd yodelled sweetly in the valleys. Then banian trees bent their long drooping branches over the boat, black swans floated on the water, and the strangest animals and flowers appeared on the shore. This was New Holland, the fifth portion of the world, which glided past them with a view of its blue mountains. They heard the song of priests, and saw the dances of the savages to the sound of drums and pipes of bone. The pyramids of Egypt reaching to the clouds, with fallen columns, and Sphynxes half buried in sand, next sailed past them. Then came the Aurora Borealis blazing over the peaks of the north; they were fireworks which could not be imitated. The Prince was so happy, and he saw a hundred times more than we have described.

" Can I stay here always? " he asked.

" That depends upon yourself," answered the Fairy. " If you do not, like Adam, allow yourself to be tempted to do what is forbidden, you can stay here always."

" I will not touch the apples on the Tree of Knowledge," said the Prince. " There are thousands of other fruits here as beautiful."

" Test yourself, and if you are not strong enough, go back with the Eastwind who brought you. He is going away now, and will not come back for a hundred years; the time will fly in this place like a hundred hours, but that is a long time for temptation and sin. Every evening when I leave you I must say ' Come with me,' and I must beckon to you, but stay behind. Do not come with me, for with every step you take your longing will grow stronger. You will reach the hall where grows the Tree of Knowledge; I sleep beneath its fragrant drooping branches. You will bend over me and I must smile, but if you press a kiss upon my lips, Paradise will sink deep down into the earth, and it will be lost to you. The sharp winds of the wilderness will whistle round you, the cold rain will drop from your hair. Sorrow and labour will be your lot."

" I will remain here! " said the Prince.

And the Eastwind kissed him on the mouth and said: " Be strong, then we shall meet again in a hundred years. Farewell! Farewell! " and the Eastwind spread his great wings, they shone like poppies at the harvest time, or the Northern Lights in a cold winter.

" Good-bye! good-bye! " whispered the flowers. Storks and pelicans flew in a line like waving ribbons, conducting him to the boundaries of the Garden.

" Now we begin our dancing! " said the Fairy; " at the end when I dance with you, as the sun goes down you will see me beckon to you and cry ' Come with me '; but do not come. I have to repeat it every night for a hundred years. Every time you resist, you will grow stronger, and at last you will not even think of following. To-night is the first time. Remember my warning! "

And the Fairy led him into a large hall of white transparent lilies, the yellow stamens in each formed a little golden harp which echoed the sound of strings and flutes. Lovely girls, slender and lissom, dressed in floating gauze which revealed their exquisite limbs, glided in the dance, and sang of the joy of living—that they would never die—and that the Garden of Paradise would bloom for ever.

The sun went down and the sky was bathed in golden light which gave the lilies the effect of roses; and the Prince drank of the foaming wine handed to him by the maidens. He felt such joy as he had never known before; he saw the background of the hall opening where the Tree of Knowledge stood in a radiancy which blinded him. The song proceeding from it was soft and lovely, like his mother's voice, and she seemed to say, " My child, my beloved child! "

Then the Fairy beckoned to him and said so tenderly, " Come with me," that he rushed towards her, forgetting his promise, forgetting everything on the very first evening that she smiled and beckoned to him.

The fragrance in the scented air around grew stronger, the harps sounded sweeter than ever, and it seemed as if the millions of smiling heads in the hall where the Tree grew, nodded and sang, " One must know everything. Man is lord of the earth." They were no longer tears of blood which fell from the Tree, it seemed to him that they were red shining stars.

" Come with me, come with me," spoke those trembling tones, and at every step the Prince's cheeks burnt hotter and hotter and his blood coursed more rapidly.

" I must go," he said, " it is no sin, I must see her asleep, nothing will be lost if I do not kiss her, and that I will not do. My will is strong."

The Fairy dropped her shimmering garment, drew back the branches, and a moment after was hidden within their depths.

" I have not sinned yet! " said the Prince, " nor will I," then he drew back the branches. There she lay asleep already, beautiful as only the Fairy in the Garden of Paradise can be.

She smiled in her dreams; he bent over her and saw the tears welling up under her eyelashes.

"Do you weep for me?" he whispered. "Weep not, beautiful maiden. I only now understand the full bliss of Paradise; it surges through my blood and through my thoughts. I feel the strength of the angels and of everlasting life in my mortal limbs! If it were to be everlasting night to me, a moment like this were worth it!" and he kissed away the tears from her eyes; his mouth touched hers.

Then came a sound like thunder, louder and more awful than any he had ever heard before, and everything around collapsed. The beautiful Fairy, the flowery Paradise sank deeper and deeper. The Prince saw it sink into the darkness of night; it shone far off like a tiny twinkling star. The chill of death crept over his limbs; he closed his eyes and lay long as if dead.

The cold rain fell on his face, and the sharp wind blew around his head, and at last his memory came back. "What have I done?" he sighed. "I have sinned like Adam, sinned so heavily that Paradise has sunk low beneath the earth!" And he opened his eyes; he could still see the star, the far away star, which twinkled like Paradise; it was the morning star in the sky. He got up and found himself in the wood near the cave of the winds, and the mother of the winds sat by his side. She looked angry and raised her hand.

"So soon as the first evening!" she said. "I thought as much; if you were my boy, you should go into the bag!"

"Ah, he shall soon go there!" said Death. He was a strong old man, with a scythe in his hand and great black wings. "He shall be laid in a coffin, but not now; I only mark him and then leave him for a time to wander about on the earth to expiate his sin and to grow better. I will come some time. When he least expects me, I shall come back, lay him in a black coffin, put it on my head, and fly to the skies. The Garden of Paradise blooms there too, and if he is good and holy he shall enter into it; but if his thoughts are wicked and his heart still full of sin, he will sink deeper in his coffin than Paradise sank, and I shall only go once in every thousand years to see if he is to sink deeper or to rise to the stars, the twinkling stars up there."

LITTLE TUK

NOW there was little Tuk; as a matter of fact his name was not Tuk at all, but before he could speak properly he called himself Tuk. He meant it for Carl, so it is just as well we should know that. He had to look after his sister Gustave, who was much smaller than he was, and then he had his lessons to do, but these two things were rather difficult to manage at the same time. The poor boy sat with his little sister on his lap and sang all the songs he knew, at the same time glancing at his geography book which was open in front of him. Before the next morning he had to know all the towns in the island of Zealand by heart, and everything there was to know about them.

At last his mother came home, for she had been out, and then she took little Gustave. Tuk ran to the window and read as hard as ever he could, for it was getting dark, and mother could not afford to buy candles.

"There's the old washerwoman from the lane," said his mother, as she looked out of the window. "She can hardly carry herself, and yet she has to carry the pail from the pump; run down little Tuk and be a dear boy. Help the old woman!"

Tuk jumped up at once and ran to help her, but when he got home again it was quite dark, and it was useless to talk about candles, he had to go to bed. He had an old turn-up

152

bed, and he lay in it thinking about his geography lesson, the island of Zealand, and all that the teacher had told him. He ought to have been learning the lesson, but of course he could not do that now. He put the geography book under his pillow, because he had heard that this would help him considerably to remember his lesson, but that can't be depended upon.

He lay there thinking and thinking, and then all at once it seemed just as if someone kissed him on his eyes and his mouth, and he fell asleep, yet he was not quite asleep either. It seemed to him as if the old washerwoman was looking at him with her kind eyes and saying: " It would be a great shame if you were not to know your lesson. You helped me, and now I will help you, and Our Lord will always help you." And all at once the book under his head went " cribble, crabble."

" Cluck, cluck, cluck! " and there stood a hen from the town of Kiöge. " I am a Kiöge hen," and then it told him how many inhabitants there were, and about the battle which had taken place there, which after all was not a very important one.

" Cribble, crabble, bang! " something plumped down; it was a wooden bird which now made its appearance—the popinjay from the Shooting Association in Præstö. It told him that there were just as many inhabitants as it had nails in its body, and it was very proud of this. " Thorvaldsen used to live close by my corner; the situation is beautiful."

Now little Tuk no longer lay in bed, he was on horseback. Gallop-a-gallop he went. He was sitting in front of a splendidly dressed knight with a shining helmet and a waving plume. They rode through the woods to the old town of Vordingborg,[1] and this was a big and populous town. The castle towered over the royal city, and the lights shone through the windows; there was dancing and singing within, and King Waldemar led out the stately young court ladies to the dance. Morning came, and as the sun rose the town sank away and the king's palace, one tower after the other; at last only one tower remained on the hill where the castle had stood, and the town had become tiny and very poor. The schoolboys came along with their

[1] Under King Waldemar a place of great importance, now insignificant, only one of the towers of its castle remaining.

books under their arms, and they said "two thousand inhabitants," but that was not true, there were not so many.

Little Tuk was still lying in his bed; first he thought he was dreaming, and then he thought he was not dreaming, but there was somebody close to him.

A sailor, a tiny little fellow, who might have been a cadet, but he was not a cadet, was saying to him, "Little Tuk! Little Tuk! I am to greet you warmly from Korsöer," which is a rising town. It is a flourishing town, which has steamers and coaches. At one time it used to be called a tiresome town,[1] but that was an old-fashioned opinion. "I lie close to the sea," says Korsöer. "I have good high-roads and pleasure-gardens, I have given birth to a poet who was amusing, and that is more than they all are. I wanted to send a ship round the world, I did not do it, but I might have done it; then there is the most delicious scent about me, because there are beautiful rose-gardens close by the gates!"

Little Tuk saw them, the green and red flowering branches passed before his eyes; and then they vanished and changed into wooded heights, sloping to the clear waters of the fiord. A stately old Church towered over the fiord, with its twin spires. Springs of water flowed from the cliff and rushed down in rapid bubbling streams. Close by them sat an old king with a golden crown round his flowing locks; this was King Hroar of the Springs and Roeskilde [2] (Hroars-springs) is now the name of the town. Down over the slopes and past the springs, walked hand in hand all Denmark's kings and queens wearing their crowns. On and on they went into the old church, to the pealing music of the organ, and the rippling of the springs. "Don't forget the Estates of the Realm," said King Hroar. All at once everything vanished—where were they? Now an old peasant woman stood before Tuk; she was a weeding woman, and came from Sorö, where the grass grows on the market-place. She had put her grey linen apron over her head and shoulders, it was soaking wet, there must have been rain. "Yes, indeed, it has been raining," she said. She knew some of the comic parts of

[1] It was a dull town on the Great Belt before the establishment of steamboats. Birthplace of the poet Baggesen.

[2] The former capital of Denmark, and the burial place of all the Danish kings and queens.

Holberg's plays, and she knew all about Waldemar and Absolom; just as she was going to tell him these stories she shrank up and wagged her head, it looked just as if she was about to take a leap. "Koax," she said, "it is wet, it is wet, it is dull as ditch-water—in good old Sorö!" She had become a frog, "koax," and then once more she was the old woman. "One must dress according to the weather!" said she. "It is wet, it is wet, my town is like a bottle, you get in by the neck, and you have to come out the same way again! I used to have beautiful fish [1] there once, now I have rosy-cheeked boys down at the bottom of the bottle; they get a great deal of wisdom there; Greek! Greek! [2] Hebrew! koax!" It was just like the croaking of frogs or the creaking of fishing boots when you walk in a swamp. It was always the same sound, so tiresome, so tiresome that little Tuk fell into a deep sleep, which was the best thing for him.

But even in this sound sleep he had a dream, or something of the sort. His little sister, Gustave, with the blue eyes and golden, curly hair, had all at once become a lovely grown up girl, and without having wings she could fly. They flew together right across Zealand, over the green woods and deep blue waters.

"Do you hear the cock crowing, little Tuk? Cock-a-doodle-doo. The hens come flying up from Kiöge town. You shall have such a big, big chicken-yard. You will be a rich and happy man! Your house shall hold up its head like King Waldemar's towers, and it shall be richly built up with marble statues, like those in Prestö. You understand me, I suppose. Your name will spread round the world with praise, like the ship which was to have sailed from Korsöer; and it will be known in Roeskilde town."

"Remember the Estates of the Realm," said King Hroar.

"You shall speak well and wisely in Parliament, little Tuk; and when you are in your grave you shall sleep as quietly as——"

"As if I were in Sorö!" said little Tuk, and then he woke up. It was bright daylight, and he remembered nothing about

---

[1] Maller, Siluris glanis, only found in Sorö Lake, and now extinct.
[2] Sorö is an old public school, founded by Holberg, the Danish Molière.

his dream; but that was as it should be, one must not look into the future.

He sprang out of bed and read his book till he knew his lesson, which he did almost at once. The old washerwoman put her head in at the door, nodded to him, and said,—

"Many thanks for your help yesterday, you dear child! May the Lord fulfil the dream of your heart!"

Little Tuk did not know a bit what he had dreamt, but One above knew all about it!

THE LITTLE MATCH GIRL

IT was late on a bitterly cold, snowy, New Year's Eve. A poor little girl was wandering in the dark cold streets; she was bareheaded and barefooted. She certainly had had slippers on when she left home, but they were not much good, for they were so huge. They had last been worn by her mother, and they fell off the poor little girl's feet when she was running across the street to avoid two carriages that were rolling rapidly by. One of the shoes could not be found at all; and the other was picked up by a boy who ran off with it, saying that it would do for a cradle when he had children of his own. So the poor little girl had to go on with her little bare feet, which were red and blue with the cold. She carried a quantity of matches in her old apron, and held a packet of them in her hand. Nobody had bought any of her during all the long day; nobody had even given her a copper. The poor little creature was hungry and perishing with cold, and she looked the picture of misery. The snowflakes fell upon her long yellow hair, which curled so prettily round her face, but she paid no attention to that. Lights were shining from every window, and there was a most delicious odour of roast goose in the streets, for it was New Year's Eve —she could not forget that. She found a corner where one house projected a little beyond the next one, and here she crouched, drawing up her feet under her, but she was colder

157

than ever. She did not dare to go home, for she had not sold any matches, and had not earned a single penny. Her father would beat her, besides it was almost as cold at home as it was here. They only had the roof over them and the wind whistled through it although they stuffed up the biggest cracks with rags and straw. Her little hands were almost dead with cold. Oh, one little match would do some good! Dared she pull one out of the bundle and strike it on the wall to warm her fingers! She pulled one out, " risch," how it spluttered, how it blazed! It burnt with a bright clear flame, just like a little candle when she held her hand round it. It was a very curious candle too. The little girl fancied that she was sitting in front of a big stove with polished brass feet and handles. There was a splendid fire blazing in it and warming her so beautifully, but—what happened—just as she was stretching out her feet to warm them, —the blaze went out, the stove vanished, and she was left sitting with the end of the burnt-out match in her hand. She struck a new one, it burnt, it blazed up, and where the light fell upon the wall, it became transparent like gauze, and she could see right through it into the room. The table was spread with a snowy cloth and pretty china; a roast goose stuffed with apples and prunes was steaming on it. And what was even better, the goose hopped from the dish with the carving knife and fork sticking in his back, and it waddled across the floor. It came right up to the poor child, and then—the match went out, and there was nothing to be seen but the thick black wall.

Again, she lit another. This time she was sitting under a lovely Christmas tree. It was much bigger and more beautifully decorated than the one she had seen when she peeped through the glass doors at the rich merchant's house this very last Christmas. Thousands of lighted candles gleamed upon its branches, and coloured pictures, such as she had seen in the shop windows, looked down to her. The little girl stretched out both her hands towards them—then out went the match. All the Christmas candles rose higher and higher, till she saw that they were only the twinkling stars. One of them fell and made a bright streak of light across the sky. "Some one is dying," thought the little girl; for her old grandmother, the only person

who had ever been kind to her, used to say, " When a star falls
a soul is going up to God."

Now she struck another match against the wall, and this
time it was her grandmother who appeared in the circle of
flame. She saw her quite clearly and distinctly, looking so
gentle and happy.

" Grandmother! " cried the little creature. " Oh, do take
me with you! I know you will vanish when the match goes
out; you will vanish like the warm stove, the delicious goose,
and the beautiful Christmas tree!"

She hastily struck a whole bundle of matches, because she
did so long to keep her grandmother with her. The light of
the matches made it as bright as day. Grandmother had never
before looked so big or so beautiful. She lifted the little girl up
in her arms, and they soared in a halo of light and joy, far, far
above the earth, where there was no more cold, no hunger, no
pain, for they were with God.

In the cold morning light the poor little girl sat there, in
the corner between the houses, with rosy cheeks and a smile
on her face—dead. Frozen to death on the last night of the
old year. New Year's Day broke on the little body still sitting
with the ends of the burnt-out matches in her hand. She must
have tried to warm herself, they said. Nobody knew what
beautiful visions she had seen, nor in what a halo she had entered
with her grandmother upon the glories of the New Year!

THE SNOW QUEEN

A TALE IN SEVEN STORIES

FIRST STORY

DEALS with a mirror and its fragments. Now we are about to begin, and you must attend; and when we get to the end of the story, you will know more than you do now about a very wicked hobgoblin. He was one of the worst kind; in fact he was a real demon. One day he was in a high state of delight, because he had invented a mirror with this peculiarity, that every good and pretty thing reflected in it shrank away to almost nothing. On the other hand, every bad and good-for-nothing thing stood out and looked its worst. The most beautiful landscapes reflected in it looked like boiled spinach, and the best people became hideous, or else they were upside down and had no bodies. Their faces were distorted beyond recognition, and if they had even one freckle it appeared to spread all over the nose and mouth. The demon thought this immensely amusing. If a good thought passed through anyone's mind, it turned to a grin in the mirror, and this caused real delight to the demon. All the scholars of the demon's school, for he kept a school, reported that a miracle had taken place: now for the

160

first time it had become possible to see what the world and mankind were really like. They ran about all over with the mirror, till at last there was not a country or a person which had not been seen in this distorting mirror. They even wanted to fly up to heaven with it to mock the angels; but the higher they flew, the more it grinned, so much so that they could hardly hold it, and at last it slipped out of their hands and fell to the earth, shivered into hundreds of millions and billions of bits. Even then it did more harm than ever. Some of these bits were not as big as a grain of sand, and these flew about all over the world, getting into people's eyes, and, once in, they stuck there, and distorted everything they looked at, or made them see everything that was amiss. Each tiniest grain of glass kept the same power as that possessed by the whole mirror. Some people even got a bit of the glass into their hearts, and that was terrible, for the heart became like a lump of ice. Some of the fragments were so big that they were used for window panes, but it was not advisable to look at one's friends through these panes. Other bits were made into spectacles, and it was a bad business when people put on these spectacles meaning to be just. The bad demon laughed till he split his sides; it tickled him to see the mischief he had done. But some of these fragments were still left floating about the world, and you shall hear what happened to them.

SECOND STORY

ABOUT A LITTLE BOY AND A LITTLE GIRL

In a big town crowded with houses and people, where there is no room for gardens, people have to be content with flowers in pots instead. In one of these towns lived two children who managed to have something bigger than a flower-pot for a garden. They were not brother and sister, but they were just as fond of each other as if they had been. Their parents lived opposite each other in two attic rooms. The roof of one house just touched the roof of the next one, with only a rain water gutter between them. They each had a little dormer window, and one only had to step over the gutter to get from one house to the other. Each of the parents had a large window-box, in which they grew pot herbs and a little rose tree. There was one in each box, and they both grew splendidly. Then it occurred to the parents to put the boxes across the gutter, from house to house, and they looked just like two banks of flowers. The pea vines hung down over the edges of the boxes, and the roses threw out long creepers which twined round the windows. It was almost like a green triumphal arch. The boxes were high, and the children knew they must not climb up on to them, but they were often allowed to have their little stools out under the rose trees, and there they had delightful games. Of course in the winter there was an end to these amusements. The windows were often covered with hoar frost; then they would warm coppers on the stove and stick them on the frozen panes, where they made lovely peep-holes as round as possible. Then a bright eye would peep through these holes, one from each window. The little boy's name was Kay, and the little girl's Gerda.

In the summer they could reach each other with one bound, but in the winter they had to go down all the stairs in one house and up all the stairs in the other, and outside there were snow-drifts.

"Look! the white bees are swarming," said the old grandmother.

"Have they a queen bee too?" asked the little boy, for he knew that there was a queen among the real bees.

"Yes indeed they have," said the grandmother. "She flies where the swarm is thickest. She is the biggest of them all, and she never remains on the ground. She always flies up again to the sky. Many a winter's night she flies through the streets and peeps in at the windows, and then the ice freezes on the panes into wonderful patterns like flowers."

"Oh yes, we have seen that," said both children, and then they knew it was true.

"Can the Snow Queen come in here?" asked the little girl.

"Just let her come," said the boy, "and I will put her on the stove, where she will melt."

But the grandmother smoothed his hair and told him more stories.

In the evening when little Kay was at home and half undressed, he crept up on to the chair by the window, and peeped out of the little hole. A few snow-flakes were falling, and one of these, the biggest, remained on the edge of the window-box. It grew bigger and bigger, till it became the figure of a woman, dressed in the finest white gauze, which appeared to be made of millions of starry flakes. She was delicately lovely, but all ice, glittering, dazzling ice. Still she was alive, her eyes shone like two bright stars, but there was no rest or peace in them. She nodded to the window and waved her hand. The little boy was frightened and jumped down off the chair, and then he fancied that a big bird flew past the window.

The next day was bright and frosty, and then came the thaw—and after that the spring. The sun shone, green buds began to appear, the swallows built their nests, and people began to open their windows. The little children began to play in their garden on the roof again. The roses were in splendid bloom that summer; the little girl had learnt a hymn, and there was something in it about roses, and that made her think of her own. She sang it to the little boy, and then he sang it with her—

" Where roses deck the flowery vale,
There, Infant Jesus, we thee hail! "

The children took each other by the hands, kissed the roses and rejoiced in God's bright sunshine, and spoke to it as if the Child Jesus were there. What lovely summer days they were, and how delightful it was to sit out under the fresh rose trees, which seemed never tired of blooming.

Kay and Gerda were looking at a picture-book of birds and animals one day—it had just struck five by the church clock—when Kay said, " Oh, something struck my heart, and I have got something in my eye! "

The little girl put her arms round his neck, he blinked his eye, there was nothing to be seen.

" I believe it is gone," he said, but it was not gone. It was one of those very grains of glass from the mirror, the magic mirror. You remember that horrid mirror, in which all good and great things reflected in it became small and mean, while the bad things were magnified, and every flaw became very apparent.

Poor Kay! a grain of it had gone straight to his heart, and would soon turn it to a lump of ice. He did not feel it any more, but it was still there.

"Why do you cry?" he asked; "it makes you look ugly; there's nothing the matter with me. How horrid!" he suddenly cried; "there's a worm in that rose, and that one is quite crooked; after all, they are nasty roses, and so are the boxes they are growing in!" He kicked the box and broke off two of the roses.

"What are you doing, Kay?" cried the little girl. When he saw her alarm, he broke off another rose, and then ran in, by his own window, and left dear little Gerda alone.

When she next got out the picture-book he said it was only fit for babies in long clothes. When his grandmother told them stories he always had a but—, and if he could manage it, he liked to get behind her chair, put on her spectacles and imitate her. He did it very well, and people laughed at him. He was soon able to imitate every one in the street; he could make fun of all their peculiarities and failings. "He will turn out a clever fellow," said people. But it was all that bit of glass in his heart, that bit of glass in his eye, and it made him tease little Gerde who was so devoted to him. He played quite different games now; he seemed to have grown older. One winter's day, when the snow was falling fast, he brought in a big magnifying glass; he held out the tail of his blue coat, and let the snow-flakes fall upon it.

"Now look through the glass, Gerda!" he said; every snow-flake was magnified, and looked like a lovely flower, or a sharply pointed star.

"Do you see how cleverly they are made," said Kay. "Much more interesting than looking at real flowers, and there is not a single flaw in them, they are perfect, if only they would not melt."

Shortly after, he appeared in his thick gloves, with his sleigh on his back. He shouted right into Gerda's ear, "I have got leave to drive in the big square where the other boys play!" and away he went.

In the big square the bolder boys used to tie their little sleighs to the farm carts and go a long way in this fashion. They had no end of fun over it. Just in the middle of their games, a big sleigh came along; it was painted white, and the occupant wore a white fur coat and cap. The sleigh drove twice round the square, and Kay quickly tied his sleigh on behind. Then off they went, faster and faster, into the next street. The driver turned round and nodded to Kay in the most friendly way, just as if they knew each other. Every time Kay wanted to loose his sleigh, the person nodded again, and Kay stayed where he was, and they drove right out through the town gates. Then the snow began to fall so heavily that the little boy could not see a hand before him as they rushed along. He undid the cords, and tried to get away from the big sleigh, but it was no use, his little sleigh stuck fast, and on they rushed, faster than the wind. He shouted aloud, but nobody heard him, and the sleigh tore on through the snowdrifts. Every now and then it gave a bound, as if they were jumping over hedges and ditches. He was very frightened, and he wanted to say his prayers, but he could only remember the multiplication tables.

The snow-flakes grew bigger and bigger, till at last they looked like big white chickens. All at once they sprang on one side, the big sleigh stopped, and the person who drove got up, coat and cap smothered in snow. It was a tall and upright lady all shining white, the Snow Queen herself.

" We have come along at a good pace, " she said; " but it's cold enough to kill one; creep inside my bearskin coat. "

She took him into the sleigh by her, wrapped him in her furs, and he felt as if he were sinking into a snowdrift.

" Are you still cold? " she asked, and she kissed him on the forehead. Ugh! it was colder than ice, it went to his very heart, which was already more than half ice; he felt as if he were dying, but only for a moment, and then it seemed to have done him good, he no longer felt the cold.

" My sleigh! don't forget my sleigh! " He only remembered it now, it was tied to one of the white chickens which flew along behind them. The Snow Queen kissed Kay again, and then he forgot all about little Gerda, Grandmother, and all the others at home.

" Now I mustn't kiss you any more," she said " or I should kiss you to death! "

Kay looked at her, she was so pretty; a cleverer, more beautiful face could hardly be imagined. She did not seem to be made of ice now, as she was outside the window when she waved her hand to him. In his eyes she was quite perfect, and he was not a bit afraid of her; he told her that he could do mental arithmetic, as far as fractions, and that he knew the number of square miles and the number of inhabitants of the country. She always smiled at him, and he then thought that he surely did not know enough, and he looked up into the wide expanse of heaven, into which they rose higher and higher as she flew with him on a dark cloud, while the storm surged around them, the wind ringing in their ears like well-known old songs.

They flew over woods and lakes, over oceans and islands, the cold wind whistled down below them, the wolves howled, the black crows flew screaming over the sparkling snow, but up above, the moon shone bright and clear—and Kay looked at it all the long, long winter nights; in the day he slept at the Snow Queen's feet.

STORY THREE

THE GARDEN OF THE WOMAN LEARNED IN MAGIC

But how was little Gerda getting on all this long time since Kay left her? Where could he be? Nobody knew, nobody could say anything about him. All that the other boys knew was, that they had seen him tie his little sleigh to a splendid big one which drove away down the street and out of the town gates. Nobody knew where he was, and many tears were shed; little Gerda cried long and bitterly. At last, people said he was dead; he must have fallen into the river which ran close by the town. Oh, what long, dark, winter days those were!

At last the spring came and the sunshine.

" Kay is dead and gone," said little Gerda.

" I don't believe it," said the sunshine.

" He is dead and gone," she said to the swallows.

" We don't believe it," said the swallows, and at last little Gerda did not believe it either.

" I will put on my new red shoes," she said one morning; " those Kay never saw; and then I will go down to the river and ask it about him! "

It was very early in the morning; she kissed the old grandmother, who was still asleep, put on the red shoes, and went quite alone, out by the gate to the river.

" Is it true that you have taken my little playfellow? I will give you my red shoes if you will bring him back to me again."

She thought the little ripples nodded in such a curious way, so she took off her red shoes, her most cherished possessions, and threw them both into the river. They fell close by the shore, and were carried straight back to her by the little wavelets; it seemed as if the river would not accept her offering, as it had not taken little Kay.

She only thought she had not thrown them far enough, so she climbed into a boat which lay among the rushes, then she went right out to the further end of it, and threw the shoes into the water again.   But the boat was loose, and her movements started it off, and it floated away from the shore: she felt it moving and tried to get out, but before she reached the other end the boat was more than a yard from the shore, and was floating away quite quickly.

Little Gerda was terribly frightened, and began to cry, but nobody heard her except the sparrows, and they could not carry her ashore, but they flew alongside twittering as if to cheer her, " We are here, we are here." The boat floated rapidly away with the current; little Gerda sat quite still with only her stockings on; her little red shoes floated behind, but they could not catch up the boat which drifted away faster and faster.

The banks on both sides were very pretty with beautiful flowers, fine old trees, and slopes dotted with sheep and cattle, but not a single person.

" Perhaps the river is taking me to little Kay," thought Gerda, and that cheered her; she sat up and looked at the beautiful green banks for hours.

Then they came to a big cherry garden; there was a little house in it, with curious blue and red windows, it had a thatched roof, and two wooden soldiers stood outside, who presented arms as she sailed past. Gerda called out to them; she thought they were alive, but of course they did not answer; she was quite close to them, for the current drove the boat close to the bank. Gerda called out again, louder than before, and then an old, old woman came out of the house; she was leaning upon a big, hooked stick, and she wore a big sun hat, which was covered with beautiful painted flowers.

"You poor little child," said the old woman, "however were you driven out on this big, strong river into the wide, wide, world alone?" Then she walked right into the water, and caught hold of the boat with her hooked stick; she drew it ashore, and lifted little Gerda out.

Gerda was delighted to be on dry land again, but she was a little bit frightened of the strange old woman.

"Come, tell me who you are, and how you got here," said she.

When Gerda had told her the whole story, and asked her if she had seen Kay, the woman said she had not seen him, but that she expected him. Gerda must not be sad, she was to come and taste her cherries and see her flowers, which were more beautiful than any picture-book; each one had a story to tell. Then she took Gerda by the hand, they went into the little house, and the old woman locked the door.

The windows were very high up, and they were red, blue, and yellow; they threw a very curious light into the room. On the table were quantities of the most delicious cherries, of which Gerda had leave to eat as many as ever she liked. While she was eating, the old woman combed her hair with a golden comb, so that her hair curled, and shone like gold round the pretty little face, which was as sweet as a rose.

"I have long wanted a little girl like you!" said the old woman. "You will see how well we shall get on together." While she combed her hair Gerda had forgotten all about Kay, for the old woman was learned in the magic art, but she was not a bad witch, she only cast spells over people for a little amusement, and she wanted to keep Gerda. She therefore went into the garden and waved her hooked stick over all the rose-bushes, and however beautifully they were flowering, all sank down into the rich black earth without leaving a trace behind them.

The old woman was afraid that if Gerda saw the roses she would be reminded of Kay, and would want to run away. Then she took Gerda into the flower-garden. What a delicious scent there was! and every imaginable flower for every season was in that lovely garden; no picture-book could be brighter or more beautiful. Gerda jumped for joy and played till the sun went down behind the tall cherry trees. Then she was put into a lovely bed with rose coloured silken coverings stuffed with violets; she slept and dreamt as lovely dreams as any queen on her wedding day.

The next day she played with the flowers in the garden again —and many days passed in the same way. Gerda knew every flower, but however many there were, she always thought there was one missing, but which it was she did not know.

One day she was sitting looking at the old woman's sun hat with its painted flowers, and the very prettiest one of them all was a rose. The old woman had forgotten her hat when she charmed the others away. This is the consequence of being absent-minded.

" What! " said Gerda, " are there no roses here? " and she sprang in among the flower beds and sought, but in vain! Her hot tears fell on the very places where the roses used to be; when the warm drops moistened the earth, the rose trees shot up again just as full of bloom as when they sank. Gerda embraced the roses and kissed them, and then she thought of the lovely roses at home, and this brought the thought of little Kay.

" Oh, how I have been delayed," said the little girl, " I ought to have been looking for Kay! Don't you know where he is? " she asked the roses. " Do you think he is dead and gone? "

" He is not dead," said the roses. " For we have been down underground, you know, and all the dead people are there, but Kay is not among them."

" Oh, thank you! " said little Gerda, and then she went to the other flowers and looked into their cups and said, " Do you know where Kay is? "

But each flower stood in the sun and dreamt its own dreams. Little Gerda heard many of these, but never anything about Kay.

And what said the Tiger lilies?

" Do you hear the drum? rub-a-dub, it has only two notes, rub-a-dub, always the same. The wailing of women and the cry of the preacher. The Hindu woman in her long red garment stands on the pile, while the flames surround her and her dead husband. But the woman is only thinking of the living man in the circle round, whose eyes burn with a fiercer fire than that of the flames which consume the body. Do the flames of the heart die in the fire? "

" I understand nothing about that," said little Gerda.

" That is my story," said the Tiger lily.

" What does the convolvulus say? "

" An old castle is perched high over a narrow mountain path, it is closely covered with ivy, almost hiding the old red walls, and creeping up leaf upon leaf right round the balcony where stands a beautiful maiden. She bends over the balustrade and looks eagerly up the road. No rose on its stem is fresher than she; no apple blossom wafted by the wind moves more lightly. Her silken robes rustle softly as she bends over and says, " Will he never come? "

" Is it Kay you mean? " asked Gerda.

" I am only talking about my own story, my dream," answered the convolvulus.

What said the little snowdrop?

" Between two trees a rope with a board is hanging; it is a swing. Two pretty little girls in snowy frocks and green ribbons fluttering on their hats are seated on it. Their brother, who is bigger than they are, stands up behind them; he has his arms round the ropes for supports, and holds in one hand a little bowl and in the other a clay pipe. He is blowing soap-bubbles. As the swing moves the bubbles fly upwards in all their changing colours, the last one still hangs from the pipe swayed by the wind, and the swing goes on. A little black dog runs up, he is almost as light as the bubbles, he stands up on his hind legs and wants to be taken into the swing, but it does not stop. The little dog falls with an angry bark, they jeer at it; the bubble bursts. A swinging plank, a fluttering foam picture—that is my story! "

" I daresay what you tell me is very pretty, but you speak so sadly, and you never mention little Kay."

What says the hyacinth?

" They were three beautiful sisters, all most delicate, and quite transparent. One wore a crimson robe, the other a blue, and the third was pure white. These three danced hand-in-hand, by the edge of the lake in the moonlight. They were human beings, not fairies of the wood. The fragrant air attracted them, and they vanished into the wood; here the fragrance was stronger still. Three coffins glide out of the wood towards the lake, and in them lie the maidens. The fire-flies flutter lightly round them with their little flickering torches. Do these dancing maidens sleep, or are they dead? The scent of the flower says that they are corpses. The evening bell tolls their knell."

" You make me quite sad," said little Gerda; " your perfume is so strong it makes me think of those dead maidens. Oh, is little Kay really dead? The roses have been down underground, and they say no."

" Ding, dong," tolled the hyacinth bells; " we are not tolling for little Kay; we know nothing about him. We sing our song, the only one we know."

And Gerda went on to the buttercups shining among their dark green leaves.

" You are a bright little sun," said Gerda. " Tell me if you know where I shall find my playfellow."

The buttercup shone brightly and returned Gerda's glance. What song could the buttercup sing? It would not be about Kay.

" God's bright sun shone into a little court on the first day of spring. The sunbeams stole down the neighbouring white wall, close to which bloomed the first yellow flower of the season; it shone like burnished gold in the sun. An old woman had brought her arm-chair out into the sun; her granddaughter, a poor and pretty little maid-servant, had come to pay her a short visit, and she kissed her. There was gold, heart's gold, in the kiss. Gold on the lips, gold on the ground, and gold above, in the early morning beams! Now that is my little story," said the buttercup.

" Oh, my poor old grandmother!" sighed Gerda. " She will be longing to see me, and grieving about me, as she did about Kay. But I shall soon go home again and take Kay with me. It is useless for me to ask the flowers about him. They only know their own stories, and have no information to give me."

Then she tucked up her little dress, so that she might run the faster, but the narcissus blossoms struck her on the legs as she jumped over them, so she stopped and said, " Perhaps you can tell me something."

She stooped down close to the flower and listened. What did it say?

" I can see myself, I can see myself," said the narcissus. " Oh, how sweet is my scent. Up there in an attic window stands a little dancing girl half dressed; first she stands on one leg, then on the other, and looks as if she would tread the whole world under her feet. She is only a delusion. She pours some water out of a teapot on to a bit of stuff that she is holding; it is her bodice. ' Cleanliness is a good thing,' she says. Her white dress hangs on a peg; it has been washed in the teapot, too, and dried on the roof. She puts it on, and wraps a saffron coloured scarf round her neck, which makes the dress look whiter. See how high she carries her head, and all upon one stem. I see myself, I see myself! "

" I don't care a bit about all that," said Gerda; " it's no use telling me such stuff."

And then she ran to the end of the garden. The door was fastened, but she pressed the rusty latch, and it gave way. The door sprang open, and little Gerda ran out with bare feet into the wide world. She looked back three times, but nobody came after her. At last she could run no further, and she sat down on a big stone. When she looked round she saw that the summer was over, it was quite late autumn. She would never have known it inside the beautiful garden, where the sun always shone and the flowers of every season were always in bloom.

" Oh, how I have wasted my time," said little Gerda. " It is autumn. I must not rest any longer," and she got up to go on.

Oh, how weary and sore were her little feet, and everything round looked so cold and dreary. The long willow leaves were quite yellow. The damp mist fell off the trees like rain, one leaf dropped after another from the trees, and only the sloe-thorn still bore its fruit, but the sloes were sour and set one's teeth on edge. Oh, how grey and sad it looked, out in the wide world.

FOURTH STORY

PRINCE AND PRINCESS

Gerda was soon obliged to rest again. A big crow hopped on to the snow, just in front of her. It had been sitting looking at her for a long time and wagging its head. Now it said " Caw, caw; good-day, good-day," as well as it could; it meant to be kind to the little girl, and asked her where she was going, alone in the wide world.

Gerda understood the word " alone " and knew how much there was in it, and she told the crow the whole story of her life and adventures, and asked if it had seen Kay.

The crow nodded his head gravely and said, " May be I have, may be I have."

" What, do you really think you have? " cried the little girl, nearly smothering him with her kisses.

" Gently, gently! " said the crow. " I believe it may have been Kay, but he has forgotten you by this time, I expect, for the Princess."

" Does he live with a Princess? " asked Gerda.

" Yes, listen," said the crow; " but it is so difficult to speak your language. If you understand ' crow's language,'[1] I can tell you about it much better."

" No, I have never learnt it," said Gerda; " but grandmother knew it, and used to speak it. If only I had learnt it! "

" It doesn't matter," said the crow. " I will tell you as well as I can, although I may do it rather badly."

Then he told her what he had heard.

" In this kingdom where we are now," said he, " there lives a Princess who is very clever. She has read all the newspapers

---

[1] Children have a kind of language, or gibberish, formed by adding letters or syllables to every word, which is called " crow's language."

in the world, and forgotten them again, so clever is she. One day she was sitting on her throne, which is not such an amusing thing to do either, they say; and she began humming a tune, which happened to be

' Why should I not be married, oh why? '

' Why not indeed? ' said she. And she made up her mind to marry, if she could find a husband who had an answer ready when a question was put to him. She called all the court ladies together, and when they heard what she wanted, they were delighted.

" ' I like that now,' they said. ' I was thinking the same thing myself the other day.'

" Every word I say is true," said the crow, " for I have a tame sweetheart who goes about the Palace whenever she likes. She told me the story."

Of course his sweetheart was a crow, for " birds of a feather flock together," and one crow always chooses another. The newspapers all came out immediately with borders of hearts and the Princess's initials. They gave notice that any young man who was handsome enough might go up to the Palace to speak to the Princess. The one who spoke as if he were quite at home, and spoke well, would be chosen by the Princess as her husband. "Yes, yes, you may believe me, it's as true as I sit here, " said the crow. " The people came crowding in; there was such running, and crushing, but no one was fortunate enough to be chosen, either on the first day, or on the second. They could all of them talk well enough in the street, but when they entered the castle gates, and saw the guard in silver uniforms, and when they went up the stairs through rows of lackeys in gold embroidered liveries, their courage forsook them. When they reached the brilliantly lighted reception rooms, and stood in front of the throne where the Princess was seated, they could think of nothing to say, they only echoed her last words, and of course that was not what she wanted.

It was just as if they had all taken some kind of sleeping powder, which made them lethargic; they did not recover themselves until they got out into the street again, and then they had plenty to say. There was quite a long line of them, reaching from the town gates up to the Palace.

" I went to see them myself," said the crow. " They were hungry and thirsty, but they got nothing at the Palace, not even as much as a glass of tepid water. Some of the wise ones had taken sandwiches with them, but they did not share them with their neighbours; they thought if the others went in to the Princess looking hungry, that there would be more chance for themselves."

" But Kay, little Kay!" asked Gerda; " when did he come? was he amongst the crowd? "

" Give me time, give me time! we are just coming to him. It was on the third day that a little personage came marching cheerfully along, without either carriage or horse. His eyes sparkled like yours, and he had beautiful long hair, but his clothes were very shabby."

" Oh, that was Kay!" said Gerda gleefully; " then I have found him!" and she clapped her hands.

" He had a little knapsack on his back!" said the crow.

" No, it must have been his sleigh; he had it with him when he went away!" said Gerda.

" It may be so," said the crow; " I did not look very particularly! but I know from my sweetheart, that when he entered the Palace gates, and saw the life guards in the silver uniforms, and the lackeys on the stairs in their gold laced liveries, he was not the least bit abashed. He just nodded to them and said, ' It must be very tiresome to stand upon the stairs. I am going inside!' The rooms were blazing with lights. Privy councillors and excellencies without number were walking about barefoot carrying golden vessels; it was enough to make you solemn! His boots creaked fearfully too, but he wasn't a bit upset."

" Oh, I am sure that was Kay!" said Gerda; " I know he had a pair of new boots, I heard them creaking in grandmother's room."

" Yes, indeed they did creak!" said the crow. " But nothing daunted, he went straight up to the Princess, who was sitting on a pearl, as big as a spinning-wheel. Poor, simple boy! all the court ladies and their attendants; the courtiers, and their gentlemen, each attended by a page, were standing round. The nearer the door they stood, so much the greater was their haughtiness; till the footman's boy who always wore slippers and stood in the doorway, was almost too proud even to be looked at."

"It must be awful!" said little Gerda, "and yet Kay has won the Princess!"

"If I had not been a crow, I should have taken her myself, notwithstanding that I am engaged. They say he spoke as well as I could have done myself, when I speak crow-language; at least so my sweetheart says. He was a picture of good looks and gallantry, and then he had not come with any idea of wooing the Princess, but simply to hear her wisdom. He admired her just as much as she admired him!"

"Indeed it was Kay then," said Gerda; "he was so clever he could do mental arithmetic up to fractions. Oh won't you take me to the Palace?"

"It's easy enough to talk," said the crow; "but how are we to manage it? I will talk to my tame sweetheart about it; she will have some advice to give us I daresay, but I am bound to tell you that a little girl like you will never be admitted!"

"Oh, indeed I shall," said Gerda; "when Kay hears that I am here, he will come out at once to fetch me."

"Wait here for me by the stile," said the crow, then he wagged his head and flew off.

The evening had darkened in before he came back. "Caw, caw," he said, "she sends you greeting, and here is a little roll for you, she got it out of the kitchen where there is bread enough, and I daresay you are hungry! It is not possible for you to get into the Palace, you have bare feet, the guards in silver and the lackeys in gold would never allow you to pass. But don't cry, we shall get you in somehow; my sweetheart knows a little back staircase which leads up to the bedroom, and she knows where the key is kept."

Then they went into the garden, into the great avenue where the leaves were, softly one by one; and when the Palace lights went out, one after the other, the crow led little Gerda to the back door, which was ajar.

Oh, how Gerda's heart beat with fear and longing! It was just as if she was about to do something wrong, and yet she only

In the morning, the strange duckling was discovered.

THE UGLY DUCKLING

Page 122

This time it was her grandmother who appeared in the circle of flame.

THE LITTLE MATCH GIRL

Page 159

wanted to know if this really was little Kay. Oh, it must be him, she thought picturing to herself his clever eyes and his long hair. She could see his very smile when they used to sit under the rose trees at home. She thought he would be very glad to see her, and to hear what a long way she had come to find him, and to hear how sad they had all been at home when he did not come back. Oh, it was joy mingled with fear.

They had now reached the stairs, where a little lamp was burning on a shelf. There stood the tame sweetheart, twisting and turning her head to look at Gerda, who made a curtsey, as grandmother had taught her.

" My betrothed has spoken so charmingly to me about you, my little miss! " she said; " your life, ' *Vita*,' as it is called, is most touching! If you will take the lamp, I will go on in front. We shall take the straight road here, and we shall meet no one."

" It seems to me that someone is coming up behind us," said Gerda, as she fancied something rushed past her throwing a shadow on the walls; horses with flowing manes and slender legs; huntsmen, ladies and gentlemen, on horseback.

" Oh, those are only the dreams! " said the crow; " they come to take the thoughts of the noble ladies and gentlemen out hunting. That's a good thing, for you will be able to see them all the better in bed. But don't forget, when you are taken into favour, that you show a grateful spirit."

" Now, there's no need to talk about that," said the crow from the woods.

They now came into the first apartment; it was hung with rose-coloured satin embroidered with flowers. Here again the dreams overtook them, but they flitted by so quickly that Gerda could not distinguish them. The apartments became one more beautiful than the other; they were enough to bewilder anybody. They now reached the bedroom. The ceiling was like a great palm with crystal leaves, and in the middle of the room two beds, each like a lily hung from a golden stem. One was white, and in it lay the Princess; the other was red, and there lay he whom Gerda had come to seek—little Kay! She bent aside one of the crimson leaves, and she saw a little brown neck. It was Kay! She called his name aloud, and held the lamp close to him.

Again the dreams rushed through the room on horseback—he awoke, turned his head—and it was not little Kay.

It was only the Prince's neck which was like his; but he was young and handsome. The princess peeped out of her lily-white bed, and asked what was the matter. Then little Gerda cried and told them all her story, and what the crows had done to help her.

" You poor little thing! " said the Prince and Princess. And they praised the crows, and said that they were not at all angry with them, but they must not do it again. Then they gave them a reward.

" Would you like your liberty? " said the Princess, " or would you prefer permanent posts about the court as court crows with perquisites from the kitchen? "

Both crows curtsied and begged for the permanent posts, for they thought of their old age, and said " it was so good to have something for the old man," as they called it.

The Prince got up and allowed Gerda to sleep in his bed, and he could not have done more. She folded her little hands and thought "how good the people and the animals are;" then she shut her eyes and fell fast asleep. All the dreams came flying back again; this time they looked like angels, and they were dragging a little sleigh with Kay sitting on it, and he nodded. But it was only a dream; so it all vanished when she woke.

Next day she was dressed in silk and velvet from head to foot; they asked her to stay at the Palace and have a good time, but she only begged them to give her a little carriage and horse, and a little pair of boots, so that she might drive out into the wide world to look for Kay.

They gave her a pair of boots and a muff. She was beautifully dressed, and when she was ready to start, there before the door stood a new chariot of pure gold. The Prince's and Princess's coat of arms were emblazoned on it, and shone like a star. Coachman, footman, and outrider, for there was even an outrider, all wore golden crowns. The Prince and Princess themselves helped her into the carriage and wished her joy. The wood crow, who was now married, accompanied her for the first three miles, he sat beside Gerda, for he could not ride with his back to the horses; the other crow stood at the door and flapped her wings, she did not go with them, for she suffered from headache since she had been a kitchen pensioner—the consequence of eating too much. The chariot was stored with sugar biscuits, and there were fruit and ginger nuts under the seat. "Good-bye, good-bye," cried the Prince and Princess; little Gerda wept and the crow wept too. At the end of the first few miles the crow said good-bye, and this was the hardest parting of all. It flew up into a tree and flapped its big black wings as long as it could see the chariot which shone like the brightest sunshine.

FIFTH STORY

THE LITTLE ROBBER GIRL

They drove on through a dark wood, where the chariot lighted up the way and blinded the robbers by its glare; it was more than they could bear.

"It is gold, it is gold!" they cried, and darting forward, seized the horses, and killed the postilions, the coachman, and footman. They then dragged little Gerda out of the carriage.

"She is fat, and she is pretty, she has been fattened on nuts!" said the old robber woman, who had a long beard, and eyebrows that hung down over her eyes. "She is as good as a fat lamb, and how nice she will taste!" She drew out her sharp knife as she said this; it glittered horribly. "Oh!" screamed the old woman at the same moment, for her little daughter had come up behind her, and she was biting her ear. She hung on her back, as wild and as savage a little animal as you could wish to find. "You bad, wicked child!" said the mother, but she was prevented from killing Gerda on this occasion.

"She shall play with me," said the little robber girl; "she shall give me her muff, and her pretty dress, and she shall sleep in my bed." Then she bit her mother again and made her dance. All the robbers laughed and said, "Look at her dancing with her cub!"

"I want to get into the carriage," said the little robber girl, and she always had her own way, because she was so spoilt and stubborn. She and Gerda got into the carriage, and then they drove over stubble and stones further and further into the wood. The little robber girl was as big as Gerda, but much stronger; she had broader shoulders, and darker skin, her eyes were quite black, with almost a melancholy expression. She put her arm round Gerda's waist and said,—

"They shan't kill you as long as I don't get angry with you; you must surely be a Princess!"

"No," said little Gerda, and then she told her all her adventures, and how fond she was of Kay.

The robber girl looked earnestly at her, gave a little nod, and said, "They shan't kill you even if I am angry with you. I will do it myself." Then she dried Gerda's eyes, and stuck her own hands into the pretty muff, which was so soft and warm.

At last the chariot stopped; they were in the courtyard of a robber's castle, the walls of which were cracked from top to bottom. Ravens and crows flew in and out of every hole, and big bull-dogs, which each looked ready to devour somebody, jumped about as high as they could, but they did not bark, for it was not allowed. A big fire was burning in the middle of the stone floor of the smoky old hall. The smoke all went up to the ceiling where it had to find a way out for itself. Soup was boiling in a big cauldron over the fire, and hares and rabbits were roasting on the spits.

"You shall sleep with me and all my little pets to-night," said the robber girl.

When they had had something to eat and drink they went along to one corner which was spread with straw and rugs. There were nearly a hundred pigeons roosting overhead on the rafters and beams. They seemed to be asleep, but they fluttered about a little when the children came in.

"They are all mine," said the little robber girl, seizing one of the nearest. She held it by the legs and shook it till it flapped its wings. "Kiss it," she cried, dashing it at Gerda's face. "Those are the wood pigeons," she added, pointing to some laths fixed across a big hole high up on the walls; "they are a regular rabble; they would fly away directly if they were not locked in. And here is my old sweetheart Be," dragging forward a reindeer by the horn; it was tied up, and it had a bright copper ring round its neck. "We have to keep him close too, or he would run off. Every single night I tickle his neck with my bright knife, he is so frightened of it." The little girl produced a long knife out of a hole in the wall and drew it across the reindeer's neck. The poor animal laughed and kicked, and the robber girl laughed and pulled Gerda down into the bed with her.

"Do you have that knife by you while you are asleep?" asked Gerda, looking rather frightened.

"I always sleep with a knife," said the little robber girl. "You never know what will happen. But now tell me again what you told me before about little Kay, and why you went out into the world." So Gerda told her all about it again, and the wood pigeons cooed up in their cage above them, the other pigeons were asleep. The little robber girl put her arm round Gerda's neck and went to sleep with the knife in her other hand, and she was soon snoring. But Gerda would not close her eyes; she did not know whether she was to live or to die. The robbers sat round the fire, eating and drinking, and the old woman was turning somersaults. This sight terrified the poor little girl. Then the wood pigeons said, "Coo, coo, we have seen little Kay, his sleigh was drawn by a white chicken and he was sitting in the Snow Queen's sleigh; it was floating low down over the trees, while we were in our nests. She blew upon us young ones, and they all died except we two; coo, coo."

"What are you saying up there?" asked Gerda. "Where was the Snow Queen going? Do you know anything about it?"

"She was most likely going to Lapland, because there is always snow and ice there! Ask the reindeer who is tied up there."

"There is ice and snow, and it's a splendid place," said the reindeer. "You can run and jump about where you like on those big glittering plains. The Snow Queen has her summer tent there, but her permanent castle is up at the North Pole, on the island which is called Spitzbergen!"

"Oh Kay, little Kay!" sighed Gerda.

"Lie still, or I shall stick the knife into you!" said the robber girl.

In the morning Gerda told her all that the wood pigeons had

said, and the little robber girl looked quite solemn, but she nodded her head and said, " No matter, no matter! Do you know where Lapland is? " she asked the reindeer.

" Who should know better than I," said the animal, its eyes dancing. " I was born and brought up there, and I used to leap about on the snow-fields."

" Listen," said the robber girl. " You see that all our men folks are away, but mother is still here, and she will stay; but later on in the morning she will take a drink out of the big bottle there, and after that she will have a nap—then I will do something for you." Then she jumped out of bed, ran along to her mother and pulled her beard, and said, " Good-morning, my own dear nanny-goat! " And her mother filliped her nose till it was red and blue; but it was all affection.

As soon as her mother had had her draught from the bottle and had dropped asleep, the little robber girl went along to the reindeer, and said, " I should have the greatest pleasure in the world in keeping you here, to tickle you with my knife, because you are such fun then; however, it does not matter. I will untie your halter and help you outside so that you may run away to Lapland, but you must put your best foot foremost, and take this little girl for me to the Snow Queen's palace, where her playfellow is. I have no doubt you heard what she was telling me, for she spoke loud enough, and you are generally eaves-dropping! "

The reindeer jumped into the air for joy. The robber girl lifted little Gerda up, and had the forethought to tie her on, nay, even to give her a little cushion to sit upon. " Here, after all, I will give you your fur boots back, for it will be very cold, but I will keep your muff, it is too pretty to part with. Still you shan't be cold. Here are my mother's big mittens for you, they will reach up to your elbows; here, stick your hands in! Now your hands look just like my nasty mother's."

Gerda shed tears of joy.

" I don't like you to whimper! " said the little robber girl. " You ought to be looking delighted; and here are two loaves and a ham for you, so that you shan't starve."

These things were tied on to the back of the reindeer; the little robber girl opened the door, called in all the big dogs, and

then she cut the halter with her knife, and said to the reindeer,
" Now run, but take care of my little girl! "

Gerda stretched out her hands in the big mittens to the
robber girl and said good-bye; and then the reindeer darted
off over briars and bushes, through the big wood, over swamps
and plains, as fast as it could go. The wolves howled and the
ravens screamed, while the red lights quivered up in the sky.

" There are my old northern lights," said the reindeer; "see
how they flash! " and on it rushed faster than ever, day and
night. The loaves were eaten, and the ham too, and then they
were in Lapland.

SIXTH STORY

THE LAPP WOMAN AND THE FINN WOMAN

They stopped by a little hut, a very poverty-stricken one;
the roof sloped right down to the ground, and the door was so
low that the people had to creep on hands and knees when they
wanted to go in or out. There was nobody at home here but
an old Lapp woman, who was frying fish over a train-oil lamp.
The reindeer told her all Gerda's story, but it told its own first;
for it thought it was much the most important. Gerda was so
overcome by the cold that she could not speak at all.

" Oh you poor creatures! " said the Lapp woman; " you've
got a long way to go yet; you will have to go hundreds of miles
into Finmark, for the Snow Queen is paying a country visit
there, and she burns blue lights every night. I will write a few
words on a dried stock-fish, for I have no paper. I will give it
to you to take to the Finn woman up there. She will be better
able to direct you than I can."

So when Gerda was warmed, and had eaten and drunk something, the Lapp woman wrote a few words on a dried stock-fish
and gave it to her, bidding her take good care of it. Then she
tied her on to the reindeer again, and off they flew. Flicker,
flicker, went the beautiful blue northern lights up in the sky all
night long;—at last they came to Finmark, and knocked on the
Finn woman's chimney, for she had no door at all.

There was such a heat inside that the Finn woman went about almost naked; she was little and very grubby. She at once loosened Gerda's things, and took off the mittens and the boots, or she would have been too hot. Then she put a piece of ice on the reindeer's head, and after that she read what was written on the stock-fish. She read it three times, and then she knew it by heart, and put the fish into the pot for dinner; there was no reason why it should not be eaten, and she never wasted anything.

Again the reindeer told his own story first, and then little Gerda's. The Finn woman blinked with her wise eyes, but she said nothing.

"You are so clever," said the reindeer, "I know you can bind all the winds of the world with a bit of sewing cotton. When a skipper unties one knot he gets a good wind, when he unties two it blows hard, and if he undoes the third and the fourth he brings a storm about his head wild enough to blow down the forest trees. Won't you give the little girl a drink, so that she may have the strength of twelve men to overcome the Snow Queen?"

"The strength of twelve men," said the Finn woman. "Yes, that will be about enough."

She went along to a shelf and took down a big folded skin, which she unrolled. There were curious characters written on it, and the Finn woman read till the perspiration poured down her forehead.

But the reindeer again implored her to give Gerda something, and Gerda looked at her with such beseeching eyes, full of tears, that the Finn woman began blinking again, and drew the reindeer along into a corner, where she whispered to it, at the same time putting fresh ice on its head.

"Little Kay is certainly with the Snow Queen, and he is delighted with everything there. He thinks it is the best place in the world, but that is because he has got a splinter of glass in his heart and a grain of glass in his eye. They will have to come out first, or he will never be human again, and the Snow Queen will keep him in her power!"

"But can't you give little Gerda something to take which will give her power to conquer it all?"

" I can't give her greater power than she already has.
Don't you see how great it is? Don't you see how both man
and beast have to serve her? How she has got on as well as she
has on her bare feet? We must not tell her what power she
has; it is in her heart, because she is such a sweet innocent child.
If she can't reach the Snow Queen herself, then we can't help
her. The Snow Queen's gardens begin just two miles from
here; you can carry the little girl as far as that. Put her down
by the big bush standing there in the snow covered with red
berries. Don't stand gossiping, but hurry back to me! " Then
the Finn woman lifted Gerda on to the reindeer's back, and it
rushed off as hard as it could.

" Oh, I have not got my boots, and I have not got my
mittens! " cried little Gerda.

She soon felt the want of them in that cutting wind, but the
reindeer did not dare to stop. It ran on till it came to the bush
with the red berries. There it put Gerda down, and kissed her
on the mouth, while big shining tears trickled down its face.
Then it ran back again as fast as ever it could. There stood
poor little Gerda, without shoes or gloves, in the middle of
freezing icebound Finmark.

She ran forward as quickly as she could. A whole regiment
of snow-flakes came towards her; they did not fall from the
sky, for it was quite clear, with the northern lights shining
brightly. No; these snow-flakes ran along the ground, and the
nearer they came the bigger they grew. Gerda remembered
well how big and ingenious they looked under the magnifying
glass. But the size of these was monstrous, they were alive, they
were the Snow Queen's advanced guard, and they took the most
curious shapes. Some looked like big, horrid porcupines, some
like bundles of knotted snakes with their heads sticking out.
Others, again, were like fat little bears with bristling hair, but all
were dazzling white and living snow-flakes.

Then little Gerda said the Lord's Prayer, and the cold was
so great that her breath froze as it came out of her mouth, and
she could see it like a cloud of smoke in front of her. It grew
thicker and thicker, till it formed itself into bright little angels
who grew bigger and bigger when they touched the ground.
They all wore helmets and carried shields and spears in their

hands. More and more of them appeared, and when Gerda had finished her prayer she was surrounded by a whole legion. They pierced the snow-flakes with their spears and shivered them into a hundred pieces, and little Gerda walked fearlessly and undauntedly through them. The angels touched her hands and her feet, and then she hardly felt how cold it was, but walked quickly on towards the Palace of the Snow Queen.

Now we must see what Kay was about. He was not thinking about Gerda at all, least of all that she was just outside the Palace.

SEVENTH STORY

WHAT HAPPENED IN THE SNOW QUEEN'S PALACE AND AFTERWARDS

The Palace walls were made of drifted snow, and the windows and doors of the biting winds. There were over a hundred rooms in it, shaped just as the snow had drifted. The biggest one stretched for many miles. They were all lighted by the strongest northern lights. All the rooms were immensely big and empty, and glittering in their iciness. There was never any gaiety in them; not even so much as a ball for the little bears, when the storms might have turned up as the orchestra, and the polar bears might have walked about on their hind legs and shown off their grand manners. There was never even a little game-playing party, for such games as " touch last " or " the biter bit "—no, not even a little gossip over the coffee cups for the white fox misses. Immense, vast, and cold were the Snow Queen's halls. The northern lights came and went with such regularity that you could count the seconds between their coming and going. In the midst of these neverending snow-halls was a frozen lake. It was broken up on the surface into a thousand bits, but each piece was so exactly like the others that the whole formed a perfect work of art. The Snow Queen sat in the very middle of it when she sat at home. She then said that she was sitting on " The Mirror of Reason," and that it was the best and only one in the world.

Little Kay was blue with cold, nay, almost black; but he did not know it, for the Snow Queen had kissed away the icy shiverings, and his heart was little better than a lump of ice. He went about dragging some sharp, flat pieces of ice, which he placed in all sorts of patterns, trying to make something out of them; just as when we at home have little tablets of wood, with which we make patterns, and call them a " Chinese puzzle."

Kay's patterns were most ingenious, because they were the " Ice puzzles of Reason." In his eyes they were first-rate and of the greatest importance: this was because of the grain of glass still in his eye. He made many patterns forming words, but he never could find out the right way to place them for one particular word, a word he was most anxious to make. It was " Eternity." The Snow Queen had said to him that if he could find out this word he should be his own master, and she would give him the whole world and a new pair of skates. But he could not discover it.

" Now I am going to fly away to the warm countries," said the Snow Queen. " I want to go and peep into the black cauldrons!" She meant the volcanoes Etna and Vesuvius by this. " I must whiten them a little; it does them good, and the lemons and the grapes too!" And away she flew.

Kay sat quite alone in all those many miles of empty ice halls. He looked at his bits of ice, and thought and thought, till something gave way within him. He sat so stiff and immovable that one might have thought he was frozen to death.

Then it was that little Gerda walked into the Palace, through the great gates in a biting wind. She said her evening prayer, and the wind dropped as if lulled to sleep, and she walked on into the big empty hall. She saw Kay, and knew him at once; she flung her arms round his neck, held him fast, and cried, " Kay, little Kay, have I found you at last?"

But he sat still, rigid and cold.

Then little Gerda shed hot tears; they fell upon his breast and penetrated to his heart. Here they thawed the lump of ice, and melted the little bit of the mirror which was in it. He looked at her, and she sang,—

" Where roses deck the flowery vale,
There, Infant Jesus, thee we hail!"

Then Kay burst into tears; he cried so much that the grain of glass was washed out of his eye. He knew her, and shouted with joy, " Gerda, dear little Gerda! where have you been for such a long time? And where have I been? " He looked round and said, " How cold it is here; how empty and vast! " He kept tight hold of Gerda, who laughed and cried for joy. Their happiness was so heavenly that even the bits of ice danced for joy around them; and when they settled down, there they lay! just in the very position the Snow Queen had told Kay he must find out, if he was to become his own master and have the whole world and a new pair of skates.

Gerda kissed his cheeks and they grew rosy, she kissed his eyes and they shone like hers, she kissed his hands and his feet, and he became well and strong. The Snow Queen might come home whenever she liked, his order of release was written there in shining letters of ice.

They took hold of each other's hands and wandered out of the big Palace. They talked about grandmother, and about the roses upon the roof. Wherever they went the winds lay still and the sun broke through the clouds. When they reached the bush with the red berries they found the reindeer waiting for them, and he had brought another young reindeer with him, whose udders were full. The children drank her warm milk and kissed her on the mouth. Then they carried Kay and Gerda, first to the Finn woman, in whose heated hut they warmed themselves and received directions about the homeward journey. Then they went on to the Lapp woman; she had made new clothes for them and prepared her sledge. Both the reindeer ran by their side, to the boundaries of the country; here the first green buds appeared, and they said " Good-bye " to the reindeer and the Lapp woman. They heard the first little birds twittering and saw the buds in the forest. Out of it came riding a young girl on a beautiful horse, which Gerda knew, for it had drawn the golden chariot. She had a scarlet cap on her head and pistols in her belt; it was the little robber girl, who was tired of being at home. She was riding northwards to see how she liked it before she tried some other part of the world. She knew them again, and Gerda recognised her with delight.

" You are a nice fellow to go tramping off! " she said to

little Kay. " I should like to know if you deserve to have some-body running to the end of the world for your sake! "

But Gerda patted her cheek, and asked about the Prince and Princess.

" They are travelling in foreign countries," said the robber girl.

" But the crow? " asked Gerda.

" Oh, the crow is dead! " she answered. " The tame sweet-heart is a widow, and goes about with a bit of black wool tied round her leg. She pities herself bitterly, but it's all nonsense! But tell me how you got on yourself, and where you found him."

Gerda and Kay both told her all about it.

" Snip, snap, snurre, it's all right at last then! " she said, and she took hold of their hands and promised that if she ever passed through their town she would pay them a visit. Then she rode off into the wide world. But Kay and Gerda walked on, hand in hand, and wherever they went, they found the most delightful spring and blooming flowers. Soon they recognised the big town where they lived, with its tall towers, in which the bells still rang their merry peals. They went straight on to grandmother's door, up the stairs, and into her room. Every-thing was just as they had left it, and the old clock ticked in the corner, and the hands pointed to the time. As they went through the door into the room they perceived that they were grown up. The roses clustered round the open window, and there stood their two little chairs. Kay and Gerda sat down upon them, still holding each other by the hand. All the cold empty grandeur of the Snow Queen's palace had passed from their memory like a bad dream. Grandmother sat in God's warm sunshine reading from her Bible.

" Without ye become as little children ye cannot enter into the Kingdom of Heaven."

Kay and Gerda looked into each other's eyes, and then all at once the meaning of the old hymn came to them.

" Where roses deck the flowery vale,
There, Infant Jesus, we thee hail! "

And there they both sat, grown up and yet children, children at heart; and it was summer—warm, beautiful summer.

A ROSE FROM HOMER'S GRAVE

THE nightingale's love for the rose pervades all the songs of the East; in those silent starlight nights the winged songster invariably brings a serenade to his scented flower.

Not far from Smyrna, under the stately plaintain trees where the merchant drives his laden camels, which tread heavily on hallowed ground, and carry their long necks proudly, I saw a blooming hedge of roses. Wild doves fluttered from branch to branch of the tall trees, and where the sunbeams caught their wings they shone like mother of pearl. There was one flower on the rose hedge more beautiful than all the rest, and to this one the nightingale poured out all the yearning of its love. But the rose was silent, not a single dew-drop lay like a tear of compassion upon its petals, while it bent his head towards a heap of stones.

"Here rests the greatest singer the world has ever known!" said the rose. "I will scent his grave and strew my petals over it when the storms tear them off. The singer of the *Iliad* returned to earth here, this earth whence I sprang!—I, a rose from Homer's grave, am too sacred to bloom for a mere nightingale!"

And the nightingale sang till from very grief his heart broke.

The camel driver came with his laden camels and his black slaves; his little boy found the dead bird, and buried the little songster in Homer's grave. The rose trembled in the wind. Night came; the rose folded her petals tightly and dreamt that it was a beautiful sunny day, and that a crowd of strange Frankish men came on a pilgrimage to Homer's grave. Among the strangers was a singer from the North, from the home of mists and northern lights. He broke off the rose and pressed it in a book, and so carried it away with him to another part of the world, to his distant Fatherland. And the rose withered away from grief lying tightly pressed in the narrow book, till he opened it in his home and said, " here is a rose from Homer's grave! "

Now this is what the flower dreamt, and it woke up shivering in the wind; a dew-drop fell from its petals upon the singer's grave. The sun rose and the day was very hot, the rose bloomed in greater beauty than ever in the warmth of Asia.

Footsteps were heard and the strange Franks whom the rose saw in its dream came up. Among the strangers was a poet from the North, he broke off the rose and pressed a kiss upon its dewy freshness, and carried it with him to the home of mists and northern lights. The relics of the rose rest now like a mummy between the leaves of his *Iliad*, and as in its dream it hears him say when he opens the book, " here is a rose from Homer's grave! "

THE EMPEROR'S NEW CLOTHES

MANY years ago there was an Emperor who was so excessively fond of new clothes that he spent all his money on them. He cared nothing about his soldiers nor for the theatre, nor for driving in the woods except for the sake of showing off his new clothes. He had a costume for every hour in the day, and instead of saying as one does about any other King or Emperor, "He is in his council chamber," here one always said, "The Emperor is in his dressing-room."

Life was very gay in the great town where he lived; hosts of strangers came to visit it every day, and among them one day two swindlers. They gave themselves out as weavers, and said that they knew how to weave the most beautiful stuffs imaginable. Not only were the colours and patterns unusually fine, but the clothes that were made of the stuffs had the peculiar quality of becoming invisible to every person who was not fit for the office he held, or if he was impossibly dull.

"Those must be splendid clothes," thought the Emperor. "By wearing them I should be able to discover which men in my kingdom are unfitted for their posts. I shall distinguish the wise men from the fools. Yes, I certainly must order some of that stuff to be woven for me."

He paid the two swindlers a lot of money in advance, so that they might begin their work at once.

They did put up two looms and pretended to weave, but they had nothing whatever upon their shuttles. At the outset

192

they asked for a quantity of the finest silk and the purest gold thread, all of which they put into their own bags while they worked away at the empty looms far into the night.

"I should like to know how those weavers are getting on with the stuff," thought the Emperor; but he felt a little queer when he reflected that anyone who was stupid or unfit for his post would not be able to see it. He certainly thought that he need have no fears for himself, but still he thought he would send somebody else first to see how it was getting on. Everybody in the town knew what wonderful power the stuff possessed, and everyone was anxious to see how stupid his neighbour was.

"I will send my faithful old minister to the weavers," thought the Emperor. "He will be best able to see how the stuff looks, for he is a clever man and no one fulfils his duties better than he does!"

So the good old minister went into the room where the two swindlers sat working at the empty loom.

"Heaven preserve us!" thought the old minister, opening his eyes very wide. "Why I can't see a thing!" But he took care not to say so.

Both the swindlers begged him to be good enough to step a little nearer, and asked if he did not think it a good pattern and beautiful colouring. They pointed to the empty loom, and the poor old minister stared as hard as he could, but he could not see anything, for of course there was nothing to see.

"Good heavens!" thought he, "is it possible that I am a fool. I have never thought so, and nobody must know it. Am I not fit for my post? It will never do to say that I cannot see the stuffs."

"Well, sir, you don't say anything about the stuff," said the one who was pretending to weave.

"Oh, it is beautiful! quite charming!" said the old minister looking through his spectacles; "this pattern and these colours! I will certainly tell the Emperor that the stuff pleases me very much."

"We are delighted to hear you say so," said the swindlers, and then they named all the colours and described the peculiar pattern. The old minister paid great attention to what they

said, so as to be able to repeat it when he got home to the
Emperor.

Then the swindlers went on to demand more money, more
silk, and more gold, to be able to proceed with the weaving;
but they put it all into their own pockets—not a single strand
was ever put into the loom, but they went on as before weaving
at the empty loom.

The Emperor soon sent another faithful official to see how
the stuff was getting on, and if it would soon be ready.   The
same thing happened to him as to the minister; he looked and
looked, but as there was only the empty loom, he could see
nothing at all.

" Is not this a beautiful piece of stuff? " said both the
swindlers, showing and explaining the beautiful pattern and
colours which were not there to be seen.

" I know I am not a fool! " thought the man, " so it must
be that I am unfit for my good post!   It is very strange though!
however one must not let it appear!   So he praised the stuff he
did not see, and assured them of his delight in the beautiful
colours and the originality of the design.   " It is absolutely
charming! " he said to the Emperor.   Everybody in the town
was talking about this splendid stuff.

Now the Emperor thought he would like to see it while it
was still on the loom.   So, accompanied by a number of selected
courtiers, among whom were the two faithful officials who had
already seen the imaginary stuff, he went to visit the crafty
impostors, who were working away as hard as ever they could at
the empty loom.

" It is magnificent! " said both the honest officials.   " Only
see, your Majesty, what a design!   What colours! "   And they
pointed to the empty loom, for they thought no doubt the
others could see the stuff.

" What! " thought the Emperor; " I see nothing at all!
This is terrible!   Am I a fool?   Am I not fit to be Emperor?
Why, nothing worse could happen to me! "

" Oh, it is beautiful! " said the Emperor.   " It has my
highest approval! " and he nodded his satisfaction as he gazed
at the empty loom.   Nothing would induce him to say that he
could not see anything.

The whole suite gazed and gazed, but saw nothing more than all the others. However, they all exclaimed with his Majesty, " It is very beautiful! " and they advised him to wear a suit made of this wonderful cloth on the occasion of a great procession which was just about to take place. " It is magnificent! gorgeous! " excellent! went from mouth to mouth; they were all equally delighted with it. The Emperor gave each of the rogues an order of knighthood to be worn in their buttonholes and the title of " Gentlemen weavers."

The swindlers sat up the whole night, before the day on which the procession was to take place, burning sixteen candles; so that people might see how anxious they were to get the Emperor's new clothes ready. They pretended to take the stuff off the loom. They cut it out in the air with a huge pair of scissors, and they stitched away with needles without any thread in them. At last they said: " Now the Emperor's new clothes are ready! "

The Emperor, with his grandest courtiers, went to them himself, and both the swindlers raised one arm in the air, as if they were holding something, and said: " See, these are the trousers, this is the coat, here is the mantle! " and so on. " It is as light as a spider's web. One might think one had nothing on, but that is the very beauty of it! "

" Yes! " said all the courtiers, but they could not see anything, for there was nothing to see.

" Will your imperial majesty be graciously pleased to take off your clothes," said the impostors, " so that we may put on the new ones, along here before the great mirror."

The Emperor took off all his clothes, and the impostors pretended to give him one article of dress after the other, of the new ones which they had pretended to make. They pretended to fasten something round his waist and to tie on something; this was the train, and the Emperor turned round and round in front of the mirror.

" How well his majesty looks in the new clothes! How becoming they are! " cried all the people round. " What a design, and what colours! They are most gorgeous robes! "

" The canopy is waiting outside which is to be carried over

your majesty in the procession," said the master of the ceremonies.

"Well, I am quite ready," said the Emperor. "Don't the clothes fit well?" and then he turned round again in front of the mirror, so that he should seem to be looking at his grand things.

The chamberlains who were to carry the train stooped and pretended to lift it from the ground with both hands, and they walked along with their hands in the air. They dared not let it appear that they could not see anything.

Then the Emperor walked along in the procession under the gorgeous canopy, and everybody in the streets and at the windows exclaimed, "How beautiful the Emperor's new clothes are! What a splendid train! And they fit to perfection!" Nobody would let it appear that he could see nothing, for then he would not be fit for his post, or else he was a fool.

None of the Emperor's clothes had been so successful before.

"But he has got nothing on," said a little child.

"Oh, listen to the innocent," said its father; and one person whispered to the other what the child had said. "He has nothing on; a child says he has nothing on!"

"But he has nothing on!" at last cried all the people.

The Emperor writhed, for he knew it was true, but he thought "the procession must go on now," so held himself stiffer than ever, and the chamberlains held up the invisible train.

THE NAUGHTY BOY

THERE was once an old poet, he was a good, honest old poet. One evening when he was sitting quietly at home a terrible storm came on; the rain poured down in torrents, but the old poet was warm and cosy in his corner beside the stove, where the fire blazed brightly and the apples were fizzling.

" There won't be a dry thread on any poor creature who is out in this rain," said he, for he was such a kind-hearted man.

" Oh, please open the door for me, I am so cold and so wet! " cried a little child outside. It kept on crying and knocking at the door, while the rain poured down and the wind shook the windows.

" Poor little creature! " said the old poet, as he went to open the door.

There stood a little boy, who was quite naked, and the water was streaming out of his yellow hair. He was shaking with cold, and if he had not been taken in he must surely have died of the cold.

" You poor little fellow! " said the old poet, taking him by the hand. " Come to me and I will soon have you warm! You shall have some wine and a roasted apple, for you are a beautiful boy! "

And so he really was. His eyes were like two bright stars, and although dripping wet, his hair hung in lovely curls. He looked like a little angel child, but the cold made him very pale, and he was shivering in every limb. He had a beautiful cross-bow in his hand, but it was quite spoilt by the rain; all the colours in the pretty arrows had run from the wet.

The old poet sat down by the stove and took the little boy on his knee; he wrung the water out of his hair, warmed his hands, and heated some sweet wine for him. He soon recovered, and the roses came back to his cheeks; he jumped down and skipped and danced round the old poet.

" You are a merry boy! " said the old man. " What is your name? "

" I am called Cupid! " he answered.   " Don't you know me?
There lies my bow—and I know how to shoot with it, I can tell
you!   Look, it is getting quite fine again, the moon is shining! "

" But your bow is spoilt," said the old poet.

" That is a pity," said the little boy, and he took it up and
looked at it.   " Oh, it is quite dry again—it is not a bit the
worse, the string is quite tight.   See, I will try it! "

He then drew his bow, put an arrow in, took aim, and shot
right into the old man's heart.

" Do you see now that my bow is not spoilt? " said he as
he ran away laughing.   The naughty boy! to shoot the old poet
who had been so kind to him, and had given him the warm wine
and the best apple.

The good old man lay upon the floor and wept, he had really
been shot right through the heart, and he said: " Fie, what a
naughty boy that Cupid is!   I will tell all the good children
about him, so that they may take care never to play with him,
or he will certainly do them some mischief."

All the good boys and girls to whom he told this story took
good care to avoid wicked little Cupid, but he cheats them over
and over again, for he is so crafty.

When the students go home from their lectures, he runs
along by their side with a black gown on and a book under his
arm.   They don't recognise him, and take hold of his arm
thinking he is a fellow-student, but then he sends a dart into
their bosoms.   When the girls go home from their classes, and
even when they are in church he lays wait for them.   He is the
same for all time and everyone alike.   He sits in the great
chandelier in the theatre, and makes such a bright hot flame;
people fancy it is a lamp, but they are soon undeceived.   He
runs about the Royal Gardens and on the ramparts; nay, once
he even shot your father and mother right through the heart!
Ask them about it and you will hear what they say.   Oh! he
is a bad boy this same Cupid.   Never have anything to do with
him!   He waylays everyone alike, and even your poor old grandmother did not escape his dart.   It was a long time ago, and the
effect has passed away, but that kind of thing is never forgotten.
Fie, fie! wicked little Cupid!   But now you know all about him,
so beware!

HOLGER THE DANE

THERE is an old castle in Denmark which is called Kronborg; it juts out into the Sound, and great ships sail past it every day by hundreds. There are Russian and English and Prussian ships, and many other nationalities; they all fire a salute when they pass the old castle; " boom," and the castle answers, " boom." That is the way cannons say " how do you do " and " thank you." No ships sail in the winter, the water is frozen over, right up to the Swedish coast, and it becomes a great high road. Swedish and Danish flags fly, and the Danes and the Swedes say " how do you do " and " thank you " to each other, not with cannons, but with a friendly shake of the hand. They buy fancy bread and cakes of each other, for strange food tastes best. But old Kronborg is always the chief feature, and down inside it, in the deep dark cellar, lives Holger the Dane. He is clad in steel and iron, and rests his head upon his strong arms, and his long beard hangs over the marble table where it has grown fast; he sleeps and dreams, but in his dreams he sees all that is happening up there in Denmark. Every Christmas Eve a holy angel comes and tells him that he has dreamt aright, and that he may go to sleep again, because Denmark is not yet in any real danger. But should danger come, then old Holger the Dane will rise up, so that the table will burst asunder when he wrenches his beard away from it, then he will come forward and strike a blow that will resound in all parts of the world,

An old grandfather was sitting telling his little grandson all this about Holger the Dane, and the little boy knew that all that his grandfather said was true. While the old man was talking, he sat carving a big wooden figure; it was to represent Holger the Dane as the figurehead of a ship; for the old grandfather was a carver, the sort of man who carves a figurehead for each ship, according to its name. Here he had carved Holger the Dane, who stood erect and proud, with his long beard. He held in his hand a great broadsword, and rested his other hand upon a shield with the Danish Arms. The old grandfather had so much to tell about remarkable Danish men and women, that the little boy at last thought he must know as much as Holger the Dane, who, after all, only dreamt about these things. When the little fellow went to bed, he thought so much about the things he had heard, and he pressed his chin so hard into the quilt, that he thought it was a long beard grown fast to it.

The old grandfather remained sitting at his work, carving away at the last bit of it, which was the arms on the shield. At last it was finished. He looked at it complete, and thought of all the things he had heard and read, and what he had been telling the little boy in the evening. He nodded, and wiped his spectacles, and put them on again, and said, " Well, I don't suppose Holger the Dane will come in my time, but perhaps the boy in bed there may see him, and have his share of the fighting when the time comes." And the old grandfather nodded again, and the more he looked at his Holger the Dane, the more plain it became to him that the figure he had made was a good one. He even fancied that the colour came into it, and that the armour shone like polished steel; the hearts in the Danish Arms [1] got redder and redder, and the crowns on the springing lions became golden.

" It's the finest coat of Arms in the world! " said the old man. " The lions are strength, and the hearts are love and tenderness! " He looked at the uppermost lion, and thought about King Knuth who bound the mighty England to Denmark's throne; and he looked at the second lion and thought of Waldemar, who united Denmark and subdued the Vandals. He looked at the third lion and thought of Margaret, who united

[1] The Danish Arms consist of three lions between nine hearts.

Denmark, Sweden and Norway; when he looked at the red hearts, they shone more brightly than ever, they became waving flames of fire, and in his thoughts he followed each of them.

The first led him into a narrow, dark prison; he saw a prisoner, a beautiful woman, Eleonora Ulfeld, daughter of Christian the Fourth. The flame placed itself like a rose on her bosom, and bloomed in harmony with her heart; she was the noblest and best of Denmark's women. "That is one heart in the Arms of Denmark," said the old grandfather.

Then his thoughts followed the next heart, which led him out to sea among the thunder of cannon and ships enveloped in smoke; and the flame attached itself like an order to Hvitfield's breast as he, to save the fleet, blew up his ship and himself with it.

The third heart led him to the miserable huts of Greenland, where Hans Egede, the priest, laboured with loving words and deeds: the flame was a star upon his breast, one heart more for the Danish Arms.

The old grandfather's heart went in advance of the waving flames, for he knew whither the flames were leading him.

Frederick the Sixth stood in the peasant woman's poor little room and wrote his name with chalk on the beams. The flame trembled on his breast, trembled in his heart; in the peasant's room his heart became a heart in Denmark's Arms. And the old grandfather wiped his eyes, for he had known King Frederick and lived for him, King Frederick with silvery hair and honest blue eyes. Then he folded his hands and sat, looking pensively before him. His daughter-in-law came and told him that it was late and he must rest, the supper was ready.

"What a grand figure you have made, grandfather," she said. "Holger the Dane and all our beautiful coat of arms— I think I have seen that face before!"

"No, that you haven't," said the old man; "but I have seen it, and often before tried to carve it in wood, just as I remember it. It was when the English lay in the roads on the 2nd day of April, and we knew we were true old Danes. Where I stood on the *Denmark* in Steen Billé's squadron I had a man by my side, it seemed as if the balls were afraid of him; there he stood singing old ballads, fighting and struggling as if he were more than a man. I remember his face still, but whence he came or whither he went, I haven't an idea, nor anyone else either. I have often thought it must have been old Holger the Dane himself, who had swum down from Kronborg to help us in the hour of danger, now that's my idea, and there stands his portrait."

The figure threw its shadow right up the wall as high as the ceiling, it looked as if it were the real Holger the Dane himself standing behind; the shadow seemed to move, but perhaps that was because the candle was not burning very steadily. The old man's daughter-in-law kissed him, and led him to the big arm-chair by the table, and she and her husband, who was the old man's son, and father of the little boy in bed, sat eating their supper and chatting.

The old grandfather's head was full of Danish lions and Danish hearts and strength and gentleness; he could talk of nothing else. He complained to them that there is another strength besides the strength of the sword, and he pointed to the shelf where his old books lay, all Holberg's plays, which were so much read, because they were so amusing; all the characters from olden times were quite familiar to him.

"You see he knew how to fight too," said the old man. "He spent all his life in showing up in his plays the follies and peculiarities of those around him!"

Then the grandfather nodded to a place above the looking-glass, where an almanac hung with a picture of the Round Tower [1] on it, and he said, "There was Tycho Brahe, he was another who used the sword; not to hack at legs and arms, but to cut out a plainer path among the stars of heaven! And then *he* whose father belonged to my calling; Thorwaldsen the old woodcarver's son. We have seen him ourselves with the silvery locks falling on his broad shoulders, whose name is known to all the world—ah, he is a sculptor, and I am only a woodcarver. Yes, Holger the Dane comes in many guises, that the strength of Denmark may be known all over the world. Shall we drink to the health of Bertel Thorwaldsen?"

The little boy in bed distinctly saw the castle of Kronborg and the real Holger the Dane, who lived down below it, with

[1] The Observatory of Copenhagen.

his beard grown fast to the marble table, and dreaming about all that happens up above. Holger the Dane also dreamt about the poor little room where the woodcarver lived; he heard everything that was said and nodded in his dreams, murmuring, "Yes, remember me, ye Danish people! Keep me in mind, I shall come in time of need."

Outside Kronborg it was bright daylight and the wind bore the notes of the huntsman's horn from the opposite shore. The ships sailed past with their greeting, "boom, boom!" with the answer from Kronborg, "boom, boom." Holger the Dane did not wake, however loud they thundered, because it was only "how do you do!" and "many thanks!" It will have to be a different kind of firing to rouse him, but he will wake, never fear; there is grit in Holger the Dane.

WHAT THE MOON SAW

IT is very extraordinary, but when my feelings are most
fervent, and at their best, my tongue and my hands alike
seem tied. I cannot reproduce my impressions either in words
or in painting, as I feel them burning within me. And yet I am
an artist, my eye tells me so, and all who have seen my sketches
and notes acknowledge the same.

I am only a poor lad, and I live in one of the narrowest
streets; but light is not wanting to me, for I live high up, and
I have a fine view over the roof. For the first few days when I
came to live in the town, it seemed very cramped and lonely.
Instead of green woods and hills, I only had chimney pots on
my horizon. I had not a single friend, and there was not even
the face of an acquaintance to greet me.

One evening I was standing sadly by the window. I opened
it and looked out, and there, how pleased I was! I saw a face I
knew, a round friendly face, my best friend at home. It was
the moon, the dear old moon, unchanged, and looking exactly
the same as he used to look, when he peeped at me there through
the willows in the marshes. I kissed my hand to him, and he
shone straight into my room and promised to look in at me
every evening he was out. This promise he has faithfully kept,
and it is only a pity that he stays so short a time. Every time
he comes he tells me something or another which he has seen
the night before.

" Now paint what I tell you! " said he, " and you will have
a very fine picture-book." I have done as he said for many
evenings, and in my own way I could give a new rendering of
the " Thousand and One Nights," but that would be too many.
Those I give here are not selected, but they come in the order in

204

which I heard them. A highly gifted painter, a poet, or a musician might perhaps make more of them; what I have given here are only hasty sketches, with my own thoughts occasionally interspersed, for the moon did not come every night, there were some evenings when he was hidden by the clouds.

FIRST EVENING

" Last evening," to give the moon's own words, " as I was gliding through the clear atmosphere of India, and reflecting myself in the Ganges, I tried to pierce the thick groves of plantain trees the leaves of which overlay each other as tightly as the horny plates on the back of the turtle. From out of the thicket came a Hindoo maiden; she was as light as a gazelle, and as beautiful as Eve. There was such an airy grace about her, and yet such firmness of purpose in this daughter of India; I could read her intention in coming. The thorny creepers tore her sandals, but she stepped rapidly onwards. The deer coming up from the river where they had quenched their thirst, bounded shyly past her, for the girl held in her hand a burning lamp. I could see the blood coursing in her delicate fingers as she bent them round the flame to form a shelter for it. She approached the river and placed the lamp upon the face of the waters, and it floated away on the stream. The flame flickered and seemed as if it would go out, but still it burned, and the dark sparkling eyes of the girl followed it with a longing glance, from under their silken fringes. She knew that if the lamp burned as long as she could follow it with her eyes, her lover lived. But if it went out, he was dead. The lamp burnt and flickered, and her heart burnt and trembled. She sank upon her knees in prayer. By her side in the grass lay a venomous snake, but she heeded it not; she only thought of Brahma, and her bridegroom. ' He lives! ' she rejoiced, and from the hills came the echo, ' He lives! ' "

SECOND EVENING

" It was yesterday," the moon told me, " I peeped down into a little court surrounded by houses; in it sat a hen with eleven chickens. A charming little girl was skipping about among them. The hen clucked and spread her wings in alarm over her brood. Then the little girl's father came out and scolded her, and I slipped away without thinking any more about it. But to-night, only a few minutes ago, I looked into the same court. At first it was quite quiet, but then the same little girl came out. She crept softly along to the chicken-house, lifted the latch and slipped in beside the hen and chickens. They cackled and flapped their wings and the little girl ran after them. I saw it all quite plainly, for I peeped in by a hole in the wall. I was quite angry with the naughty child, and felt pleased when her father came and scolded her, more angrily than yesterday. He took her by the arm, and she bent back her head, showing her big blue eyes full of tears. ' What are you doing here? ' asked he. She cried and said, ' I only wanted to get into the hen to kiss her, and to ask her to forgive me for frightening her yesterday, but I was afraid to tell you.'

" The father kissed the sweet innocent upon the forehead, and I kissed her on the eyes and lips."

THIRD EVENING

" In the narrow street close by—it is so narrow that I can only let my beams glide down for a few minutes, but in those minutes I see enough to know what the people are who move about there—I saw a woman sixteen years ago; she was a child; away in the country she played in the old vicarage garden. The rose hedges were old and past flowering. They were running wild over the paths and sending up long shoots into the apple trees. Here and there grew one poor rose, not lovely as the queen of flowers should be, but the colour was there, and the fragrance. The parson's little daughter seemed to me a far sweeter flower, sitting upon her footstool under the wild hedge, kissing the battered cheeks of her doll.   Ten years later I saw her again.   I saw her in a brilliant ballroom; she was the lovely bride of a rich merchant.   I was delighted with her happiness, and I often sought her in those quiet evenings.   Alas! no one thought of my clear eye or my sharp glances.   My rose was also sending out wild shoots like the roses in the vicarage garden. There are tragedies in everyday life too.   To-night I saw the last act.   There, in the narrow street, on a bed, she lay at death's door.   The wicked landlord, rough and cruel, her only protector, tore aside the coverlet.   'Get up!' he said.   'Your face is a sight.   Dress yourself up, paint your face, and get some money, or I will turn you into the street.   Get up at once!'   'Death is in my heart!' she said.   'Oh, let me rest!'   But he forced her to get up, and painted her cheeks, and put a wreath of roses in her hair.   Then he seated her by the window, with the light close by, and left her.   I gazed upon her as she sat motionless, with her hands in her lap.   The window flew back, and one of the panes cracked, but she did not move.   The curtain fluttered round her like a flame.   She was dead.

"The dead woman at the open window preached a moral to me: My rose from the vicarage garden."

FOURTH EVENING

"I went to a German play last night," said the moon.   "It was in a little town; a stable had been turned into a theatre, that is to say, the stalls were left standing and furnished up to make boxes.   All the woodwork was covered up with bright paper.   A little iron chandelier hung from the low ceiling, and so that it might disappear into the roof, as in a big theatre at the sound of the prompter's bell, an inverted tub was fixed above it. 'Ring-a-ting' went the bell, and the little chandelier made a spring of about a foot, and then one knew that the play had begun.   A young prince and his consort, who were travelling through the town, were present at the performance.   The house was crammed; only the place under the chandelier was left like a little crater; not a creature sat there, for the grease dropped.

' Drop, drop.'   I saw it all, for it was so warm that all the loop-
holes had been opened.   The lads and lasses outside were peeping in, notwithstanding that the police inside kept threatening
them with their sticks.   The noble pair sat in a couple of old arm-
chairs close to the orchestra.   The burgomaster and his wife
usually occupied these, but on this occasion they were obliged
to sit on the wooden benches, just as if they had been ordinary
citizens.   ' There, you see there is rank above rank! ' was the
quiet remark of the goodwives; and this incident gave a special
air of festivity to the entertainment.   The chandelier gave its
little hops; the crowd was wrapped over the knuckles, and I——.
Yes, the moon saw the whole entertainment."

FIFTH EVENING

" Yesterday," said the moon, " I looked down upon the life
of Paris, and my eye penetrated to some of the apartments in
the Louvre.   An old grandmother poorly clad, belonging to the
lower classes, accompanied by some of the subordinate attendants
entered the great empty throne-room.   She wanted to see it,
she must see it!   It had cost her many small sacrifices and
much persuasiveness before she had attained her wish.   She
folded her thin hands and looked about her as reverently as if
she were in a church.   ' It was here,' she said, ' here,' and she
approached the throne with its rich embroidered velvet hangings.
' There! ' she said, ' there! ' and she fell upon her knees and kissed
the purple carpet; I believe she wept.   ' It was not this very
velvet,' said the attendant, a smile playing round his mouth.
' But it was here! ' said the woman, ' it looked the same.'   ' The
same,' he answered, ' yet not the same; the windows were
smashed to atoms, the doors torn off, and there was blood upon
the floors! '   ' But still you may say that my grandson died
upon the throne of France.   Died! ' repeated the old woman.
I don't think anything more was said; they left the room soon
after.   The twilight faded, and my light grew stronger upon the
rich velvet on the throne of France.   Who do you think the old
woman was?   I will tell you a story.   It was evening, on the
most brilliant day of victory in the July revolution, when every

She took him in, wrapped him in her furs, and he felt as
if he were sinking into a snowdrift.

THE SNOW QUEEN

Page 165

He sends a shower of milk into their eyes and they can't keep their eyes open after it.

OLÉ LUKÖIÉ, THE DUSTMAN

Page 283

house was a fortress, every window an embrasure. The populace stormed the Tuileries, even women and children fought among the combatants; they pressed through the apartments of the palace. A poor half-grown lad in rags fought bravely among the other insurgents; he fell fatally wounded by bayonet thrusts, and sank to the ground in the throne-room itself, and his bleeding form was laid upon the throne where his blood streamed over the imperial purple! What a picture that was! The noble room, the struggling groups, a torn banner upon the ground, the tricolour floating from the bayonets; and on the throne the poor dying boy with his pale transparent face and eyes turned towards heaven, while his limbs were already stiffening in death. His naked breast and torn clothing were half hidden by the purple velvet decked with the lilies of France. It had been prophesied at his cradle that ' he should die on the throne of France.' The mother's heart had dreamt of a new Napoleon. My beams have kissed the wreath of Immortelles on the lad's grave, and this night they kissed the forehead of the old grandmother while she dreamt and saw the picture you may sketch here, ' The poor boy upon the throne of France! ' "

SIXTH EVENING

" I have been in Upsala," said the moon. " I looked down upon the great plain covered with coarse grass and the barren fields. I looked at myself in the waters of the Fyris river, while the steamers frightened the fishes in among the rushes. The clouds chased each other below me, and threw their shadows on to Odin's, Thor's, and Freya's graves, as they are called. Names have been cut all over the mounds in the short turf. There is no monument here, where travellers can have their names carved, nor rock walls where they may be painted, so the visitors have had the turf cut away, and their names stand out in the bare earth. There is a perfect network of these spread all over the mounds. A form of immortality which only lasts till the fresh grass grows. A man was standing there, a poet. He emptied the mead horn with its broad silver rim and whispered a name, telling the wind not to betray it; but I heard it and knew it. A count's coronet sparkles over it, and therefore he did not speak it aloud. I smiled; a poet's crown sparkles over his! Eleanora d'Este's nobility gains lustre from Tasso's name. I knew, too, where this Rose of Beauty blooms!" Having said this the moon was hidden by a cloud. May no clouds come between the poet and his rose!

SEVENTH EVENING

"Along the shore stretches a great forest of oak and beech; sweet and fragrant is its scent. It is visited every year by hundreds of nightingales. The sea is close by, the ever changing sea, and the broad high road separates the two. One carriage after another rolls by; I do not follow them, my eye rather rests on one particular spot. It is a tumulus, or barrow; brambles and wild sloes grow among its stones. Here is real poetry in nature. How do you think people in general interpret it? I will tell you what I heard only last night.

"First two rich farmers drove by. 'There are some fine trees,' said one. 'There are ten loads of wood in each,' answered the other. 'This will be a hard winter, and last winter we got fourteen dollars a cord,' and they were gone. 'This is a bad bit of road,' said the next man who drove along. 'It's those cursed trees,' answered his companion. 'You don't get a current of air, you only have the breeze from the sea,' and then they rolled by. Next, the diligence came along. The passengers were all asleep at the prettiest part of the road. The driver blew his horn; he only thought 'how well I am blowing it, and it sounds well here; I wonder what they think of it,' and then the diligence, too, was gone. The next to pass were two lads on horseback. Here we have youth and champagne in the blood, I thought. And indeed they looked with a smile at the moss-grown hill and the dark thicket. 'Shouldn't I like a walk here with the miller's Christine!' said one, and then they rushed on. The flowers scented the air, and every breeze was hushed, it looked as if the sea was a part of the heavens outspread over a deep valley. A carriage drove by in which were six travellers, four of them were asleep, the fifth was thinking of his new summer coat, and whether it became him. The sixth leant forward and asked the driver if there was anything remarkable about that heap of stones. ' No,' answered the man, ' it's only a heap of stones; but those trees are remarkable.' ' Tell me about them.' ' Well, they are very remarkable; you see, sir, in winter when the snow lies deep, and every place looks alike, these trees are a landmark to me, and I know I must keep close to them so as not to drive into the sea. In that way, you see, they are remarkable,' then he drove on. Now an artist came along and his eyes sparkled, he did not say a word, but he whistled and the nightingales sang, the one louder than the other. ' Hold your tongues,' he cried, and took out his notebook and began noting down the colours in the most methodical manner, ' Blue, lilac, dark brown. It will make a splendid picture.' He saw it as a mirror reflects a scene, and in the meantime he whistled a march by Rossini. The last to come by was a poor girl, she rested a moment by the barrow and put down her burden. She turned her pale pretty face towards the wood and her eyes shone when she looked upwards to the sky over the sea. She folded her hands and I think she whispered a prayer. She did not herself understand the feelings which penetrated her, but I know that in years to come this night will often recur to her with all the lovely scene around her. It will be much more beautiful and truer to nature in her memory than the painter's picture will be with his exact colouring noted down in a book. My beams followed her till the dawn kissed her forehead."

EIGHTH EVENING

There were heavy clouds in the sky, and the moon did not appear at all. I was doubly lonely in my little room, looking up into the sky where the moon ought to have been. My thoughts wandered up to the kind friend who had told me stories every evening and shown me pictures. What had he not experienced? He had sailed over the angry waters of the flood and looked down upon the ark, as he now did upon me, bringing consolation to the new world which was to arise. When the children of Israel stood weeping by the waters of Babylon, he peeped sadly through the willows where their harps were hung. When Romeo climbed on to the balcony and young love's kiss flew like a cherub's thought from earth to heaven, the round moon was hidden behind the dark cypresses in the transparent air.   He saw the hero at St. Helena where he stood on the rock gazing out over the illimitable ocean, while great thoughts stirred his breast.   Nay, what could not the moon tell us?   The life of the world is a story to him.   To-night I do not see you, old friend; and I have no picture to draw in remembrance of your visit.   But as I looked dreamily up at the clouds, there appeared one beam from the moon—but it was soon gone, the black clouds swept over it.   Still it was a greeting, a friendly evening greeting, to me from the moon.

NINTH EVENING

The air was clear again, several evenings had passed, while the moon was in its first quarter.   Then I got a new idea for a sketch: hear what the moon told me.   " I have followed the polar birds and the swimming whales to the east coast of Greenland.   Gaunt ice-covered rocks, and dark clouds overhung a valley where willows and bilberry bushes stood in thick bloom, and the scented lychnis diffused its fragrance; my light was dim and my crescent pale as the leaf of the water-lily which has been floating for weeks upon the waters after being torn away from its stem.   The corona of the northern lights burned with a fierce light.   The rays spread out from its wide circle over the heavens like whirling columns of fire playing in green and red light.   The inhabitants were assembled for dancing and merry-making, but they had no wonder to bestow on the glorious sight, so accustomed to it were they.   ' Let the souls of the dead play at ball with the walrus' head as much as they like,' they thought, according to their superstitions.   Their attention was entirely centred on the dancing and singing.   A Greenlander without his fur coat stood in the middle of the circle, with a small drum in his hand, on which he played, and at the same time sang a song in praise of seal hunting;   the chorus answered him with ' Eia, eia, a ! ' and at the same time hopped round the circle in their white fur coats looking like polar bears. They wagged their heads and rolled their eyes in the wildest way. Then they held a mock court of justice. The litigants stepped forward and the plaintiff rehearsed his opponent's faults all in a bold and mocking manner; the rest meanwhile dancing to the music of the drum. The defendant replied in the same spirit, and the assemblage laughingly gave their judgment. Thunders resounded from the mountains when portions of the ice fields slipped away, and great masses broke off shivering into dust. It was a typical Greenland summer night.

" A hundred paces away, under a tent of skins, lay a sick man; life was still coursing through his veins, yet he was to die. He knew it himself, and those standing round him knew it too, so much so that his wife was already sewing up the skin robe around him so as not to have to touch the dead man later. She asked him, ' Will you be buried on the Fells, in the hard snow, or would you rather be sunk in the sea? ' ' In the sea,' he whispered, and nodded with a sad smile. ' Yes, the sea is a cosy summer tent,' said the woman. ' Thousands of seals sport about in it, and the walrus will sleep at your feet; the chase is certain and plenty of it.' The children howled, and tore away the tightened skin from the window, so that the dying man might be borne down to the sea, the swelling ocean which gave him food for life, and now in death a resting-place! His headstone was the floating iceberg which changes from day to day. Seals slumber on the ice, and the albatross spreads its great wings above it."

TENTH EVENING

" I knew an old maid," said the moon; " she used to wear a yellow satin pelisse in winter. It was always new, and she never varied the fashion of it. Every summer she used to wear the same straw hat and, I believe, a bluish grey dress. She only used to go and see one old friend, who lived across the street; but for the last few years she did not go, for her friend was dead. My old friend bustled about in her loneliness by her window, which was always full of beautiful flowers in summer, and in the winter she grew splendid mustard and cress on a piece of felt. For the last few months she has not appeared at the window, but I knew that she still lived, for I had not seen her take the great journey about which she and her friend talked so much. ' Yes,' she used to say, ' when my time comes to die, I shall travel much further than I have ever done in my whole life. Our family burial place is twenty miles from here, and I am to be taken there for my last sleep with the rest of my family!' Last night a van stopped at the door, and a coffin was carried out, so I knew that she was dead. They put straw round the coffin and drove off. In it slept the quiet old maid, who for the last few years had not been outside the house. The van rattled quickly out of the town, as if bent on a pleasure trip. They went faster still when they reached the high road. The driver looked over his shoulder every now and then; I believe he was half afraid of seeing the old lady sitting there, on the top of the coffin, in her yellow pelisse. Then he whipped up the horses mercilessly and held them in so tightly that they foamed at the mouth, a hare darted across the road, and they got beyond the man's control. The quiet old maid, who, year in year out, had moved so slowly in her daily round, now that she was dead, was being hurried at a headlong pace over stock and stone along the road. The coffin, which was wrapped in mats, slipped off the van and fell on to the road, while driver, horses, and van rushed away in their wild flight. A little lark flew up from the field and burst into its morning song, right over the coffin. It perched on it and pecked at the matting, as if to tear the shell asunder, then it rose gaily warbling into the air, and I drew back behind the rosy clouds of dawn! "

ELEVENTH EVENING

" It was a bridal feast! " said the moon. " Songs were sung, toasts were drunk, everything was gay and festive. The guests went away; it was past midnight. The mothers kissed the bride and the bridegroom. Then I saw them alone, but the curtains were almost closely drawn; the comfortable room was lit up by a lamp. ' Thank goodness they are all gone,' said he, kissing her hands and her lips. She smiled and wept and leant her head upon his breast, trembling like the lotus flower upon the flowing waters. They talked together in tender glowing words. ' Sleep sweetly! ' he exclaimed, and she drew aside the window curtain. ' How beautifully the moon is shining! ' she said; ' see how still and clear it is! ' Then she put out the lamp, and the cosy room was dark, except for my beams, which shone as brightly as his eyes. Oh womanhood, kiss thou the poet's lyre, when he sings of the mysteries of life! "

TWELFTH EVENING

" I will give you a picture of Pompeii," said the moon. " I was in the outskirts of the town, in the street of Tombs, as it is called, where the beautiful monuments stand; it is the place where once joyous youths crowned with roses danced with the fair sisters of Lais. Now the stillness of death reigns. German soldiers in the Neapolitan pay keep guard and play at cards and dice. A crowd of strangers from the other side of the mountains came into the town with guides. They wanted to see this city risen from the grave under my full beams. I showed them the chariot tracks in the streets paved with slabs of lava; I showed them the names on the doors and the signboards still hanging. In the small courtyards they saw the basins of the fountains decorated with shells, but no stream of water played, and no songs resounded from the richly painted chambers where the metal dog guarded the doors. It was indeed a city of the dead, only Vesuvius thundered forth its everlasting hymn, the several verses of which are called by man, ' a new eruption.' We went to the Temple of Venus, built of dazzling white marble, with its high altar in front of the broad steps, and the weeping-willow shooting up among the pillars. The air was blue and transparent, and in the background stood Vesuvius, inky black, with its column of fire like the stem of a pine tree. In the darkness the cloud of smoke looked like the crown of the tree, only it was blood-red illuminated by the internal flames. A songstress was among the company, a great and noted one; I have seen the homage paid to her in the various capitals of Europe. When they reached the tragic theatre, they all sat down on the stone steps of the amphitheatre. They filled up a little corner of it as in centuries gone by. The stage still stood with its walled side scenes, and two arches in the background through which one sees the same decoration as was seen then—nature herself, the hills between Amalfi and Sorrento. For a joke the singer mounted the stage and sang, for the place inspired her. I thought of the wild Arab horse, when it neighs, tosses its mane, and tears away—her song was so light and yet so assured. I also thought of the suffering mother beneath the cross of Golgotha, it was so full of deep feeling and pain. Round about echoed, just as it had done a thousand years ago, the sound of applause and delight. ' Happy, gifted creature! ' they all cried. Three minutes later the stage was empty and not a sound was to be heard. The company departed, but the ruins stood unchanged, as they will stand for centuries, and no one will know of the momentary burst of applause, the notes of the beautiful songstress and her smiles; they are past and gone. Even to me they are but a vanished memory."

THIRTEENTH EVENING

" I peeped through the windows of an editor's office," said the moon. " It was somewhere in Germany. It was well furnished; there were many books and a perfect chaos of papers. Several young men were present, and the editor stood by the desk. Two small books, both by young authors, were to be reviewed. ' This one has been sent to me,' he said; ' I have not read it yet, but it is nicely got up; what do you say about the contents? ' ' Oh,' said one, who was himself a poet, ' it is pretty good, a little drawn out perhaps, but he is a young man still. The verses might be better, but the thoughts are sound, if a little commonplace. What are you to say? you can't always think of something new. You will be quite safe in praising him, though I don't suppose he will ever be a great poet. He is well read, a first rate Oriental scholar, and he has judgment. It was he who wrote that nice article on my " Reflections on Domestic Life." One must be kind to a young man.'

" ' But he must be a regular ass! ' said another man in the room; ' nothing is worse in poetry than mediocrity, and he will never rise above it.'

" ' Poor fellow! ' said a third, ' and his aunt is so delighted with him; it is she, Mr. Editor, who found so many subscribers to your last translation.'

" ' Oh, the good woman. Well, I have reviewed the book quite briefly. Unmistakable talent — a welcome offering — a flower in the garden of poetry—well got up—and so on. But the other book! I suppose the author wants me to buy it. I hear it is being praised. He has genius, don't you think so? '

" ' Oh, they all harp upon that,' said the poet; ' but he talks rather wildly! And the punctuation is most peculiar.'

" ' It would do him good to pull him to pieces a bit and enrage him, or he will think too highly of himself! '

" ' But that would be rather unreasonable,' cried another; ' don't let us carp at his small faults, rather let us rejoice over his good points: and he has many. He beats all the others.'

" ' Heaven preserve us! If he is such a genius he will be able to stand some rough handling. There are plenty of people to praise him in private. Don't let us make him mad! '

" ' Unmistakable talent,' wrote the editor, ' with the usual want of care; that he can write incorrect verses may be seen on page 25, where there are two false quantities. A study of the Ancients is recommended, and so on! '

" I went away," said the moon, " and peeped through the window into the aunt's room where the cherished poet sat, the *tame* one. He was worshipped by all the guests, and quite happy. I sought the other poet, the *wild* one, he was also at a large party, in the house of one of his admirers, where they were talking of the other poet's book. ' I mean to read yours too,' said Mæcenas; ' but you know I never tell you anything but what I think, and to tell the truth, I do not expect great things of you, you are too wild and too fantastic; but I acknowledge, that as a man you are very respectable.'

" A young girl sat in a corner, and she read in a book these words:

> ' Let stifled genius lie below,
> While you on dulness praise bestow,
> So has it been from ages past
> And aye will be, while earth doth last.' "

FOURTEENTH EVENING

The moon said to me: " There are two cottages by the roadside in the wood, the doors are low and the windows crooked, but the buckthorn and the berberis cluster round them. The roofs are overgrown with moss, yellow flowers, and houseleek. There are only cabbages and potatoes in the little garden, but near the fence is a flowering elder-bush, and beneath it sat a little girl; her brown eyes were fixed upon the old oak between the cottages. It had a great gnarled trunk, and the crown had been sawn off, and the stork had built his nest on the top of the trunk. He was standing there now clattering his beak. A little boy came out and placed himself beside the girl, they were brother and sister.

" ' What are you looking at? ' he asked.

" ' I am looking at the stork,' she said; ' the woman next door has told me that he is going to bring us a little brother or sister to-night, and I am watching to see them come.'

" ' The stork won't bring one,' said the boy; ' our neighbour told me the same thing, but she laughed when she said it, and I asked if she dared swear by the name of God, and she dared not, so I know very well that all that nonsense about the stork is just something they make up for us children! '

" ' Where will the little baby come from then? ' asked the girl.

" ' Our Lord will bring it,' said the boy. ' God has it under His mantle; but nobody can see God, and so we shall not see Him bring it.'

" Just then a gust of wind rustled through the leaves of the elderbush, and the children clasped their hands and looked at each other. It must be God sending the baby!—they took hold of each other's hands. The cottage door opened, and a woman appeared. 'Come in now,' she said; 'come in and see what the stork has brought; it is a little brother!'

"The children nodded, they knew well enough he had come."

FIFTEENTH EVENING

"I was passing over Limborg heath," said the moon, "and I saw a lonely hut by the wayside. Some leafless trees grew round it, on one of which a nightingale was singing; it had lost its way. I knew that it must die of the cold, and that it was its swan-song I heard. At daybreak a caravan came along, of emigrant peasants, on their way to Bremen or Hamburg to take ship for America, where good fortune, the fortune of their dreams, was awaiting them. The women were carrying the babies, and the bigger children skipped along beside them. A wretched horse drew a van on which were a few miserable articles of furniture. A cold wind blew, and a little girl clung closer to her mother, who looked up at my waning disc, and thought what bitter need they had endured at home, and of the heavy taxes which could not be paid. Her thoughts were those of the whole caravan, so the red dawn shone upon them, like a glimmer from that sun of fortune which was about to arise. They heard the song of the dying nightingale, and to them it was no false prophet, but rather a harbinger of good fortune. The wind whistled sharply, and they did not understand its song. Sail on securely over the ocean! you have given all that you possessed in return for the journey; poor and helpless you will land upon the shores of your Canaan. You must sell yourself, your wife, and your children, but you shall not suffer long. The goddess of death lurks behind the broad, fragrant leaves, her kiss of welcome will breathe pestilential fever into your blood! Sail on, sail on over the surging waters! But the travellers listened happily to the song of the nightingale, for it promised them good fortune. Daylight shone through the floating clouds, and peasants were wending their way over the heath to church. The women in their black dresses, and with white kerchiefs round their heads, looked as if they might have stepped down out of the old pictures in the church. Round about there was only the great dead plain, covered with brown withered heather and the white sand hills beyond. The women held their prayer-books in their hands and wandered on towards the church. Ah, pray, pray for those whose steps are leading them to the grave beyond the rolling waters!"

SIXTEENTH EVENING

"I know a Punchinello," said the moon. "The public shout directly they see him, each of his movements is so comic that the whole house roars when he appears; his personality makes them laugh, not his art. Even when he was little, playing about with the other boys, he was already a Punchinello. Nature had made him one; she had given him a hump on his back and one on his chest. But the inner man, the soul, ah, that was richly endowed. No one had deeper feelings or greater elasticity of mind than he. The theatre was his ideal world. If he had been slender and well made he would have been the first tragedian on any stage. The great and the heroic filled his soul, and yet he had to be a Punchinello. Even his pain and his melancholy increased the comic dryness of his sharply-cut features, and called forth laughter from the multitudes who applauded their favourite. The pretty Columbine was kind and friendly, but she preferred marrying the Harlequin. It would have been far too comic in real life if Beauty and the Beast had joined hands. When Punchinello was in low spirits she was the only person who could make him smile, nay, even laugh outright. At first she would be melancholy too, then gay, and at last full of fun. 'I know what is the matter with you, well enough!' said she; 'you are in love.' 'I and love,' he exclaimed; 'we should be a nice pair! How the public would applaud us!' 'You are in love,' she repeated, 'you are in love with me.' That might very well be said when one knew there was no question of love. Punchinello laughed, and bounded into the air, all his melancholy was gone. Yet she had spoken the truth; he loved her, worshipped her, as he worshipped all that was highest and best in Art. At her wedding he was the merriest person there, but at night he wept bitter tears. Had the public seen his distorted face they would indeed have applauded.

" Quite lately Columbine had died, and on the day of her burial Harlequin had a holiday; was he not a sorrowing widower? The manager was obliged to produce something more than usually merry, so that the public should not miss pretty Columbine. Therefore Punchinello had to be doubly lively; he danced and bounded with despair in his heart, and he was more applauded than ever. ' Bravo! Bravissimo! ' Punchinello was called forward, he was indeed above all price.

" Last night after the performance the little hunchback wandered out of the town to the lonely churchyard. The wreaths were already withering on Columbine's grave. He sat down upon it. It would have made a touching picture, with his hand under his chin, his eyes turned towards me; he was like a monument, a Punchinello on a grave, characteristic and comical. If the public had seen their favourite, how they would have shouted, ' Bravo! Bravissimo! Punchinello.' "

SEVENTEENTH EVENING

Listen to what the moon told me.

" I have seen the cadet become an officer, and for the first time put on his handsome uniform. I have seen the young girl in her ball dress, and I have seen a royal bride rejoicing in her festal robes; but I have never seen greater delight than I saw last night in a child, a little four year old girl. She had on a new blue frock and a pink hat! they had just been put on, and the bystanders were calling for lights. The moon shining through the window gave too faint a light, they must have something brighter altogether. There stood the little girl as stiff as any doll, holding her arms away from the dress, each finger stuck stiffly out! Oh! how her eyes glistened, and her whole face beamed with delight. ' To-morrow you shall go out in them,' said the mother; and the little one looked down at her frock and smiled contentedly. ' Mother! ' she said, ' what will the dogs think when they see me in all my pretty things! ' "

EIGHTEENTH EVENING

"I have told you," said the moon, "about Pompeii, that city of the dead resuscitated, and again ranking among living places. I know another town even more fantastic; it is not so much the corpse as it is the ghost of a city. I seem to hear the romance of the floating city wherever the fountains play into their marble basins. Yes, water must tell its story, the waves of the sea sing its song! A mist often floats over the stretches of its waters; that is its veil of widowhood. The bridegroom of the sea is dead; his palace and town are now his mausoleum. Do you know this city? Never has the roll of wheels or the clatter of horses' hoofs been heard in its streets. The fish swim in them, and the black gondola skims over the surface of its green waters. I will show you," continued the moon, "the Forum of the town, its grand square, and you may imagine yourself to have been in Fairyland. The grass grows between its broad flags, and at dawn thousands of tame pigeons flutter round its solitary lofty tower. On three sides of it you are surrounded by colonades; under their shelter the silent Turk sits smoking his long pipe. A handsome Greek boy leans against the columns, and looks up at the trophies and lofty masts raised around, memorials of its ancient power. The flags droop from them like mourning scarves. Here a girl is resting; she has put down her heavy water-pails, and the yoke in which she carried them hangs on her shoulders; she supports herself against the column of Victory. That is no fairy palace there in front of you; it is a church; its gilt cupolas and balls glitter in my beams. Those majestic bronze horses have travelled, like the bronze horse in the fairy tale. They came hither, went hence, and again returned. Do you see the gorgeous colouring on the walls and in the window panes? It looks as if genius had given way to the whims of some child in adorning the wonderful temple. Do you see the winged lion on its column? The gold still glitters, but its wings are bound; the lion is dead, for the king of the sea is dead; his great halls are empty, and there are only bare walls now where costly pictures used to hang. The Lazzaroni sleep now under the arches, on whose floor only the highest nobles in the land dared at one time to tread. From the deep wells—or does it come from the leaden chambers near the Bridge of Sighs?—sounds a groan, just as in the days when tambourines sounded from the gondolas with their gay trappings, when the bridal ring flew from the brilliant Bucentaur to Adria, queen of the sea. Oh, Adria, wrap thyself in the mist! Let thy widow's veil cover thy bosom! Hang it over the mausoleum of the bridegroom, oh Venice, thou city of ghostly marble palaces."

NINETEENTH EVENING

"I come from Rome," said the moon. "There in the middle of the town, on the summit of one of the seven hills, stands the ruins of the palace of Cæsars. The wild fig grows now in the crevices of the walls, covering their nakedness with its broad greyish green leaves. The ass treads down its laurel hedges among the heaps of stones, and browses on the barren thistle. Here, whence once the eagles of Rome fluttered—came, saw, and conquered—there is now the entrance to a poor little hovel plastered up with clay between the two broken marble columns. The vine hangs like a mourning wreath over its crooked windows. An old woman lives in it with her little granddaughter; they now rule in the palace of the Cæsars, and show its treasures to visitors. There is only a bare wall left standing of the rich throne-room; the dark cypress points with its long shadows to where the throne once stood. The earth is heaped high over the ruined floor, and the little girl, now sole daughter of the Cæsars, often brings her footstool there when the evening bells ring. She calls the keyhole in the door close by her balcony, for she can see half Rome through it, as far as the mighty dome of St. Peter's. Silence reigned, as always, this evening when the little girl came out into the full light of my beams. She was carrying a water jar of antique shape on her head: her feet were bare, her short skirt and the sleeves of her little chemise were ragged. I kissed the child's delicately rounded shoulders, her dark eyes, and black shining hair. She climbed up the steps to the little house, they were steep and made of sharp bits of marble from the broken columns. Gaily coloured lizards darted about among her feet, but they did not startle her. She was just raising her hand to the bell-pull, this was a hare's foot at the end of a piece of string, such is the bell now in the palace of the Cæsars. She paused a moment—what was she thinking about? Perhaps about the beautiful Infant Jesus wrapped in gold and silver down in the chapel, where the silver lamps gleamed, and where her little friends took part in singing the hymns which she knew too; I do not know—she moved forward again, tripped, and the jar fell from her head on to the steps, where it was broken to atoms upon the fluted marble. She burst into tears. The beautiful daughter of the Cæsars, weeping over the poor broken jar. There she stood with her bare feet, weeping, and dared not pull the string —the bell-rope of the palace of the Cæsars."

TWENTIETH EVENING

The moon had not shone for over a fortnight, but now I saw it again; it rose round and bright above the slowly moving clouds. Listen to what it told me.

" I followed a caravan from one of the towns of the Fezzan. They made a halt near the desert by one of the salt plains; it shone like a sheet of ice, and was covered only in parts with quicksands. An elder among them, with a water-bottle hanging at his belt, and a bag of unleavened bread lying by him, drew a square with his staff in the sand, and wrote in it some words from the Koran. After this the whole caravan entered within the consecrated space. A young merchant, a child of the sun—I saw it in his eyes and in the beautiful lines of his figure—rode his fiery white steed thoughtfully. Was he perhaps thinking of his fair young wife? It was only two days since a camel covered with skins and costly shawls carried her, his lovely bride, round the walls of the town to the sound of drums and pipes. Women sang, and festive salvoes were fired; the loudest and most frequent were fired by the bridegroom himself, and now—now he was leading the caravan through the desert. I followed them for many nights; I saw them rest by the walls among the dwarf palms. They stuck their knives into the breast of the fallen camel, and roasted the meat by the fire. My beams cooled the burning sand, my beams showed them the buried rocks like submerged islands in a sea of sand. They encountered no unfriendly tribes on the trackless plain, no storms arose, and no sand-storm swept mercilessly over the caravan. At home the lovely wife prayed for her husband and her father. ' Are they dead? ' she asked my golden horns. ' Are they dead? ' she asked my shining disc. Now the desert lies behind them, and this evening they sit beneath the lofty palm trees, where the crane spreads its broad wings and the pelican watches them through the branches of the mimosa. The luxuriant thicket is trodden down by the heavy feet of the elephant; a troop of negroes are returning from the market far inland. The women have copper beads twisted round their heads of frizzled hair, and they are clad in skirts of indigo blue. They drive the heavily laden oxen, on whose backs the naked black children lie sleeping. A negro leads by a rope a young lion which he has bought; they approach the caravan. The young merchant sits motionless and silent, thinking of his lovely bride; dreaming in the land of the blacks of his white flower beyond the desert, he lifts his head!"——

A cloud passed over the moon, and then another; I heard no more that evening.

TWENTY-FIRST EVENING

" I saw a little girl crying," said the moon. " She was crying at the wickedness of the world. The loveliest doll in the world had been given to her. Oh, it was most delicate and fragile, and certainly not fit to face adversity. But the little girl's brothers, great big boys, had taken the doll away and put it up into a high tree, and then had run away. The poor little girl could not get it down, or get at it in any way, so she sat down and cried. The doll no doubt was crying too; it stretched out its arms among the branches, and looked most unhappy. Yes, this must be the adversity of the world, about which mama talked so much. Oh, the poor doll! Evening was coming on, it was getting dark, and it would soon be night. Was it to stay out there all alone in the tree for the whole night? No, the little girl could not endure the thought. ' I will stay with you,' she said, although she was not at all courageous, and she fancied already that she could see the little Brownies in their high-pointed caps peeping through the bushes, and there were long ghostly shadows dancing about in the dark walk. They came nearer and nearer, and stretched out their hands towards the tree where the doll was sitting; and they laughed and pointed their fingers at her. Oh! how frightened the little girl was. ' But if one has committed no sin,' she thought, ' evil can do one no harm. I wonder if I have sinned! ' Then she began to think. ' Oh, yes ' she said, ' I laughed at the poor duck with a red rag round its leg, it looked so funny limping along, so I laughed, and it is a sin to laugh at dumb animals.' Then she looked up at her doll. ' Have you ever laughed at dumb animals? ' And the doll seemed to shake its head."

TWENTY-SECOND EVENING

" I looked down in the Tyrol," said the moon. " I let the dark pine trees throw their long shadows on to the rocks. I saw St. Christopher with the child Jesus on his back, as they are painted on the walls of the houses; they are colossal in size, reaching from the ground to the tops of the gables. There is also St. Florian pouring water on the burning house, and the Saviour hanging bleeding on the cross at the roadside. These are old pictures to the new generation, but I saw their origin. There is a solitary convent perched upon the mountain-side like a swallow's nest. Two of the sisters were standing up in the tower ringing the bell; they were both young, so their glances roamed over the mountains into the wide world beyond. A travelling carriage drove along the high-road; the post horn sounded gaily, and the poor nuns fixed their eyes, filled with the same thoughts, upon the carriage; a tear stood in those of the youngest. The sound of the horn grew fainter and fainter till its dying notes were drowned by the convent bell."

TWENTY-THIRD EVENING

Hear what the moon told me.

" Several years ago I was in Copenhagen; I peeped in at the window of a poor little room. The father and mother were both asleep, but their little son was awake. I saw the flowered chintz curtains stirring and the child peeped out. I thought at first that he was looking at the grandfather's clock from Bornholm. It was gaily painted in red and green, and a cuckoo sat at the top; it had heavy laden weights, and the pendulum, with its shining brass disc, swung backwards and forwards, ' Tick, tack '; but that was not what he was looking at. No, it was his mother's spinning-wheel which stood under the clock. It was the boy's dearest treasure in all the house, but he dared not touch it or he would be rapped over the knuckles. He would stand for hours, while his mother was spinning, looking at the whirling spindle and the whizzing wheel, and he had his own thoughts about them. Oh, if only he dared spin with that wheel; father and mother were asleep; he looked at them, he looked at the wheel, and soon he put one bare little foot out of bed, and then another little bare foot followed by two little legs—bump, there he stood upon the floor. He turned round once more to see if father and mother were still asleep. Yes, they were fast asleep; so he went softly, very softly, in his short little shirt, to the wheel and began to spin. The cord flew off, and the wheel ran faster and faster. I kissed his yellow hair and his large blue eyes. It was a pretty picture.

" His mother woke just then. She put the curtain aside and looked out, and thought she saw a Brownie or some other little sprite. ' In Heaven's name,' she said, pushing her husband; he opened his eyes, rubbed them, and looked at the busy little figure. ' Why, it is our Bertel! ' he said. And my eye turned away from the poor little room. My glances extend so far that at the same moment I looked in at the galleries of the Vatican where the sculptured gods stand. I flooded the Laocoon group with my light, and the marble seemed to sigh. I pressed a gentle kiss upon the bosom of the muses; they almost seemed to move.

But my glance rested longest upon the great Nile-group with the colossal god. He leant pensively against the Sphinx, dreamy and thoughtful, as if he was pondering on the bygone years. Little Cupids played around him sporting with the crocodiles. One tiny little Cupid sat inside the cornucopia with his arms folded looking at the great solemn river-god. He was a true picture of the little boy at the spinning-wheel, his features were the same. This little marble child was life-like, and graceful in the extreme, yet the wheel of time had turned more than a thousand times since he sprang from the marble. Just so many times as the little boy turned the spinning-wheel in the humble little room had the greater wheel of time whirled round, and yet will whirl, before the present time creates marble gods like these.

"Now all this happened years ago," continued the moon. "Yesterday I looked down on to a bay on the east coast of Zealand. The cliffs round it were beautifully wooded, and in the midst of the woods stood an old red castle, with swans swimming in the moat. A little country town lay near, with its church buried among apple trees. A procession of boats with blazing torches glided over the smooth waters; these torches were not lighted for spearing eels. No, it was a great festivity; there were sounds of music and singing, and in one of the boats stood the object of all the homage. He was a tall powerful man wrapped in a cloak; he had blue eyes and long white hair. I knew him, and thought of the Vatican and the Nile-group among all the sculptured gods. Then I thought of the poor little room; I believe it was in ' Grönné-gade ' where little Bertel sat spinning in his little shirt. The wheel of time had been turning, and new gods have arisen from the marble since then. From the boats came ' Hurrah, hurrah for Bertel Thorwaldsen! ' "

TWENTY-FOURTH EVENING

" I will give you a picture from Frankfort," said the moon. " I looked at one building in particular. It was not Goethe's birthplace, not the old Townhall, where, through the grated windows, may still be seen the horns of the oxen which were roasted and given to the people at the coronation of the Emperor.

No, it was a burgher's house I looked at; it was painted green, and was quite plain; it stood at the corner of the narrow Jews' street. It was Rothschild's house. I looked in through the open door, the staircase was brightly lighted, footmen stood there holding burning lights in massive silver candlesticks, bending low before the old woman who was being carried down in a carrying chair. The owner of the house stood with bared head, and pressed a respectful kiss upon her hand. She was his mother; she nodded kindly to him and the footmen, and they carried her into a little house in the dark narrow street. Here she lived, here she had borne her children, from here their fortune had blossomed forth. If she now left the little house in the mean street perhaps their luck would leave them. This was her belief."

The moon told me no more; her visit to-night was far too short, but I thought of the old woman in the narrow mean street. One word from her and she might have a palace on the banks of the Thames; one word, and she would have had a villa on the Bay of Naples. "Were I to leave this humble house where the fortunes of my sons originated, their fortune might forsake them." It is a superstition, but a superstition of such a kind that, if one knows the story and sees the picture, it only needs two words to understand it—" A Mother."

TWENTY-FIFTH EVENING

" Yesterday at daybreak," these were the moon's own words, " not a chimney was yet smoking in the great town, and it was these very chimneys I was looking at, when suddenly a little head popped out at the top of one of them, followed by the upper part of a body, with the arms resting on the edge of the chimney. 'Hurrah!' It was a little chimney sweep who had gone right up a chimney for the first time in his life, and got his head out at the top. 'Hurrah!' this was a very different matter from creeping about in the narrow flues and smaller chimneys. A fresh breeze met his face, and he could see right out over the town away to the green woods beyond. The sun was just rising, big and round, and it shone straight into his face which beamed with delight, although it was thoroughly smudged with soot. ' Now the whole town can see me,' said he, ' and the moon can see me, and the sun too, hurrah! ' and he waved his brush above his head.''

TWENTY-SIXTH EVENING

" Last night I looked down upon a town in China," said the moon; " my beams illumined the long blank walls which border the streets. Here and there you certainly find a door, but it is always tightly shut, for what does the Chinaman care about the outside world! The windows of the houses behind the walls are closely covered with jalousies. The Temple was the only place whence a dim light shone through the windows. I looked in upon its gorgeous colours. The walls from floor to ceiling are covered with pictures in strong colours and rich gilding. They are representations of the labours of the gods here on earth. There is an image of a god in every niche, almost hidden by gorgeous draperies and floating banners. Before each of the gods—which are all made of tin—stands a little altar with holy water, flowers, and burning wax tapers. At the upper end of the Temple stands Fu, the chief of all the gods; he is draped in silk of the sacred yellow. At the foot of the altar sat a living being, a young priest. He seemed to be praying, but in the midst of his prayers to fall into a reverie; and no doubt that was a sin, for his cheeks burnt, and his head sank lower and lower. Poor Soui-houng! was he in his dream seeing himself behind those dreary walls in a little garden of his own working at the flower beds? Perhaps a labour much dearer to him than this of tending wax tapers in the Temple. Or was it his desire to sit at a richly spread table, wiping his lips between each course with tissue paper? Or was his sin so great that did he dare to express it the Heavenly powers would punish him with death? Did his thoughts venture to stray with the barbarians' ships to their home in far distant England? No, his thoughts did not fly so far a-field, and yet they were as sinful as only the hot blood of youth can conceive them. Sinful, here in the Temple, before the image of Fu and the other gods. I know whither his thoughts had wandered.

" In the outskirts of the town, upon the flat flagged roof of a house where the parapet seemed to be made of porcelain, and among handsome vases full of large white bell-shaped flowers, sat the lovely Pé, with her narrow roguish eyes, full lips, and tiny feet.   Her shoes pinched, but the pressure at her heart was far greater, and she wearily raised her delicately modelled arms in their rustling satin sleeves.   In front of her stood a glass bowl with four gold-fish in it; she slowly stirred the water with a little painted and lacquered stick, slowly, oh very slowly, for she was musing.   Was she thinking how richly the fish were clad in gold, and how securely they lived in their glass bowl with all their plentiful food, and yet how much happier they would be if they had their freedom?   Ah, yes, the fair Pé thoroughly comprehended that.   Her thoughts wandered from her home and sought the Temple, but not for the sake of God!   Poor Pé! Poor Soui-houng!   their earthly thoughts met, but my cold beams fell between them like an angel's sword! "

TWENTY-SEVENTH EVENING

" It was a dead calm," said the moon; " the water was as transparent as the pure air that I was traversing.   I could see the curious plants down under the water, they were like giant forest trees stretching towards me, many fathoms long.   The fish swam over their tops; a flock of wild swans were flying past high up in the air; one of them sank with outspread wings lower and lower.   It followed with its eyes the aerial caravan, as the distance between them rapidly increased.   It held its wings outspread and motionless, and sank as a soap bubble sinks in the quiet air; when it touched the surface of the water, it bent its head back between its wings, and lay as still as the white lotus blossom on a tranquil lake.   A gentle breeze rose and swelled the glittering surface of the phosphorescent water, brilliant as ether itself rolling on in great broad billows.   The swan lifted its head, and the sparkling water dashed over its back and breast like blue flames.   Dawn shed its rosy light around, and the swan soared aloft with renewed vigour towards the rising sun, towards the faint blue coast line whither the aerial caravan took its flight. But it flew alone with longing in its breast. Solitary it flew over the swelling blue waters.''

TWENTY-EIGHTH EVENING

'' I will give you one more picture from Sweden,'' said the moon. '' Among gloomy forests near the melancholy shores of the Roxen stands the old convent church of Wreta. My beams fell through a grating in the wall into a spacious vault where kings slumber in their marble tombs. A royal crown glitters on the wall above them as an emblem of earthly glory; a royal crown, but it is made of painted wood, and kept in place by a wooden peg driven into the wall. Worms have gnawed through the gilded wood; the spider has spun its web from the crown to the coffin. It is a mourning banner, frail and transient as the grief of mortals. How calm their slumber! I remember them distinctly. I still see the confident smile around those lips which, so authoritatively and decidedly, uttered words of joy or grief.

'' When the steamer comes up among the mountains like a bark from fairyland, many a stranger comes to the church and pays a visit to this burial vault. He asks the kings' names, and they echo with a dead and forgotten sound. He looks at the worm-eaten crown, and if he has a pious mind, there is sadness in his smile. Sleep on, ye Dead! The moon remembers you, the moon sends her cold beams in the night into your silent kingdom over which the wooden crown hangs.''

TWENTY-NINTH EVENING

'' Close to the high road,'' said the moon, '' stands an inn, and immediately opposite to it is a great waggon shed, the roof of which was being thatched. I looked through the rafters, and through the open trap door into the uncomfortable space below. A turkey cock was asleep on a beam, and a saddle was resting in an empty crib. A travelling carriage stood in the middle of the shed. Its owners slept in it as safely as possible, while the horses were being fed and watered, and the driver stretched his legs, although—and I know it for a certainty—he had been fast asleep for more than half the way. The door of the groom's bedroom was open, the bed was topsy-turvy, and a candle guttered on the floor. The wind whistled cold through the shed, it was nearer daybreak than midnight. A party of strolling musicians were asleep in a stall. The father and mother, I daresay, were dreaming of the drops of liquid fire in their flask, and the pale girl about the tear-drop in her eye; a harp lay at their head, and a dog at their feet."

THIRTIETH EVENING

" It was in a little country town," said the moon. " I saw it last year, but that doesn't matter, for I saw it so distinctly. To-night I read about it in the papers, but the story is not nearly so intelligible in them. A bear-leader was sitting in the bar of a public-house eating his supper; his bear was tied up outside behind the wood-shed. Poor bear! he wouldn't harm a creature, though he looked fierce enough. Three little children were playing in the light of my beams up in an attic, the eldest was perhaps six years old, the youngest not more than two! Flop, flop! a muffled sound was heard coming up the stairs, who could it be? The door flew open—it was the bear, great shaggy Bruin! He was bored by standing out there in the yard, and he had found his way upstairs. I saw it all," said the moon. " The children were very much frightened when they first saw the big furry animal; they each crept into a different corner, but he found them out. He snuffed at them all, but did not hurt them. ' Why it must be a great big dog,' they thought, and they began to pat him. He lay down upon the floor, and the smallest boy rolled about on the top of him, and played at hiding his golden locks in the bear's long black coat. Then the biggest boy got out his drum, and played upon it as hard as ever he could; as soon as he heard it the bear got up on his hind legs and danced; it was a pretty sight. Each boy shouldered his gun, and the bear, of course, had to have one too, and he held it as tightly as any of them. This was indeed a rare playmate they had got, and no mistake. They marched up and down, 'one, two; one, two!' Just then someone came to the door and opened it, it was the children's mother. You should have seen the terrible, speechless agony in her ashen face, with open mouth, and starting eyes. But the smallest boy nodded to her, he was ever so pleased, and cried out loud, in his baby way, 'We are only playing soldiers, mother.' And then the bear-leader made his appearance."

THIRTY-FIRST EVENING

The wind blew strong and cold, the clouds were chasing by, and the moon only appeared now and then.

"I look down upon the flying clouds from the silence of space above!" said he. "I can see the clouds chasing over the earth. Just lately I was looking down into a prison, outside which stood a closed carriage; a prisoner was about to leave. My beams penetrated the grated window, and shone upon the inside wall. The prisoner was tracing some lines upon the wall; it was his farewell. He did not write words but a tune; the outpouring of his heart on his last night in this place. The door opened, and he was conducted to the carriage, he looked up at my round disc—clouds flew between us, as if he might not see my face nor I his. He got into the carriage, the door was shut, the whip cracked, and off they went through the thick forest, where my beams could not reach. I looked in through the prison grating again, and my beams fell once more upon the wall where the melody was traced—his last farewell: where words fail, melody may often speak!—But my rays only lighted up a few isolated notes, the greater part will always remain dark to me. Was it a death hymn he wrote? or were they carolling notes of joy? Was he driving to meet his death, or to the embrace of his beloved? The beams of the moon cannot read all that even mortals write. I look down on the flying clouds, from the silence of space above, and I see big clouds chasing across the earth."

THIRTY-SECOND EVENING

" I am very fond of children," said the moon, " the little
ones especially are so amusing.   I often peep at them through
the curtains when they least think I see them.   It is so amusing
to see them trying to undress themselves; first, a little round
naked shoulder appears out of the frock, then one arm slips out.
Or I see a stocking pulled off a dimpled little leg, firm and round,
and then comes out a little foot made to be kissed, and I kissed
it," said the moon.   " I must tell you what I saw to-night.   I
looked in at a window where the blind did not reach the bottom,
for there were no opposite neighbours.   I saw a whole flock of
little ones, brothers and sisters.   One little girl is only four years
old, but she knows ' Our Father ' as well as any of them, and
her mother sits by her bed every evening to hear it.   Then she
kisses her and sits by her till she falls asleep, which generally
happens as soon as she shuts her eyes.

" To-night the two eldest were rather wild; one of them
hopped about on one leg in his long white nightgown.   The
second one stood on a chair with the clothes of all the others
heaped upon him; he said it was a tableau, and they must guess
what it meant.   The third and fourth were putting their toys
carefully away in a drawer, and, of course, that has to be done,
but their mother said they must be quiet, for the little one was
going to say her prayers.   I peeped in over the lamp," said the
moon.   " The little four year old girl lay in bed among all the
fine white linen, her little hands were folded, and her face quite
grave and serious, and she began, ' Our Father,' aloud.   ' But
what is this,' said her mother, interrupting her in the middle.
' When you have said, " give us this day our daily bread," you
say something more which I can't quite hear; what is it?   You
must tell me.'   The little girl hesitated, and looked shyly at her
mother.   ' What do you say after " give us this day our daily
bread? " '   ' Don't be angry, mother, dear,' said the little one;
' I say, please put plenty of butter on it.' "

THE TINDER BOX

A SOLDIER came marching along the high road. One, two! One, two! He had his knapsack on his back and his sword at his side, for he had been to the wars, and he was on his way home now. He met an old witch on the road, she was so ugly, her lower lip hung right down on to her chin.

She said, "Good-evening, soldier! What a nice sword you've got, and such a big knapsack; you are a real soldier! You shall have as much money as ever you like!"

"Thank you kindly, you old witch!" said the soldier.

"Do you see that big tree!" said the witch, pointing to a tree close by. "It is hollow inside! Climb up to the top and you will see a hole into which you can let yourself down, right down under the tree! I will tie a rope round your waist so that I can haul you up again when you call!"

"What am I to do down under the tree?" asked the soldier.

"Fetch money!" said the witch. "You must know that when you get down to the bottom of the tree you will find yourself in a wide passage; it's quite light there, for there are over a hundred blazing lamps. You will see three doors which you can open, for the keys are there. If you go into the first room you will see a big box in the middle of the floor. A dog is sitting on the top of it, and he has eyes as big as saucers, but you needn't mind that. I will give you my blue-checked apron, which you can spread out on the floor; then go quickly forward, take up the dog and put him on my apron, open the box and take out as

236

much money as ever you like. It is all copper, but if you like silver better, go into the next room. There you will find a dog with eyes as big as millstones; but never mind that, put him on my apron and take the money. If you prefer gold you can have it too, and as much as you can carry, if you go into the third room. But the dog sitting on that box has eyes each as big as the Round Tower. He *is* a dog, indeed, as you may imagine! But don't let it trouble you; you only have to put him on to my apron and then he won't hurt you, and you can take as much gold out of the box as you like!"

"That's not so bad!" said the soldier. "But what am I to give you, old witch? For you'll want something, I'll be bound."

"No," said the witch, "not a single penny do I want; I only want you to bring me an old tinder box that my grandmother forgot the last time she was down there!"

"Well! tie the rope round my waist!" said the soldier.

"Here it is," said the witch, "and here is my blue-checked apron."

Then the soldier climbed up the tree, let himself slide down the hollow trunk, and found himself, as the witch had said, in the wide passage where the many hundred lamps were burning.

Now he opened the first door. Ugh! There sat the dog with eyes as big as saucers staring at him.

"You are a nice fellow!" said the soldier, as he put him on to the witch's apron, and took out as many pennies as he could cram into his pockets. Then he shut the box, and put the dog on the top of it again, and went into the next room. Hallo! there sat the dog with eyes as big as millstones.

"You shouldn't stare at me so hard; you might get a pain in your eyes!" Then he put the dog on the apron, but when he saw all the silver in the box he threw away all the coppers, and stuffed his pockets and his knapsack with silver. Then he went into the third room. Oh! how horrible! that dog really had two eyes as big as the Round Tower, and they rolled round and round like wheels.

"Good-evening!" said the soldier, saluting, for he had never seen such a dog in his life; but after looking at him for a bit he thought, "that will do," and then he lifted him down on to the

apron and opened the chest.   Preserve us!   What a lot of gold!
He could buy the whole of Copenhagen with it, and all the sugar
pigs from the cake-woman, all the tin soldiers, whips, and rock-
ing-horses in the world!   That was money indeed!   Now the
soldier threw away all the silver he had filled his pockets and his
knapsack with, and put gold in its place.   Yes, he crammed all
his pockets, his knapsack, his cap, and his boots so full that he
could hardly walk!   Now, he really had got a lot of money.   He
put the dog back on to the box, shut the door, and shouted up
through the tree, " Haul me up, you old witch! "

" Have you got the tinder box? "

" Oh! to be sure! " said the soldier.   " I had quite forgotten
it."   And he went back to fetch it.   The witch hauled him up,
and there he was standing on the high road again with his pockets,
boots, knapsack, and cap full of gold.

" What do you want the tinder box for? " asked the soldier.

" That's no business of yours," said the witch.   " You've
got the money; give me the tinder box! "

" Rubbish! " said the soldier.   " Tell me directly what you
want with it, or I will draw my sword and cut off your head."

" I won't! " said the witch.

Then the soldier cut off her head; there she lay!   But he tied
all the money up in her apron, slung it on his back like a pack,
put the tinder box in his pocket, and marched off to the town.

It was a beautiful town, and he went straight to the finest
hotel, ordered the grandest rooms and all the food he liked best,
because he was a rich man now that he had so much money.

Certainly the servant who had to clean his boots thought
they were funny old things for such a rich gentleman, but he
had not had time yet to buy any new ones; the next day he
bought new boots and fine clothes.   The soldier now became a
fine gentleman, and the people told him all about the grand
things in the town, and about their king, and what a lovely
princess his daughter was.

" Where is she to be seen? " asked the soldier.

" You can't see her at all! " they all said; " she lives in a
great copper castle surrounded with walls and towers.   Nobody
but the king dare go in and out, for it has been prophesied that
she will marry a common soldier, and the king doesn't like that! "

" I should like to see her well enough!" thought the soldier. But there was no way of getting leave for that.

He now led a very merry life; went to theatres, drove about in the King's Park, and gave away a lot of money to poor people, which was very nice of him; for he remembered how disagreeable it used to be not to have a penny in his pocket. Now he was rich, wore fine clothes, and had a great many friends, who all said what a nice fellow he was—a thorough gentleman—and he liked to be told that.

But as he went on spending money every day and his store was never renewed, he at last found himself with only two pence left. Then he was obliged to move out of his fine rooms. He had to take a tiny little attic up under the roof, clean his own boots, and mend them himself with a darning needle. None of his friends went to see him, because there were far too many stairs.

One dark evening when he had not even enough money to buy a candle with, he suddenly remembered that there was a little bit in the old tinder box he had brought out of the hollow tree, when the witch helped him down. He got out the tinder box with the candle end in it and struck fire, but as the sparks flew out from the flint the door burst open and the dog with eyes as big as saucers, which he had seen down under the tree, stood before him and said, " What does my lord command? "

" By heaven! " said the soldier, " this is a nice kind of tinder box, if I can get whatever I want like this! Get me some money," he said to the dog, and away it went.

It was back in a twinkling with a big bag full of pennies in its mouth.

Now the soldier saw what a treasure he had in the tinder box. If he struck once, the dog which sat on the box of copper came; if he struck twice, the dog on the silver box came, and if he struck three times, the one from the box of gold.

He now moved down to the grand rooms and got his fine clothes again, and then all his friends knew him once more, and liked him as much as ever.

Then he suddenly began to think: After all, it's a curious thing that no man can get a sight of the princess! Everyone says she is so beautiful! But what is the good of that when she always has to be shut up in that big copper palace with all the towers. Can I not somehow manage to see her? Where is my tinder box? Then he struck the flint, and, whisk, came the dog with eyes as big as saucers.

" It certainly is the middle of the night," said the soldier, " but I am very anxious to see the princess, if only for a single moment."

The dog was out of the door in an instant, and before the soldier had time to think about it, he was back again with the princess. There she was, fast asleep on the dog's back, and she was so lovely that anybody could see that she must be a real princess! The soldier could not help it, but he was obliged to kiss her, for he was a true soldier.

Then the dog ran back again with the princess, but in the morning, when the king and queen were having breakfast, the princess said that she had had such a wonderful dream about a dog and a soldier. She had ridden on the dog's back, and the soldier had kissed her.

" That's a pretty tale," said the queen.

After this an old lady-in-waiting had to sit by her bed at night to see if this was really a dream, or what it could be.

The soldier longed so intensely to see the princess again that at night the dog came to fetch her. He took her up and ran off with her as fast as he could, but the old lady-in-waiting put on her galoshes and ran just as fast behind them; when she saw that they disappeared into a large house, she thought now I know where it is, and made a big cross with chalk on the gate. Then she went home and lay down, and presently the dog came back, too, with the princess. When he saw that there was a cross on the gate, he took a bit of chalk, too, and made crosses on all the gates in the town; now this was very clever of him, for the lady-in-waiting could not possibly find the gate when there were crosses on all the gates.

Early next morning the king, the queen, the lady-in-waiting, and all the court officials went to see where the princess had been.

" There it is," said the king, when he saw the first door with the cross on it.

" No, my dear husband, it is there," said the queen, who saw another door with a cross on it.

" But there is one, and there is another! " they all cried out.

They soon saw that it was hopeless to try and find it.

Now the queen was a very clever woman; she knew more than how to drive in a chariot. She took her big gold scissors and cut up a large piece of silk into small pieces, and made a pretty little bag, which she filled with fine grains of buckwheat. She then tied it on to the back of the princess, and when that was done she cut a little hole in the bag, so that the grains could drop out all the way wherever the princess went.

At night the dog came again, took the princess on his back, and ran off with her to the soldier, who was so fond of her that he longed to be a prince, so that he might have her for his wife.

The dog never noticed how the grain dropped out all along the road from the palace to the soldier's window, where he ran up the wall with the princess.

In the morning the king and the queen easily saw where their daughter had been, and they seized the soldier and threw him into the dungeons.

There he lay! Oh, how dark and tiresome it was, and then one day they said to him, " To-morrow you are to be hanged." It was not amusing to be told that, especially as he had left his tinder box behind him at the hotel.

In the morning he could see through the bars in the little window that the people were hurrying out of the town to see him hanged. He heard the drums, and saw the soldiers marching along. All the world was going; among them was a shoe-maker's boy in his leather apron and slippers. He was in such a hurry that he lost one of his slippers, and it fell close under the soldier's window where he was peeping out through the bars.

" I say, you boy! Don't be in such a hurry," said the soldier to him. " Nothing will happen till I get there! But if you will run to the house where I used to live, and fetch me my tinder box, you shall have a penny! You must put your best foot foremost! "

The boy was only too glad to have the penny, and tore off to get the tinder box, gave it to the soldier, and—yes now we shall hear.

Outside the town a high scaffold had been raised, and the soldiers were drawn up round about it, as well as crowds of the townspeople. The king and the queen sat upon a beautiful throne exactly opposite the judge and all the councillors.

The soldier mounted the ladder, but when they were about to put the rope round his neck, he said that before undergoing his punishment a criminal was always allowed the gratification of a harmless wish, and he wanted very much to smoke a pipe, as it would be his last pipe in this world.

The king would not deny him this, so the soldier took out his tinder box and struck fire, once, twice, three times, and there were all the dogs. The one with eyes like saucers, the one with eyes like millstones, and the one whose eyes were as big as the Round Tower.

" Help me! Save me from being hanged! " cried the soldier.

And then the dogs rushed at the soldiers and the councillors; they took one by the legs, and another by the nose, and threw them up many fathoms into the air; and when they fell down, they were broken all to pieces.

" I won't! " cried the king, but the biggest dog took both him and the queen and threw them after all the others. Then the soldiers became alarmed, and the people shouted, " Oh! good soldier, you shall be our king, and marry the beautiful princess! "

Then they conducted the soldier to the king's chariot, and all three dogs danced along in front of him and shouted " Hurrah! " The boys all put their fingers in their mouths and whistled, and the soldiers presented arms. The princess came out of the copper palace and became queen, which pleased her very much. The wedding took place in a week, and the dogs all had seats at the table, where they sat staring with all their eyes.

MA

THE GOLOSHES OF FORTUNE

CHAPTER I

A GRAND party was assembled one evening in a big house in East Street, Copenhagen. It was one of those parties given, no doubt, in the expectation that invitations would be received in return. Half the company were already seated at the card tables, and the other half were waiting to see what would be the result of a remark of their hostess—" Now we must see what we can do to amuse ourselves."

They were at this point, and the conversation was getting on as well as it could. Among other subjects, it fell upon the Middle Ages; some considered that period far superior to our own, nay, Mr. Councillor Knap defended this view so vigorously that he won over the hostess to his side, and both inveighed against Oersted's article in the Almanack on Ancient and Modern Times, in which the preference is given to our own. The Councillor considered the times of King Hans [1] as the noblest and happiest.

During all this talk, which was only interrupted for a moment by the arrival of the newspaper in which there was nothing worth reading, we will retire into the ante-room which was given up to cloaks, sticks, umbrellas, and goloshes.

[1] He died in 1513.

243

Two maidens were sitting here, one young and one old; it might be supposed that they had come to accompany their mistresses home, some old maid or widow lady. If, however, one looked a little closer, one soon saw that they were not ordinary maids; their hands were too white, their bearing and their movements were too distinguished for that, and then the cut of their clothes was too elegant and uncommon.

They were in fact two fairies, the youngest, though not Dame Fortune herself, was the messenger of one of her maids-of-honour, used to carry about the smaller gifts of fortune. The elder one looked very serious; she was Sorrow, and she always goes about herself, to do her errands in person, for then she knows they are well done.

They were telling each other where they had been during the day; she who was the handmaid of Fortune had only been employed on some trifling matters, such as saving a new hat from a downpour of rain, and procuring a greeting for an honest man from a grand Nobody, and so on. What she still had left to do was quite out of the ordinary way.

" I must tell you," she said, " that to-day is my birthday, and in honour of it I have had intrusted to me a pair of goloshes which I am to convey to mankind. These goloshes have this property, that whoever puts them on will immediately find himself in whatever place or period he would like; every wish with regard to time or place will be at once gratified, and the wearer will thus for once find perfect happiness in this world! "

" A likely story! " said Sorrow; " he will be sorely unhappy, and will bless the moment when he can get rid of the goloshes! "

" What nonsense you are talking," said the other; " I will place them here near the door, and someone will take them by mistake, and in putting them on will find happiness." Thus ended the conversation.

CHAPTER II

WHAT HAPPENED TO THE COUNCILLOR

It was late when Councillor Knap, lost in thought about the good old times of King Hans, wanted to go home, and Fate willed it so that instead of his own goloshes, he put on those of

Fortune, and went out into East Street.   But, by the magic power of the goloshes, in doing so he stepped straight back three hundred years into the reign of King Hans, and therefore his feet sank into the mud and slush of those times, the streets then not being paved.

"Oh! this is terrible!" he said; "what mud; and what has become of the footpath?   And the lamps are extinguished!"

The moon had not yet risen, and it was rather foggy, so that everything melted away into darkness.   At the nearest street corner, however, hung a lantern in front of an image of the Madonna, but the light it gave was as good as none, he only saw it when he was close under it and his eyes fell on the figures of the Mother and Child.

"It is most likely a Museum of Art, and they have forgotten to take down the sign."

Two persons in the dress of the Middle Ages passed him.

"Who on earth are these?   They must be coming from a Masquerade."

All at once he heard drums and fifes, and blazing torches shone around him; the Councillor stopped to look, while the extraordinary procession passed him.   First came a whole troop of drummers, beating their drums very cleverly; they were followed by halberdiers with long bows and cross-bows.   The principal person in the procession wore a clerical dress.   In astonishment the Councillor asked what was the meaning of all this, and who the man was?

"It is the Bishop of Zealand!" he was answered.

"Good gracious!" he exclaimed, "whatever has the Bishop taken into his head?"   Then he shook his head and murmured that it could not possibly be the Bishop.   Musing over this, and without looking either to the right or the left, the Councillor walked on down East Street and over the High Bridge Place. He could not find the bridge to Palace Square at all, but only saw a shallow stream, and at last came upon two men with a boat.

"Does the gentleman want to be put over to Holm?" asked they.

"Over to Holm?" said the Councillor, who had no idea in what Age he was now living.   "I want to go to Christian's Haven in Little Turf Street."

The men stared at him.

"Only tell me where to find the bridge," he said. "It's shameful that there are no lamps lighted, and then it's so muddy one might be walking in a swamp."

But the more he talked to the boatmen, the less they understood each other.

"I don't understand your jargon," he cried at last, and turned his back on them. The bridge, however, he could *not* find, nor any railing. "What a scandalous condition the place is in," he said. Never certainly had he found his own Age so miserable as on this evening. "I think it will be better for me to take a coach; but where are they?" There was not one to be seen. "I must go back to the King's New Market Place, where there is a stand, or I shall never get back to Christian's Haven."

So then he walked back to East Street, and had nearly traversed the length of it, when the moon burst through a cloud.

"Good gracious! Whatever is that erection?" he exclaimed, as he caught sight of the East Gate which in olden times used to stand at the end of East Street. At last he found a wicket gate, and passed through on to what is now the New Market Place. Nothing was to be seen but a great open meadow, a few solitary bushes stood here and there, and a wide stream flowed across it. On the opposite bank stood a few miserable wooden booths used by the Dutch watermen, whence it gained its name of the Dutch meadow.

"Either I see a Fata Morgana, as they call it, or else I am drunk!" the Councillor groaned. "What can it be? What is the matter with me?" He turned back again, firmly convinced that he must be ill. On entering the street again, he looked more closely at the houses, most of them were timbered, and with thatched roofs.

"I am certainly quite out of sorts," he sighed, "and yet I only drank one glass of punch. But I can't stand even that! and it really is too bad to give us punch with hot salmon! I shall have to tell our hostess so! Shall I go straight back and tell them what a condition I am in? It would look so foolish, and I should hardly expect anyone to be up now!" He tried to find the house, but in vain.

"This is desperate! I don't know East Street again! Not

a shop to be seen, only miserable, tumble-down hovels such as one might find in Roeskilde or Ringsted. Oh! how ill I am, it's no good standing on ceremony. But where in the world is the agent's house? There is a house, but it's not like itself! There are still some people up in it, I can hear them. O dear, I feel very queer!''

He found a half-open door through which the light streamed. It was a tavern of the olden times, and seemed to be a kind of beer-house. The room looked like one of the old-fashioned house places of Holstein with a clay floor. A number of good folks, consisting mostly of seamen, Copenhagen burghers, and a few scholars, sat in deep conversation over their mugs, and took very little notice of him as he stepped in.

'' Pardon me!'' said the Councillor to the landlady; '' I do not feel very well, and I should be much obliged if you would send for a coach to take me home to Christian's Haven.''

The woman stared at him and shook her head; then she spoke to him in German, from which the Councillor concluded that she did not understand Danish, and repeated his request in German. This, as well as his strange dress, convinced the woman that he was a foreigner. She soon understood that he felt ill, and brought him a mug of water which was certainly rather brackish, as it came from the well outside.

The Councillor rested his head on his hand, drew a deep breath, and pondered over all the wonders around him.

'' Is that this evening's *Day?*'' he asked, for the sake of saying something, as he saw the woman folding a large sheet of paper.

She did not understand what he meant, but handed him the sheet. It was a woodcut representing a comet seen in the city of Cologne.

'' That is very old,'' said the Councillor, becoming quite excited at discovering this ancient woodcut. '' Wherever did you get this rare print? It is very interesting, although the whole affair is a fable. Comets are easily explained in these days; they are northern lights, and are no doubt caused by electricity.''

Those who sat near him and heard what he said, looked at him in astonishment, and one of them rose, took off his hat respectfully, and said in a very serious manner, " You must be a very learned man, monsieur."

" Oh no! " replied the Councillor; " I can only discourse a little on topics which everyone should understand."

" *Modestia* is a beautiful virtue," said the man; " otherwise I must say to your speech *mihi secus videtur*, yet in this case I willingly suspend my *judicium*."

" May I ask whom I have the pleasure of addressing? " said the Councillor.

" I am Baccalaureus Scripturæ Sacræ," said the man.

This answer was enough for the Councillor, for the title agreed with the dress. Some old village schoolmaster, he thought, an odd fellow, such as one still may find in Jutland.

" This is certainly not a *locus docendi*," began the man; " still I must beg you to continue the conversation. You must be deeply read in the ancient writings."

" Oh, pretty well," replied the Councillor. " I am very fond of reading useful old books and modern ones as well, with the exception of ' Everyday Stories,' [1] of which we really have more than enough in real life! "

" Everyday Stories? " asked the Baccalaureus.

" Yes; I mean these new novels."

" Oh," replied the man with a smile, " and yet they are very witty, and are much read at Court. The King is especially fond of the ' Romance of Iwain and Jawain,' which describes King Arthur and his knights of the Round Table. He has joked about it with the gentlemen of his Court."

" Well, I have certainly not read that; I suppose it is a new one which Heiberg has just published."

" No," answered the man; " It is not by Heiberg. Gottfred von Gehman brought it out."

" Oh, is he the publisher? That is a very old name! Why, he was the first printer we had in Denmark! "

" Yes; he is our first printer," said the man.

So far, all had passed off very well. Now one of the burghers began to speak of a terrible pestilence which had been raging a year or two before, meaning the plague of 1484. The Councillor

---

[1] " Everyday Stories," popular stories of the day, edited by Heiberg, written by Fru Gyllembourg.

supposed that he alluded to the cholera, and they got on without finding out their mistake. The Freebooter's War of 1490 was still so near that it was the next topic. The English Freebooters had taken ships on the Rheden, said they. The Councillor, who was well up in the incident of 1801, was quite at one with them against the English. After that the conversation was not so pleasant, every moment one contradicted the other. The honest Baccalaureus was so ignorant that the simplest utterances of the Councillor sounded to him wildly fantastic. They looked at each other, and when they became quite incomprehensible to each other, Baccalaureus spoke Latin, in the hope of being better understood, but it was all of no use.

" How are you now? " asked the landlady, pulling the Councillor by the sleeve. This brought him to himself, for while he had been talking he had entirely forgotten what had passed before.

" Where am I? " he said, his brain reeling as he tried to think.

" We will have claret, mead, and Bremen beer," shouted one of the guests, " and you shall drink with us! "

Two maids came in, one of them wore a parti-coloured hood.[1] They filled the glasses and curtsied: a cold shiver ran down the Councillor's back.

" What is this? What does it mean? " said he, but he was obliged to drink with them. They quite overpowered the good man; he was in despair, and when one of them said he was drunk he never doubted the man's words, but begged them to fetch him a " droschky," and then they thought he was speaking the Muscovite tongue.

Never had he been in such low, coarse company; one might have thought the country had gone back to heathendom again. Said he to himself, " This is the most terrible moment of my life! " Just then it came into his head to stoop down under the table, creep to the door, and so try to get away, but just as he reached the door the others perceived his intention and seized him by the feet, when, luckily for him, off came the goloshes, and with them all the enchantment.

[1] In the time of King Hans, chambermaids were obliged to wear caps of two colours.

The Councillor now saw quite plainly a brightly burning lamp in front of him, and behind it a large house; every house round was familiar to him, he was in East Street just as we know it. He was lying with his feet against a gate, and the watchman sat opposite fast asleep.

"Good heavens! Have I lain here dreaming in the street!" he said. "Yes, to be sure, this is East Street, as bright and well lighted as usual. It is terrible that one glass of punch should have had such an effect on me."

Two minutes later he was comfortably seated in a coach on his way to Christian's Haven. He thought of all the terror and anxiety he had undergone, and with a full heart he prized the happy reality of his own time, which, with all its shortcomings, was so much better than that of which he had lately made trial. Now this was very wise of the Councillor.

CHAPTER III

THE WATCHMAN'S ADVENTURE

"Why, here is a pair of goloshes!" said the watchman. "They must belong to the Lieutenant who lives up there, they are close to the door." The honest man would willingly have rung the bell and handed them in, for there were still lights burning, but he was afraid of disturbing the other people in the house.

"It must be nice and warm to have those things on," he said, "the leather is so soft!" He slipped his feet into them. "How odd things are in this world! Now the Lieutenant might be in his comfortable bed, but see if he is! No! he is marching up and down the room. He's a happy man, he has neither wife nor bairns, he goes out to parties every night, shouldn't I like to be in his place, then I should be a happy man!"

As he uttered his wish the goloshes began to have their effect, and the watchman became the Lieutenant in body and soul. There he stood upstairs in his room holding a little pink paper between his fingers upon which was written a poem he had just completed. Who at some time in his life has not been impelled to write poetry? One writes poetry when one is in love, but a wise man does not print it. The words Lieutenant, Love, and Lack of gold form a triplet, or better still, a half of Fortune's shattered die. The Lieutenant felt this also, and so, as he leant against the window, he said with a sigh,—

" The poor watchman out in the street is far happier than I! He does not know privation as I do! He has a home, wife, and children who weep with him in his sorrow and rejoice with his joy! Oh, I should be happier than I am if I could change places with him! "

At this moment the watchman again became a watchman because it was through the goloshes of Fortune that he had become a Lieutenant. As we see, he felt far less happy, and preferred to be what he really was, so the watchman was again a watchman.

" That was an ugly dream! " said he; " but curiously enough I thought I was the Lieutenant up there, and there was no pleasure in it. I missed my old woman and the little ones; they're always ready to smother me with kisses."

Then he sat nodding again, he could not get the dream quite out of his head, for he still had the goloshes on. A shooting star darted across the sky.

" There it goes! " he said; " there are plenty of them. I should like well enough to see those affairs a bit nearer, especially the moon; it wouldn't slip through my fingers. The student for whom my wife washes says that when we die we fly from one to the other of them. It's a lie, of course, but it wouldn't be bad. If I could have a little trip up there, I'd willingly leave my body behind." Now there are certain things in the world we should beware of expressing, especially if we have Fortune's goloshes on our feet. Just listen to the watchman's adventure.

Few amongst us are not acquainted with the rapidity of steam-travelling either on land by railway, or at sea by boat, but these flights are only like the wanderings of the sloth, or the march of the snail, compared with the velocity of light. Light travels nineteen million times faster than the best racehorse, but it is again outstripped by electricity. Death is an electric shock which touches the heart; the soul when freed is borne on the wings of electricity. The sunlight takes eight minutes and some seconds to perform a journey of over twenty millions of miles, but the soul performs the same distance in an infinitely shorter space of time. The space between the heavenly bodies is, for it, not greater than would be to us the distance between our friends' houses in a town, even if these were rather close together. In the meantime this electric shock entirely deprives us of the use of our bodies, unless, like the watchman, we are wearing the goloshes of Fortune. In a few seconds the watchman had traversed the 52,000 miles to the moon, which is, as we know, made of a much softer material than our earth; it is more like new fallen snow. He found himself on one of the numerous mountains which we all know from Dr. Mädler's large map of the moon. The interior of the mountain was like a large cauldron, a whole Danish mile in depth. At the bottom of this cauldron lay a town, of whose appearance an idea may be formed by putting the white of an egg into a glass of water, the substance of which it was made being quite as soft, while similar towers with cupolas and hanging balconies, all perfectly transparent, hovered in the thin clear air. Our earth floated above his head like a great blood-red ball.

Crowds of beings, all no doubt what we should call persons, moved about; but their appearance was very different from ours. They also had a language which nobody could expect the soul of the watchman to understand, this however it did. The soul of the watchman understood the language of the moon-dwellers perfectly well. They were disputing about our earth, and doubting whether it could be inhabited; the air, they thought, must be too thick for any sensible moon-being to live in it. Most of them were of opinion that the moon alone was inhabited, it was the original globe in which the old-world people lived.

Now we must return to East Street to see what has become of the watchman's body.

Lifeless on the steps it lay; the Morning Star [1] had fallen out of its hand, and the eyes looked up towards the moon, where its honest companion the soul was wandering.

"What o'clock is it, watchman?" asked a passer by. But the watchman did not answer, so the enquirer gently tapped him on the nose, and away went his balance, the body fell down full

---

[1] His badge of office, a club armed with iron spikes.

length, for the watchman was dead, you know. A great fright
had come over the man who had pushed him, the watchman
was dead, and dead he remained. The death was notified, and
at dawn the body was taken to the hospital.

It might be a rare joke for the soul when it came back, if, as
in all probability, it went to East Street to look for the body, and
failed to find it there. Probably it would first go to the police-
station, then to the lost property office to advertise for it among
other things lost or stolen; and last of all it might go to the
hospital. However, it may console us to know that the soul is
wisest when left to itself; it is the body which makes it stupid.

As we said before, the watchman's body went to the hospital,
where it was first taken into the bathroom and the goloshes were,
of course, taken off. Then the soul had to come back again; it
immediately took possession of the body, and the man came to
life at once. He declared that it had been the most terrible
night of his life, and not for a shilling would he go through it
again. However, all was over now. He was discharged the
same day, but the goloshes were left at the hospital.

CHAPTER IV

A CRITICAL MOMENT—AN EVENING'S DRAMATIC READING—A MOST UNUSUAL JOURNEY

Everyone in Copenhagen knows what the Frederik's Hospital
looks like, but, as probably some strangers may read this tale,
we must give a short description of it.

The hospital is separated from the street by a rather high
railing, of which the thick iron bars are just so far apart that a
thin student—so the story goes—could squeeze through them,
and so pay little visits to the outside world. The part of the
body most difficult to squeeze through was the head; in this case,
as so often in the world, a small head was the most convenient.
This will be a sufficient introduction.

One of the young medical students, of whom only in a physical
sense could it be said that he was thick-headed, happened to be
on duty that night; it was pouring with rain. Notwithstanding
these two hindrances he pined to get out, if only for a quarter of

an hour. It was not worth while, he thought, confiding in the porter, if he could slip out through the railings. There lay the goloshes the watchman had forgotten; little did he think that they were Fortune's, but they might be useful in such weather; so he slipped them on. Now came the question whether he could slip through the railings; he had never tried it before. There he stood.

" How I wish I had my head through," he said, and immediately, although it was far too big, it slipped through quite easily. The goloshes understood all about it. Now to get the body through. " Ugh! I am too stout," said he. " I thought the head was the greatest difficulty. I shall never get through."

Then he tried to draw his head back quickly, but it wouldn't come. He could move his neck about, but that was all he could do. He first felt very angry, and then his spirits sank below zero. The goloshes of Fortune had brought him into a terrible position, and unfortunately it never occurred to him to wish himself free again. Instead of wishing, he struggled to free himself, but in vain. The rain poured down, not a creature was to be seen in the street. He could not reach the bell by the gate; how was he to get away. He foresaw that he might have to stand there till morning, then a smith would have to be fetched to file the bars, and it would be a very slow business. All the blue coat boys from the school opposite would be on the move, the people from Nyboder would appear on the scene for the fun of seeing him in the pillory. There would be a much bigger crowd than there was at the meeting for the wrestling championship last year. " Ugh! " he cried, " the blood is rushing to my head; I shall go mad. Oh! if I were only free again I should be all right."

Now he should have said this before; no sooner was the wish expressed than it was fulfilled, his head was free. He rushed into the hospital quite distracted by the terror which the goloshes of Fortune had caused him.

We must not suppose that his adventures were over. No indeed, the worst is to come.

The night passed and the following day, but no one sent for the goloshes.

In the evening there was to be a performance in the small theatre in Kannicke Street. The house was crammed, and between the acts a new poem was to be recited. It was called "My Aunt's Spectacles." It was the story of a pair of spectacles which enabled the wearer to look into futurity. The poem was excellently recited, and it was received with much applause. Among the audience was the medical student, who seemed entirely to have forgotten his adventure of the previous evening. Again he was wearing the goloshes, as no one had claimed them, and the streets being very muddy, they would do him good service, he thought.

He was much taken with the poem, and the idea of it haunted him. He would like such a pair of spectacles well enough himself. Perhaps, if they were rightly used, one might be able to look straight into people's hearts, and this would be much more interesting, he thought, than to know what would happen next year. Future events must, in due course, be revealed, whereas the secrets of the heart would never be divulged.

"I can picture to myself the whole row of ladies and gentlemen on the front bench, if one could only look straight into their hearts—what a revelation there would be! A sort of shop would open before me, and how I should use my eyes! In the heart of that lady opposite, for instance, I should expect a whole millinery establishment! The next one would be quite empty, but it would be none the worse for a thorough cleaning. There would also be shops of a more substantial nature! Ah, yes!" he sighed, "I know one in which everything is substantial and good, but unfortunately there is already a shopman in it, more is the pity! From many I should hear the words, 'Be so good as to walk inside.' Ah! if only he could walk in, as a nice little thought passes through the heart!"

This was quite enough for the goloshes, the student shrank up into nothing, and began a journey of a most unusual kind, right through the hearts of the people in the front row. The first heart he entered was that of a lady, but at first he imagined himself to be in an Orthopædic Hospital, where people go to have their limbs straightened, and to be cured of their deformities. He was in a room hung round with plaster casts of misshapen limbs! but the difference here was, that whereas in the hospital the casts were taken when the patients were admitted, these in the heart were taken and preserved after the originals had left. They were, in fact, the casts of the bodily and mental deformities of her friends, thus carefully preserved.

Quickly he passed on into the heart of another woman; this one appeared to him as a great sacred church. The white dove of Innocence hovered over the altar. How gladly would he have fallen on his knees before it, and worshipped, but he was hurried on into the next heart. Still, however, the notes of the organ echoed in his heart, and he seemed to have become another and a better man, and not utterly unworthy to enter the next sanctuary. Here was revealed to him a poor little attic, where lay a sick mother. Poor though it was, God's warm sunshine streamed brightly in; lovely roses nodded their heads from the little wooden box on the roof, while two blue birds warbled sweetly of the joys of childhood, and the sick mother called down a blessing on her daughter.

Now he crept on hands and knees through an over-crowded butcher's shop. Flesh, flesh, and nothing but flesh; it was the heart of a rich respectable man, whose name no doubt will be found in the directory.

He next entered the heart of the man's wife. It was an old deserted dove-cot; the husband's portrait was used as a weather-cock, which was connected with the doors, so that these opened and shut as the man turned about.

Thence he passed into a cabinet of mirrors such as we have in the Castle of Rosenborg, only these had the power of magnifying to an extraordinary extent. In the middle of the room, on the floor, like the grand Llama of Thibet, sat the insignificant "Ego" of the person, astonished with the contemplation of his own greatness. After this he found himself in a narrow needle-case, full of sharp needles. "This must surely be the heart of some old maid!" he thought, but this was not the case, it was the heart of quite a young officer with many medals and orders, and who was considered a man of spirit and refinement.

The wretched student passed out of the last heart in a state of great bewilderment, he could not collect his thoughts at all, but fancied that his vivid imagination had run away with him.

"Good heavens!" he sighed, "I must be on the high road to madness! It is so desperately hot here, it makes the blood rush to my head!" All at once he remembered the terrible events of the night before, how his head had been stuck between the bars of the railing at the hospital. " I must have brought it on there," he said. " There's nothing like taking things in time. A turkish bath would be the best thing. I wish I were on the upper shelf there! "

Accordingly he found himself on the upper shelf in the " Sudarium," but he lay there in all his· clothes, boots and goloshes; the drops of hot water trickled on to his face from the ceiling.

" Hallo! " he shouted, and rushed down to get a shower-bath. The attendant also shouted when he saw a man with all his clothes on in the shower-bath.

The student collected himself sufficiently to whisper, " It's a wager! " The first thing he did when he got home was to put a blister on to his neck and his back, to draw out the madness.

The next morning his back was raw, and that was all he gained by the goloshes.

CHAPTER V

THE METAMORPHOSIS OF THE COPYING CLERK

In the meantime the watchman, whom we have not forgotten, remembered the goloshes he had found, which had gone to the hospital with him. He fetched them away, but as neither the Lieutenant nor anyone else in the street would own them, they were left at the police station.

" They're exactly like my own goloshes," said one of the clerks, as he examined the castaways and measured them with his own. " You would have to have a keener eye than a shoemaker to see any difference between them! "

" Mr. Clerk! " said an attendant who came in with some papers.

The clerk returned to speak to the man, and when he was gone and he returned to his examination of the goloshes, he could no longer remember whether the right hand pair or the left hand pair were his. " Those which are wet must be mine! " he thought, but in this he made a mistake for they were Fortune's.

Surely the police may make mistakes sometimes, as well as other people!

So he put them on, stuffed some papers into his pockets and took some others under his arm, for they were to be read and revised at home.   It happened to be Sunday morning, and a very fine day, so he thought a walk in Frederiksborg garden would do him good, and out he went.

No one could be a quieter or more industrious person than this young man, and right glad are we that he should have this little walk, it could only do him good after so much sitting.

At first he walked along not thinking of anything in particular, so the goloshes had no opportunity of exercising their magic power.   He met a friend in the Avenue, a young poet, who told him that his summer holiday was to begin on the following day.

" Hallo! are you off again? " said the clerk.   " You are a lucky fellow.   You can fly off whenever you like, we others are tied by the leg! "

" Ah! but one end of the chain is attached to the bread fruit tree, you must remember," answered the poet.   " You have no cares about your daily bread, and then you have a pension."

" Still you are far better off! " said the clerk; " you can sit writing poetry, what a pleasure that is.   Everybody says pleasant things to you, and you are your own master.   I should like you to sit writing about all these trivial affairs in an office! "

The poet shook his head, the clerk shook his too, and neither of them changed their opinions in the least.   They then took leave of each other.

" They're queer cattle these poets," said the clerk.   " I should like to understand them and their ways, and to become a poet myself; I'm certain I shouldn't write such lackadaisical rhymes as other people.   What a lovely spring day this is, a perfect poet's day! the air is so clear, and the clouds are so beautiful, and there is such a delicious scent from the flowers and shrubs.   I have not felt as I do to-day for years! "

We already perceive that he has become a poet, though there was no great outward change in him, for it is a foolish idea that poets look different from other people.   There may be many far more poetical natures among persons who are not known as poets, than in those of the acknowledged poets. The only difference is that the poet has a better memory, he can hold fast to a feeling or an idea till it comes forth clearly embodied in beautiful words, and this the others cannot do. But to pass from a commonplace person into one of originality must always be a great change, and this is what had now befallen the clerk.

"What fragrant air!" he said; "it reminds me of Aunt Magdalene's violets; ah! that was when I was a little boy! What an age it is since I thought about her, my good old aunt. She used to live there, behind the Exchange. She always had a few buds, or green shoots in water, however severe the winter might be. I used to smell the violets while I put the heated pennies on the frozen window panes to make peep holes. What a view that was; there were the ships frozen up in the canal deserted by the sailors, one cawing crow being the whole crew in charge. As soon as the fresh spring breezes returned, everything received new life. Amid songs and merriment the ice was sawn up, the ships were tarred and rigged, and then off they went to foreign parts. I have remained here, and always must remain, sitting at the office seeing other people taking their passports for foreign countries. Such is my lot!" he said, sighing deeply; but suddenly he stopped. "Good Heavens! what is the matter with me? I have never felt like this before! It must be the effect of the spring air, it gives me almost as much pain as pleasure!" He felt in his pockets for the papers. "These will give me something else to think about," he said, running his eyes over the first page. "'Dame Sigbrith,' an original tragedy in five acts," he read. "Why, what is this, yet it is in my own handwriting. Did I write this tragedy? 'The Intrigue on the Ramparts,' a comedy—where on earth did this come from, someone must have put it into my pocket; here is a letter too!" It was from the manager of a theatre, the pieces were rejected, and the letter was anything but civil. "Hum! hum!" said the clerk, sitting down on a bench; his ideas were so fresh and his heart so softened. Mechanically he plucked a flower growing near; it was a simple little daisy, yet what botanists can only explain to us in several lectures, this little flower teaches us at once. She related the myth of her birth, she told him about the power of the sun, which unfolded her tender leaves and drew forth her fragrance; this made him reflect on the battle of life, which in like manner rouses the slumbering feelings in our breasts. Light and air both woo the flower, but light is the favoured lover, and to him she turns continually; when light disappears she shuts up her petals and sleeps in the safe guardianship of air. "It is light which makes me so beautiful," said the flower. "But it is air which gives light!" whispered the poet's voice.

Close by stood a boy stirring up the mud in a ditch with a stick; the water splashed up into the green branches above. The clerk thought of the millions of invisible insects hurled up in the drops of water, and to whom such an evolution must have been as terrible as it would be for us to be whirled about the clouds. As these thoughts came into his head, and all the changes which had taken place in him, he smiled. "I must be fast asleep and dreaming! But how wonderful it is! how naturally one dreams, knowing all the time that it is but a dream. If only I could remember when I wake all that I have been dreaming. I seem to be wonderfully clear headed just now; I see everything plainly, but I am sure in the morning, if I have any recollection of my dreams at all, they will be nothing but nonsense. I have tried it before. All the clever and brilliant things one says and hears in dreams are like the gold of the underground gnomes; rich and bright when it is given you, but see it by daylight, and you have nothing but stones and dead leaves. Alas!" he said, sighing sadly, as he looked at the little birds singing gaily and hopping from branch to branch. "They are much better off than I am. Flying is a delightful accomplishment if you are born to it! If I were to change into anything else it should be into a little lark like that!"

At once the sleeves and tails of his coat stuck together and became wings, his clothes changed to feathers, and his goloshes to claws. He perceived the change at once, and laughed inwardly. "Now I am sure I am dreaming," he said; "but such a stupid dream as this I have never had before." He flew up among the branches with a song, but there was no poetry in it, for his poet's nature was gone. The goloshes, like everyone who does anything thoroughly, could only do one thing at a time. The clerk wished to be a poet, and he became one; now he wanted to be a little bird, and a bird he became; but on becoming a bird he lost his previous characteristics.

" This is nice enough," he said; " during the day I can sit at the office attending to the gravest matters, and at night I can dream that I am flying about like a lark in Frederiksborg gardens. What a capital farce it would make!" Then he flew down on to the grass, twisting and turning his head about among the waving stalks, which, in proportion to his present size, were as tall as the palms of Northern Africa.

It was but for a few minutes; all at once it grew as dark as night around him; a huge object, as it seemed to him, was thrown over him. It was a big cap with which a schoolboy from Nydober had covered him. A hand crept in and clutched the clerk by the back and wings, so tightly that he piped, and in his terror called out quite loud, " You impudent young puppy, I am a clerk in the police service!" but to the boy it only sounded like peep-peep, and he hit him on the beak and walked off with him.

In the Avenue he met two schoolboys of the upper classes— in rank at least; in learning they were amongst the lowest in the school. They bought the bird for a few pence, and in this way the clerk got back to Copenhagen, where he was taken to a house in Goth Street.

" It's well that I'm only dreaming," said the clerk, " or I should be in a fine rage! First I was a poet, now I am a lark! It was my poetical temperament which made me change into a bird; but it's a miserable business when one falls into the hands of boys. I should like to know what the end of it will be."

The boys took him into a very elegantly furnished room, where a stout, merry lady received them, but she was by no means pleased at their bringing in a common little field-bird, as she called the lark. She would let them keep it for to-day, she said, and they might put it in the empty cage near the window; " Perhaps it would please Polly-parrot!" added she, laughing at a big green parrot which was swinging backwards and forwards in a stately manner in its gorgeous brass cage. " It is Polly's birthday," she added, with affected gaiety, " so the little field-bird must come and congratulate!"

Polly did not answer a word, but went on swinging. A pretty

little canary in the next cage, which had been brought from its own warm fatherland, began singing loudly.

" Be quiet, screamer! " said the lady, throwing a handkerchief over the cage.

" Peep-peep! " it sighed; " what a fearful snow-storm."

The clerk, or, as the lady called him, the field-bird, was put into a little cage close to the canary, and not far from the parrot. The only words the parrot could chatter, and which often came in oddly enough, were, " Now let us be men! " All its other utterances were just as incomprehensible as the twittering of the canary, except to the clerk, who, being a bird himself, understood his companions perfectly.

" I used to fly about under green palms and flowering almonds," sang the canary. " I used to fly with my brothers and sisters, among gorgeous flowers and over the glassy lake, where the plants at the bottom nodded to us. There were lots of bright parrots, who used to tell us the funniest stories in the world."

" They were wild birds," answered the parrot; " they had no education. Now let us be men! "

" Do you remember the pretty girls dancing in the great outspread tent under the flowering trees? Do you remember the luscious fruits and the cooling juice of the wild grapes? "

" Oh yes! " said the parrot; " but I'm far better off here; I have good food, and I am treated with great consideration. I know how clever I am, and I desire nothing more. Now let us be men! You have a poet's soul, as they call it; I have sound accomplishments and wit. You have genius, but no discretion; you give yourself away by bursting out into those piercing notes of yours, and then they smother you. They never presume to cover me up, for I cost them so much; then I impress them with my beak, and confound them all with my wit! wit! wit! Now let us be men! "

" Oh, my beloved, flowery fatherland! " sang the canary. " I will pipe of your dark green trees, of your little bays, where the drooping branches kiss the waters. I will ever sing of the rejoicing of my brilliant brothers and sisters hovering over the cactus plants, ' Wells of the desert,' as they are called! "

" Oh, stop that lackadaisical strain! " said the parrot. " Say something that one can laugh at. Laughter is a sign of the highest mental cultivation. Can a dog or a horse laugh? No, they can cry, but laughter is only given to mankind. Ho! ho! ho! " laughed the parrot, adding its usual phrase, " Now let us be men! "

" You little grey Danish bird," said the canary, " they have made a captive of you too! It must be cold in your woods, but still there is freedom in them. Fly away! they have forgotten to fasten your cage, and the window is open at the top. Fly! fly! " The clerk immediately hopped out of his cage. Just at that moment the half-open door to the next room creaked, and the cat crept stealthily in with green shining eyes, and gave chase.

The canary fluttered in its cage: the parrot flapped its wings and shouted, " Let us be men! " The clerk was terribly frightened, and flew off through the window, over the house-tops and over the streets; at last he was obliged to take a little rest.

There was something familiar about the opposite house; there was an open window, and he flew in, it was his own room, and he perched upon the table.

" Let us be men! " he said, without thinking of what he was saying, only repeating the parrot's phrase mechanically; at the same moment he became the clerk again, there he was sitting on the table.

" Good heavens! " said he, " however did I get here sleeping on the table, and very disturbed dreams I've been having too! Stupid nonsense the whole story! "

CHAPTER VI

THE LAST BEST GIFT OF THE GOLOSHES

Next day in the early morning, while the clerk was still in bed, someone knocked at the door. It was his neighbour, the Divinity Student, who lived on the same floor, and now walked in.

" Lend me your goloshes," he said, " it's so wet in the garden, but the sun is shining, and I want to smoke a pipe."

He put on the goloshes and went down into the garden, which possessed one apple and one pear tree. Even that was a great treasure in the heart of the town.

The student walked up and down the path, it was only six o'clock; a post horn sounded in the street.

" Oh, to travel, to travel! surely it is the most delightful thing in the world. It is the great desire of my heart! If I could travel, this restlessness which comes over me would be quieted. But it must be far away! I should like to see beautiful Switzerland, travel in Italy, and——"

It was a good thing that the goloshes began to have an effect at once, or he would have travelled about too much either for himself or for us. Well, he travelled. He was in the heart of Switzerland, but packed into a diligence with eight other people. He had a headache and a crick in his neck, his legs were swollen from sitting so long, and his boots pinched him. He was half asleep and half awake. He had a letter of credit in his right hand pocket, and his passport in the left, and a little leather purse with some Louis-d'Ors sewn up in it in his breast-pocket. Every time he dropped off, he dreamt that one or other of these was lost, and he started up in feverish haste; the first movement of his hand was a triangle from right to left, and up to his breast, to feel if they were still there. Umbrellas, sticks, and hats swayed about in the net above their heads, and considerably impaired the view, which was grand in the extreme. He stole glances at it, while his heart sang jubilantly words which we know at least one other poet has sung, but which have not up to the present time been printed.

The landscape was stupendous, dark, and solemn. The pine-woods looked like mere heather on the high mountains, whose summits were lost in wreaths of mist. Soon it began to snow, and a piercing wind sprang up.

" Oh! " he shuddered, " if only we were on the other side of the Alps, it would be summer, and I should have got some money on my letter of credit, the fear of losing it spoils all my pleasure in Switzerland! Oh! if only I were on the other side."

And there he was on the other side, far in the interior of Italy between Florence and Rome. The lake of Thrasymene lay before him like a flaming sheet of gold, amidst the dark blue mountains. Here, where Hannibal defeated Flaminius, the vines now entwined their graceful tendrils; charming half-naked children guarded a flock of coal-black pigs among a group of scented laurels by the wayside. If we could paint this picture so as to do it justice, everyone who saw it would rejoice over " beautiful Italy! " but neither the student nor any of his companions in the carriage would have said it.

Thousands of poisonous flies and gnats swarmed around them, and in vain they attempted to drive them out with myrtle branches; they bit all the same. Not a man in the carriage but his face was swollen and disfigured from the bites. The poor horses looked like carrion, the flies settled in masses upon them; they only had a moment's relief, when the driver got down and scraped them off. When the sun went down, a sharp wind whistled round, which was anything but pleasant, but a beautiful green light rested on mountains and clouds—you must go and see it thoroughly to appreciate it. It was wonderful! The travellers thought so too, only—their stomachs were empty, their limbs weary, and all their thoughts turned towards quarters for the night. But where were these? They looked much more anxiously for an inn than at the beautiful view.

Their road ran through an olive wood, just as at home it might have wound through stunted willows; here lay the solitary inn. Half a score of crippled beggars were encamped outside, the best of whom looked like " Famine's " eldest son, " Snarleyyow," in Captain Marryat's *Dog Fiend*. The others were either blind, or had withered feet and crept on their hands, or contracted arms and fingerless hands. It was indeed misery in rags.

" Eccellenza, miserabili," they moaned, stretching out their maimed limbs. The hostess herself had bare feet, uncombed hair, and was clad in a dirty blouse. The doors were tied up with string, the floors consisted of half uprooted cobble stones, bats flew about under the ceiling, and the odour——

" It would be as well if we had the supper served in the stable," said one of the travellers; " there at least one knows what the air is one breathes."

The windows were opened to let in a little fresh air, but quicker than the air, in came the withered arms and the everlasting whines, " Miserabili, Eccellenza." There were many inscriptions on the walls, many of them uncomplimentary to " La bella Italia."

The dinner was brought; it consisted of water soup flavoured with pepper and rancid oil. The same oil figured in the salad; stale eggs and roasted cockscombs were the grandest dishes, even the wine had a disagreeable taste; it was a nauseous mixture.

At night the boxes were piled against the door, and one of the travellers kept watch while the others slept. The student had the first watch. Oh! how close it was! The heat was oppressive, the gnats stung, and the miserabili outside whined in their sleep.

"Travelling would be well enough," sighed the traveller, "if one had no body. If it could rest and the spirit soar alone. Wherever I go there is always something wanting which oppresses the heart, something better than the present, and that I must have. Something better, the best of all, but where, and what is it? I know very well what I want. I want to reach a happy goal, the happiest of all!"

As the words escaped his lips, he found himself back at home; long white curtains hung before the windows, and a coffin stood in the middle of the floor, and he himself lay in it, in the quiet sleep of death. His wish was fulfilled, his body was at rest, and his spirit free. "Call no man happy before he is in his grave," were Solon's words, which here received a fresh confirmation.

Every corpse is an enigma to Immortality, neither could this sphinx before us answer the question which the living man had written down two days before—

> "Strong Death, thy very silence wakes our dread,
> As to the grave our wandering steps are led.
> Shall now my soul up Jacob's ladder pass
> Into Death's garden, there but to spring as grass?

> "Our greatest suffering oft the world sees not.
> O Thou! to whom fell sad and lonely lot,
> Thou knowst, that heavier are our woes passed by,
> Than all the earth that on our graves doth lie."

Two figures were moving about in the room; we know them both. They were Sorrow and Fortune's handmaid; they bent over the dead man.

"Seest thou now," said Sorrow, "what sort of happiness thy goloshes brought to mankind!"

" They at least brought him who sleeps here, good of a lasting kind," answered Joy.

"Oh, no!" said Sorrow; "he went of his own accord; he was not called away! His spiritual powers were not given strength enough to accomplish the task which had been set him. I will do him a true kindness!" saying which she took off the goloshes; the sleep of death was over—the dead man rose to life again with renewed strength.

Sorrow vanished, taking with her the goloshes; she seemed to look upon them as her property.

THE BRONZE BOAR

IN the town of Florence, not far from the Piazza del Granduca, runs a little cross street, I think it is called Porta Rossa. In front of a kind of market in this street, where green stuff is sold, stands a skilfully worked bronze boar. A stream of fresh clear water gushes out of its mouth; it has turned dark green from age, only its snout shines as if it had been polished; and so it has by the many hundreds of children and poor people who take hold of it with their hands and put their mouths to its mouth to drink the water. It is a picture in itself to see the well-formed animal embraced by a handsome half-naked boy putting his fresh lips to its snout.

Most people who go to Florence find the place; one only has to ask the first beggar one sees about the bronze boar and he will find it.

It was late on a winter evening; the mountains were covered with snow, but it was moonlight, and the moon in Italy gives a light which is as good as that of a dark winter's day in the north. Nay, it is better, for the clear air seems to raise us above the earth, while in the north the cold, grey, leaden clouds press us to the ground—the cold, wet ground which one day will press upon our coffins.

Along in the ducal gardens, under the shelter of the stone pines, where thousands of roses bloom in the winter, a little ragged boy had been sitting all day. A boy who might have stood for typical Italy; he was so handsome, so merry, and yet so suffering. He was hungry and thirsty, but no one gave him a copper, and when it got dark and the gardens were to be closed, the porter drove him away. He stood for a long time dreaming on the bridge over the Arno, looking at the glittering stars reflected in the water beneath the stately marble bridge. He took the road to the bronze boar, knelt before it, threw his arms round its neck, and put his little mouth to its shining snout and drank great draughts of the fresh water. Close by lay a few salad leaves and some chestnuts, and these were his supper. There was not a creature in the street; he was quite alone, he got on to the boar's back, leant forward so that his little curly head rested on the animal's head, and before he knew what he was about he fell fast asleep.

It was midnight, the bronze boar moved. He heard it say quite plainly, " Hold tight, for I am going to run off, you little boy! " Then off it ran with him. What an odd ride that was! First they came to the Piazza del Granduca, and the bronze horse which carried the duke's statue neighed aloud. The many-coloured coats of arms on the old Town Hall shone like transparent pictures, and Michael Angelo's David slung his sling; it was a curious mixture of life! The bronze groups of Perseus, and of the Rape of the Sabines, were only too much alive; a death shriek from them resounded through the stately, solitary, Piazza. The bronze boar stopped by the Uffizi palace under the colonnade where the nobles assemble during Lent for the carnival.

" Hold tight," said the animal, " hold tight, for now I am going up the stairs."

The little fellow had not yet said a word, he was half frightened, half delighted. They stepped into a long gallery, he knew it well, he had been there before. The walls were crowded with pictures, and the statues and busts were all in as bright a light as if it were day; but the most splendid sight of all was when the door to one of the adjoining rooms was opened. The little boy remembered the splendours here, but to-night everything was positively magnificent.

Here stood the statue of a woman, as beautiful as only the costliest marble and the master hand of the sculptor could make her; she moved her lovely limbs, dolphins sprang at her feet, and immortality shone from her eyes. She is known to the world as the Venus de Medici. Marble statues of splendid men were grouped around her; one of them was whetting his sword, he is called the Grinder. The next group was the Wrestling Gladiators;

the sword was whetted, and the giants struggled for the goddess of beauty.

The boy was dazzled by the glitter; the walls were radiant with colour, and everything there was full of life and movement. The picture of Venus, the earthly Venus with her rounded limbs and glowing with life as Titian saw her, shone out in redoubled splendour. Near her the portraits of two beautiful women, stretched upon soft cushions, with heaving bosoms and luxuriant locks falling over their rounded shoulders, while their dark eyes betrayed their burning thoughts; but none of all these pictures ventured quite out of their frames. The goddess of beauty herself, the Gladiators, and the Grinder remained in their places, subdued by the halo round the Madonna, with the infant Jesus and St. John. The sacred pictures were no longer pictures, they were the saints themselves.

What brilliance and what beauty as they passed from gallery to gallery! the little boy saw them all; the bronze boar went slowly through all the glories. One sight crowded out the previous one; one picture only really took hold of his thoughts, and that chiefly because of the happy children in it; once by daylight the little boy had nodded to them.

Many probably pass this picture lightly, and yet it contains a treasury of poetry; it is a Christ descending to the nether regions, but He is not surrounded by souls in torment, no, these are the heathen. The picture is by the Florentine Angiolo Bronzino; most beautiful is the expression of the children's faces in their certainty that they are going to heaven. Two little creatures are already embracing each other, one little one stretches out a hand to a companion below, pointing to himself as much as to say, "I am going to heaven!" All the older people stand round doubting, or hoping, or bending humbly before the Saviour. The boy looked longer at this picture than at any of the others; the bronze boar stood still before it, a gentle sigh was heard. Did it come from the picture, or from the animal's breast? The boy held out his hand towards the smiling children; then the animal tore off with him, tore away through the open gallery.

"Thank you, thank you, you beautiful animal!" said the little boy patting the boar, which went bump, bump, down the stairs with him.

"Thank you!" said the bronze boar. "I have helped you, and you have helped me, because I only get strength to run when I have an innocent child on my back! Nay, I dare even step under the rays of the lamp before the Madonna. I can carry you anywhere except into a church, but when you are with me I can stand outside, and look in at the open door! Don't get down off my back, if you do that I shall be dead, just as you see me in the daytime in the Porta Rossa!"

"I will stay with you, my beloved creature," said the little boy, and then they rushed at a furious pace through the streets of Florence to the Piazza before the church of Santa Croce. The folding doors flew open, and the lights on the altar streamed through the church, and out into the solitary Piazza.

There was a wonderful blaze of light from a sculptured tomb in the left aisle; thousands of twinkling stars formed a kind of halo round it. The tomb was surmounted by a coat of arms, a red ladder gleaming like a flame of fire on a blue field. It was the grave of Galileo. It is a simple monument; the red ladder might be emblematic of Art, signifying that the way to fame is always upwards on a flaming ladder. All genius soars to heaven, like Elias of old.

In the right aisle of the church, every statue on the costly sarcophagi seemed endowed with life. Here stood Michael Angelo, there Dante, with a wreath of laurel round his brows; Alfieri, Machiavelli, these great men rest side by side—the pride of Italy. It is a very beautiful church, far more beautiful, if not so large as the marble Cathedral of Florence.

The marble garments appeared to move, as if their great wearers once again raised their heads, and looked towards the glowing altar with its many lights, where the white-robed boys swung their golden censers, amid song and music, while the fragrance of the incense filled the church, and streamed out into the Piazza.

The boy stretched out his hands towards the light, but at the same moment the bronze boar rushed on again, and he had to clutch it tightly. The wind whistled in his ears, he heard the church doors creak on their hinges as they were shut, he seemed to lose consciousness, and felt a rush of icy air—and then he opened his eyes.

It was morning; he had half slipped off the bronze boar, which stood in its usual place in the Porta Rossa. Fear and trembling seized the lad as he thought of the woman he called his mother. She had sent him out yesterday to get money, and he had got none. He was hungry and thirsty, and again he flung his arms round the boar's neck, kissed its snout, nodded to it, and walked off to one of the narrowest streets, only wide enough for a well-laden ass. A big iron-studded door stood half open; he went in here, and up some stone steps by a dirty wall with a greasy rope for a hand-rail, till he reached an open gallery hung with rags. A flight of steps led into a courtyard where there was a fountain; the water was drawn up from the fountain to the different floors by means of a thick iron wire, where the buckets hung side by side. Sometimes the pulley jerked the buckets and splashed the water all over the court. Another broken-down staircase led still higher up, and two Russian sailors running down almost upset the boy. They were coming from their nightly carousals. A strongly-built woman, no longer young, with thick black hair, followed them.

" What have you brought home? " she asked the boy.

" Don't be angry! " he pleaded, taking hold of her dress as if to kiss it. " I've got nothing, nothing at all."

They passed on into a little room. I need not describe it, but only say that in it stood an earthen pot with handles for holding fire, called a " marito." She hung this on her arm, warmed her fingers, and pushed the boy with her elbow.

" You must have got some money," she said.

The boy began to cry, and then she kicked him, making him cry out loud.

" Will you be quiet? or I'll break your screaming head! " and she swung the pot at him. The boy ducked his head and shrieked.

Then a neighbour came in, and she also had her marito on her arm.

" What are you doing to the child, Felicita? " she said.

" The child is my own," answered Felicita, " and I can murder him if I like, and you too, Gianina! "

Then she swung the fire-pot again. The other woman raised hers to parry it, and the two pots clashed together, smashing them to atoms and scattering fire and ash all over the room.

The boy seized the opportunity to escape; he rushed across the courtyard and out of the gate. The poor child ran till he had no breath left. At last he stopped by the church of Santa Croce, whose great doors had opened to him last night. He went in; everything here was bright. He knelt down by the first tomb. It was Michael Angelo's, and very soon he sobbed as if his heart would break. People came and went, mass was celebrated, nobody took any notice of him but an old citizen, who stopped and looked at him for a moment, and then passed on like the rest. The poor child was quite overpowered by hunger and thirst; he became faint and ill. After a time he crept into a corner behind the monuments and fell asleep. Towards evening he was awakened by someone shaking him. He started up, and saw the same old citizen standing before him.

" Are you ill? Where is your home? Have you been here all day? " were some of the questions asked by the old man.

After hearing what he had to say, the old man took him with him to a little house in a side street near. It was a glovemaker's, and a woman was sitting busily at work when they entered. A little white poodle, so closely clipped that the pink skin shone through, jumped upon the table and sprang towards the little boy.

" The innocents soon make friends with each other! " said the woman, patting both the dog and the boy.

The good people fed him, and said he should stay the night. Next day old Father Giuseppe would go and speak to his mother. He only had a homely little bed, but it was regal to him, who so often slept upon the hard stones, and he slept sweetly and dreamt about the pictures and the bronze boar.

Father Giuseppe went out early next morning, and the poor boy was not glad to see him go, for he knew that he had gone to his mother, and that he might have to go back. He cried at the thought, and kissed the lively little dog; the woman nodded to them both.

What did Father Giuseppe say when he came back? He talked to his wife for a long time, and she nodded and patted the boy.

"He's a beautiful child!" she said; "what a clever glove-maker he will be, just like you; see what fingers he has, they're so delicate and flexible! Madonna intended him to be a glove-maker!" So the little boy stayed in the house, and the woman taught him to sew; he had plenty to eat, and got plenty of sleep. He grew quite merry, and at last began to tease Bellissima, as the little dog was called. This made the woman angry, she scolded him and shook her finger at him, so he went sadly to his own room. It faced the street, and the skins were hung up in it to dry; there were thick iron bars across the windows. That night he could not sleep, his head was full of the bronze boar. Suddenly he heard "scramble, scramble," outside, could it be the boar? He rushed to the window, but there was nothing to be seen.

"Help the Signor to carry his box of colours," said his mistress in the morning, as their neighbour, a young artist, came down carrying his colour box as well as a huge roll of canvas. The child took the box, and followed the painter. They took the road to the picture gallery, and mounted the same stairs which he remembered so well, from the night when he rode the bronze boar. He remembered all the statues and the pictures, the beautiful marble Venus, and the painted ones too. Again he looked at the Madonna, with the infant Jesus and St. John. They stopped before the picture of Bronzino, where Christ is represented as standing in the under world, with the children smiling around Him, in their certainty of entering heaven. The poor boy smiled too, for he was in his heaven.

"Now you may go home," said the painter to him, when he had put up his easel.

"Might I stay to see the Signor paint?" said the boy; "might I see you put the picture on this canvas?"

"I'm not painting yet," said the artist, taking out a piece of charcoal. His hand moved quickly, and his eye rapidly took the measures of the great picture; though he only made a few light strokes, there stood the figure of the Saviour, as in the painting.

"Why don't you go!" said the painter.

Then the boy wandered dreamily home again, sat down on the table—and learnt to make gloves.

His thoughts were all day in the gallery, and therefore he was clumsy and pricked his fingers; but he did not tease Bellissima.

In the evening when he found the house door open, he crept out; it was cold, bright starlight, and very clear. He wandered away through the quiet streets, and soon found himself before the bronze boar; he bent over it, kissed its shining snout, and then seated himself upon its back.

"You beloved creature!" he said, "how I have been longing for you! we must have another ride to-night! But the boar remained motionless. The little boy still sat astride of it, when he felt something pull his clothes. He looked down and saw the little naked, clipped Bellissima. The little dog had followed him, without having been noticed by anyone. Bellissima barked, as much as to say, "Do you see I am here? what are you sitting up there for?"

A fiery dragon could not have frightened the boy more than the little dog at that place. "Bellissima in the street and not dressed!" as the old lady called it, "what would be the end of it?" The dog never went out in the winter without a little sheep-skin coat which had been made for it. It was fastened round the neck and body with a red ribbon, and decorated with little red bows and jingling bells. It almost looked like a little kid when it went out in the winter, tripping after its mistress. Now here was Bellissima in the cold without her coat; what would be the consequences? All his fancies were quickly put to flight, yet he stopped to kiss the boar before getting down, and then he took the shivering little dog in his arms. Oh how cold she was, the boy ran off with her as fast as he could.

"What are you running off there with?" shouted two policemen he met, and Bellissima barked. "Where did you steal that pretty dog?" they asked, and took it away from him.

"Oh, give it back to me!" cried the boy.

"If you didn't steal it, you can tell them at home that it can be fetched from the police station," and off they walked with Bellissima. This was a terrible business. He did not know whether he had better jump into the river or go home and confess everything. They would certainly kill him, he thought. "But I would gladly be killed; then I should go to heaven." So he hurried home almost hoping to be killed. The door was fastened, and he could not reach the knocker. There was no one in the street, so he took a stone and hammered at the door with it.

"Who is there?" said someone inside.

"It is I," he said. "Bellissima is lost; let me in and kill me!"

Then, indeed, there was an uproar, his mistress was so very fond of Bellissima; she looked at the wall where his coat ought to hang, and there it was, in its proper place.

"Bellissima at the police station!" she cried; "you bad child! Why did you take him out! he will die of cold! That delicate little animal among all those rough men!"

Father Giuseppe had to go off at once, his wife scolded, and the boy cried; everybody in the house came to see what was the matter, among them the painter. He took the boy on his knee and questioned him. Bit by bit he got out the whole story about the bronze boar, and the picture gallery. It was rather difficult to understand; but the painter comforted the child and talked over the woman, but she would not be happy till Giuseppe came back with Bellissima, who had been in the hands of the police. Then there was great rejoicing, and the painter patted the boy on the head, and gave him a few pictures.

Oh, what splendid pictures they were! comical heads; and above all the bronze boar himself. Oh, nothing could be more delightful. It was sketched in a few strokes, and even the house behind it appeared too.

"Oh, if one could only draw and paint! one would have the whole world before one."

Next day, in his first quiet moment, the little fellow got a pencil and tried to copy the drawing of the bronze boar, and he succeeded too! it was a little crooked, a little on one side, one leg thick and another leg thin, still it was like the copy, and he was delighted. Only the pencil would not go as straight as he meant it to go. The next day another boar stood beside the first one, and this one was a hundred times better; the third one was so good that anyone could see what it was meant for.

But the glovemaking went on badly; he did the errands very slowly; he had learnt from the bronze boar that any picture might be put on paper, and the town of Florence is a complete picture-book, if you only turn over the leaves.

On the Piazza della Trinità stands a slender column, and upon it stands Justice blindfolded, with the scales in her hand. She was also soon put upon paper by the glovemaker's little apprentice. His collection grew, but as yet they were only copies of inanimate objects, when one day Bellissima came hopping towards him. " Stand still! " he said. " I will make a beautiful portrait of you to put among my pictures! " But she would not stand still, so he had to tie her up. He tied her by the head and tail; she did not like it, and barked and jumped about and strained at the cord; just then her mistress came in.

" You wicked boy! the poor animal! " was all she had time to say. She pushed the boy aside, kicked him, and called him an ungrateful, good-for-nothing, wicked boy. She almost smothered Bellissima with her kisses and tears.

At this moment the painter came up the stairs, and—this is the turning point of the story.

.   .   .   .

In 1834 there was an exhibition in the Academy of Arts at Florence. Two pictures hung side by side attracted much attention from the spectators. In the smaller of the two a merry little boy sat at a table drawing; his model was a closely clipped, little white poodle; as the animal would not stand, it was tied up by the head and tail with string. The whole picture was so full of life and truth to nature that it could not fail to interest all who looked at it. The story went that the painter was a young Florentine, who had been found in the streets and brought up by an old glovemaker; and that he had taught himself to draw. A now celebrated artist discovered his talent at a time when he was about to be turned out of the glovemaker's house for having tied up his mistress's favourite, the little poodle, when he wanted a model. The glovemaker's apprentice had become a great painter, as the picture plainly proved. The larger picture was an even greater proof of his talent. There was only a single figure in it, that of a handsome ragged boy, fast asleep, leaning against the bronze boar of the Via Porta Rossa. All the spectators knew the spot well. The child's arm rested on the boar's head, and he slept sweetly; the lamp in front of the Madonna was a beautiful picture. A handsome gilt frame surrounded it, and a wreath of laurel was hung on one corner; but a black ribbon was entwined among the leaves, and long black streamers hung down from it. The young painter was just—dead!

THE BELL

IN the evening, at sunset, when glimpses of golden clouds could just be seen among the chimney pots, a curious sound would be heard, first by one person, then by another; it was like a church bell, but it only lasted a moment because of the rumble of vehicles and the street cries.

"There is the evening bell," people would say; "the sun is setting."

Those who went outside the town where the houses were more scattered, each with its garden or little meadow, saw the evening star, and heard the tones of the bell much better. It seemed as if the sound came from a church buried in silent, fragrant woods, and people looked in that direction, feeling quite solemn.

Time passed, and still people said one to the other, "Can there be a church in the woods! that bell has such a wonderfully sweet sound; shall we go and look at it closer." The rich people drove and the poor ones walked, but it was a very long way; when they reached a group of willows which grew on the out-skirts of the wood, they sat down and looked up among the long branches, thinking that they were really in the heart of the forest. A confectioner from the town came out and pitched a tent there, and then another confectioner, and he hung a bell up over his tent. This bell was tarred so as to stand the rain, and the clapper was wanting. When people went home again they said it had been so romantic, and that meant something beyond mere tea. Three persons protested that they had penetrated right through the forest to the other side, and that they had heard the same curious bell all the time, but that then it sounded as if it came from the town.

One of them wrote a poem about it, and said that it sounded like a mother's voice to a beloved child, no melody could be sweeter than the chimes of this bell.

The Emperor's attention was also drawn to it, and he promised that anyone who really discovered where the sound came from should receive the title of " the world's bell-ringer," even if there were no bell at all.

A great many people went to the woods for the sake of earning an honest penny, but only one of them brought home any kind of explanation. No one had been far enough, not even he himself, but he said that the sound of the bell came from a very big owl in a hollow tree; it was a wise owl, which perpetually beat its head against a tree, but whether the sound came from its head or from the hollow tree he could not say with any certainty. All the same he was appointed " world's bell-ringer," and every year he wrote a little treatise on the owl, but nobody was much the wiser for it.

Now on a certain Confirmation day the priest had preached a very moving sermon, all the young people about to be confirmed had been much touched by it; it was a very important day for them. They were leaving childhood behind and becoming grown-up persons, the child's soul was, as it were, to be transformed into that of a responsible being. It was a beautiful sunny day, and after the Confirmation the young people walked out of the town and they heard the sound of the unknown bell more than usually loud coming from the wood. On hearing it they all felt anxious to go further and see it; all except three. The first of these had to go home to try on her ball-dress; it was this very dress and this very ball which were the reason of her having been confirmed this time; otherwise it would have been put off. The second was a poor boy, who had borrowed his tail-coat and boots of the landlord's son, and he had to return them at the appointed time. The third said that he had never been anywhere without his parents, that he had always been a good child and he meant to continue so, although he was confirmed; nobody ought to have made fun of this resolve, but he did not escape being laughed at.

So these three did not go; the others trudged off. The sun shone and the birds sang, and the newly-confirmed young people took each other by the hand and sang with them; they had not yet received any position in life, they were all equal in the eye of the Lord on the day of their Confirmation. Soon two of the smallest ones got tired and they returned to town; two little girls sat down and made wreaths, so they did not go either. When the others reached the willows where the confectioners had their tents, they said, " Now, then, here we are; the bell doesn't exist, it is only something people imagine! "

Just then the bell was heard in the wood, with its deep rich notes; and four or five of them decided after all to penetrate further into the wood. The underwood was so thick and close that it was quite difficult to advance. The woodruff grew almost too high, convolvulus and brambles hung in long garlands from tree to tree, where the nightingales sang and the sunbeams played. It was deliciously peaceful, but there was no path for the girls, their clothes would have been torn to shreds. There were great boulders over-grown with many-coloured mosses, and fresh springs trickled among them with a curious little gurgling sound.

" Surely that cannot be the bell! " said one of the young people, as he lay down to listen.

" This must be thoroughly looked into." So he stayed behind and let the others go on.

They came to a little hut made of bark, and branches over-hung by a crab-apple, as if it wanted to shake all its bloom over the roof, which was covered with roses. The long sprays clustered round the gable, and on it hung a little bell. Could this be the one they sought? Yes, they were all agreed that it must be, except one; he said it was far too small and delicate to be heard so far away as they had heard it, and that the tones which moved all hearts were quite different from these. He who spoke was a king's son, and so the others said, " That kind of fellow must always be wiser than anyone else."

So they let him go on alone, and as he went he was more and more overcome by the solitude of the wood; but he still heard the little bell with which the others were so pleased, and now and then when the wind came from the direction of the confectioners he could hear demands for tea.

But the deep-toned bell sounded above them all, and it

seemed as if there was an organ playing with it, and the sounds came from the left, where the heart is placed.

There was a rustling among the bushes, and a little boy stood before the king's son; he had wooden shoes on, and such a small jacket that the sleeves did not cover his wrists. They knew each other, for he was the boy who had had to go back to return the coat and the boots to the landlord's son. He had done this, changed back into his shabby clothes and wooden shoes, and then, drawn by the deep notes of the bell, had returned to the wood again.

" Then we can go together," said the king's son.

But the poor boy in the wooden shoes was too bashful. He pulled down his short sleeves, and said he was afraid he could not walk quickly enough, besides which he thought the bell ought to be looked for on the right, because that side looked the most beautiful.

" Then we shan't meet at all," said the king's son, nodding to the poor boy, who went into the thickest and darkest part of the wood, where the thorns tore his shabby clothes and scratched his face, hands, and feet till they bled. The king's son got some good scratches too, but he at least had the sun shining upon his path. We are going to follow him, for he is a bright fellow.

" I must and will find the bell," said he, " if I have to go to the end of the world."

Some horrid monkeys sat up in the trees grinning and showing their teeth.

" Shall we pelt him? " said they. " Shall we thrash him; he is a king's son."

But he went confidently on further and further into the wood, where the most extraordinary flowers grew. There were white star-like lilies with blood-red stamens, pale blue tulips which glistened in the sun, and apple-trees on which the apples looked like great shining soap-bubbles. You may fancy how these trees glittered in the sun. Round about were beautiful green meadows, where stags and hinds gambolled under the spreading oaks and beeches. Mosses and creepers grew in the fissures where the bark of the trees was broken away. There were also great glades with quiet lakes, where white swans swam about flapping their wings. The king's son often stopped and listened, for he sometimes fancied that the bell sounded from one of these lakes; but then again he felt sure that it was not there, but further in the wood.

Now the sun began to go down, and the clouds were fiery red; a great stillness came over the wood, and he sank upon his knees, sang his evening psalm, and said, " Never shall I find what I seek, now the sun is going down, the night is coming on— the dark night; perhaps I could catch one more glimpse of the round, red sun before it sinks beneath the earth. I will climb up on to those rocks; they are as high as the trees."

He seized the roots and creepers, and climbed up the slippery stones where the water-snakes wriggled and the toads seemed to croak at him; but he reached the top before the sun disappeared. Seen from this height, oh! what splendour lay before him! The ocean, the wide, beautiful ocean, its long waves rolling towards the shore. The sun still stood like a great shining altar, out there where sea and sky met. Everything melted away into glowing colours; the wood sang, the ocean sang, and his heart sang with them. All Nature was like a vast holy temple, where trees and floating clouds were as pillars, flowers and grass the woven tapestry, and the heaven itself a great dome. The red colours vanished as the sun went down, but millions of stars peeped out; they were like countless diamond lamps, and the king's son spread out his arms towards heaven, sea, and forest. At that moment, from the right-hand path came the poor boy with the short sleeves and wooden shoes. He had reached the same goal just as soon by his own road. They ran towards each other, and clasped each other's hands in that great temple of Nature and Poetry, and above them sounded the invisible holy bell; happy spirits floated round it to the strains of a joyous Hallelujah.

OLÉ LUKÖIÉ, THE DUSTMAN

THERE is nobody in all the world who can tell so many stories as Olé Luköié! And such stories as he can tell! When night is drawing on, and the children are sitting round the table as good as possible, or on their little footstools, in walks Olé Shut-eyes. He comes so quietly up the stairs without his shoes, and opens the door so softly that nobody hears him; and puff! he sends a shower of milk into their eyes in such fine spray as to be invisible; but they can't keep their eyes open after it, and so they never see him. He steals behind them and breathes upon their necks, making their heads as heavy as lead; but he never hurts them; he does it all from kindness to the children. He only wants them to be quiet, and the best way to make them quiet is to have them in bed; when they are settled there, he can tell them his stories.

Then as soon as the children are asleep, Olé Luköié seats himself upon their beds. He is well dressed; his clothes are all of silk, but it is impossible to say what colour they are, for it shimmers green, red, and blue every time he turns. He has an umbrella under his arm, one with pictures on it, and this he holds over the good children, and then they dream the most delightful stories all night long. The other umbrella has no pictures on it, and he holds this one over the children who have been naughty, and then they sleep heavily till the morning and have no dreams at all.

I am now going to tell you about a little boy to whom Olé Luköié went every night for a whole week. His name was Hialmar. There are just seven stories, because there are seven days in a week.

MONDAY

"Now, just listen!" said Olé Luköié, in the evening, when he had got Hialmar to bed. "First I will smarten things up a

283

bit," and then all the plants in pots became big trees, with their branches stretching right up to the ceiling and along the walls, so that the room looked like a delightful arbour. The branches were covered with flowers, and the flowers were more beautiful than roses; they had the most delightful scent, and, if you tried to eat them, were more delicious than the very nicest jam. The fruit shone like gold, and then there were buns bursting with plums; they were splendid!

All at once the most miserable grumbles came from the table-drawer where Hialmar's schoolbooks were kept.

"What is that now?" said Olé Luköié, going along and opening the drawer.

It was the slate groaning and writhing because there was a wrong figure in the sum set on it, and it was ready to fall to pieces.

The pencil was hopping and skipping at the end of its piece of string, just as if it had been a little dog which would like to try and do the sum, but it couldn't! Then there was Hialmar's copybook clamouring away inside its covers most pitifully. There was a row of capital letters down each side on every leaf, each with a little one beside it; then beside them letters which imagined that they looked like them, but these were written by Hialmar. They looked almost as if they had tumbled over the line on which they ought to have been standing upright.

"See, this is how you ought to hold yourselves!" said the headlines, "so—to one side with a brisk flourish!"

"Oh, we should like nothing better," said Hialmar's letters, "but we can't, we are so crooked!"

"Then you shall have a dose of medicine," said Olé Luköié.

"Oh, no!" they cried, and then they stood up as stiffly as possible.

"Well, now we can't tell any stories!" said Olé Luköié. "I must drill them! One, two! One, two!" and then he drilled the letters and they stood up stiffer than any headlines could stand. But when Olé Luköié went away and Hialmar woke up in the morning they were as crooked as ever.

TUESDAY

As soon as Hialmar was in bed, Olé Luköié touched all the furniture in the room with his little wooden wand, and everything began to talk. They all talked about themselves except the spittoon, which was silent and much annoyed that they were all so vain as only to talk about themselves, and to pay no attention to him, standing so modestly in the corner and allowing himself to be spat upon. There was a big picture in a gilt frame hanging over the chest of drawers; it was a landscape in which one saw tall, old trees, flowers growing in the grass, and a great piece of water, with a river flowing from it round behind a wood, past many castles and away to the open sea.

Olé Luköié touched the picture with his wand, and the birds in it began to sing, the branches of the trees moved, and the clouds scudded along; you could see their shadows passing over the landscape.

Now Olé Luköié lifted little Hialmar up close to the frame, and Hialmar put his leg right into the picture among the long grass, and there he stood; the sun shone down upon him through the branches of the trees. He ran to the water and got into a little boat which lay there, it was painted red and white, and the sails shone like silver. Six swans, all with golden crowns round their necks, and a shining blue star upon their heads, drew the boat past the dark green woods, where the trees told stories about robbers and witches; and the flowers told other stories about the pretty little elves, and all that the butterflies had told them.

Beautiful fish with gold and silver scales swam after the boat; every now and then they sprang out of the water and back again with a splash. Red and blue birds, large and small, flew in two long lines behind them; the gnats buzzed, and the cockchafers boomed; they all wanted to go with Hialmar, and each of them had a story to tell.

That was a sailing trip indeed! Now the woods were thick and dark, now they were like beautiful gardens full of sunshine and flowers, and among them were castles of glass and marble. Princesses stood upon the balconies, and they were all little girls whom Hialmar knew and used to play with.

They stretched out their hands, each one holding the most beautiful sugar pig which any cakewoman could sell. Hialmar took hold of one end of the pig as they sailed by, and the princess held the other tight, and each had a share, she the smaller and Hialmar the bigger! Little princes stood sentry by each castle; they saluted with golden swords, and showered down sugar plums and tin soldiers; they were princes indeed.

Now he sailed through a wood, now through great halls, or right through a town; he passed through the one where his nurse lived, she who used to carry him about when he was quite a little boy and who was so fond of him. She nodded and waved her hand to him, and sang a pretty little song which she had written herself and sent to Hialmar:

> " I dream of thee for many an hour,
>   Hialmar, my own, my sweeting;
> My kisses once fell like a shower,
>   Thy brow and red cheeks greeting.
>
> " Mine ear thy first formed word addressed,
>   Thy last must be in parting;
> May you on earth by Heaven be blessed,
>   Angel, from Heavenward darting! "

All the birds sang too, the flowers danced upon their stalks, and the old trees nodded, just as if Olé Luköié were telling them stories.

WEDNESDAY

How the rain was pouring down outside! Hialmar could even hear it in his sleep, and when Olé Luköié opened the window, the water stood right up to the sill; it was a regular lake, and a beautiful ship lay close up to the house.

" Will you sail with me, little Hialmar? " said Olé Luköié; " if you will, you can go to distant countries to-night, and be back here again in the morning! "

Then all at once Hialmar found himself in his best Sunday clothes on board the beautiful ship; it was heavenly weather, and they sailed through the streets, past the church, till they reached a wild open sea. They sailed so far that there was no more land to be seen. They saw a flock of storks leaving home on their way to the warm countries, flying in a line, one behind the other; they had already flown a long, long way. One of them was so tired that his wings could hardly carry him any further; he was the last one in the row, and soon he was a long way behind. At last he sank, with outspread wings, lower and lower; he flapped his wings feebly for a few strokes, but it was no use. Now he touched the rigging of the ship with his feet, and slid down the sail with a flop on to the deck.

Then the cabin boy picked him up and put him into the henhouse, with the chickens, and ducks and turkeys; the poor stork stood among them looking quite depressed.

"What a creature!" said all the hens. The turkey-cock puffed himself up as big as he could, and asked who he was; and the ducks waddled backwards, pushing against each other, saying, "Quack, quack!"

Then the stork told them about sunny Africa, and the pyramids, and the ostrich running across the deserts like a wild horse; but the ducks did not understand him, and they pushed each other and said, "Are we agreed that he is an idiot?"

"Yes, indeed, he's an idiot," said the turkey-cock with a gobble. Then the stork became quite silent, and thought about his beloved Africa.

"Nice thin legs you've got!" said the turkey-cock; "how much a yard?"

"Quack, quack, quack!" grinned all the ducks, but the stork appeared not to hear them.

"You're quite at liberty to laugh too," said the turkey-cock to him; "it was a very witty remark, or perhaps it was too low for you, gobble, gobble. He's not many-sided," he said to the others; "it's good enough to amuse us!" Then all the hens clucked and the ducks quacked; it was tremendous the amusement they got out of it.

But Hialmar went along to the henhouse, opened the door, and called the stork, and it hopped out on to the deck to him. It was rested now, and it seemed to nod to Hialmar to thank him; thereupon it spread its wings and flew away to the warm countries. But the hens clucked, the ducks quacked, and the turkey-cock's head got as red as fire.

"To-morrow we'll make you into soup," said Hialmar, and

then he woke up and found himself lying in his own little bed. That was an extraordinary journey Olé Luköié had taken him.

THURSDAY

" I'll tell you what! " said Olé Luköié; " don't be frightened, and I will show you a little mouse." And he stretched out his hand with the tiny little animal in it. " It has come to invite you to a wedding. There are two little mice who intend to enter the wedded state to-night. They live under the floor of your mother's larder, which they say is a most delightful residence."

" But how can I get through a little mouse-hole in the floor? " said Hialmar.

" Leave that to me," said Olé Luköié; " I'll soon make you small enough! "

Then he touched Hialmar with his wand, and he quickly grew smaller and smaller; at last he was not as tall as one's finger.

" Now you may borrow the tin soldier's clothes; I think they'll just fit you, and it looks so smart to have on a uniform when one's in company."

" Yes indeed! " said Hialmar, and in a moment he was dressed like the grandest tin soldier.

" Be so good as to take a seat in your mother's thimble," said the little mouse, " and I shall have the honour of drawing you! "

" Heavens! are you going to take that trouble yourself, young lady? " said Hialmar, and off they drove to the mouse's wedding.

First they went down under the floor into a long passage, which was just high enough for them to drive through, and the whole passage was lighted up with touch-wood.

" Isn't there a delicious smell here? " said the mouse who was drawing him; " the whole passage has been smeared over with bacon fat! Nothing could be nicer."

Then they came to the bridal hall, where all the little lady mice stood on the right whispering and giggling, as if they were making fun of each other, and on the left stood all the gentlemen mice stroking their whiskers with their paws. The bridal pair stood in the middle of the room, in the hollow rind of a cheese, kissing each other most energetically before all the other people, but then they were engaged, you know, and just about to be married.

More and more visitors poured in, the mice were almost crushing each other to death, and the bridal pair had taken their place in the doorway, so that one could neither get in nor out. The whole room, like the passage, was smeared with bacon fat; there were no other refreshments, but for dessert a pea was produced, in which one of the little mice of the family had bitten the name of the bridal pair; that is to say the first letter of it, and this was something quite extraordinary.

All the mice said it was a delightful wedding, and the conversation most entertaining.

And then Hialmar drove home again; he had been in very grand company, but in order to get there he had been obliged to shrink wonderfully, to make himself small enough to get into the uniform of a tin soldier.

FRIDAY

" It is astounding what a number of grown-up people would like to get hold of me! " said Olé Luköié, " especially those with a bad conscience. ' Good little Olé,' they say to me, ' we can't close our eyes, and there we lie all night with all our bad deeds staring us in the face. They are like naughty elfins; they come and sit on our beds and squirt hot water over us. Won't you come and chase them away so that we may have a good sleep? ' and then they sigh deeply. ' We will gladly pay you, Olé; goodnight. You will find the money on the window-sill.' But I don't do it for money! " said Olé Luköié.

" What are we going to do to-night? " asked Hialmar.

" Well, I don't know whether you would like to go to a wedding again to-night; it's a different kind from yesterday's. Your sister's big doll, the one which looks like a man, and is called Herman, is to be married to Bertha; besides which, it is her birthday, so there will be no end of presents."

"Oh, I know all about that; whenever the dolls want new clothes my sister lets them have a birthday or a wedding. It has happened hundreds of times!"

"Yes, but to-night it's the hundred and first wedding, and the hundred and first is the end of all things, so that's why this one will be so grand. Just look!"

Hialmar looked along at the table; there was the little pasteboard house with lights in the windows, and all the tin soldiers presenting arms outside. The bridal pair sat upon the floor leaning against the leg of the table; they were very thoughtful, and they had reason to be. Olé Luköié, dressed in grandmother's black skirt, married them; when the ceremony was over, all the furniture in the room joined in singing the following pretty song which had been written by the pencil; it went to the tune of the tattoo.

> " Our song shall swing like the wind, like the wind,
> Till the bridal pair are enshrin'd, are enshrin'd,
> And they curtsey both like a stick, do you mind?
> For they're wood inside with kid for a rind.
> Hurrah! hurrah! wood and skin well combin'd,
> We'll sing it aloud to the rain and the wind!"

Then the presents were given, but they had declined any eatables: love was enough for them without anything else.

"Shall we go into the country or travel abroad?" asked the bridegroom, and then they consulted the swallow which had travelled so much, and the old mother hen which had reared five broods of chickens. The swallow told them all about the delightful warm countries where the grapes hung in luscious clusters, and where the air was so mild, and the colours on the mountains were such as were not to be found elsewhere.

"But they haven't got our green cabbage," said the hen. " I was in the country all one summer with my chicks; there was a gravel pit that we scratched in all day, and then we got admission to a garden where the cabbage grew! Oh, how green it was! I can't imagine anything more beautiful."

"But one cabbage is just like another," said the swallow, " and then there's so much bad weather here!"

" Oh, we're used to that," said the hen.

" But it's so cold, it freezes."

" That's good for the cabbage," said the hen. " Besides, sometimes it is warm enough. Four years ago didn't we have a summer with tremendous heat, for five weeks one could hardly breathe! And then we don't have all the poisonous creatures they have abroad, and there are no robbers. Anyone who doesn't think our own country the best, must be a fool! He doesn't deserve to live here." And the hen began to cry. " I've had my journeys too; I once travelled twelve miles in a barrel, and there's no pleasure in travelling."

" Ah, the hen is a wise woman!" said Bertha the doll. " I don't like travelling among mountains either, for first you go up and then you go down! No, we will move out by the gravel pit and take our walks in the cabbage garden."

And that was the end of it.

SATURDAY

" Are we going to have some stories?" asked little Hialmar, as soon as Olé Luköié had got him to bed.

" We haven't time for any to-night," said Olé, as he opened his prettiest umbrella. " Just look at these Chinese!" The whole umbrella looked exactly like a big Chinese bowl, with blue trees all over it, and arched bridges on which stood little people nodding their heads. " We must have the whole world polished up for to-morrow," said Olé; " it is a holiday, for it is Sunday. I must go up into the church tower to see if the little church brownies are polishing the bells so that they may sound well. I must go into the fields to see if the wind has blown the dust off the grass and leaves. My biggest piece of work is to get down all the stars to polish them; I take them in my apron; but first I have to number each one, and the holes they belong to have to be numbered too, so that they may go back into their proper places, or they wouldn't stick, and then we should be having too many falling stars, one after the other would drop out."

" Now, I say, Mr. Luköié," said one of the old portraits hanging on the wall, " I am Hialmar's great-grandfather; I am

much obliged to you for telling him stories, but you mustn't
puzzle his brains.   The stars can't be taken down to be polished!
The stars are planets just like our own earth, and that's the best
of them! "

"Much obliged to you, old great-grandfather," said Olé
Luköié. "My best thanks to you; you are the head of the
family; you are an antiquity, but I am older than you!   I am
an old heathen; the Greeks and Romans call me the Dream-god!
I have my footing in the grandest houses; I can get on both
with big and little!   You may tell the stories yourself! "   And
then Olé Luköié went away and took his umbrella with him.

"I suppose one mayn't give an opinion now! " said the old
portrait.

And then Hialmar woke.

SUNDAY

"Good-evening," said Olé Luköié, and Hialmar nodded; and
then he jumped up and turned great-grandfather's portrait with
its face to the wall, so that it should not talk as it did last time.

"Now you must tell me some stories about ' The five green
peas which lived in a peaspod,' and about the ' Cock paying
his addresses to the hen,' and about the ' Darning-needle ' which
was so fine that it fancied it was an ordinary needle! "

"You may have too much of a good thing," said Olé Luköié;
"I would rather show you something you know!   I will show
you my brother; he is also called Olé Luköié, but he never
comes more than once to anybody, and when he comes he takes
them away with him on his horse, and tells them stories.   He
only knows two, one which is so beautiful that nobody on earth
can imagine it, and one which is too horrible to be described! "
And then Olé lifted little Hialmar up to the window, and said,
"Now you can see my brother, the other Olé Luköié!   He is
also called Death; you see he doesn't look at all bad, as he
sometimes does in pictures, all bones and joints!   No, he has a
silver embroidered border round his coat; it is a Hussar's uniform, and a black velvet cloak streams out behind over his
horse's back!   See how they are galloping."

And Hialmar saw how Olé Luköié rode off, taking both old and young with him on his horse. He put some of them before him and some behind, but he always asked first, "What character have you in your mark book?" They all said "good." "Let me see myself," said he, and then they had to show him the book. All those who had "very good" or "excellent" against their names were put up in front of him, and were told the most delightful stories; but those who had only "pretty good" or "tolerable," had to sit behind him, and were told horrible stories. They shivered, and cried, and tried to get off the horse, but they couldn't do that, because they grew fast to it at once.

"But Death is a beautiful Olé Luköié," said Hialmar. "I am not a bit afraid of him!"

"Nor need you be," said Olé Luköié; "if only you take care to have a good character in your book."

"Ah, now, that's instructive!" mumbled great-grandfather's portrait. "It's some good after all to speak one's mind!" and he was quite pleased.

Now this is the story about Olé Luköié! To-night he can tell you some more himself.

THE SWINEHERD

THERE was once a poor Prince; he had only quite a tiny kingdom, but it was big enough to allow him to marry, and he was bent upon marrying.

Now, it certainly was rather bold of him to say to the Emperor's daughter, "Will you have me?" He did, however, venture to say so, for his name was known far and wide; and there were hundreds of Princesses who would have said "Yes," and "Thank you, kindly," but see if *she* would!

Just let us hear about it.

A rose tree grew on the grave of the Prince's father, it was such a beautiful rose tree; it only bloomed every fifth year, and then only bore one blossom; but what a rose that was! By merely smelling it one forgot all one's cares and sorrows.

Then he had a nightingale which sang as if every lovely melody in the world dwelt in her little throat. This rose and this nightingale were to be given to the Princess, so they were put into great silver caskets and sent to her.

The Emperor had them carried before him into the great Hall where the Princess was playing at "visiting" with her ladies-in-waiting; they had nothing else to do. When she saw the caskets with the gifts she clapped her hands with delight!

"If only it were a little pussy cat!" said she—but there was the lovely rose.

"Oh, how exquisitely it is made!" said all the ladies-in-waiting.

" It is more than beautiful," said the Emperor; " it is neat."
But the Princess touched it, and then she was ready to cry.
" Fie, papa! " she said; " it is not made, it is a real one! "
" Fie," said all the ladies-in-waiting; " it is a real one! "

" Well, let us see what there is in the other casket, before
we get angry," said the Emperor, and out came the nightingale.
It sang so beautifully that at first no one could find anything
to say against it.

" *Superbe ! charmant !* " said the ladies-in-waiting, for they
all had a smattering of French, one spoke it worse than the other.

" How that bird reminds me of our lamented Empress's
musical box," said an old courtier. " Ah, yes, they are the
same tunes, and the same beautiful execution."

" So they are," said the Emperor, and he cried like a little
child.

" I should hardly think it could be a real one," said the
Princess.

" Yes, it is a real one," said those who had brought it.

" Oh, let that bird fly away then," said the Princess, and
she would not hear of allowing the Prince to come. But he was
not to be crushed; he stained his face brown and black, and,
pressing his cap over his eyes, he knocked at the door.

" Good-morning, Emperor," said he; " can I be taken into
service in the palace? "

" Well, there are so many wishing to do that," said the
Emperor; " but let me see!—yes, I need somebody to look after
the pigs, for we have so many of them."

So the Prince was made imperial swineherd. A horrid little
room was given him near the pig-sties, and here he had to live.
He sat busily at work all day, and by the evening he had made
a beautiful little cooking pot; it had bells all round it, and when
the pot boiled they tinkled delightfully and played the old tune:

" Ach du lieber Augustin,
Alles ist weg, weg, weg! " [1]

But the greatest charm of all about it was, that by holding
one's finger in the steam one could immediately smell all the

[1] Alas! dear Augustin,
All is lost, lost, lost!

dinners that were being cooked at every stove in the town. Now this was a very different matter from a rose.

The Princess came walking along with all her ladies-in-waiting, and when she heard the tune she stopped and looked pleased, for she could play " Ach du lieber Augustin " herself; it was her only tune, and she could only play it with one finger.

" Why, that is my tune," she said; " this must be a cultivated swineherd. Go and ask him what the instrument costs."

So one of the ladies-in-waiting had to go into his room, but she put pattens on first.

" How much do you want for the pot," she asked.

" I must have ten kisses from the Princess," said the swineherd.

" Heaven preserve us! " said the lady.

" I won't take less," said the swineherd.

" Well, what does he say? " asked the Princess.

" I really cannot tell you," said the lady-in-waiting, " it is so shocking."

" Then you must whisper it."   And she whispered it.

" He is a wretch! " said the Princess, and went away at once. But she had only gone a little way when she heard the bells tinkling beautifully:

" Ach du lieber Augustin."

" Go and ask him if he will take ten kisses from the ladies-in-waiting."

" No, thank you," said the swineherd; " ten kisses from the Princess, or I keep my pot."

" How tiresome it is," said the Princess. " Then you will have to stand round me, so that no one may see."

So the ladies-in-waiting stood round her and spread out their skirts while the swineherd took his ten kisses, and then the pot was hers.

What a delight it was to them. The pot was kept on the boil day and night. They knew what was cooking on every stove in the town, from the chamberlain's to the shoemaker's. The ladies-in-waiting danced about and clapped their hands.

" We know who has sweet soup and pancakes for dinner, and who has cutlets; how amusing it is."

" Highly interesting," said the mistress of the robes.

" Yes, but hold your tongues, for I am the Emperor's daughter."

" Heaven preserve us! " they all said.

The swineherd—that is to say, the Prince, only nobody knew that he was not a real swineherd—did not let the day pass in idleness, and he now constructed a rattle. When it was swung round it played all the waltzes, galops and jig tunes which have ever been heard since the creation of the world.

" But this is *superbe!* " said the Princess, as she walked by. " I have never heard finer compositions. Go and ask him what the instrument costs, but let us have no more kissing."

" He wants a hundred kisses from the Princess! " said the lady-in-waiting.

" I think he is mad! " said the Princess, and she went away, but she had not gone far when she stopped.

" One must encourage art," she said; " I am the Emperor's daughter. Tell him he can have ten kisses, the same as yesterday, and he can take the others from the ladies-in-waiting."

" But we don't like that at all," said the ladies.

" Oh, nonsense! If I can kiss him you can do the same. Remember that I pay your wages as well as give you board and lodging." So the lady-in-waiting had to go again.

" A hundred kisses from the Princess, or let each keep his own."

" Stand in front of me," said she, and all the ladies stood round, while he kissed her.

" Whatever is the meaning of that crowd round the pigsties? " said the Emperor as he stepped out on to the verandah; he rubbed his eyes and put on his spectacles. " Why, it is the ladies-in-waiting, what game are they up to? I must go and see! " so he pulled up the heels of his slippers for they were shoes which he had trodden down.

Bless us, what a hurry he was in! When he got into the yard, he walked very softly and the ladies were so busy counting the kisses, so that there should be fair play, and neither too few nor too many kisses, that they never heard the Emperor. He stood on tiptoe.

" What is all this? " he said when he saw what was going

on, and he hit them on the head with his slipper just as the swineherd was taking the eighty-sixth kiss.

"Out you go!" said the Emperor, for he was furious, and both the Princess and the Prince were put out of his realm.

There she stood crying, and the swineherd scolded, and the rain poured down in torrents.

"Oh, miserable creature that I am! if only I had accepted the handsome Prince. Oh, how unhappy I am!"

The swineherd went behind a tree, wiped the black and brown stain from his face, and threw away his ugly clothes. Then he stepped out dressed as a Prince, he was so handsome that the Princess could not help curtseying to him.

"I am come to despise thee," he said. "Thou wouldst not have an honourable prince, thou couldst not prize the rose or the nightingale, but thou wouldst kiss the swineherd for a trumpery musical box! As thou hast made thy bed, so must thou lie upon it!"

Then he went back into his own little kingdom and shut and locked the door. So she had to stand outside and sing in earnest—

> "Ach du lieber Augustin,
> Alles ist weg, weg, weg!"

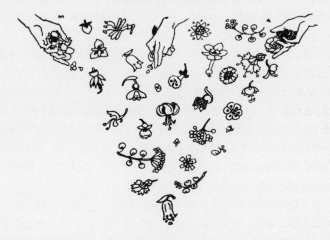

THE TRAVELLING COMPANIONS

POOR John was very sad, his father was ill and he knew that he could not recover. There was no one else in the little room besides these two; it was quite late at night and the lamp had nearly burnt out.

"You have been a good son, John," said the dying man. "I am sure the Lord will help you on in the world!" and he fixed his mild, gentle eyes upon his son, drew a long breath and passed away so quietly, he only seemed to be asleep. John wept bitterly, for now he had nobody in the world belonging to him, neither father nor mother, sister nor brother. Poor John! he knelt by the bedside and kissed his dead father's hands and shed many tears; but at last his eyes closed, and he fell asleep with his head against the hard bed-post.

He had a wonderful dream; he saw the sun and moon bowing before him, and he saw his father quite well and strong again; he laughed as he always used to laugh when he was very pleased. A lovely girl with a golden crown on her long, beautiful hair, stretched out her hand to John, and his father said, "See what a beautiful bride you have won. She is the loveliest maiden in the world." Then he woke up, and all the beautiful things were gone; his father lay on the bed dead and cold, and there was no one else there, poor John!

The dead man was buried in the following week; John walked close behind the coffin, and he could no longer see his good father who had loved him so much. He heard the earth fall upon the coffin lid, and watched it till only a corner was left, and then the last shovelful fell upon it, and it was entirely hidden. He was so miserable, he felt as if his heart would break.

A beautiful psalm was being sung which brought the tears into his eyes, he wept, and this brought him relief. The sun was shining brightly on the green trees, and seemed to say, " Do not be so sad, John! See how blue the sky is; your good father is up there, and he will pray to God that all may be well with you."

" I will always be good! " said John, " and then I shall go to Heaven some time to my father, and what joy it will be to see each other again. How much I shall have to tell him; and he will have so much to show me, and to teach me about the bliss of Heaven, just as he used to teach me here on earth. Oh, what joy it will be! "

John saw it all so vividly that he smiled at the thought, although the tears still ran down his cheeks. The little birds in the chestnut tree twittered with joy although they had been at the funeral, but they knew that the dead man was in Heaven, and that he now had wings larger and more beautiful than their own. They knew, too, that he was happy, because he had been a good man here on earth, and they were glad of it. John saw them fly away from the trees out into the world, and he felt a strong desire to fly away with them. But first he made a wooden cross to put up on his father's grave; when he brought it along in the evening he found the grave covered with sand and decorated with flowers. This had been done by strangers for love of his father.

Early next morning John packed his little bundle and stowed away his sole inheritance in his belt; it only consisted of fifty dollars and a few silver coins, and with these he started out into the world. But first he went to the churchyard to his father's grave, where he knelt and said the Lord's prayer, and then added, " Farewell, dear father! I will always be good, and then you won't be afraid to pray to the good God that all may go well with me! "

The fields that John passed through were full of bright flowers nodding their heads in the warm sunshine as much as to say,

" Welcome into the fields! Is it not lovely here? " but John turned round once more to look at the old church where he had been baptised, and where he had gone every Sunday and sung the psalms with his good old father. On looking back he saw standing in one of the loop-holes of the tower the little church-Nissé with his pointed red cap, shading his eyes from the sun with his arm. John nodded good-bye to him, and the little Nissé waved his hand and kissed his fingers to him to show that he was sending his good wishes for a pleasant journey.

John now began to think how many beautiful things he would see in the great beautiful world before him, and he went on and on till he found himself much further away than he had ever been before. He did not know the towns through which he passed, or the people he met, he was quite among strangers. The first night he had to sleep under a haystack in a field, for he had no other bed. But he thought it was lovely, no king could have had a better. The field by the river, the haystack, and the deep blue sky above made a charming room. The green grass dotted with red and white flowers was the carpet, the elders and the rose bushes were growing bouquets, and he had the whole river for a bath, with its clear fresh water, and the rushes which nodded their heads bidding him both " Good-night " and " Good-morning." The moon was a great night light high up under the blue ceiling, one which would never set fire to the curtains. John could sleep quite quietly without fear, and this he also did. He only woke when the sun was high up in the sky and all the little birds were singing, " Good-morning! Good-morning! Are you not up yet? "

The bells were ringing for church; people were on their way to hear the parson pray and preach, and John went with them. He sang a psalm and listened to the word of God, and he felt as if he were in his own old church, where he had been christened, and where he had sung the psalms with his father. There were a great many graves in the churchyard, and some of them were overgrown with long grass. John thought of his father's grave, which some day might look like these when he was no longer there to weed and trim it. So he knelt down, pulled up the long grass, and raised the wooden crosses which had fallen down. He picked up the wreaths which had been blown away and replaced them, thinking that perhaps someone would do the same for his father's grave now he was away.

An old beggar was standing outside the churchyard leaning on a crutch, and John gave him the few silver coins he had left, and then went happily and cheerfully on into the wide world. Towards evening a fearful storm came on and John hurried to get under shelter, but it soon grew dark. At last he reached a little church standing on a solitary hill; the door was ajar, and he slipped in to take shelter till the storm was over.

" I will sit down here in a corner till the storm is over," he said; " I am quite tired and in need of a rest! " so he sat down, folded his hand, and said his evening prayer; and before he was aware he was asleep and dreaming, while it thundered and lightened outside.

When he woke up it was the middle of the night and the storm was over: the moon was shining in upon him through the windows. In the middle of the aisle stood an open coffin with a dead man in it who was not yet buried. John was not at all afraid, for he had a good conscience, and he knew that the dead can do no harm; it is living wicked people who do harm to others. There were two such bad men standing by the coffin. They had come to do harm to this poor dead man; to turn him out of his coffin and throw the body outside the church door.

" Why do you want to do this? " asked John. " It is very wicked and disgraceful; let the man rest for Heaven's sake! "

" Oh nonsense! " replied the wretches; " he cheated us, he owed us money which he could not pay, and now he has gone and died into the bargain, and we shall never see a penny, so we want to revenge ourselves. He shall lie like a dog outside the church doors! "

" I have not got more than fifty dollars," said John; " it is my whole inheritance, but I will gladly give it to you if you will honestly promise me to leave the poor dead man in peace. I shall manage very well without the money, I have good strong limbs, and the Lord will always help me."

" Well," said the bad men, " if you are ready to pay his debt like that, we won't do him any harm, we can assure you! "

And they took the money John gave them, laughing at him for being such a simpleton, and then they went away. John put the body straight again, folded the hands, said good-bye, and went away through the woods in a state of great satisfaction. Around him, where the moon pierced through the trees, he saw numbers of little elves playing about merrily. They did not disturb themselves on his account, they knew very well that he was a good innocent person, and it is only bad people who never see the fairies. Some of them were no bigger than one's finger, and they had long yellow hair fastened up with golden combs. They swung hand in hand upon the big dewdrops which covered the leaves and the long grass. Sometimes the dewdrops rolled down, and then they fell with it down among the grass, and this caused great noise and laughter among the little folks. It was very amusing. They sang all the pretty little songs John used to know when he was a little boy. Great spiders with silver crowns upon their heads spun their webs from branch to branch like bridges connecting palaces. They glittered in the moonlight like glass where the dew had fallen on them. They went on with their sports till the sun rose, and the little creatures crept away into the flower buds, and the wind caught the bridges and palaces and swept them away into the air like cobwebs.

John had just got through the wood, when a strong man's voice called out behind him, " Hallo, comrade! whither away? "

" Out into the wide world," said John. " I have neither father nor mother, I am only a poor lad, but the Lord will protect me."

" I am going out into the wide world too! " said the stranger; " shall we go together? "

" By all means," said John, and so they walked on together.

They soon grew much attached to each other, for they were both good men, but John soon saw that the stranger was much wiser than himself, he had been round the greater part of the world, and he was well able to describe all that he had seen.

The sun was already high when they sat down under a big tree to eat their breakfast, and just then an old woman came up. She was very old and bent, and walked with a crutch; she had a bundle of sticks she had picked up in the wood on her back, and her apron was fastened up, and John could see in it three bundles or faggots of dried fern and some willow twigs. When she got near them, her foot slipped and she fell with a loud shriek; the poor old woman had broken her leg.

John wanted to carry her home, but the stranger opened his knapsack, and took out a little pot of salve, which he said would make her leg well directly, and she would be able to walk home as well as if she had never broken it. But in payment for it he wanted the three bundles of fern she had in her apron.

"That is very good payment," said the old woman, nodding her head rather oddly; she did not want to part with her three bundles of fern, but it was not so pleasant to lie there with a broken leg, so she gave him the faggots. As soon as he had rubbed on the salve, the old woman got up and walked away faster than she had been able to do before. This was all the effect of the salve; but no such ointment as this was to be had at any chemist's.

"Whatever do you want with those bundles of fern?" said John to his companion.

"They make very good birch rods, and they are just what I like. I am a very queer fellow, you know!"

Then they walked on for a good bit.

"What a storm is drawing up there!" said John, pointing before him; "those are terribly black clouds."

"No," said his fellow-traveller, "those are not clouds, they are mountains, beautiful high mountains, where you can get right above the clouds into the fresh air. It is splendid up there! To-morrow we shall just reach them."

They were not so near, however, as they seemed to be; it took them a whole day to reach the mountains, where the dark forests grew right up towards the sky, and where there were great boulders as big as houses, or even towns. It would be a heavy task to climb over all these, and so John and his fellow-traveller went into an inn to rest and refresh themselves before they made the ascent next day. There were a number of people in the parlour at the inn, for there was a man showing off some marionettes. He had just put up his little theatre, and the people were sitting round waiting for the play to begin. A fat old butcher had taken up his place in the middle of the front row, and he had a ferocious looking bulldog by his side, and it sat staring just as hard as anybody else.

Then the comedy began, and it was a very pretty play, with a King and a Queen in it. They sat on a velvet throne with golden crowns on their heads, and trains, for they could well afford it. The prettiest little wooden dolls stood by all the doors, they had bright glass eyes and big whiskers, and they were employed in opening and shutting the doors to let in the fresh air. It was a capital play, and not at all a tragic one, but just as the Queen got up to walk across the floor—Heaven knows what idea entered the bulldog's head, but finding that the butcher was not holding him, he made a great leap forward right into the middle of the theatre and seized the Queen by the slender waist, and crunched her head up. It was a terrible disaster!

The poor showman was quite frightened and also very sad about his Queen, for she was his prettiest doll, and the horrid bulldog had entirely ruined her. But when all the people had gone away John's fellow-traveller said he could make her all right again, and he took out his little pot and rubbed some of the same ointment on to the doll which had cured the poor old woman who had broken her leg. As soon as ever the doll had been rubbed over with the ointment she became whole again, nay, she could even move all her limbs herself; it was no longer necessary to pull the wires. The doll was exactly like a living being, except that she could not speak. The showman was delighted, because now he did not have to hold the wires at all for this doll, as she could dance quite well by herself, and none of the others could do that.

At night, when everybody had gone to bed, someone was heard sighing most dolefully, and it went on so long that everybody got up to see who it could be. The showman went along to his theatre, because that was where the sighs seemed to come from. All the wooden dolls were lying in a heap; it was the King and his guards who were sighing so dismally and staring with their glass eyes. They all wanted to be rubbed with some of the same ointment as the Queen, so that they might be able to move their limbs as well as she did. She threw herself down on her knees and stretched out her hands with her golden crown, saying, " Pray, take this, but do, please, rub some of the ointment on to my consort and the courtiers! " The poor man who owned the theatre and the marionettes could not help crying, he was so sorry for them. He immediately promised the travelling-companion that he would give him all the money he possessed if he would only anoint five or six of the prettiest dolls. But the travelling-companion said that he did not want anything except the big sword that the showman wore at his side, and as soon as it was given him he anointed six dolls. They began to dance about at once so prettily that all the real, living girls who saw them began to dance too. The coachman and the cook, the waiter and the chambermaid, and all the strangers joined in, as well as the shovel and the tongs: but those two fell on the top of each other just as they were making their first bound. It was indeed a lively night!

Next morning John and his travelling-companion went away from them all, up the high mountains and through the great pine forests. They got so high that at last the church towers far below looked like little red berries among all the green; and they could see far away for many, many miles, to places where they had never been! John had never seen so many of the beauties of this beautiful world all together before. The warm sun shone brightly in the clear blue sky, and the huntsman was heard winding his horn among the mountains; it was all so peaceful and sweet that it brought tears to his eyes, and he could not help exclaiming, " Great God, I could fall down and kiss the hem of Thy garment out of gratitude for all Thy good gifts to us! "

His travelling-companion also stood with folded hands looking at the woods and the villages basking in the warm sunshine. They heard a wonderful and beautiful sound above their heads, and looked up; a great white swan was hovering in the air above them. It sang as they had never heard any bird sing before; but the song became fainter and fainter, and the swan gradually sank down before their feet, where it lay dead—the beautiful bird.

" Two such beautiful wings," said the travelling-companion. " Such big white ones are worth a lot of money; I will take them with me. Now, you see what a good thing it was that I got this sword! " and with one blow he struck off both the wings of the dead swan, for he meant to keep them.

They travelled many, many miles over the mountains, till at

last they saw before them a great town with over a hundred towers, which glittered like silver in the sunshine. In the middle of the town was a splendid marble palace, thatched with red gold, in which the King lived.

John and his travelling-companion did not want to go into the town at once; they stopped at an inn outside to change their clothes, as they wished to look their best when they walked through the streets. The host told them that the King was such a good old man, he never did any harm to anyone; but his daughter—Heaven preserve us! she was a wicked Princess.

Beauty she had more than enough of; nobody could be so beautiful and fascinating as she was, but what was the good of it when she was such a bad, wicked witch, who was the cause of so many handsome Princes having lost their lives. She had given permission to anybody to court her. Anyone who would might come, were he Prince or beggar—it was all the same to her; he only had to guess three riddles she asked him. If he could answer them, she would marry him, and he would be king over all the land when her father died; but if he failed to answer them, he either had to be hanged or to have his head cut off. So bad and so wicked was this beautiful Princess. Her father, the old King, was much grieved by it, but he could not prevent her from being so wicked, for he had once said that he would never have anything to do with her lovers; she must deal with them herself as she liked. Every Prince who had yet come to guess the riddles so as to gain the Princess had failed, and so he had either been hanged or had his head cut off. Each one had been warned, and he need not have paid his addresses unless he had liked. The old King was so grieved by all this trouble and misery that he and his soldiers spent a whole day every year on their knees praying that the Princess might become good. But she had no intention of so doing. The old women who drank brandy dyed it black before they drank it; that was their way of mourning, and what more could they do!

"That vile Princess!" said John, "she ought to be well birched, that would be the best thing for her. If I were the King I would make the blood run!" Just then they heard all the people in the streets shouting "Hurrah!" The Princess was passing, and she was really so beautiful that when they saw her everybody forgot how wicked she was, and so they all shouted " Hurrah." Twelve beautiful maidens clothed in white silk, with golden tulips in their hands, rode twelve coal-black horses by her side. The Princess herself was on a snow-white horse, adorned with diamonds and rubies; her riding dress was of pure gold, and the whip in her hand looked like a sunbeam. The golden crown on her head seemed to be made of little twinkling stars from the sky; and her cloak was sewn all over with thousands of beautiful butterflies' wings. But she was far, far more beautiful than all her clothes.

When John saw her his face became as red as blood, and he could hardly say a single word; the Princess was the image of the beautiful girl with the golden crown whom he had seen in his dream, the night his father died. He thought her so beautiful that he at once fell in love with her. It certainly could not be true, he thought, that she could be a wicked witch who allowed people to be hanged or executed if they could not guess her riddles. " Anyone may pay his addresses to her, even the poorest peasant: I will go to the Palace myself! I can't help going! "

They all said that he ought not to go as he would only meet the same fate as the others. His travelling-companion also advised him against going, but John thought he would be sure to get on all right; so he brushed his coat and his shoes, washed his hands and face, and combed his yellow hair, and then went quite alone to the town and straight up to the Palace.

" Come in," said the old King when John knocked at the door. He opened it, and the old King in his dressing-gown and slippers came towards him. He had his gold crown on his head, the sceptre in one hand, and the golden ball in the other. " Wait a moment," said he, tucking the ball under his arm so as to be able to shake hands with John. But as soon as he heard that John was a suitor he began to cry so much that both the ball and the sceptre rolled on to the floor, and he had to wipe his eyes with his dressing-gown. The poor old King!

" Leave it alone! " said he; " you are sure to fail just like the others, I am convinced of it! " Then he led John into the Princess' pleasure garden, which was a ghastly sight. From every tree hung three or four King's sons who had come to court the

Princess, but who had all been unable to guess her riddles. With every gust of wind the bones rattled so that all the little birds were frightened away and they never dared come into the garden; all the flowers were tied up to human bones in the place of stakes, and human skulls grinned out of every flower pot. It was indeed a nice garden for a Princess.

"Here you see," said the old King, "your fate will be just the same as all these. Do give it up. It makes me most unhappy, I take it so much to heart." John kissed the old King's hand and said he thought it would be all right for he was so fond of the beautiful Princess.

Just then the Princess came herself with all her ladies driving into the Palace gardens, so they went up to her and said "Goodmorning." She was certainly very beautiful as she shook hands with John, and he was more in love with her than ever; it was impossible that she could be the wicked witch people said she was. They all went up into the hall and the little pages brought jam and gingerbread nuts to them; but the old King was so sad that he could eat nothing, besides the ginger nuts were too hard for him.

It was now decided that John was to come up to the Palace the next morning, when the judges and all the council would be assembled to hear if he could guess the first riddle. If he succeeded the first time, he would have to come twice more, but nobody yet had ever guessed the first riddle—he had lost his life at once.

John was not a bit alarmed about himself; he was delighted, and only thought of the lovely Princess. He felt quite certain that the good God would help him, but in what manner it would be he had not the slightest idea, nor did he trouble his head about it. He danced along the highway, when he went back to the inn where his travelling-companion was waiting for him. John was never tired of telling him how charming the Princess had been towards him, and how lovely she was. He was longing for the next day to come, when he was to go to the Palace to try his luck with the riddles. But his travelling-companion shook his head and was quite sad.

"I am so fond of you," he said; "we might have been companions for a long time yet, and now I shall lose you directly!

My poor dear John, I could weep over you, but I will not spoil your pleasure on the last evening we perhaps may spend together. We will be merry, as merry as possible; to-morrow when you are gone I can be sad! "

Everybody in the town had heard directly that a new suitor had come for the Princess, and there was general mourning. The theatre was closed, and all the cakewomen tied black crape round the sugar pigs. The King and the priests were praying on their knees in the churches, and there was universal grief, for they all knew that there could be no better fate in store for John than for the other suitors.

Late in the evening the travelling-companion made a great bowl of punch, and said to John that they must be merry now and drink the Princess' health. But when John had drunk two glasses he became so sleepy that he could not hold up his head, and he fell fast asleep. His travelling-companion lifted him quietly up from his chair, and laid him on his bed. As soon as it was dark he took the two big wings which he had cut off the swan, and tied them on to his own shoulders; then he put the biggest bunch of twigs he had got from the old woman who had broken her leg into his pocket, opened the window, and flew over the roofs of the houses right up to the Palace, where he sat down in a corner under the window of the Princess' bedroom.

The whole town was quiet. As the clock struck the quarter before twelve the window was opened, and the Princess flew out in a great white cloak and long black wings. She flew over the town to a great mountain, but the travelling-companion made himself invisible and flew behind her, raining blows on her back with his birch rod, till the blood flowed. Oh, what a flight that was through the air; the wind caught her cloak, which spread out on every side like the sail of a ship, and the moon shone through it.

" How it hails, how it hails! " said the Princess at every blow, but she richly deserved it.

At last they reached the mountain and knocked; there was a rumble as of thunder, the side of the mountain opened, and the Princess went in, closely followed by the travelling-companion. No one saw him, as he was quite invisible. They went through a long passage which glittered curiously, owing to thousands of shining spiders which swarmed over the walls, shedding a fiery light. They next reached a great hall built of gold and silver, with red and blue flowers as big as sunflowers all over the walls. No one could pick these flowers, for the stems were poisonous snakes, and the flowers were flames coming out of their mouths. The ceiling was covered with shining glow-worms and pale blue bats which flapped their transparent wings. This had an extraordinary effect. In the middle of the floor was a throne supported on four horses' legs with harness of the red fiery spiders. The throne itself was of milky glass, and the cushions were made of little black mice holding on to each other by the tails. There was a canopy above it of rose-coloured spider's web, dotted with the most exquisite little green flies which glittered like diamonds.

A hideous old ogre sat in the middle of the throne with a crown on his ugly head and a sceptre in his hand. He kissed the Princess on her forehead, and made her sit down by him on the costly throne, then the music began! Great black grasshoppers played upon Jews' harps, and the owl beat upon his own stomach in place of a drum. It was a most absurd concert. Numbers of tiny little elves, each with a firefly on their little caps, danced round the hall. No one could see the travelling-companion, but he could see and hear everything from behind the throne, where he had placed himself. The courtiers who now made their appearance looked most grand and proper, but anyone who could really see perceived at once what they were. They were merely broomsticks with cabbages for heads, into which the ogre had put life by his magic powers and dressed them up in embroidered clothes. But this did not matter a bit, for they were only used on grand occasions.

After the dancing had gone on for a time, the Princess told the ogre that she had another suitor, and asked him what she had better think of to put as a riddle the next day.

" Listen! " said the ogre; " I will tell you what, you must think of something very simple, and then he will never think of it. Let us say one of your own shoes; he will never guess that. Then have his head chopped off, but don't forget when you come here to-morrow night to bring me his eyes. I want to eat them."

The Princess curtsied low, and said that she would not forget the eyes. The ogre opened the mountain, and she flew home again; and, as before, the travelling-companion followed her closely and beat her so hard with the birch rod that she groaned at the terrible hailstorm and hurried back as fast as she could to her bedroom window. The travelling-companion flew back to the inn, where he found John still fast asleep. He took off his own clothes and went to bed too, for he had good right to be tired.

John woke up early in the morning, and the travelling-companion got up at the same time, and told him that he had had a wonderful dream about the Princess and her shoe; and he begged John to ask the Princess if she had not thought of her shoe. This was of course what he had heard the ogre say in the mountain, but he did not want to tell John anything about that, and so he merely told him it was a dream.

" I may just as well ask that as anything else!" said John. " perhaps your dream will come true, for I always think God will help me! All the same I will say good-bye, for if I guess wrong you will never see me again."

So they kissed each other, and John went to the town and up to the Palace. The hall was full of people; the judges were seated in their arm-chairs, and they had down pillows under their heads for they had so much to think about. The old King stood near wiping his eyes with a white pocket handkerchief. Then the Princess came in, greeting everyone very pleasantly, and she was even lovelier than yesterday. She shook hands with John and said, " Good-morning to you." Now John had to guess what she had thought of. She looked at him most sweetly, but as soon as she heard him say the word shoe, she turned as white as a sheet and trembled all over; but that was no good, for he had guessed aright.

Preserve us! how pleased the old King was, he turned head over heels without stopping, and everybody clapped their hands both on his account and on John's, whose first guess had been right.

The travelling-companion beamed with delight when he heard how successful John had been. But John folded his hands and thanked God, who no doubt would also help him on the two following occasions. The next day was fixed for the second riddle.

The evening passed just as the previous one had done. When John had gone to sleep the travelling-companion flew behind the Princess to the mountain, and he beat her harder than ever, for this time he had taken two birch rods with him. Nobody could see him, and he heard everything as before. The Princess was to think of her glove, and this he told John just as if it had been a dream. John of course could easily guess aright, and again there was great delight at the Palace. The whole court turned somersaults, as they had seen the King do the first time; but the Princess lay on the sofa and would not say a single word. Now all turned upon whether John guessed the third riddle or not. If he did, he would win the Princess and inherit the whole kingdom when the old King died; but if he was wrong, he would lose his life, and the ogre would eat his beautiful blue eyes.

The evening before, John went early to bed, said his prayers, and slept as peacefully as possible; but the travelling-companion tied the wings on to his back, and bound the sword round his waist, took all the birch rods, and flew off to the Palace.

It was a pitch dark night. There was such a gale that the tiles flew off the roofs, and the trees in the garden of bones bent like reeds before the wind. The lightning flashed every moment, and the thunder rolled continuously the whole night long. The window burst open and the Princess flew out; she was as pale as death, but she laughed at the storm as if it were not bad enough; her white mantle swirled about in the wind like the sails of a ship. The travelling-companion beat her with his three birches till the blood dripped on to the ground. She could hardly fly any further. At last they reached the mountain.

"What a hailstorm there is!" she said as she entered. "I have never been out in such a bad one!"

"One may even have too much of a good thing!" said the ogre.

Then she told him that John's second guess had been right, and if he was successful again in the morning she would never be able to come and see him again in the mountain. Nor would she ever be able to do any more of the sorcerer's tricks as before, and she was very sad about it.

" He shall never guess it," said the ogre.

" I shall think of something that will never enter his head. But we will have some fun first! " And he took the Princess by both hands and they danced round the room with all the little elves and the fireflies. The red spiders ran merrily up and down the walls, and the fire flowers seemed to give out sparks. The owls played their drums, the crickets chirped, and the grasshoppers played their harps. It was a very gay ball.

After they had danced some time the Princess was obliged to go home or she would be missed, and the ogre said he would go with her so as to have more of her company.

So away they flew through the storm, and the travelling-companion wore out his birch rods on their backs; never had the ogre been out in such a hailstorm. He said good-bye to the Princess outside the Palace, and whispered to her, " Think of my head," but the travelling-companion heard what he said, and at the very moment when the Princess slipped in at her window, and the ogre was turning away to go back, he seized him by his long black beard, and before he had time to look round, cut off his head close to the shoulders with his big sword. He threw the body into the sea to be food for fishes, but he only dipped the head into the water, and tied it up in his silk handkerchief and took it back to the inn, and he then went to bed.

Next morning he gave John the handkerchief, but said he must not open it before the Princess asked him what she had thought about.

There were so many people in the hall that they were packed as close together as a bundle of radishes. The judges were sitting in their arm-chairs with the soft down cushions; and the old King had his new clothes on, and his crown and sceptre had been polished up and looked quite festive. But the Princess was very, very pale, and she was dressed in black, as if for a funeral.

" What have I thought of ? " she asked John; and he immediately untied the handkerchief, and was very much frightened himself when he saw the hideous ogre's head. A shudder ran through the whole assemblage, but the Princess seemed turned to stone, and could not say a single word. At last she got up and gave her hand to John, for he had guessed all the riddles;

she looked neither to the right nor to the left, but sighed deeply, and said, "You are my master now; our wedding shall take place to-night." "I like that," said the old King; "that is just as it should be." All the people shouted hurrah, the guard's band played in the streets, the bells rang, and the cakewomen took the crape off the sugar pigs, because all was now rejoicing. Three oxen stuffed with chickens and ducks were roasted whole in the market-place, and everyone could cut off a portion for themselves. The fountains played wine instead of water, and anyone who bought a penny roll had six large buns full of plums given in.

In the evening the whole town was illuminated. The soldiers fired salutes, and the boys let off squibs and crackers. At the Palace all was eating and drinking, toasting and dancing. The grand gentlemen danced with the pretty ladies, and the singing could be heard far and wide.

But the Princess was still bewitched, and she did not care a bit about John; the travelling-companion knew this, and gave him three feathers out of the swan's wings and a little bottle with a few drops of liquid in it. He told John to have a large bath full of water placed by the side of the bed, and when the Princess was going to get into bed he must give her a little push so that she fell into the water, where he was to dip her three times, first having thrown the three feathers and the drops of liquid into it. She would then be released from the spell and would grow very fond of him.

John did everything as he was told. The Princess shrieked when he dipped her into the water, and struggled in his hands in the form of a black swan with glittering eyes. The second time she came up as a white swan, except for a black ring round the neck. John prayed humbly to God, and the third time she came up as a lovely Princess. She was more lovely than she had been before, and thanked him, with tears in her eyes, for having released her from the spell.

Next morning the old King came with all his courtiers to offer their congratulations, and this went on all day. Last of all came the travelling-companion; he had his stick in his hand and his knapsack on his back. John kissed him over and over, and said that he must not go away; he must stay with them, as he was the cause of all their happiness. But the travelling-companion shook his head, and said gently and tenderly, "No; my time is up. I have only paid my debt. Do you remember the dead man whom you prevented the wicked men from disturbing. You gave all that you possessed so that he might have rest in his grave. I am the dead man!" And then he immediately vanished.

The wedding festivities lasted a whole month. John and the Princess were devoted to each other, and the old King had many happy days in which to let their little children play " ride a cock-horse " on his knee and to play with his sceptre. But John was King over the whole country.

THE FIR-TREE

FAR down in the forest, where the warm sun and the fresh air made a sweet resting-place, grew a pretty little fir-tree; and yet it was not happy, it wished so much to be tall like its companions—the pines and firs which grew around it. The sun shone, and the soft air fluttered its leaves, and the little peasant children passed by, prattling merrily, but the fir-tree heeded them not. Sometimes the children would bring a large basket of raspberries or strawberries, wreathed on a straw, and seat themselves near the fir-tree, and say, " Is it not a pretty little tree? " which made it feel more unhappy than before. And yet all this while the tree grew a notch or joint taller every year; for by the number of joints in the stem of a fir-tree we can discover its age. Still, as it grew, it complained, " Oh! how I wish I were as tall as the other trees, then I would spread out my branches on every side, and my top would over-look the wide world. I should have the birds building their nests on my boughs, and when the wind blew, I should bow with stately dignity like my tall companions." The tree was so discontented, that it took no pleasure in the warm sunshine, the birds, or the rosy clouds that floated over it morning and evening. Sometimes, in winter, when the snow lay white and glittering on the ground, a hare would come springing along, and jump right over the little tree; and then how mortified it would feel! Two winters passed, and when the third arrived, the tree had grown so tall that the hare was obliged to run round it. Yet it remained unsatisfied, and would exclaim, " Oh, if I could but keep on growing tall and old! There is nothing else worth caring for in the world! " In the autumn, as usual, the wood-cutters came and cut down several of the tallest trees, and the young fir-tree, which was now grown to its full height, shuddered as the noble trees fell to the earth with a crash. After the branches were lopped off, the trunks looked so slender and bare, that they could scarcely be recognized. Then they were placed upon wagons, and drawn by horses out of the forest. "Where were they going? What would become of them?" The young fir-tree wished very much to know; so in the spring, when the swallows and the storks came, it asked, "Do you know where those trees were taken? Did you meet them?"

The swallows knew nothing, but the stork, after a little reflection, nodded his head, and said, "Yes, I think I do. I met several new ships when I flew from Egypt, and they had fine masts that smelt like fir. I think these must have been the trees; I assure you they were stately, very stately."

"Oh, how I wish I were tall enough to go on the sea," said the fir-tree. "What is the sea, and what does it look like?"

"It would take too much time to explain," said the stork, flying quickly away.

"Rejoice in thy youth," said the sunbeam; "rejoice in thy fresh growth, and the young life that is in thee."

And the wind kissed the tree, and the dew watered it with tears; but the fir-tree regarded them not.

Christmas-time drew near, and many young trees were cut down, some even smaller and younger than the fir-tree who enjoyed neither rest nor peace with longing to leave its forest home. These young trees, which were chosen for their beauty, kept their branches, and were also laid on wagons and drawn by horses out of the forest.

"Where are they going?" asked the fir-tree.   "They are not taller than I am: indeed, one is much less; and why are the branches not cut off? Where are they going?"

"We know, we know," sang the sparrows; "we have looked in at the windows of the houses in the town, and we know what is done with them. They are dressed up in the most splendid manner. We have seen them standing in the middle of a warm room, and adorned with all sorts of beautiful things,—honey cakes, gilded apples, playthings, and many hundreds of wax tapers."

"And then," asked the fir-tree, trembling through all its branches, "and then what happens?"

"We did not see any more," said the sparrows; "but this was enough for us."

" I wonder whether anything so brilliant will ever happen to me," thought the fir-tree. " It would be much better than crossing the sea. I long for it almost with pain. Oh! when will Christmas be here? I am now as tall and well grown as those which were taken away last year. Oh! that I were now laid on the wagon, or standing in the warm room, with all that brightness and splendor around me! Something better and more beautiful is to come after, or the trees would not be so decked out. Yes, what follows will be grander and more splendid. What can it be? I am weary with longing. I scarcely know how I feel."

" Rejoice with us," said the air and the sunlight. " Enjoy thine own bright life in the fresh air."

But the tree would not rejoice, though it grew taller every day; and, winter and summer, its dark-green foliage might be seen in the forest, while passers by would say, " What a beautiful tree!"

A short time before Christmas, the discontented fir-tree was the first to fall. As the axe cut through the stem, and divided the pith, the tree fell with a groan to the earth, conscious of pain and faintness, and forgetting all its anticipations of happiness, in sorrow at leaving its home in the forest. It knew that it should never again see its dear old companions, the trees, nor the little bushes and many-colored flowers that had grown by its side; perhaps not even the birds. Neither was the journey at all pleasant. The tree first recovered itself while being unpacked in the courtyard of a house, with several other trees; and it heard a man say, " We only want one, and this is the prettiest."

Then came two servants in grand livery, and carried the fir-tree into a large and beautiful apartment. On the walls hung pictures, and near the great stove stood great china vases, with lions on the lids. There were rocking-chairs, silken sofas, large tables, covered with pictures, books, and playthings, worth a great deal of money,—at least, the children said so. Then the fir-tree was placed in a large tub, full of sand; but green baize hung all around it, so that no one could see it was a tub, and it stood on a very handsome carpet. How the fir-tree trembled! " What was going to happen to him now? " Some young ladies came, and the servants helped them to adorn the tree. On one branch they hung little bags cut out of colored paper, and each bag was filled with sweetmeats; from other branches hung gilded apples and walnuts, as if they had grown there; and above, and all round, were hundreds of red, blue, and white tapers, which were fastened on the branches. Dolls, exactly like real babies, were placed under the green leaves,—the tree had never seen such things before,—and at the very top was fastened a glittering star, made of tinsel. Oh, it was very beautiful!

"This evening," they all exclaimed, "how bright it will be!" "Oh, that the evening were come," thought the tree, "and the tapers lighted! then I shall know what else is going to happen. Will the trees of the forest come to see me? I wonder if the sparrows will peep in at the windows as they fly? shall I grow faster here, and keep on all these ornaments summer and winter?" But guessing was of very little use; it made his bark ache, and this pain is as bad for a slender fir-tree, as headache is for us. At last the tapers were lighted, and then what a glistening blaze of light the tree presented! It trembled so with joy in all its branches, that one of the candles fell among the green leaves and burnt some of them. "Help! help!" exclaimed the young ladies, but there was no danger, for they quickly extinguished the fire. After this, the tree tried not to tremble at all, though the fire frightened him; he was so anxious not to hurt any of the beautiful ornaments, even while their brilliancy dazzled him. And now the folding doors were thrown open, and a troop of children rushed in as if they intended to upset the tree; they were followed more silently by their elders. For a moment the little ones stood silent with astonishment, and then they shouted for joy, till the room rang, and they danced merrily round the tree, while one present after another was taken from it.

"What are they doing? What will happen next?" thought the fir. At last the candles burnt down to the branches and were put out. Then the children received permission to plunder the tree.

Oh, how they rushed upon it, till the branches cracked, and had it not been fastened with the glistening star to the ceiling, it must have been thrown down. The children then danced about with their pretty toys, and no one noticed the tree, except the children's maid who came and peeped among the branches to see if an apple or a fig had been forgotten.

"A story, a story," cried the children, pulling a little fat man toward the tree.

" Now we shall be in the green shade," said the man, as he seated himself under it, " and the tree will have the pleasure of hearing also, but I shall only relate one story; what shall it be? Ivede-Avede, or Humpty Dumpty, who fell down stairs, but soon got up again, and at last married a princess."

" Ivede-Avede," cried some. " Humpty Dumpty," cried others, and there was a fine shouting and crying out. But the fir-tree remained quite still, and thought to himself, " Shall I have anything to do with all this? " but he had already amused them as much as they wished. Then the old man told them the story of Humpty Dumpty, how he fell down stairs, and was raised up again, and married a princess. And the children clapped their hands and cried, " Tell another, tell another," for they wanted to hear the story of " Ivede-Avede; " but they only had " Humpty Dumpty." After this the fir-tree became quite silent and thoughtful; never had the birds in the forest told such tales as " Humpty Dumpty," who fell down stairs, and yet married a princess.

" Ah! yes, so it happens in the world," thought the fir-tree; he believed it all, because it was related by such a nice man. " Ah! well," he thought, " who knows? perhaps I may fall down too, and marry a princess; " and he looked forward joyfully to the next evening, expecting to be again decked out with lights and playthings, gold and fruit. " To-morrow I will not tremble," thought he; " I will enjoy all my splendor, and I shall hear the story of Humpty Dumpty again, and perhaps Ivede-Avede." And the tree remained quiet and thoughtful all night. In the morning the servants and the housemaid came in. " Now," thought the fir, " all my splendor is going to begin again." But they dragged him out of the room and upstairs to the garret, and threw him on the floor, in a dark corner, where no daylight shone, and there they left him. " What does this mean? " thought the tree, " what am I to do here? I can hear nothing in a place like this," and he had time enough to think, for days and nights passed and no one came near him, and when at last somebody did come, it was only to put away large boxes in a corner. So the tree was completely hidden from sight as if it had never existed. " It is winter now," thought the tree, " the ground is hard and covered with snow, so that people cannot plant me. I shall be sheltered here, I dare say, until spring comes. How thoughtful and kind everybody is to me! Still I wish this place were not so dark, as well as lonely, with not even a little hare to look at. How pleasant it was out in the forest while the snow lay on the ground, when the hare would run by, yes, and jump over me too, although I did not like it then. Oh! it is terrible lonely here."

"Squeak, squeak," said a little mouse, creeping cautiously toward the tree; then came another; and they both sniffed at the fir-tree and crept between the branches.

" Oh, it is very cold," said the little mouse, " or else we should be so comfortable here, shouldn't we, you old fir-tree? "

" I am not old," said the fir-tree, " there are many who are older than I am."

" Where do you come from? and what do you know? " asked the mice, who were full of curiosity. " Have you seen the most beautiful places in the world, and can you tell us all about them? and have you been in the storeroom, where cheeses lie on the shelf, and hams hang from the ceiling? One can run about on tallow candles there, and go in thin and come out fat."

" I know nothing of that place," said the fir-tree, " but I know the wood where the sun shines and the birds sing." And then the tree told the little mice all about its youth. They had never heard such an account in their lives; and after they had listened to it attentively, they said, " What a number of things you have seen! you must have been very happy."

"Happy!" exclaimed the fir-tree, and then as he reflected upon what he had been telling them, he said, " Ah, yes! after all those were happy days." But when he went on and related all about Christmas-eve, and how he had been dressed up with cakes and lights, the mice said, " How happy you must have been, you old fir-tree."

" I am not old at all," replied the tree, " I only came from the forest this winter, I am now checked in my growth."

" What splendid stories you can relate," said the little mice. And the next night four other mice came with them to hear what the tree had to tell. The more he talked the more he remembered, and then he thought to himself, " Those were happy days, but they may come again. Humpty Dumpty fell down stairs, and yet he married the princess; perhaps I may marry a princess too." And the fir-tree thought of the pretty little birch-tree that grew in the forest, which was to him a real beautiful princess.

"Who is Humpty Dumpty?" asked the little mice. And then the tree related the whole story; he could remember every single word, and the little mice were so delighted with it, that they were ready to jump to the top of the tree. The next night a great many more mice made their appearance, and on Sunday two rats came with them; but they said, it was not a pretty story at all, and the little mice were very sorry, for it made them also think less of it.

"Do you know only one story?" asked the rats.

"Only one," replied the fir-tree; "I heard it on the happiest evening of my life; but I did not know I was so happy at the time."

"We think it is a very miserable story," said the rats. "Don't you know any story about bacon, or tallow in the storeroom?"

"No," replied the tree.

"Many thanks to you then," replied the rats, and they marched off.

The little mice also kept away after this, and the tree sighed, and said, "It was very pleasant when the merry little mice sat round me and listened while I talked. Now that is all passed too. However, I shall consider myself happy when some one comes to take me out of this place." But would this ever happen? Yes; one morning people came to clear out the garret, the boxes were packed away, and the tree was pulled out of the corner, and thrown roughly on the garret floor; then the servant dragged it out upon the staircase where the daylight shone. "Now life is beginning again," said the tree, rejoicing in the sunshine and fresh air. Then it was carried down stairs and taken into the courtyard so quickly, that it forgot to think of itself, and could only look about, there was so much to be seen. The court was close to a garden, where everything looked blooming. Fresh and fragrant roses hung over the little palings. The linden-trees were in blossom; while the swallows flew here and there, crying, "Twit, twit, twit, my mate is coming,"—but it was not the fir-tree they meant. "Now I shall live," cried the tree, joyfully spreading out its branches; but alas! they were all withered and yellow, and it lay in a corner amongst weeds and nettles. The star of gold paper still stuck in the top of the tree and glittered in the sunshine. In the same courtyard two of the merry children were playing who had danced round the tree at Christmas, and had been so happy. The youngest saw the gilded star, and ran and pulled it off the tree. "Look what is sticking to the ugly old fir-tree," said the child, treading on the branches till they crackled under his boots. And the tree saw all the fresh bright flowers in the garden, and then looked at itself, and wished it had remained in the dark corner of the garret. It thought of its fresh youth in the forest, of the merry Christmas evening, and of the little mice who had listened to the story of " Humpty Dumpty." " Past! past!" said the old tree; " Oh, had I but enjoyed myself while I could have done so! but now it is too late." Then a lad came and chopped the tree into small pieces, till a large bundle lay in a heap on the ground. The pieces were placed in a fire under the copper, and they quickly blazed up brightly, while the tree sighed so deeply that each sigh was like a pistol-shot. Then the children, who were at play, came and seated themselves in front of the fire, and looked at it and cried, " Pop, pop." But at each " pop," which was a deep sigh, the tree was thinking of a summer day in the forest; and of Christmas evening, and of " Humpty Dumpty," the only story it had ever heard or knew how to relate, till at last it was consumed. The boys still played in the garden, and the youngest wore the golden star on his breast, with which the tree had been adorned during the happiest evening of its existence. Now all was past; the tree's life was past, and the story also,—for all stories must come to an end at last.

THE BEETLE WHO WENT
ON HIS TRAVELS

THERE was once an Emperor who had a horse shod with gold. He had a golden shoe on each foot, and why was this? He was a beautiful creature, with slender legs, bright, intelligent eyes, and a mane that hung down over his neck like a veil. He had carried his master through fire and smoke in the battle-field, with the bullets whistling round him; he had kicked and bitten, and taken part in the fight, when the enemy advanced; and, with his master on his back, he had dashed over the fallen foe, and saved the golden crown and the Emperor's life, which was of more value than the brightest gold. This is the reason of the Emperor's horse wearing golden shoes.

A beetle came creeping forth from the stable, where the farrier had been shoeing the horse. "Great ones, first, of course," said he, "and then the little ones; but size is not always a proof of greatness." He stretched out his thin leg as he spoke.

"And pray what do you want?" asked the farrier.

"Golden shoes," replied the beetle.

"Why, you must be out of your senses," cried the farrier. "Golden shoes for you, indeed!"

"Yes, certainly; golden shoes," replied the beetle. "Am I not just as good as that great creature yonder, who is waited upon and brushed, and has food and drink placed before him? And don't I belong to the royal stables?"

"But why does the horse have golden shoes?" asked the farrier; "of course you understand the reason?"

"Understand! Well, I understand that it is a personal slight to me," cried the beetle. "It is done to annoy me, so I intend to go out into the world and seek my fortune."

"Go along with you," said the farrier.

"You're a rude fellow," cried the beetle, as he walked out of the stable; and then he flew for a short distance, till he found himself in a beautiful flower-garden, all fragrant with roses and lavender. The lady-birds, with red and black shells on their backs, and delicate wings, were flying about, and one of them said, " Is it not sweet and lovely here? Oh, how beautiful everything is."

" I am accustomed to better things," said the beetle. " Do you call this beautiful? Why, there is not even a dung-heap." Then he went on, and under the shadow of a large haystack he found a caterpillar crawling along. " How beautiful this world is!" said the caterpillar. " The sun is so warm, I quite enjoy it. And soon I shall go to sleep, and die as they call it, but I shall wake up with beautiful wings to fly with, like a butterfly."

" How conceited you are!" exclaimed the beetle. " Fly about as a butterfly, indeed! what of that. I have come out of the Emperor's stable, and no one there, not even the Emperor's horse, who, in fact, wears my cast-off golden shoes, has any idea of flying, excepting myself. To have wings and fly! why, I can do that already; " and so saying, he spread his wings and flew away. " I don't want to be disgusted," he said to himself, " and yet I can't help it." Soon after, he fell down upon an extensive lawn, and for a time pretended to sleep, but at last fell asleep in earnest. Suddenly a heavy shower of rain came falling from the clouds. The beetle woke up with the noise and would have been glad to creep into the earth for shelter, but he could not. He was tumbled over and over with the rain, sometimes swimming on his stomach and sometimes on his back; and as for flying, that was out of the question. He began to doubt whether he should escape with his life, so he remained, quietly lying where he was. After a while the weather cleared up a little, and the beetle was able to rub the water from his eyes, and look about him. He saw something gleaming, and he managed to make his way up to it. It was linen which had been laid to bleach on the grass. He crept into a fold of the damp linen, which certainly was not so comfortable a place to lie in as the warm stable, but there was nothing better, so he remained lying there for a whole day and night, and the rain kept on all the time. Towards morning he crept out of his hiding-place, feeling in a very bad temper with the climate. Two frogs were sitting on the linen, and their bright eyes actually glistened with pleasure.

" Wonderful weather this," cried one of them, " and so refreshing. This linen holds the water together so beautifully, that my hind legs quiver as if I were going to swim."

" I should like to know," said another, " If the swallow who flies
so far in her many journeys to foreign lands, ever met with a better
climate than this. What delicious moisture! It is as pleasant as
lying in a wet ditch. I am sure any one who does not enjoy this has
no love for his fatherland."

"Have you ever been in the Emperor's stable?" asked the
beetle. "There the moisture is warm and refreshing; that's the
climate for me, but I could not take it with me on my travels. Is
there not even a dunghill here in this garden, where a person of
rank, like myself, could take up his abode and feel at home?" But
the frogs either did not or would not understand him.

"I never ask a question twice," said the beetle, after he had
asked this one three times, and received no answer. Then he went
on a little farther and stumbled against a piece of broken crockery-
ware, which certainly ought not to have been lying there. But as it
was there, it formed a good shelter against wind and weather to
several families of earwigs who dwelt in it. Their requirements
were not many, they were very sociable, and full of affection for
their children, so much so that each mother considered her own
child the most beautiful and clever of them all.

"Our dear son has engaged himself," said one mother, "dear
innocent boy; his greatest ambition is that he may one day creep
into a clergyman's ear. That is a very artless and loveable wish;
and being engaged will keep him steady. What happiness for a
mother!"

"Our son," said another, "had scarcely crept out of the egg,
when he was off on his travels. He is all life and spirits, I expect he
will wear out his horns with running. How charming this is for a
mother, is it not Mr. Beetle?" for she knew the stranger by his
horny coat.

"You are both quite right," said he; so they begged him to walk
in, that is to come as far as he could under the broken piece of
earthenware.

"Now you shall also see my little earwigs," said a third and a
fourth mother, "they are lovely little things, and highly amusing.
They are never ill-behaved, except when they are uncomfortable
in their inside, which unfortunately often happens at their age."

Thus each mother spoke of her baby, and their babies talked
after their own fashion, and made use of the little nippers they
have in their tails to nip the beard of the beetle.

"They are always busy about something, the little rogues," said the mother, beaming with maternal pride; but the beetle felt it a bore, and he therefore inquired the way to the nearest dung-heap.

"That is quite out in the great world, on the other side of the ditch," answered an earwig, "I hope none of my children will ever go so far, it would be the death of me."

"But I shall try to get so far," said the beetle, and he walked off without taking any formal leave, which is not considered a polite thing to do.

When he arrived at the ditch, he met several friends, all them beetles; "We live here," they said, "and we are very comfortable. May we ask you to step down into this rich mud, you must be fatigued after your journey."

"Certainly," said the beetle, "I shall be most happy; I have been exposed to the rain, and have had to lie upon linen, and cleanliness is a thing that greatly exhausts me; I have also pains in one of my wings from standing in the draught under a piece of broken crockery. It is really quite refreshing to be with one's own kindred again."

"Perhaps you came from a dung-heap," observed the oldest of them.

"No, indeed, I came from a much grander place," replied the beetle; "I came from the emperor's stable, where I was born, with golden shoes on my feet. I am travelling on a secret embassy, but you must not ask me any questions, for I cannot betray my secret."

Then the beetle stepped down into the rich mud, where sat three young-lady beetles, who tittered, because they did not know what to say.

"None of them are engaged yet," said their mother, and the beetle maidens tittered again, this time quite in confusion.

"I have never seen greater beauties, even in the royal stables," exclaimed the beetle, who was now resting himself.

"Don't spoil my girls," said the mother; "and don't talk to them, pray, unless you have serious intentions."

But of course the beetle's intentions were serious, and after a while our friend was engaged. The mother gave them her blessing, and all the other beetles cried "hurrah."

Immediately after the betrothal came the marriage, for there was no reason to delay. The following day passed very pleasantly, and the next was tolerably comfortable; but on the third it became necessary for him to think of getting food for his wife, and, perhaps, for children.

"I have allowed myself to be taken in," said our beetle to himself, "and now there's nothing to be done but to take them in, in return."

No sooner said than done. Away he went, and stayed away all day and all night, and his wife remained behind a forsaken widow.

"Oh, said the other beetles, "this fellow that we have received into our family is nothing but a complete vagabond. He has gone away and left his wife a burden upon our hands."

"Well, she can be unmarried again, and remain here with my other daughters," said the mother. "Fie on the villain that forsook her!"

In the mean time the beetle, who had sailed across the ditch on a cabbage leaf, had been journeying on the other side. In the morning two persons came up to the ditch. When they saw him they took him up and turned him over and over, looking very learned all the time, especially one, who was a boy. "Allah sees the black beetle in the black stone, and the black rock. Is not that written in the Koran?" he asked.

Then he translated the beetle's name into Latin, and said a great deal upon the creature's nature and history. The second person, who was older and a scholar, proposed to carry the beetle home, as they wanted just such good specimens as this. Our beetle considered this speech a great insult, so he flew suddenly out of the speaker's hand. His wings were dry now, so they carried him to a great distance, till at last he reached a hothouse, where a sash of the glass roof was partly open, so he quietly slipped in and buried himself in the warm earth. "It is very comfortable here," he said to himself, and soon after fell asleep. Then he dreamed that the emperor's horse was dying, and had left him his golden shoes, and also promised that he should have two more. All this was very delightful, and when the beetle woke up he crept forth and looked around him. What a splendid place the hothouse was! At the back, large palm-trees were growing; and the sunlight made the leaves look quite glossy; and beneath them what a profusion of luxuriant green, and of flowers red like flame, yellow as amber, or white as new-fallen snow! "What a wonderful quantity of plants," cried the beetle; "how good they will taste when they are decayed! This is a capital store-room. There must certainly be some relations of mine

living here; I will just see if I can find any one with whom I can
associate. I'm proud, certainly; but I'm also proud of being so."
Then he prowled about in the earth, and thought what a pleasant
dream that was about the dying horse, and the golden shoes he had
inherited. Suddenly a hand seized the beetle, and squeezed him,
and turned him round and round. The gardener's little son and his
playfellow had come into the hothouse, and, seeing the beetle,
wanted to have some fun with him. First, he was wrapped in a
vine-leaf, and put into a warm trousers' pocket. He twisted and
turned about with all his might, but he got a good squeeze from the
boy's hand, as a hint for him to keep quiet. Then the boy went
quickly towards a lake that lay at the end of the garden. Here the
beetle was put into an old broken wooden shoe, in which a little
stick had been fastened upright for a mast, and to this mast the
beetle was bound with a piece of worsted. Now he was a sailor, and
had to sail away. The lake was not very large, but to the beetle it
seemed an ocean, and he was so astonished at its size that he fell
over on his back, and kicked out his legs. Then the little ship sailed
away; sometimes the current of the water seized it, but whenever
it went too far from the shore one of the boys turned up his trousers,
and went in after it, and brought it back to land. But at last, just
as it went merrily out again, the two boys were called, and so
angrily, that they hastened to obey, and ran away as fast as they
could from the pond, so that the little ship was left to its fate. It was
carried away farther and farther from the shore, till it reached the
open sea. This was a terrible prospect for the beetle, for he could
not escape in consequence of being bound to the mast. Then a fly
came and paid him a visit. " What beautiful weather," said the fly;
" I shall rest here and sun myself. You must have a pleasant time
of it."

"You speak without knowing the facts," replied the beetle;
" don't you see that I am a prisoner? "

"Ah, but I'm not a prisoner," remarked the fly, and away
he flew.

"Well, now I know the world," said the beetle to himself; " it's
an abominable world; I'm the only respectable person in it. First,
they refuse me my golden shoes; then I have to lie on damp linen,
and to stand in a draught; and to crown all, they fasten a wife upon
me. Then, when I have made a step forward in the world, and
found out a comfortable position, just as I could wish it to be, one of

these human boys comes and ties me up, and leaves me to the mercy of the wild waves, while the emperor's favorite horse goes prancing about proudly on his golden shoes. This vexes me more than anything. But it is useless to look for sympathy in this world. My career has been very interesting, but what's the use of that if nobody knows anything about it? The world does not deserve to be made acquainted with my adventures, for it ought to have given me golden shoes when the emperor's horse was shod, and I stretched out my feet to be shod, too. If I had received golden shoes I should have been an ornament to the stable; now I am lost to the stable and to the world. It is all over with me."

But all was not yet over. A boat, in which were a few young girls, came rowing up. " Look, yonder is an old wooden shoe sailing along," said one of the younger girls.

" And there's a poor little creature bound fast in it," said another.

The boat now came close to our beetle's ship, and the young girls fished it out of the water. One of them drew a small pair of scissors from her pocket, and cut the worsted without hurting the beetle, and when she stepped on shore she placed him on the grass. " There," she said, " creep away, or fly, if thou canst. It is a splendid thing to have thy liberty." Away flew the beetle, straight through the open window of a large building; there he sank down, tired and exhausted, exactly on the mane of the emperor's favorite horse, who was standing in his stable; and the beetle found himself at home again. For some time he clung to the mane, that he might recover himself. " Well," he said, " here I am, seated on the emperor's favorite horse,—sitting upon him as if I were the emperor himself. But what was it the farrier asked me? Ah, I remember now,—that's a good thought,—he asked me why the golden shoes were given to the horse. The answer is quite clear to me, now. They were given to the horse on *my* account." And this reflection put the beetle into a good temper. The sun's rays also came streaming into the stable, and shone upon him, and made the place lively and bright. " Travelling expands the mind very much," said the beetle. " The world is not so bad after all, if you know how to take things as they come."

THE SHEPHERDESS AND THE CHIMNEY-SWEEP

HAVE you ever seen an old wooden cupboard quite black with age, and ornamented with carved foliage and curious figures? Well, just such a cupboard stood in a parlor, and had been left to the family as a legacy by the great-grandmother. It was covered from top to bottom with carved roses and tulips; the most curious scrolls were drawn upon it, and out of them peeped little stags' heads, with antlers. In the middle of the cupboard door was the carved figure of a man most ridiculous to look at. He grinned at you, for no one could call if laughing. He had goat's legs, little horns on his head, and a long beard; the children in the room always called him, "Major general-field-sergeant-commander Billy-goat's-legs." It was certainly a very difficult name to pronounce, and there are very few who ever receive such a title, but then it seemed wonderful how he came to be carved at all; yet there he was, always looking at the table under the looking-glass, where stood a very pretty little shepherdess made of china. Her shoes were gilt, and her dress had a red rose for an ornament. She wore a hat, and carried a crook, that were both gilded and looked very bright and pretty. Close by her side stood a little chimney sweep, as black as coal, and also made of china. He was, however, quite as clean and neat as any other china figure; he only represented a black chimney-sweep, and the china workers might just as well have made him a prince, had they felt inclined to do so. He stood holding his ladder quite handily, and his face was as fair and rosy as a girl's; indeed, that was rather a mistake, it should have had some black marks on it. He and the shepherdess had been placed close together, side by side; and, being so placed, they became engaged to each other, for they were very well suited, being both made of the same sort of china, and being equally fragile. Close to them stood another figure, three times as large as

332

they were, and also made of china. He was an old Chinaman, who could nod his head, and used to pretend that he was the grandfather of the shepherdess, although he could not prove it. He however, assumed authority over her, and therefore when " Major-general-field-sergeant-commander Billy-goat's legs" asked for the little shepherdess to be his wife, he nodded his head to show that he consented. " You will have a husband," said the old Chinaman to her, " who I really believe is made of mahogany. He will make you a lady of Major-general-field-sergeant-commander Billy-goat's-legs. He has the whole cupboard full of silver plate, which he keeps locked up in secret drawers."

" I won't go into the dark cupboard," said the little shepherdess. " I have heard that he has eleven china wives there already."

" Then you shall be the twelfth," said the old Chinaman. " To-night as soon as you hear a rattling in the old cupboard, you shall be married, as true as I am a Chinaman; " and then he nodded his head and fell asleep.

Then the little shepherdess cried, and looked at her sweetheart, the china chimney-sweep. " I must entreat you," said she, " to go out with me into the wide world, for we cannot stay here."

" I will do whatever you wish," said the little chimney-sweep; " let us go immediately: I think I shall be able to maintain you with my profession."

" If we were but safely down from the table!" said she; " I shall not be happy till we are really out in the world."

Then he comforted her, and showed her how to place her little foot on the carved edge and gilt-leaf ornaments of the table. He brought his little ladder to help her, and so they contrived to reach the floor. But when they looked at the old cupboard, they saw it was all in an uproar. The carved stags pushed out their heads, raised their antlers, and twisted their necks. The major-general sprung up in the air; and cried out to the old Chinaman. " They are running away! They are running away !" The two were rather frightened at this, so they jumped into the drawer of the window-seat. Here were three or four packs of cards not quite complete, and a doll's theatre, which had been built up very neatly. A comedy was being performed in it, and all the queens of diamonds, clubs, and hearts, and spades, sat in the first row fanning themselves with tulips, and behind them stood all the knaves, showing that they had heads above and below as playing cards generally have. The play was about two lovers, who were not allowed to marry, and the shepherdess wept because it was so like her own story. "I cannot bear it," said she, "I must get out of the drawer;" but when they reached the floor, and cast their eyes on the table, there was the old Chinaman awake and shaking his whole body, till all at once down he came on the floor, "plump." "The old Chinaman is coming," cried the little shepherdess in a fright, and down she fell on one knee.

"I have thought of something," said the chimney-sweep; "let us get into the great pot-pourri jar which stands in the corner; there we can lie on rose-leaves and lavender, and throw salt in his eyes if he comes near us."

"No, that will never do," said she, "because I know that the Chinaman and the pot-pourri jar were lovers once, and there always remains behind a feeling of good-will between those who have been so intimate as that. No, there is nothing left for us but to go out into the wide world."

"Have you really courage enough to go out into the wide world with me?" said the chimney-sweep; "have you thought how large it is, and that we can never come back here again?"

"Yes, I have," she replied.

When the chimney-sweep saw that she was quite firm, he said, "My way is through the stove and up the chimney. Have you courage to creep with me through the fire-box, and the iron pipe? When we get to the chimney I shall know how to manage very well. We shall soon climb too high for any one to reach us, and we shall come through a hole in the top out into the wide world." So he led her to the door of the stove.

"It looks very dark," said she; still she went in with him through the stove and through the pipe, where it was as dark as pitch.

"Now we are in the chimney," said he; "and look, there is a beautiful star shining above it." It was a real star shining down upon them as if it would show them the way. So they clambered, and crept on, and a frightful steep place it was; but the chimney-sweep helped her and supported her, till they got higher and higher. He showed her the best places on which to set her little china foot, so at last they reached the top of the chimney, and sat themselves down, for they were very tired, as may be supposed.

The sky, with all its stars, was over their heads, and below were the roofs of the town. They could see for a very long distance out into the wide world, and the poor little shepherdess leaned her head on her chimney-sweep's shoulder, and wept till she washed the gilt off her sash; the world was so different to what she expected. "This is too much," she said; "I cannot bear it, the world is too large. Oh, I wish I were safe back on the table again, under the looking glass; I shall never be happy till I am safe back again. Now I have followed you out into the wide world, you will take me back, if you love me."

Then the chimney-sweep tried to reason with her, and spoke of the old Chinaman, and of the Major-general-field-sergeant-commander Billy-goat's-legs; but she sobbed so bitterly, and kissed her little chimney-sweep till he was obliged to do all she asked, foolish as it was. And so, with a great deal of trouble, they climbed down the chimney, and then crept through the pipe and stove, which were certainly not very pleasant places. Then they stood in the dark fire-box, and listened behind the door, to hear what was going on in the room. As it was all quiet, they peeped out. Alas! there lay the old Chinaman on the floor; he had fallen down from the table as he attempted to run after them, and was broken into three pieces; his back had separated entirely, and his head had rolled into a corner of the room. The major-general stood in his old place, and appeared lost in thought.

"This is terrible," said the little shepherdess. "My poor old grandfather is broken to pieces, and it is our fault. I shall never live after this;" and she wrung her little hands.

"He can be riveted," said the chimney-sweep; "he can be riveted. Do not be so hasty. If they cement his back, and put a good rivet in it, he will be as good as new, and be able to say as many disagreeable things to us as ever."

"Do you think so?" said she; and then they climbed up to the table, and stood in their old places.

"As we have done no good," said the chimney-sweep, "we might as well have remained here, instead of taking so much trouble."

"I wish grandfather was riveted," said the shepherdess. "Will it cost much, I wonder?"

And she had her wish. The family had the Chinaman's back

mended, and a strong rivet put through his neck; he looked as good as new, but he could no longer nod his head.

"You have become proud since your fall broke you to pieces," said Major-general-field-sergeant-commander Billy-goat's-legs. "You have no reason to give yourself such airs. Am I to have her or not?"

The chimney-sweep and the little shepherdess looked piteously at the old Chinaman, for they were afraid he might nod; but he was not able: besides it was so tiresome to be always telling strangers he had a rivet in the back of his neck.

And so the little china people remained together, and were glad of the grandfather's rivet, and continued to love each other till they were broken to pieces.

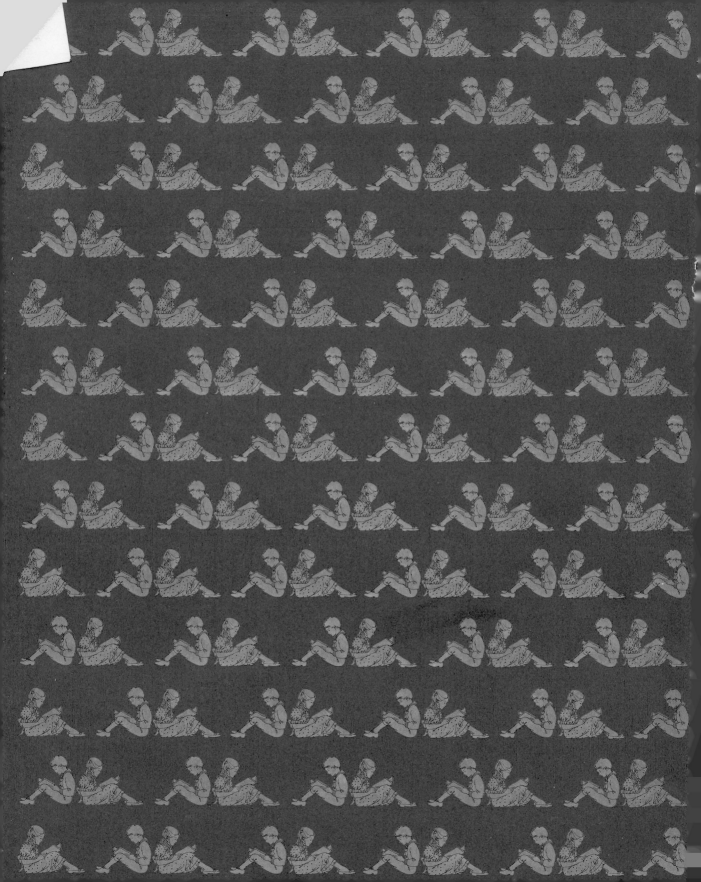